EW YORK TIMES, SATURDAY, SEPTEMBER 11, 1948.

DICTMENT CALLS XIS SALLY TRAITOR

S.-Born Woman Accused of iding Nazis in Campaign of Psychological Warfare

VASHINGTON, Sept. 10 UP— American-born woman accused roadcasting a series of "Home, eet Home" programs over the man radio to American troops Europe was indicted for treason ay.

nown to wartime GI's as "Axis y," the defendant is Mildred abeth Gillars, 47, a native of tland, Me.

INDICTED FOR TREASON

"I don't think Ethel Barrymore could have received the verdict any better."

'AXIS SA SHE BE

Tells Jury S veal Milita If It

SATURDAY EVENI

No Other Ga Like Axis S

'AXIS SA WHY S

FRANKF Germany, Gillars said become "Ax German rad let for the had always

Axis Sally To Testify

Wins Right to Call Nazis Forced Her to

xis Sally' Portrayed as Dupe Of Former Teacher at Hunter

fense Counsel Identifies Max Koischewitz s 'Svengali' Who Swayed Broadcaster

TIME

E WEEKLY NEWSMAGAZINE

BROADCASTER GILLARS

Sirupy and defeatist. Last week xis Sally" and "Tokyo Rose" were rted home to face trial for treason. Their stories were almost identical. laine-born Mildred Elizabeth Gillars, 47, ent to Europe in 1929 to study music. When war came she stayed on in Berlin, broadcasting a mixture of sirupy music and defeatist propaganda to U.S. troops

'AXIS SALLY' FAINTS ON HEARING OWN VOICE

EX-ACTOR OUTLINES 'AXIS SALLY' ROLE

Tells Capital Jury He and She Took Part in Nazi Broadcast to Discoura

NEWSWEEK

COLLIERS MA

TOKYO ROSE, Axis Sally glamor girls of the Axis ra with American troops in bo eaters. Their excellent recorde hilarious propaganda

W YORK TIMES, FRIDAY, MARCH 26, 1

XIS SALLY' GETS TO 30-YEAR TERM

itor Also Fined $10,000, akes Sentence With No Display of Emotion

SENT

XIS SA CQUITT

ge Rejects Comment—D 'Mere Words'

Sally is a Solid Sender

During World War II, Allied soldiers listened to Mildred Gillars broadcast Nazi-authored propaganda and American hit parade tunes. Whether in barracks, POW camps or fox-holes, they laughed at the ridiculous, obviously Nazi-authored propaganda while enjoying her sexy voice and the great music she played. The testimonials of hundreds of these men, taken in Normandy on the fiftieth anniversary of D-Day, surprised this author. The mention of the name "Axis Sally" brought a wry smile and, invariably: "You mean 'My Gal Sal?' What ever happened to her? I hope they let her go."

AXIS SALLY

M. WILLIAMS FULLER

PARADISE
WEST

ParadiseWest Publishing
P.O. Box 30398
Santa Barbara, CA 93130-0398
(805) 682-6185

website: www.axissally.net
email address: axissally@cox.net

For information, or additional copies, please contact: Special Markets Department, ParadiseWest Publishing, P.O. Box 30398, Santa Barbara, California 93130-0398 or visit www.axissally.net

FIRST EDITION

Library of Congress Cataloging-in-Publication Data
2002094049
Fuller, M. Williams.
Axis Sally
ISBN 0-9723675-7-8

Retail Price: $19.95

Axis Sally is based, with few exceptions, on the lives of real people and events. Names of certain individuals and organizations have been altered in order to protect them from undo exposure and embarrassment. Although certain storytelling liberties have been taken, particularly in portraying minor characters, relationships and conversations, the author has taken great care to remain faithful to the main characters and essential chronology of the twentieth century.

Research in both the United States and Europe has included perusal of documents available under the U.S. Freedom of Information Act, Federal Court Records and Alderson Federal Prison Records.

It was a moment that forever sealed my fate... that first moment our eyes met. He is... was... my destiny.

– Mildred Gillars
(United States vs Gillars, 1947)

1

New York City – September, 1925

The strap of the book bag bit into her shoulder as, late for class, she raced across campus. Her first day at Hunter and she'd overslept. Off to the right, brick buildings swallowed streams of college girls. Catching the sound of their chatter and excited giggles, she came to a halt. "I must be an idiot," she muttered, "thinking I'd fit in. They'll take me for a dunce... a fool."

A stirring of the wind urged her on. Arriving at the lecture hall, she paused but a moment to catch her breath before sprinting up a dozen or so marble steps. She tugged on the huge door and flew inside. Transitioning from bright sunlight to the dark interior, she didn't see the small table stacked high with pamphlets and collided with it head on, sending it crashing to the floor. Necks craned as she righted the table. Eyes stared. A collective sigh and a buzz of protests rose from the vortex.

"Shhhh! You've interrupted the professor's lecture!"

"Clumsy!"

"Quiet!"

"For goodness sake!"

A softer, kinder voice: "There's a seat in down front."

Dry-mouthed, her face burning with embarrassment, she started down the concrete stairs.

At the midpoint of her descent she felt the book bag's bottom seam begin to rupture. Pen and pencil fell out first and, upon striking the hard floor, bounced away like tiny pogo sticks. A silver compact escaped next. Striking the floor, it cracked open and expelled a white cloud.

"Oh, brother!" groused a student from an aisle seat. "Now she's sending smoke signals!"

Clutching the bag more firmly only made the tear grow. One book after another slammed to the floor. Fighting an urge to vomit, she squatted to retrieve the compact. As she reached for it, her knee slipped inside the loop of her necklace and glass beads exploded in every direction, pouring from one level of seats to the next in an endless cascade.

Her gaping mouth evoked a flurry of giggles.

"Wow! What an encore!"

"Shall we applaud?"

"This is college, Miss Klutz, not kindergarten!"

From her squat she pitched onto her knees, her face inches from the floor, and groped for beads still within her reach. As she withdrew her head from the tight dark space under a seat, her nose nearly brushed his shoes—shiny black wingtips with pointed toes, heels snapping together with a sharp, military click.

"Professor Koischwitz at your service, Fraulein. And you, my dear, you are?"

Remaining on all fours, she started at his feet. "Mildred."

"Ah! Yes, Mildred! You have, I presume, a surname?"

"Gillars..."

"Tell me, Fraulein Mildred Gillars, do you anticipate being

settled soon?" With an almost imperceptible wink and a crooked smile, he extended his hand. "Please, allow me."

She thought him too young to be a professor of German literature. Perfect, almost rigid posture suggested a proud streak; the mop of black tousled hair contempt for the slicked-down style of the day. An oversized nose complimented his sharply defined jaw and cleft chin.

He spoke to the student seated nearest them. "Fraulein Krantz, at the end of my lecture will you be so kind as to help our lovely latecomer retrieve her belongings?" He then placed Mildred's hand on his arm and escorted her on down the stairs to the empty seat. "Fraulein," he said with a curt bow, "I trust I may now resume my lecture?"

She gazed up at him as though at an apparition.

"Oh yes, please..."

He turned sharply and marched back to the podium. "My dear students," he said, his eyes scanning the eager faces, his voice hard and charged with authority, "it would seem I must impose a rule. After today, tardiness will not, under any circumstances, be tolerated. As a true German, I insist on order and punctuality."

Ignoring groans and the odd squeaking of a seat, he resumed his lecture on Germany's pre-eminent place in world literature. At precisely five minutes to the hour, he placed his papers in his briefcase and snapped it shut. Then, like a Wagnerian knight exiting the stage after battling to a great victory, he strode smartly from the room.

Two weeks passed before he summoned her to his private office. A Persian carpet and the golden glow of a lamp lent coziness to the otherwise dark room. Framed diplomas, awards and charcoal sketches covered every wall. Heaps of books overflowed an oak desk. Against a sepia-colored screen stood a sofa. In front of it, a coffee table offering a basket of bright red apples.

"Ah, Fraulein Gillars, wunderbar!" He led her to the sofa. "Please, my dear, sit."

"Thank you, Professor." With every nerve in her body alert, she perched stiffly on the cushion's edge.

He turned and walked to a cabinet. With a key taken from his pocket, he unlocked a drawer, withdrew a crystal decanter and two dainty goblets. "A taste of sherry, Fraulein?"

"Oh no, thank you, thank you very much. I don't—well that is, I don't usually... well, only on special occasions... I..."

He smiled at her wide-eyed stammering. "Ah..." A gold ring on the little finger of his right hand glinted as he set the goblets on the table and filled them to the brim. "Would you not say this is a special occasion?"

"Oh yes! Certainly! It certainly is!"

He lifted a goblet and waited for her to do the same. When she just stared at him, he held his drink up. "Cheers!"

Watching him take a long, slow sip aroused her. As if she had taken the very same sip, she could taste the sweetness and feel the amber spirits burn her mouth as its fire spread to the lining of her cheeks. As her tongue peeked out to lick the aftertaste from her lips, her hand touched her throat to conceal a swallow.

Her expression sent him toward the window. "You are perhaps a bit warm? Here, let me open this..."

A breeze rustled then blew papers from his desk. Ignoring them, he returned to the sofa, sat beside her and took her hand. "You are perhaps wondering why I have sent for you?"

His moist, sherry-tinged breath caressed her face and caused a shiver of anticipation. Her heart racing, she lowered her eyes.

"I have sent for you because it is my custom to interview that student who, on the first examination of the semester, has scored the lowest."

Her mouth flew open. "What?"

"Perhaps if I knew something about your background..."

"You... you sent for me because... I scored the lowest?"

He picked up the full goblet and placed it in her hands. "Perhaps a taste or two would help you collect your thoughts..." She took a sip, then, at his urging, another. "Tell me about yourself, Fraulein. Your father was, I presume, well-educated?"

She stiffened. Her hand, hidden in the fold of her skirt, balled into a fist. Without thinking, she drained half the goblet. "Mother was a talented artist..."

"Was? She's..."

"No, no... she's alive, she just doesn't paint anymore. She lives in Conneaut... Ohio."

"And your father?"

She gripped the goblet so tightly that her fingertips turned white.

"Sorry, I didn't mean to upset you. Forgive me."

He talked about all manner of things until the sherry found its mark and she relaxed. Coaxed, she began telling of her childhood, of happy summers at her grandfather's old mansion in Bar Harbor, Maine. She'd starred in plays in Conneaut High School and studied drama in Ohio's Wesleyan College. Then, her full lips pouting, she told of having to drop out for lack of funds.

He held up his hands. "Hardship strengthens character, my dear. Tell me, what are your aspirations—where do you see yourself five years from now? Married and with six children, I suppose?"

She reared back. "Heavens *no*! I don't see myself like that at all. My first love is, and will always, *always be* the theater. My dream of dreams is to become a great dramatic actress."

His forehead knit. "An actress? You're highest goal is to become... an actress?"

"It's the best, most magical profession in the entire world. On stage I can be anyone! I can make the audience love me!"

He gazed upon her like a fly in a spider web. "And you find being Mildred Gillars so terrible?" He held his empty goblet up to the light and, rotating it, watched a last drop of sherry chase an irregular ellipse. "So, my dear, you come to academia at the advanced age of twenty-four... a rather circuitous route to the stage, wouldn't you say?"

"Oh, I'll get back behind the footlights—you may be sure of that. If it's the very last thing I do, I'll get there."

"You're very determined, I see."

"These last five years I've done everything from waitressing to selling pencils door-to-door to get the money to pay for acting lessons. Last spring I played the part of "Martha" in Hatcher Hughes' newest play, *Hell Bent for Heaven.*"

"I don't believe I've heard of it."

Her smile faded. "Well, it wasn't exactly on Broadway..."

"It was a success, this *Hell Bent for Heaven?*"

"Actually, no." She straightened. "But a reviewer for *The Village Voice* saw it and liked my performance. He even put my name in the newspaper in bold print! He said I was someone to watch—someone with promise!"

"And indeed you are! But, I am a bit confused. Tell me, my lovely and promising Fraulein, how is it that I am blessed with your presence in my class?"

She gave her long blonde tresses a flip and explained. With the play's closing, she'd fallen on hard times. Unable to land another part in a play, she'd taken a secretarial job with an agency which, for a fee, arranged for introductions of lonely gentlemen to single young women of good repute. Unfortunately the agency closed before she could collect her first paycheck. Just as she'd hit bottom, the letter came notifying her of a bequest in the will of her recently deceased grandmother. Regarding actresses akin to prostitutes, Grandmother Hewitson had tied a string to the bequest: Mildred could use the inheritance solely to complete college—not necessarily Wesleyan—any accredited college.

Amazed by the melodrama, the professor smiled. "So, life has dealt you one challenge after another! No wonder you seem the most mature of my students! Tell me, what do the young women with whom you live call you? 'The Relic of the Dormitory?'"

"They call me no such thing."

He rose and gazed out the window. "Forgive me, Fraulein. My jest offends you."

"I don't live with those... children. I have a small apartment off campus."

He spun around, a look of delight on his face. "Ah! In that case, I might be able to... Obviously you will need extra help if you are to succeed here at Hunter. Since you live alone it might be possible for me to tutor you privately."

Mildred's pulse quickened. "Why that sounds wonderful! I would be ever so grateful, Professor... so indebted."

"No! No! No! It is not good to feel indebted!"

"But..."

"Perhaps, in return for my tutoring, you could..."

"Anything, I'll do anything..."

"You could help me to speak with less of an accent. It is essential to my career that I become more Americanized."

"Oh, yes, of course..."

"If your schedule permits, shall we say... Wednesday evenings?"

It is the most important point, you know,
that the tutor should be dignified and
at a distance from the pupil, and that the pupil
should be as much as possible degraded...

– Lewis Carroll (1832–1898)

2

Retired vaudevillian Sophie Goldblat was a no nonsense landlady. She rented tiny apartments in the clapboard three-story structure to single females and insisted on strict adherence to house rules. One violation and you were in for it; two and you were out.

Having just witnessed the eviction of a young lady who'd twice entertained a young man after hours, Mildred knocked softly on Sophie's door.

The door opened just a crack. "Yes, Miss Gillars, what do you want?"

"Mrs. Goldblat, I... I just thought you should know that my brother will be visiting me on Wednesday evenings. He's a professor of literature–German literature. He will be tutoring me."

The door flew open and framed the hefty, bath-robed Sophie who had yet to remove the fat, shiny curlers from her hair. Her arms were folded over her chest, resting on huge, sagging breasts. "Look, dearie, I've heard 'em all–so don't think you're pullin' the wool over my eyes. It makes no difference to me whether he's your brother, your lover, or Pope Pius. My rules stand: NO MEN—OF ANY DESCRIPTION—AFTER NINE P.M."

Professor Koischwitz, impeccably dressed even to his black Homburg hat and perfectly knotted silk necktie, arrived exactly on time. Mildred opened the door at his first knock. He hesitated before entering to take a cautious look up and down the hallway. Satisfied that no one was about, he stepped inside. "My, you look beautiful this evening!"

A silk flower in her hair matched her dress's red trim. Silk stockings gave a luster to her shapely legs and high-heeled pumps an extra sexiness to her stance. Three silver bracelets encircling her wrist jingled as she motioned him to the sofa. "Please, have a seat while I set the kettle on for tea."

He sat and studied the room. "Nice quarters you have here. Good lighting." He peered at the lone picture, a faded print of ballerinas by the artist Degas. "*Before the Dance*—delightful! You enjoy the ballet?"

Her reply, muted by the sound of running water and clinking cups, "I've never been."

A glance at the window and he darted to it. She returned as he finished pulling down the shade. "Why, Professor, what's the matter? Is something wrong?"

He took her hand. "My dear, are there not gossips here in America just as there are gossips in my homeland?"

"Gossips?"

"And their wagging tongues, do they not ruin reputations? End careers?"

Stirred by a note of urgency in his voice, Mildred nodded repeatedly. "Yes, they do. They most certainly do."

"Then you understand why we must be discreet?"

"Discreet?"

He rolled his eyes at her naïveté. "My dear, although you

may find it impossible to comprehend, there are those who might misunderstand."

"Oh."

"And since they might misunderstand, you must tell no one of these meetings. Should we encounter one another beyond these walls, it must appear to be the encounter of strangers." Her nod struck him as that of a puppet. "No, I must have your promise! Do you promise to refrain from doing anything and from saying anything that might in any way jeopardize my position at Hunter?"

"Oh dear, no! I mean, yes! I absolutely promise!"

While tea steeped and scones warmed, the professor spoke at length of his family and childhood. "I was born in Jauer, a small hamlet in the mountains of Silesia. My first name, Max, is of course after the great Maximillian. My middle name, Otto, came from my grandfather. My dear father is a brilliant physician and an accomplished artist. My beloved mother, the soul of my family, once danced with the Bolshoi. I miss her very much and write to her every day."

Aware of Mildred's eyes on him, he got up and, with a deft flare of his hand, struck a match to light a cigarette. Holding her gaze, he sucked the smoke into his lungs and held it until, cheeks flushed, he exhaled a slow, steady stream of white. Two more drags and a cough rumbled up from his chest. He turned from her until it subsided, then snuffed the cigarette as if determined to make it his last. He declined her offer of water. "Coughing is an old enemy. Except for mother's care, I would not have survived my childhood. The bronchitis still plagues me."

His expression, as he talked of his home in Silesia, reminded her of Raphael's *Homesick Angel.* "The townspeople called me 'nature boy'—a 'hermit.' They considered me odd, when all I wanted was to spend my time alone, in my beloved mountains reading, meditating... losing myself in metaphysical thought."

That he'd not touched his scone concerned her for he seemed so thin, almost gaunt. She asked if he'd prefer a slice of toast.

"No, this is fine. I'm not much of an eater. Could you bring me a pencil and paper?"

Thinking he wanted to get started on their tutoring, she hurried to her desk. "I hope this paper will do—it's unlined."

"Perfect!" He took the pencil, positioned the paper just so in front of him and, to her amazement, began to sketch. "Please, Fraulein, sit down and do not look over my shoulder. And, none of your chatter until I am finished."

"Chatter?"

"Shhhh."

He finished the sketch, signed it and handed it across the table. "For you, my dear, a bouquet of Edelweiss."

She gazed at the delicately drawn flowers. "Why, they're beautiful! Magnificent!" A tear glinted her eye. "I shall frame this!"

He got up, strode to the bookcase and squatted to read the titles in her miniscule library. He clicked his tongue. "It's no wonder you are doing so poorly in my class. We *are* what we read, Fraulein. We must not squander our time on books such as these. Great books—that's what we must read! Great books were the cornerstones of my adolescence. From them I learned of Germany's great philosophers and valiant soldiers. To this day they are my most admired heroes, those gods of Valhalla who defined the German psyche and bore arms for the Fatherland." His eyes, as though reflecting a heavenly sunrise, filled with a strange light. "My ancestors have earned their rest in Valhalla. Great-grandfather, for bearing arms against Napoleon and Grandfather, for fighting against France in the Franco-Prussian war."

She listed more attentively when he switched to current history. "I graduated—with highest honors of course—from the College de Royal Françoise. My first teaching assignment was at Ottilienhaus, a girls' college in Berlin. Believe me, the pay was terrible."

"And the girls?"

"Ah, not so terrible!"

Insisting she leave the tidying-up until later, he led her back to the sofa. He sat beside her and brought his arm around to rest on her shoulders. As he continued the saga of his early career, his fingertips came to rest lightly on her breast.

With hope of landing a better paying teaching position, he had left Ottilienhaus to study medieval German literature at the University of Berlin. Adding a list of new classes–all passed with the highest grades–to a resume reflecting a lack of experience didn't help. Inexperienced teachers lucky enough to find jobs were earning no more than dish washers.

Distracted from his tale by a shifting of her weight, he pulled the fob leading to his vest pocket and withdrew a golden timepiece. "Perhaps you will find this more interesting–it's my most precious possession. See, the cover is engraved with my family's crest. Father presented this watch to me on the day I sailed for America."

She marveled at the intricate engraving: two lions standing erect at either side of an ornate, heart-shaped shield. "He must miss you terribly."

Max's forehead creased. "He is ill with tuberculosis."

"Oh, I'm terribly sorry, I..."

"Where was I? Ah yes, telling you how impossible it was to find decent wages in Germany. But then, when I least expected it, the gods smiled on me. My application was accepted and I was invited to come to America–to stay at International House. You've heard of International House?"

"On Long Island?"

"No, on Riverside Drive. Your famous philanthropist John D. Rockefeller built it to promote international good will and understanding. Half of the students admitted to International House must be foreigners taking at least eight college credits or devoting equal time to academic research."

"I'll bet you fit right in."

He nodded. "And fortunately for me, for I had so little money, Hunter College gave me a part-time position teaching German literature." He cupped her chin. "So you see, Fraulein Gillars, I've had to bide my time for a whole year before you came my way. Do you know that you have the most beautiful hair?"

"I do?"

"It's the color of flax that grows in Silesia's meadows. And your face—seldom have I seen such perfect symmetry. Beauty such as yours begs to be captured on an artist's canvas. How I should love to sketch you in a variety of poses!" With great gentleness he then tilted her face toward his and kissed her.

A loud, persistent knock at the door stunned her back to reality. "Dearie? Do I hear a man's voice in there? It's almost midnight!"

"Shhhh! Don't make a sound," Mildred whispered, "it's Mrs. Goldblat!"

The landlady's voice boomed through the door again, this time loud enough to wake everyone in the building. "Better not be a man in there! You know the rules, dearie."

"It's just the radio, Mrs. Goldblat. Sorry, it won't happen again. I'll turn it off."

The professor pressed Mildred closer, nibbled her ear and whispered, "Can you... turn it off?"

"You'd better," Mrs. Goldblat threatened, her voice growing fainter as her footsteps disappeared down the hall. "You'd better turn it off... whatever it is!"

Stifling giggles, Mildred nuzzled her tutor's cheek. "You really must... leave now, Max."

He stiffened. "Very well, you may call me Max—but *only* when we are here in your apartment. Outside these walls I am 'Professor Koischwitz'—always, in public, I am 'Professor Koishwitz.'"

"It's late... Max."

He took his hat and, while kissing her, allowed himself to be nudged toward the door. His hand cupped her buttock. "Mmmm. Very nice."

"Watch out," she teased. "Mrs. Goldblat's a tough cookie, she doesn't tolerate any hanky-panky."

He rolled his eyes and did some teasing of his own. "Hanky-panky? Fraulein Gillars, vas ist dis *hanky-panky*?"

"I suspect you could write a book on the subject. And please, call me 'Mildred.'"

"'Mildred'? Oh no. For the rest of my life I shall call you 'Liebling.'" Then, like a rube in a melodrama, he opened the door and, with great caution, scanned the hall.

She gave his back a playful tap. "The coast is clear I take it?"

"Wunderbar! Ah, yes, this expression I like. The coast is clear!"

No human being is master of his fate...
we are all motivated far more than we care to admit
by characteristics inherited from our ancestors
which individual experiences of childhood
can modify, repress, or enhance... but cannot erase.

– Agnes E. Meyer (1887–1970)

3

She dreamed of him until dawn and awoke with a smile. Sitting up, she hugged herself and began to hum. The aroma of frying bacon wafted through the window. "I'm famished!" she exclaimed to the empty room, "Madly in love and utterly famished!" She jumped out of bed and dressed in a rush. She would splurge on this most exquisite of mornings. She would have ham and eggs at The Galloping Hen and then, no matter if it did cost more than two dollars to phone Conneaut, she would call Momma and tell her the news.

The phone in Rosen's Hidden Treasures rang incessantly as Mary Gillars unlocked the shop's front door. "Hold your horses! I'm coming!" A stream of excited chatter poured from the receiver as she lifted it to her ear. "Mildred? Is this you? Slow down! What's wrong? What's happened?"

"Nothing's wrong, Momma! I'm in love and I think he loves me, too!"

"Oh."

"Momma, he's the handsomest, most brilliant, kindest

man in the whole world! And hold onto your hat, Momma, are you sitting down?"

"Why?"

"He's a professor!"

"A what? I think we have a poor connection."

"No, Momma, you heard right! He's a professor of German literature! Professor Max Otto Koischwitz. He came to my apartment last night to tutor me. Oh Momma, I haven't slept a wink since. I just had to tell you. I never dreamed there was such a man. I'm walking on clouds!"

"Write me all about it, Mildred. It's cheaper."

"But..."

"Write me. I'm happy for you. I have to go now... to open the shop." Hanging the receiver back in its holder, she looked up and spoke to the shop-worn owl hovering over the cash register. "My daughter," she muttered to the dusty creature, "she's known him no time and already she's walking on clouds."

Mary put on her smock, the one she always wore while opening shop and, chagrined at her daughter's elation, set to work placing sale items on the front table. "We women are such fools!" Her mind flew back a quarter of a century, back to her elopement with Vincent Sisk.

Knowing how her father detested him, Vincent had come to Mary's home in New Brunswick in the dark of night and whisked her off to Portland, Maine where a justice of the peace married them. Wedded bliss soon turned nightmare. About to get into bed with him for the first time, he'd made her swear, on a hotel-room bible, that he was the only one she'd ever love and that she would not, under any circumstance, bear a child to come between them.

Six months later when she told him she was pregnant, he became enraged, upset every piece of furniture and smashed every dish in the house. His tantrum ended with a hard slap to her face.

It sleeted all day and into the night of November 29, 1900—the night Mildred was born. A midwife washed and bundled the new arrival and took her to be admired by her father. Vincent took one look at the squalling, wrinkled infant, cursed and set out for the corner tavern.

Mary, her eyes smarting with memory-caused tears, pulled a hanky from the pocket of her smock and blew her nose. How she'd prayed, as Mildred grew into an attractive, bright child, for Vincent to turn from the sin of rejecting his daughter. But he didn't, not when at the age of five Mildred mastered advanced piano pieces, not when she composed songs to sing or bowed to the applause of an imaginary audience, not ever.

Mary saw a spider and swiped at it with a vengeance meant for Vincent who'd fly off the handle at the least provocation! The beatings he'd give Mildred if she'd dare cover her ears against his insults! Pushing Vincent from her mind, Mary thought of her parents. They'd emigrated from New Brunswick to Maine three years after her elopement with Vincent. Her father, retired sea captain Elijah Hewitson soon bought a ship's chandlery in Bar Harbor. For his wife, Estelle, he bought "Greystone," a grand old estate overlooking the Atlantic.

Elijah feared for his granddaughter Mildred. "It's her only means of escape," he counseled Mary about her daughter's constant daydreaming. "She's created a world of make-believe as a sanctuary from that monster's abuse. I tell you, you don't have a marriage—you have a disaster waiting to happen. If you value your sanity you'll leave him—the sooner, the better."

It was Vincent who left. On Mildred's seventh birthday he put on his hat and, without a backward glance, disappeared out the back door forever.

The three and a half years between Vincent's leaving and her second trip down the aisle were the happiest Mary ever knew. Determined to pursue her art, she moved with

Mildred to Greenwich Village. The Bohemian life fostered her talent. She became a street artist and began to attract customers eager to buy her black-paper silhouettes. Refusing her father's financial help, she managed, at first, to make expenses with a few pennies left over. Every spare cent went into the tin can labeled "Betterment," a fund for Mildred's piano lessons, matinees, trips on the Staten Island Ferry and trolley fare for Sunday visits to the Bronx Zoo.

Those halcyon days came to an abrupt end with Mary's marriage to another man she thought she knew. At a dance given to raise money for children orphaned by the disastrous fire in the Triangle Shirtwaist Factory, she met Robert Gillars, Doctor of Dental Surgery. Impressed by his seeming flamboyance, she thought him charming and high-spirited.

Held at Greystone, the wedding was a quiet affair. Smiling broadly as the ceremony concluded, Doctor Gillars, bolstered by a double shot of whiskey, made a stunning announcement. Although he had yet to travel further west than Pennsylvania, he'd just purchased, sight unseen, the house and dental practice of a dentist in Conneaut, Ohio. Ignoring his bride's shock, bridegroom Gillars opened an envelope and withdrew three train tickets.

One look at the place and all three faces fell. Located on Grant Street near Conneaut's historic Octagon Barn, the dilapidated cottage clearly needed major repair—chimney work, paint and a new roof. The new family ventured inside.

The living room served as dental office and contained a drilling apparatus, instrument cabinet, dental chair and spit-sink. Behind the living room was a dining room, two small bedrooms, a kitchen with a wood stove and a screened-in, tilting back porch.

After a week spent getting things in order by day, and nipping by night, Doctor Gillars hung out his shingle. The citizens of Conneaut, he soon discovered, were a suspicious lot and didn't quite know what to think of this "outsider" dentist with the sad-eyed wife—and little girl he was quick to tell everyone wasn't his. The practice of Robert Gillars, DDS grew like a leaky balloon.

In Conneaut less than a year, Mary bore a second child, Edna Mae Gillars. That his stepdaughter went by the surname "Sisk" evoked embarrassing questions and annoyed the doctor. Teased once too often that he was his wife's "second choice," the good doctor sent the patient packing, seized the family Bible and, with a flourish of his pen, changed Mildred's last name to "Gillars."

Mary gave a start at the tinkling of the bell above the shop's door. She looked up, expecting to greet the day's first customer. Her eyes twinkled to see instead the shop's owner, Ira Rosen. He hurried to her, enclosed her in his arms and planted a long passionate kiss on her lips.

"Oh, Ira."

He held her at arm's length. "I named this shop well—you are indeed my 'Hidden Treasure.'"

"Mildred called."

"Oh?"

"She's walking on clouds."

Falling in love consists merely in uncorking the imagination and bottling the common-sense.

– Helen Rowland (1875-1950)

4

Mildred appraised her outfit as she half-listened to Thaddeus Walker, Hunter's long-time professor of Early American History. Her brown skirt felt too tight in the hips. The tangerine-colored sweater gave her skin a nice glow, but it clung so that her nipples practically stuck out. She stretched her legs and admired the shapeliness of them. The white silk stockings were a good choice. And her feet did look smaller in the Cuban-heeled suede pumps.

Irritated that Professor Koischwitz's lectures had been rescheduled to late afternoon, she frowned at the clock. Were its hands stuck? Could it still be more than an hour before she would see him again?

A quick exit from Professor Walker's lecture on the Boston Tea Party and she made it back to her apartment in record time. There was time for a shampoo, if she hurried, maybe even time for a fresh lemon juice rinse to give her blonde tresses extra shine. She glanced into the hall mirror and scowled. Dark discs underscored her eyes. One look at them and he'd guess the truth—that she'd slept scarcely a wink since their last meeting. She made mental notes: *Lay tea bags soaked in ice water over eyes, whiten teeth with baking soda, wear the new panties, the blue lace bra...*

Early for his class, she thought the echo of her footsteps too loud as she descended the stairs to the front row. She took the first seat and, consumed with excitement, closed her eyes.

He arrived seconds later. Rushing to her side, he took her hand, lifted it to his lips and kissed it. "Liebling! At last I can breathe again. My heart can resume its beating."

"Professor, I..."

He touched her cheek. "Shhh... your eyes do the talking." A flash of light on the wall alerted him. He straightened, stepped back and nodded. "That is correct, Miss Gillars, your assignment for this class was to read the next two chapters in the text." He looked up at the young woman coming down the stairs. "Fraulein Scott! You must be very interested in German literature to arrive so early!"

Well into the hour's lecture on Goethe's early writings, he posed several questions. Many hands, but not Mildred's, shot up. While ostensibly listening to less than brilliant answers, he subtly positioned himself beside Mildred's chair, leaning his hip ever so slightly against her upper arm. He remained there for the rest of his lecture, enthralling his listeners, titillating Mildred with his closeness, driving her mad every time his fingers brushed her shoulder.

For the second Wednesday night tutoring session Max arrived fifteen minutes early and slipped in without knocking. He found her primping in front of the mirror, scooped her up into his arms and, without a word, carried her to bed.

They undressed one another with abandon. He caressed and covered her naked body with wet kisses. They came together like two merging, molten streams. He cupped her buttocks to him, riding her, slamming his body into hers. At last she cried out and fell back, a woman completely, spectacularly and for the first time, sated.

"Did I hurt you?" He smiled down on her face as she rested in the crook of his arm. "I would never want to hurt you."

She touched his cheek and closed her eyes. As she drifted, snippets of scenes played in her mind. One second she and Max were holding hands, fleeing from pitchfork wielding farmers; the next, dancing and cavorting at a medieval faire. In the final scene they appeared as sackcloth-garbed wretches crying out for mercy. Chilled, she sat up and gathered the sheet to her throat.

"Is something wrong, Liebling?"

"You'll think me mad."

"Never!"

"Could we have... no, I can't."

He kissed her. "Never say *can't*, my darling. I find the word intolerable."

She inhaled deeply. "Could we have possibly lived before? Could we have been...?"

"Lovers?" He drew her close. "Liebling, did you not know that our coming together in my lecture hall was not our first meeting?"

"It wasn't?"

"We are much more than casual lovers, my dear. Our love has rekindled itself down through the centuries and will continue to do so through eternity. You know that now, don't you? You are convinced?"

"Oh, yes! With all my heart I..."

He silenced her with a kiss then took her again until every fiber of her being convulsed in a singular, soul-grabbing orgasm.

Max taught her far more than she cared to know about Germany's glorious past. The subject electrified him. His face lit up when he described Walter von der Vogelweide, the Prince of Minnesingers. The heroic days of the Nibelungenleid moved him to tears. So fond was he of Wagner's *Die Valkyrie* that when "The German Hour" aired the epic during one of his Wednesday evening visits, he infuriated Mildred by begging off their love-making to listen.

To make amends, he arrived early for their next "tutoring" session. And he came well prepared—with rice paper and charcoal—to sketch her in the nude.

With her coaching, Max became an avid student of Americana. Gifted with a razor sharp mind, he grasped the most-subtle nuances of idiom and retained everything, even the smallest detail. He particularly loved American folklore and trivia.

Once, during class he astounded Mildred by veering from a discussion of Parsifal to impress his students with his knowledge of things American. Teddy Roosevelt, he told them, had, at the wheel of a motorcar, raced a train from Los Angeles to Santa Barbara. When students applauded this digression, he was spurred to add, with absolute certainty, that the first Indianapolis 500 took place on a track constructed of *exactly* 3.2 million bricks.

Keeping their affair a secret required elaborate planning. Max thought it prudent that she drop his class—perhaps switch to one held at such a location that they wouldn't be running into each other. When she refused, they reached a settlement: she would remain in his class, sit in the seat farthest from his lectern and continue to refrain from raising her hand when he posed questions.

Max worked out a strategy for them to be together in public while appearing not to be. Only then did they dare venture out to see a motion picture. Max arrived at the theater alone, entered to the right and found a seat. Mildred arrived minutes later, entered and sat on the far left. The house lights dimmed. Then, cautiously, they made their way through the flickering darkness to sit together. The movie's star, in blackface, smiled down on them from the screen.

Max hated the film. He stood it as long as he could before stunning those seated nearby with his outburst. "Such a stupid story this is! A white man paints his face black and struts like a Negro! Preposterous!"

Leaving the theater at this point was not in keeping with his plan. A believer in strict adherence to order, he stayed in his seat fidgeting until the film ended and the newsreel began. He then put on his hat, pulled the brim down over his eyes and gave Mildred's thigh a squeeze. Shying away from her offer of a kiss, he stepped into the aisle, hurried up to the lobby and exited to the street. He'd arranged for a cab. Finding it waiting for him down the block, he got in and waited.

As ordered, Mildred stayed through the newsreel. It contained gruesome footage. Half-starved wretches paraded across the screen as subtitles offered a litany of hardships ravaging inflation-plagued Germany. Berlin's riots exploded on the screen together with superimposed rolling text:

> *These fascists threaten world peace. They must be reckoned with if democracy is to prevail!*

Disturbed by the film's hysterical bent, Mildred hurried outside, ran down the street and ducked into the cab. "My God, Max! I had no idea!"

"You saw something disturbing?"

"Disturbing? It was horrible! Brutal! These fascists, are they really such a threat to world peace?"

"Clark and Montgomery," Max said to the cabbie.

Mildred fell silent as the cab coursed along the dark streets. "Clark and Montgomery? But that's blocks from my apartment? You're not seeing me home?"

Max enfolded her in his arms. "It's best, Liebling. Now, to answer your questions about fascists: Rest assured, my dear, Americans are too intelligent to be drawn into another European conflict. Yours is a great country, it offers hope to dreamers and opportunity to those with determination."

"My country? But Max, you're intelligent, you've got determination—surely you've come to consider this *your* country..."

Mildred was right on two counts that night. Max was intelligent and, he did indeed have determination. During those, his first years at Hunter, he also had hope. His highest and most lofty goal was to earn the recognition and respect of his superiors in academia. But his was a part-time assignment at Hunter. If his talents were to be recognized, he must cultivate people of influence—people who could help him land a full-professorship.

A charismatic charmer who carried himself well, he reached high for a hand up the academic ladder. He wheedled invitations to premiers and kept score at polo matches. He read the society page, finagled invitations to opulent parties and volunteered to serve on committees of the elite.

Max took great pride in his appearance. Spartan when it came to diet and exercise, he scrimped to buy expensive suits. Shirts and sweaters he selected to highlight the steel-blue intensity of his eyes; overcoats to pad his slight build and make him appear taller. His wardrobe included two tuxedos, a dinner jacket, several pairs of black patent leather shoes and all the accessories of formal attire.

An avid sailor, he also had the perfect apparel for yacht cruises on the Hudson. Society columnists pegged him: "The Continental—a stylish libertine in yachtsman's cap and gold-braided blazer."

He also drew the eye of a reporter for the campus newspaper who wrote: "Careful, girls, or a certain very colorful and intriguing professor will steal your hearts!"

His reputation, particularly as an intellectual, grew. Astute and often controversial opinions earned him invitations to elegant black-tie affairs.

Predictably, Mildred reacted. "Not again, Max! I'm sick and tired of staring at these four walls! Besides, how do I know you're not escorting some beautiful woman to these shindigs?"

Unruffled, he sat her down on his lap and pressed his head to her bosom. "Always remember, Liebling, every step I take is a step toward *our* future. Bear with me, dearest. I 'trip the light fantastic' as you say, always alone—always with my heart left here with you in our little love nest."

Academically, Max began to shine as one of Hunter's brightest stars. He published widely and held office in many professional organizations. Important journals cited him as an expert on tests and methods of measuring student potential, progress and achievement.

Working with the Institute of School Experimentation, he turned thirty-four of his students, including Mildred, into "literary guinea pigs." First he exposed them to a broad range of contemporary plays then, by means of an ingenious examination he had devised, tested and measured their "literary absorption" against the student's background in contemporary literature. For his success with this highly acclaimed effort, his colleagues applauded him. Hunter's Board gave him a small raise.

"But no promotion," he complained to Mildred following a reception in his honor. "Always and unjustly they withhold from me a full-professorship." He poured himself a large brandy and collapsed onto her sofa. "Liebling, you don't know how I suffer. They give me crumbs, never a promotion."

"*Why*, Max? Why not a full-professorship?"

"If only I knew! Perhaps they think I'm a Jew."

The first time he failed to keep their Wednesday night rendezvous, Mildred came apart. She paced the floor, peeped out the window and checked the hallway every five minutes. Certain he had met with an accident, she wept. Desperate, she called International House.

"We give out no information regarding our residents, Miss Gillars," came the house operator's reply. Mildred cried herself to sleep.

The next morning a pounding on the door startled her awake. Before she could open it, Max burst in, pushed past her and hurled his hat at the sofa. "How dare you–you idiot!"

"Idiot?"

"You've betrayed me!"

Mildred reeled toward the sink. She turned on the faucet and bending, let a blast of cold water strike her face.

Max came up behind her, seized her shoulders and spun her around. "How dare you call International House! Is your head filled with feathers? Are you stupid? Have you no regard for my career?"

"Oh, Max. I am so sorry, so very sorry. Please... oh, please forgive me. You have my word of honor, I will never, never again inquire after you."

The next time Max pulled a no-show, Mildred responded differently. The instant the walls started to close in, she made a phone call. "Is this Harry?"

"That's me, baby. Harry Horatio Schwartz the Fourth." Hunter's Assistant Registrar, he'd been the first person she'd met on campus. Since he liked to sit in on various classes, she'd seen him again in History and then in Beginning French. Although she'd not mentioned it to Max, she'd had coffee with this newfound friend and had once accompanied him to an evening lecture. He was a gold mine of campus gossip, knew the vices of faculty members, which administrators nipped and the latest on student pregnancies.

Unlike men Mildred had befriended in the past, Harry never made sexual overtures. He could be counted on for a good laugh, casual rather than academic conversation and interesting theories on popular music. Harry had sat in on a few of Max's lectures and had found every one of them annoying. "The guy's a crackpot! A nervous zealot! He goes off on all sorts of wild tangents."

Careful not to tip her hand, Mildred tried to defend her lover. "Come on now, Professor Koischwitz isn't all that bad."

"No? I'll say this, if that fascist doesn't reign himself in and stick to German literature he'll get his walking papers!"

"Being pro-German doesn't make him a fascist."

"So what is he trying to do? Rub our noses in Germany's greatness? I say we buy Herr Koischwitz a one-way ticket back to der Vaterland!"

That he had some inkling of Mildred's involvement with the professor leaked from his next sentence. "Watch yourself around that Kraut, kid. Don't be a sucker."

Lured by the vast array of exciting nightspots, Mildred, without mentioning it to Max, began frequenting the most popular ones with Harry. The friendly twosome became drunk on the pulsing brew of jazz clubs and speakeasies. Dancing, especially dancing the Tango, became their passion. Many evenings ended with a visit to Harlem's Cotton Club to hear King Oliver's band.

Excited to have won a dance contest, Mildred detailed the affair in a letter to her sister. Edna Mae wrote back—how she would love to visit New York—to get away from the deadly boredom of Conneaut High. Her postscript: Momma and I worry that you've turned into a flapper. Please let us know you haven't.

Mildred replied by return mail:

> Dearest Momma and Edna Mae,
>
> According to Funk & Wagnall: A flapper is a modern woman who shows disdain for conventional dress and behavior. She rouges her knees, wears short, fringed skirts to road-houses and frequents speakeasies to dance the Black Bottom and the Charleston.
>
> Brace yourself beloveds, that description suits me to a tee!
>
> (signed) Millie the Flapper

Love called, and I could not linger,
But sought the forbidden tryst,
As music follows the finger
Of the dreaming lutanist...

– James Russell Lowell (1819-1891)

5

Eager to enhance Max's visits, Mildred spent hours converting her tiny apartment into a love-nest. She bought roses to assure a supply of petals to sprinkle on the bed and little gifts to tuck under his pillow. Minutes before his arrival she would burn Egyptian incense, turn the radio dial to a soft love song, fluff pillows and, after lighting and placing candles, shut off the electric bulbs.

To celebrate their fourth Wednesday evening she presented Max with a beautifully wrapped box containing small tubes of body paint. Tickled by his delight, she watched as he mixed them to achieve a dazzling palette of reds, purples, yellows and pinks.

He undressed her as though lifting layers of gossamer from a statue of Venus. He had brought a bottle of bootleg champagne. They sipped it by candlelight while in a bathtub filled with bubbles and jasmine-scented water. They bathed together, splashing and squealing like children. Max blew mounds of soapsuds from her shoulders until the water grew too cold for him. Shivering, he got out and wrapped himself in a towel. At length he blotted her dry, picked up the palette and led her to bed.

Her body would be his canvas. He commenced sketching. Edelweiss blossoms spread over her breasts and next, on her shoulder he sketched a cherub. His face intent, he decorated her thigh with a spray of shooting stars. His sketching complete, he set the paint with a fine dusting of powdered lavender. That his subject moaned with delight aroused him. "Look, Liebling! Your nipples stand up like luscious cherries! They beg to be tasted!"

"Oh, Max!" Overwhelmed with passion, she pulled him toward her until their bodies fused and, writhing, smeared the edelweiss, cherub, shooting stars and powdered lavender into an abstract masterpiece.

Punctual to a fault, Max arrived every Wednesday evening at the stroke of seven and left promptly at nine. They paced their lovemaking, smoked Turkish cigarettes and shared details of the separate lives they'd lived in the week past.

She yearned to see where he lived. He flatly refused to let her attend the annual public tour of International House. "But sweetheart, I do so want to see where you spend so much of your time. I'll go all by myself—no one there knows me."

"No!" he said through clenched teeth, his nostrils flaring, his hand vise-like as it gripped her arm. "Under no circumstances are you to go anywhere near International House!"

Except for Wednesdays and occasional outings with Harry, Mildred spent most evenings reading or doing homework. Weekends she worked part-time as an usher at a playhouse in downtown Manhattan. Max claimed a busier schedule—one devoted weeknights to preparing lectures, devising tests and grading student papers. He described his weekends to Mildred as packed with seminars, research and dull but important parties given by academia's elite.

Only once while she attended Hunter did they spend a whole day together. It was during a freak late-October heat wave. To escape the city, Max borrowed a friend's Model-T Ford and drove Mildred to Rockaway Beach.

"Sweetheart," she said as they bounced over trolley tracks, "this is exciting! In case you haven't heard, Rockaway has the reputation of being a 'Sodom by the Sea!'"

"Is that so? You don't say. Swell!" Max replied, combining three newly acquired American expressions. "We shall indeed enjoy ourselves!"

A hot offshore breeze buffeted the Model-T as Max eased into Rockaway's gravel-topped parking lot. They ducked into separate cabanas, changed into swimsuits and, upon emerging, found a sandy spot. As they spread their blanket, a fracas erupted on the pier—one seeming to involve a group of scantily clad women and a jeering crowd.

Mildred and Max arrived on the scene just in time to see the women lock arms and return the catcalls of detractors. "*We're the Rockaway Rockettes!*" they chanted in unison. "*We wear what we ple-ease... even if we free-eze.*"

The taunting escalated as the angry mob of conservatively dressed beach-goers advanced toward the young women. Vulgar insults led to shouting and shoving. "Serves the floozies right!" an old man shouted. "Them and their skimpy bathing suits! It's the work of the devil they're doin'—the work of the devil!"

One beauty whose knees were clearly visible below her form-fitting bathing suit shouted back. "Old man, I don't see you swimming in a long taffeta dress! Where are *your* bloomers and stockings?"

A member of the conservative group, a plump matron dressed in a long, black bathing dress, pointed at Mildred. "There's another one! Look at that suit! Disgraceful!"

The fracas boiled over into a full-blown riot. Max and Mildred came under fire. Pelted with sand, doused with salt water and swung at with beach umbrellas, they locked hands and ran for the car. Once inside, they gawked dumbfounded through the windsheild as the parking lot swarmed with police cars. A black van arrived and spit out six police matrons. Armed with measuring tapes, the husky, long-skirted law-enforcers set to work arresting and escorting dress-code violators to paddy wagons. Max and Mildred watched wide-eyed until, with siren wailing, a paddy wagon carted off the last of the Rockaway Rockettes.

After the crowd dispersed Max and Mildred returned to the beach. They chose a sandy spot, this one closer to the parking lot—just in case. They spread the blanket and reclined on it. Max chuckled and pointed to a city ordinance posted on a nearby pole. He jumped to his feet. "It's a good thing I brought my camera!" Ignoring Mildred's protests, he pulled her to her feet and toward the sign. He stood her under it and insisted she strike a provocative pose. She obliged, grudgingly at first but then, feeling quite the seductress in her flesh-colored swimsuit, began to camp it up. Her hand went to her hip. A bare leg snaked around the pole. She looked up and, with her free hand, began thumbing her nose at the sign which decreed: "White and flesh-colored bathing suits are banned. Violators will be arrested on sight." Max snapped the picture and crowed with delight, completely unaware that another camera had captured, not only the lovers smooching on the blanket, but also Mildred in full flaunt.

The next evening the door of Mildred's apartment burst open and Max flew in, pale and trembling. He hurled a newspaper at her. "This ends it!"

"Ends what?"

He gathered the newspaper up from the floor. "Look—pictures of us spread across the front page. My God, here we're lying together for all the world to see!" His finger moved to the photo of Mildred thumbing her nose at the sign. "And this one! My God, you look naked."

"But you bought me that suit. You said it looked..."

"This has got to stop!" He gave the footstool a kick. "We can't go on like this. I'll be ruined!"

Mildred bent closer to the grainy photo of the recumbent couple and studied it. "Goodness, you'd need a magnifying glass to make out your face."

He brought his fist to his mouth and, chewing a knuckle, paced the room. At length he slumped onto the sofa. "I just can't risk it–not when I'm this close to being awarded a full-professorship..."

Max stepped up his efforts to achieve recognition for his academic excellence. To add to his prestige he took on, in addition to his job at Hunter, a part-time teaching position at Columbia University. He started by teaching classes under the supervision of Fraulein Holtz, the sole member of Columbia's German Department and a pioneer in redesigning intercultural studies. He was an immediate success, lauded for his teaching and recognized for his tireless research. This success was the shot in the arm he needed.

With his star rising he became even more obsessed with his academic future and, since he had more to lose, even more obsessed with keeping his and Mildred's affair a secret. A set of hard, fast rules–that's what was needed. Mildred received his dictum by mail. The first of his "Relationship Axioms" he had drummed into her many times: "You must never, in public, acknowledge me or in any way betray our intimacy." The second read: "Starting this fall, you may audit but not enroll in my class." Last and worst: "Henceforth our Wednesday night encounters shall be curtailed to one hour, thirty minutes."

Cast further into the shadows, Mildred became depressed

and jittery. Food lost its taste. Crying jags preceded every night's fitful sleep. Her grades plummeted. Then, one Wednesday as she anticipated Max's arrival, she hit upon a solution.

"Max!" she exclaimed the moment he came through the door, "we won't have to live like moles anymore!" She ignored the way his shoulders heaved, the way his eyes studied the ceiling as though scanning the sky for lightening. "I'm quitting Hunter, Max. They can't accuse you of fraternizing—not if I'm not a student—not if I quit."

His hand shook as it went to cover his heart. "Quit? We Germans never quit! Never!"

Taken aback, she swallowed hard. "I'm only one-eighth German."

He grabbed her to him until their noses nearly touched. "You listen to me. If I am to succeed, I must have a sensible, educated woman at my side, not a... not a QUITTER!"

Measles struck Hunter with a vengeance. The disease tore into Mildred with full fury. Her entire body become covered with pustules, each erupting through the skin like a molten volcano. Alone in her apartment and burning with fever, she called the landlady. Mrs. Goldblat summoned a doctor.

Quarantined in Hunter's infirmary, Mildred grew glassy-eyed and then delirious. It was Harry and not Max who defied the quarantine to sneak into her room late at night to apply cold cloths to her face, neck and arms.

"Don't fret," he said when she rallied and moaned for Max. "I'm sure he's just dying to visit you. It's just... well, measles can make a man sterile. Heavens, honey—you don't want 'Professor Casanova' to become sterile, do you?"

Mildred's confinement lasted ten days. Weak and wobbly-legged upon her discharge, she had to be wheeled to Harry's car. He drove her home and, with considerable puffing, carried her up the two flights to her apartment.

Mrs. Goldblat took charge of Mildred's recuperation. She dosed her with all sorts of tonics and advice. She chided Mildred only once, for sobbing over a picture of Max. "You silly girl! For such a schlemiel you shed tears? May beets grow in the schmuck's belly!"

Two weeks into Mildred's recuperation, Harry arrived carrying a bottle of fresh orange juice and a potted plant with clustered white flowers and flat, gray leaves. "What's this my sweet malingerer? Rosy cheeks? A sparkle in the eyes? A smile on that beautiful face?"

As he poured her a glass of juice, Mildred sniffed the flowers. "I don't get it—they smell like violets but they're the wrong color."

"*Allium tuberosum*—Chinese Chives, to you—also known as Garlic Chives. Make yourself a few cups of tea from the leaves and you'll feel better in no time."

"I hate garlic. Besides, I feel much better today—downright frisky."

He bent over and kissed her forehead. "Frisky enough to stop playing hooky?"

On Mildred's first morning back at Hunter she spotted Max strolling across campus. Surrounded by a gaggle of gushing girls, his black mane glistening in the early sunlight, he appeared to have not a care in the world. He joshed with them, clearly encouraging their adulation. When, with a sideward glance, he saw Mildred, he flinched.

She waved.

The smile left his face and, for a moment, his hand clasped his forehead. Then, as though suddenly remembering a matter of utmost urgency, he gave his admirers a sober nod, turned and hurried off.

Stunned by the snubbing Mildred returned home, threw herself across the bed and wept. By mid-morning hurt turned to anger; by noon, when she arrived back on campus, the anger turned to rage. She hurried to Max's office and began pounding on the door, her threats and curses filling the corridor. An elderly custodian rushed up. "Why, miss, please... calm down." He gaped at her bleeding knuckles. "I'll call someone..."

"No!"

"But can't I help?"

"Not unless you have a gun."

"A gun, miss?"

She fled from him, ran out of the building and raced to Iroquois Pond. Halfway across the footbridge, she leaned over the rail and vomited.

At precisely 7:00 P.M. that Wednesday evening she rose in the darkness of her apartment to answer a soft knock at the door. Max stood there, flowers in hand. "Bastard!" she screamed, slamming the door in his face. When he knocked again she opened the door, tore the flowers from his grasp, sent them flying down the corridor and, with a "Get lost!"—again slammed the door in his face.

"Liebling? Please, I have come to say goodbye. I'll be going away soon—far away. Perhaps forever."

It was more than she could bear. She opened the door and, weeping, fell into his arms.

Her grades, poor enough to warrant academic probation even before her illness, continued to slip. Unable to catch up as the semester dragged on, she saw no reason to prolong the inevitable. This time when she told Max that she was going to quit Hunter, he reacted very differently. "Yes! I concur completely. It's for the best!" He nuzzled her neck. "Nothing is more important to me than your happiness, my darling! I am desperately concerned about your health."

"My *health*? But Max, last time I mentioned quitting..."

"Liebling, you must promise me something... on your word of honor."

"Of course, sweetheart... have I ever turned you down?"

He sighed with relief. "You will return to your family for a while."

"To my family? To Conneaut?" She pushed him away. "No!"

"Please, try to understand. I am concerned about your health—especially in light of these winter storms. They're predicting one blizzard after another. You have been so very ill. Please, my darling, we mustn't risk a relapse."

Mildred extracted a cigarette from the pack in his shirt pocket. She placed it between her lips. Max produced a lighter and lit it. She inhaled deeply, then blew a stream ceiling-ward. "Max, none of this makes sense. If you want a brutal winter, spend one on the shores of Lake Erie. No, I'd be warmer here in New York."

"But dearest—a few months with your family—with your mother taking care of you..."

"No."

"Mildred, in the foreseeable future I won't have a moment to spend with you. I'll be traveling to international conferences, teaching, doing research, holding seminars." Tears rose in his eyes, turning them to liquid sapphires. "Please, Liebling, I beg of you, don't add the guilt of neglecting you to my burden."

"What do you mean by *the foreseeable future?*"

"Winter and spring will pass before you will have a chance to miss me. We can announce our engagement to your family in June, when I come to Ohio to fetch you."

"Our engagement? Oh, Max!" It was the first time he'd even hinted at marriage.

The next afternoon, despite a threatening sky, Mildred traveled by trolley downtown to have her valise repaired and to pick up a train schedule at Grand Central Station.

The storm broke minutes after she left the repair shop. Bone chilling wind penetrated her coat. Shivering, she wound her wool scarf tighter around her pulled-up collar. To lessen the sting of icy, wind-whipped raindrops, she kept her face down and, with eyes cast on the slippery sidewalk, proceeded with care.

Up ahead, directly in her path, a knot of people, the women bundled in furs, poured from the Ritz Carlton. They seemed a cheery lot. A familiar voice and high-pitched laugh came from their midst. Stunned, she saw Max standing at the center of the knot, his right arm around a beautiful young woman whose hair, more than anything, caught her eye. A rich copper fashioned in a flattering bouffant style, it shone like a new penny.

Mildred pivoted and ducked into a shadowy recess. Afraid Max might see her, she drew her scarf up to her eyes. She watched.

Those surrounding Max congratulated him. "You're a lucky chap... a lucky chap indeed!" A lanky, bearded man delivered a playful slap to Max's back.

A woman swathed in silver fox turned to the young woman at Max's side. "Now Erna, don't take too long getting settled."

"That's right, Mrs. Koischwitz!" The stout woman's escort nodded. "We want to hear all about Constantinople!"

Max laughed heartily and hugged the copper-haired beauty. A cab spun up to the curb. Max opened its door. He kissed the beauty on the lips and helped her in. Remaining on the sidewalk, he waved her off. Mildred watched the cab until it disappeared. The well-wishers started for waiting limousines.

Only when the street emptied did Max turn and, to Mildred's horror, march straight toward her.

"My God!" He snatched the scarf from her face. "It *is* you! What are you *doing* here? *Spying?*"

"What am *I* doing here? Who is that *woman*? Why were

those people congratulating you? My God, Max, are you... are you *married?*"

His eyes turned incredulous. "Married? What? What are you talking about? You're mad!"

"But... they called her Mrs. Koischwitz. And you... you *kissed* her!"

"Of course I kissed her! Since when is it a sin to kiss my brother's wife?"

"Oh sure... your brother's wife."

"Who else would she be? Erna arrived this morning from Constantinople."

"Erna...?"

"Honestly, Mildred, you do need a rest. Have you forgotten about my brother Otto?"

"But your name is Otto."

His eyes rolled. "It is my middle name just as it is his first name... after our grandfather. What is wrong with you? Don't you remember? I've mentioned how much Otto loves teaching at the American University in Constantinople."

Mildred's mind spun as it sought to recall and sort out all the things Max had told her about his family. His old Uncle Herbert came to mind, as did descriptions of cousins. There had been a sister... she had died an infant. He had described boyhood pranks he'd pulled on his younger brother Claus. But Otto? Had Max ever mentioned a brother named Otto?

Max's jaw worked. "Those people you saw me with... most of them are on Hunter's Board of Directors. What if they've seen you stalking me?"

"Stalking you?"

"You've probably ruined my career! You know I can't be involved with a student."

"You're being ridiculous! What difference does it make if they see me? Max, I'm not a student anymore. Don't you remember? I *quit*."

He blanched. "Scheiss!" Nostrils flaring, he seized her arm, hurting her. "Scheiss!"

She had learned long ago, in fact before she was seven, how to steel herself against pain and how, in the blink of an eye, to become someone else. "Now, now, Professor," she said, her voice taunting. "Let's not be crude. I take it the lovely Mrs. Koischwitz is enjoying her stay in New York?"

He gritted his teeth and propelled her toward the curb. His right arm shot into the air as though commanding the world to stop. A cab pulled over. He opened its rear door, pushed her onto the back seat and jumped in beside her.

"Where are we going my dear professor?"

"You, my suspicious wench, are going to meet Erna. If you don't believe me, perhaps you will believe her."

"Really, this isn't necessary."

"The poor soul comes thousands of miles to visit her dying father and now she must deal with a jealous, crazy woman!"

His indignation drained the last of her strength. "Oh Max, please, don't. I'll never doubt you again—I promise."

They traveled a mile or more before he leaned forward and told the cab driver to pull over. He tossed a five-dollar bill into the front seat. "I'll get out here—take the lady home." Then, to Mildred: "Go back to your apartment. Don't ever spy on me again. If you don't trust me, leave me."

Late that night he paid her an unscheduled visit. As they reclined on the bed, he stroked her naked body. "You must love me as much as I love you, Liebling... with the same ever-lasting, ever-trusting love."

Two days before she left for Conneaut, Max treated her to a night in the bridal suite of the Waldorf Astoria Hotel. Discretion, he insisted, precluded him from meeting her in the lobby.

She arrived by cab, entered an elevator and ascended to

the tenth floor. Arriving at the door, she took a moment to admire it. Done in plaster relief and painted gold, two cherubs caressed. Above the door and covered in gold leaf, a nymph winked.

Max opened the door and surveilled the hall. The coast clear, he gathered her up into his arms and carried her over the threshold. "My bride of brides!" He kicked the door shut.

The opulence of the suite took Mildred's breath. Flower arrangements decorated every table. Rose petals adorned the carpet. A crystal chandelier sparkled and reflected the glow of a hundred flickering candles. The bed peeped out from the next room. On it, crimson pillows formed a giant heart. He carried her to the window to behold New York's endless sea of lights.

"Oh Max, it's all so beautiful!"

He bore her past the white marble fireplace and with the gentleness of a prince, set her on the red velvet chaise lounge. "Close your eyes, Liebling."

As she obeyed, he fetched a stack of brightly wrapped packages from behind the sofa and placed them at her feet. A waiter, his eyes discreetly averted, carried in a tray of hors d'oeuvres. Another wheeled in a masterpiece of exotic food chilled by an exquisite ice sculpted gazelle.

"Max, this is too much! It must have cost you a fortune! Where in the world did you get the money for all this?"

"A certain publisher has given me a large advance. A very large advance."

A gypsy violinist appeared, his red blouse billowing, his gold-threaded sash glinting. To the strains of Sheherazade, Hungarian Dances and selections from Don Juan, the lovers sipped champagne from crystal flutes and licked pate from each other's fingers. Max popped pickled dove's eggs into her mouth. They gorged themselves on goose liver collared in truffles from France, picked at smoked sparrows from Spain and nibbled white caviar imported from Budapest.

Later, with the aroma of cherries jubilee still sweet in the room, Mildred sat on Max's lap and began to open the gifts. The first was a silk, sunset-colored gown. Next, a matching peignoir trimmed with exquisite marabou.

He smiled. "Well, say something!"

She smothered him with kisses. Then, pulsing with desire, she jumped to her feet, peeled off her clothes and let him slip the gown over her naked body. "Oh Max, it's from Paris!"

He lunged for her and, with the flourish of a bullfighter commanding a cape, enclosed her in the peignoir. His breath, brandied and moist, warmed her throat.

She spun free and, aping the famous dancer Isadora Duncan, cavorted about playing an imaginary tambourine, gyrating like a belly dancer. "Look, I'm your harem girl!" she cried. The sheer silk wed itself to her breasts.

Slowing the tempo, she became a vixen, slinking ever closer, taking slow, seductive steps in new, ermine-trimmed slippers. Placing her toe on Max's inner thigh, she showed off another of his gifts, a gold ankle-bracelet.

"You're driving me wild!" he shouted, his face flushed. He swept her up into his arms. Kissing her hungrily, he whisked her toward the bed.

"Oh Max, my heart is bursting with happiness! So many gifts, such exquisite, naughty lingerie—I feel like a bride!" They made love that night until exhausted and fell asleep in each other's arms.

The first to awaken, Mildred crept to the window to watch dawn bring down the curtain on that "night-of-nights." The moon, spent on lovers, grew feeble. A wash of light filled the lower sky and, as Max snored softly, strands of clouds rushed southward like wisps of a fleeing bride's veil.

I sing to use the waiting,
My bonnet but to tie,
And shut the door unto my house;
No more to do have I...

– Emily Dickinson (1830-1886)

6

Soon after their "night-of-nights," the professor and his mistress parted. Snow blanketed New York as he waved her off to Conneaut swearing his undying love and promising to write every day. She waved back, blew kisses and beseeched him to make the days hurry until he would come to Conneaut to make her his wife.

A pretty, dark-haired girl came running to meet the train as it pulled in to Conneaut's station. "Sis! Sis!"

"Edna Mae? No, it can't be..."

The girl danced about like an excited colt, grabbed Mildred and spun her around and around. "Who'd you expect? The ugly duckling?"

Mildred held her at arm's length. "You've turned into a beautiful swan!"

She rolled her eyes as a young man wearing bib overalls and a baseball cap ran up to them and slid to a stop. "This is Howie. Isn't he great? He's borrowed his father's truck to take you home."

Mildred extended her hand. "Howie! Your father's truck? How very sweet of you!"

The young man blushed and seemed not to know what to do with Mildred's hand once he took it. Edna Mae saved him by seizing Mildred's other hand and pulling her toward the truck. "Come on! Let's go!"

Howie set the suitcase atop the pile of lumber in the truck's bed, helped Edna Mae and then Mildred up into the cab, took his place behind the wheel and fired up the engine. Delighted to be seen with two such pretty females, he tooted the horn the entire length of Main Street.

Edna Mae giggled. "The old hometown looks great, doesn't it? Mayor Burton claims business has never been better! Look, Gunderson's Mercantile is adding a second story and the Roxy Theater is packing them in day and night. There goes Missus Van der Veer in her new mink–pretty good, huh, for the wife of a dairy farmer."

Howie waved to a friend and, forgetting himself, squeezed Edna Mae's knee. He pointed to a line of stevedores outside Fitzpatrick's Freight. "It's payday for those guys–they've never had it so good–Lake Erie must be the busiest port in the world, why..."

Edna Mae interrupted. "And Sis, a lot's happened since I last wrote you. Mrs. Hartley's husband ran off with her sister Grace. The bank got robbed by two guys wearing Halloween masks!"

"That ain't all," Howie said. "Sheriff Wilson, 'used to run Saturday night Bingo? Got himself arrested swindling the widow Koontz!"

The truck turned onto Grant Street, bounced over a series of potholes and skidded to a stop. Seeing something new in front of the house where she'd been raised, Mildred clamped a hand to her jaw. Where else but in this hick town, she thought, would a dentist solicit business by mounting in his front yard a pole from which hung a giant wooden tooth.

The door opened and Momma came flying out onto the front porch. "Millie! Millie, my baby!" She beckoned to the shadowy figure lurking just inside the doorway. "Robert! Come, greet Mildred!"

He stayed put as his wife greeted her daughter with hugs and kisses. Arm in arm they mounted the steps and approached him. He grudgingly stepped back to let them enter.

Mildred's forced smile faded the moment her eyes met his. "Hello, Doctor."

"So, kid, back under my roof again, huh?"

Hating to disappoint her as he had every delivery since she'd come home, old Silas "Si" Jenkins trudged past the wooden tooth and hoisted his mailbag up the stairs. From their chats he'd gotten to know more than he cared to about this German for whom the pretty blonde pined. Si found the situation so perplexing that he'd discussed it with friends at his Friday night poker game. "The damn Kraut—he promises to write her every day and forgets her the minute she's outta' sight."

Ed Whelan, the cobbler, had put off declaring three-of-a-kind to voice his indignation. "He must be a real rat to string along such a nice girl."

Now, seeing her hurry toward him, Si feigned preoccupation with his handful of mail for this address. "Mornin' missy."

"Anything for me?"

He handed her the envelopes and looked away as she whipped through them. "Mildred, honey, I know it isn't my business to say so, but maybe you should re-think tying the knot with this professor."

"Never!"

Every day she mailed a letter to Max. Not one was

answered nor returned. Thinking it would take Mildred's mind off the professor, Momma insisted she get out of the house and look for a job. The good doctor wholeheartedly concurred.

Times were good. With the unemployment rate the lowest in a decade, every store window along Conneaut's Main Street displayed a "Help Wanted" sign. The first place she applied, a seamstress's shop, hired her to hem napkins and tablecloths. Unable to stop daydreaming about Max and, prone to running home at midmorning to check the mail, she lasted less than a week.

The small town monotony of Conneaut enervated the former tripper of New York's light fantastic. She missed the city's hum, the excitement, the sophistication and the high-stepping nightlife.

Edna Mae tried everything to cheer her sister—pantomiming, dressing in crazy costumes, singing ribald songs, telling jokes and reading outlandish newspaper articles. "Get this one in the *Conneaut Gazette*, Sis..." she read:

> *AIMEE'S FLOCK RETURNS*
>
> *Choosing to forgive and forget, followers of the ebullient, platinum-haired preacher flock back to her extravagant religious services. Miss McPherson made headlines when lawmen, after concluding that she had neither died nor been resurrected, found her not in heaven but occupying a shack in the desert with her disciple-lover...*

"Sounds like heaven to me," Mildred replied, "...shear heaven!"

A letter of deliverance arrived before she started her second job—typing invoices at the foundry. Inside the house and locked in a shouting match with her stepfather over her "freeloading," she didn't see Si come bounding up onto the porch waving the envelope. "You got something, missy!"

She raced to the porch and grabbed the letter from Si's hand. Her face fell. It was not from Max. When at last she made out her grandfather's scrawl, her face brightened. Could she, old Captain Elijah Hewitson wanted to know, possibly come to Bar Harbor for a spell and give him a hand? Past eighty now and at loose ends since his wife's passing, he yearned to see Mildred once more before his eyesight left altogether. Besides, Greystone could use a woman's touch. He admitted to ailing a bit... "but please, Millie, don't mention that 'ailing' part to Aaron... he's off studying to be a doctor."

The name *Aaron* jumped off the page. Mention that Grandpa was ailing to Aaron? How ridiculous! She hadn't seen, much less thought of Aaron Stern in ages, not since she visited Greystone as a teenager and played with the eight-year-old imp. She had lived at Greystone, in her earliest years, and again after Momma's failed attempt at independent living in Greenwich Village. She'd been happy there until that awful day Momma married her dashing dentist. Back then, Aaron, the son of Grandfather's servant girl Golda, was just a tot. Although it was an innocent enough question, Mildred had angered her grandmother on that long ago day. "Grandmother, why doesn't Aaron have a father?"

The reprimand had been like a slap in the face. "Shame on you, Mildred! How dare you ask such a question! Suffice it to say that Golda is a Jew—her child doesn't require a father."

Grandfather Hewitson had, from the day of Aaron's birth, taken the boy under his wing. During summers spent at Greystone, Mildred and Edna Mae had come to love "Grampa's boy," the bright lad with the snapping dark eyes and mop of red curls.

Mildred folded the letter, put it in her pocket and went inside to pack. The next day, using the train ticket Elijah had enclosed in his letter, she left for Bar Harbor, Maine.

No one answered her knock on Greystone's massive front door. Sensing he was at home, she walked around the house and let herself in through the back door. A blast of cold, garbage-scented air led her to the kitchen where she found counters littered with half-empty cans of baked beans and chicken soup. Several dishes of moldy cat food lay about the floor. Unwashed dishes and utensils sat mute on the table. She found her grandfather feverish and half asleep in an unkempt downstairs bedroom.

Despite doctor prescribed pills and attempts to nourish him with rich broths, the old man grew worse. His last request, whispered moments before he died, came from a hallucinating mind. "Wife, anchor and sell all my ships. Give everything to my good Aaron."

She buried him in the family plot on a drizzling, overcast day. A few old friends, having read the obituary in the *Bar Harbor News*, attended. Among them was Elijah's banker. When Mildred asked him about a will, he drew a blank. "Don't think he had one, miss. Your grandfather liked to keep track of things himself."

"Can you tell me something about his finances?"

The banker sighed. "Poor Elijah. I know he didn't mean to leave me holding a hefty mortgage on Greystone and the several other loans I've foolishly made to him over the years. Unless someone can come up with enough to satisfy the bank, I'm afraid Greystone is headed for foreclosure."

She returned to the old mansion to box her grandfather's belongings. To her surprise she found, sandwiched between pages of her grandfather's book of accounts, five one-hundred dollar bills. Looking over the accounts netted something far more shocking–the secret of her grandfather's relationship to Aaron Stern. Going by entries ranging back to the date of Aaron's birth, entries that read: "For my son

Aaron," she knew at last who had fathered the son of the fiery maidservant Golda.

Within a month Greystone went on the auction block. On the day of the sale a letter arrived from Max:

> Berlin, Germany – June 1926
> Liebling,
>
> As you can tell by this stationery, I am not in New York. Dearest, at the invitation of the Board of Directors, I have returned to Germany for the summer to teach at the University of Berlin. Surely you would not have wanted me to pass up this spectacular opportunity.
>
> Germany is abysmal. The country, owing to the Treaty of Versailles, is on its knees. Inflation skyrockets. The problems of restoring industry, rebuilding cities and creating employment seem insurmountable. It is impossible for my homeland to pay the insane amount the Allies insist on for war damages. Imagine, thirty billion dollars plus interest!! My parents suffer deprivation of the worst kind. I am filled with anxiety for my beloved homeland.
>
> Liebling, it is only the thought of you that sustains me. Our hearts beat now and will always beat as one, my love. We are never truly apart. Although we must put our wedding plans on hold, I take this summer assignment knowing it will make our future together more secure. Take heart! We will be reunited when autumn kisses the trees and turns them gold.
>
> Keep me in your heart, meine Liebchen.
>
> (signed) Max

For an actress to be a success,
she must have the face of Venus,
the brains of Minerva,
the grace of Terpsichore,
the memory of a Macaulay,
the figure of June,
and the hide of a rhinoceros.

– Ethel Barrymore (1879-1959)

7

She returned to New York to await her lover's arrival. The money she'd managed to salvage from Greystone dwindling fast, she settled into a cheap rented room and set out to find an acting job. Each day, as she pounded the pavement between auditions, she posted a letter to Professor Koischwitz in care of the University of Berlin. Returning each evening from a day of turndowns, she checked the mailbox.

A friend's tip sent her to the Roxy Theater. If nothing else, her pitch was improving. "Honestly, mister, I can sing, dance, act, do slapstick, walk-ons, carry signs—you name it, I'll do it!"

The director's shiny-head reflected the footlights. As if she were invisible, he kept his eyes locked on the line of high-kicking chorus girls. "Yeah? So what makes you different from a million other dames? Leave your number."

Subsequent tips resulted in three upcoming auditions. Success in the first would lead to a speaking part in Eugene

O'Neill's *Desire Under the Elms.* A walk-on bit in Sean O'Casey's *The Plough and the Stars* might come of the second. The one she hoped most to get meant becoming "the other woman" in W. Somerset Maugham's *The Constant Wife.*

The first audition went sour as the director thought her "too tall" for *Desire.* Nor did the second pan out. "You won't do—you're too Scandinavian for O'Casey. Next!"

Mildred's temper flared. "Too Scandinavian? No problem! I'll just dye my hair red and tattoo a jillion freckles on my face, you idiot!"

Jeffrey Tuttle held the audition for *The Constant Wife.* He sensed Mildred's desperation. "Your delivery's not bad, kid, not bad. But I don't see you as 'the other woman.' How about trying out for another part, something more in keeping with your talent? Come back Thursday at five."

Mildred woke on the day before her call back and set out on a buying spree, resolved to spend her last penny if that's what it took to land the part. At an upscale dress shop near Times Square, she plunked down fifty dollars for a figure-clinging, knee-skimming creation of aquamarine Canton crepe. Against the advice of the saleswoman, she ordered it shortened another two inches to show off her long, shapely legs. From a millinery shop on Fifth Avenue she purchased the perfect picture hat, a wide-brimmed Panama banded with silk cornflowers. At a department store she bought four-inch high heels, elbow length gloves, a jeweled cigarette holder, sheer stockings, a lacy garter belt and a satin, extra-uplift brassiere.

On the way home she stopped at "Beauty Salon of the Stars." She ordered the works—mudpack, facial, manicure, pedicure and eyebrow tweezing. The operator posed to do her hair raised an eyebrow at Mildred's insistence, "I want the very same shampoo you use on Gloria Swanson."

"I've never done Miss Swanson."

"All right then, Mary Pickford. Now, for the final rinse

you're to use the juice of two fresh lemons. And don't leave me under the dryer too long–I snarl less while still slightly damp. Now, as to the style... I want something sexy–not brassy. Bouncy but sophisticated. Perhaps a hint of playfulness."

"Anything else?"

"Yes. Tomorrow I'm auditioning for a leading role on Broadway. Send me out of here looking good enough to get the director's nod and you'll get an extra ten bucks and a front row seat on opening night."

A case of jitters kept her awake the entire night. Puffy-eyed, she drank coffee all morning. At noon, her stomach knotted, she began grooming for the audition. Her face, blotched from a reaction to the mudpack, took forever. The seams of her nylons insisted on marching a crooked path up the backs of her legs. She broke a fingernail trying to straighten them. A quick repair and an eternity for the new polish to dry, she began to dress. She flipped on the radio. Hearing the time announced, she let out a shriek. Her clock had stopped! With less than ten minutes to get to the theater, she raced downstairs as fast as her high heels would allow and hailed a cab to the theater.

Mr. Tuttle not only arrived late, he had no idea who she was. When she explained that she had come at his request to try out for the lead, he rolled his eyes. "You got your wires crossed, girlie."

"But you said..."

He tossed her a script. "Here, read the maid's part."

Tears made her eyes smart. Her mascara began to run. Little black rivulets seeped from her eyes and, smeared by her fingertips, grew to fat black smudges. Bewildered by Mr. Tuttle's smirk, she poured over the script in search of the maid's part. There it was: *MAID–enter stage left, cross to the door. Open it.*

A man stood in the wings. Amused by the intensity of the tall, shapely blonde sporting a fighter's shiner, he couldn't resist. "Ready slugger? Now, when I push this button it don't mean ya' should come out for round two." He pushed the button. The theater filled with the sound of door chimes.

Mildred took a deep breath and, hips swaying, walked across the stage and paused in front of the door. Her hand seized the knob and pulled. The door wouldn't budge. She tightened her grip and pulled harder. The flimsy fake wall quivered. She seized the doorknob with both hands and pulled with all her might.

It sprung toward her as though pushed in by a tornado. Thrown off balance, she reeled backwards. Her backward flight blocked by an overstuffed chair, she regained sufficient composure to recite her line. "May I take your hat, sir?"

"No! No! No!" Tuttle jumped to his feet, flung his green visor to the floor and marched toward the stage. "Fer chrissakes woman! Where'd ya' ever learn to open a door like that?"

"Well, I..."

"You what? Look kid, a maid opens a door gently, not like a wrestler trying to pull somebody's arm off!"

"Sorry. I'll try again."

"Nah, I don't think so. Your diction stinks."

"Stinks? But I only said six words..."

"Next!"

She returned to her apartment in a daze, flopped across the bed and cried herself to sleep. A nightmare brought fits of tossing and turning. Resplendent in a wedding gown, she repetitively floated down the aisle toward Max. Every time she reached his side he pushed her back. "No! No! No! You are all wrong for the constant wife! Your diction stinks!"

A knock at the door caused her to wake with a start. She slipped on her robe and opened the door.

"Hi slugger, mind if I come in?"

"What?"

"I wanna make ya' an offer."

"What kind of offer?"

"Look, I'm not just some dummy who stands in the wings pressin' buttons for Tuttle." He shot out his hand. "Cecil 'The Brains' Cerruti at yer service, sweetheart. I'm here to offer ya' a big part in my movie. Tuttle and me don't see eye-to-eye on lots of things. I say ya' have talent. He says ya' don't. So we made a little bet."

She let him in and listened to his proposal. He wanted her for his first motion picture, *Unwelcome Children*. The film, he assured her, would be a landmark. It would set the record straight regarding illegitimacy and unwed mothers.

He started pacing, waving a smoldering cigar. "See kid, a movie's no good unless it delivers a message... and my picture delivers one helluva message. It takes the blame off bastard kids and puts it right smack where it belongs, on whoring mothers!" The anger in his voice suggested a personal vendetta.

"Where are you *from* Mr. Cerruti?"

"Me? What's it to ya'? Ya' want the part or don't ya'? And don't expect to earn much 'cuz you won't. But, ya'll get great exposure. I suppose ya' know exposure's everything in this business."

"When do I start?"

He withdrew a contract and handed her a pen. His finger tapped the dotted line. "Put yer John Hancock right here, ."

"But it's a contract, shouldn't I read it first?"

"Nah, it's just a bunch of boilerplate. They all say the same thing. Just sign here."

She signed.

Illegitimacy was never, not even in the roaring twenties, mentioned in polite society. Movies dealing with unwed mothers, promiscuity, gambling, fornication, adultery or divorce were taboo.

Mildred, down to her last few dollars, couldn't afford to be choosy. When a friend asked if she had any qualms about signing to do *Unwelcome Children*, Mildred gave a candid reply. "Sure I do, but let's face it, one has to eat. Honey, my back's so up against the wall I'd do a film written by the devil himself."

The camera can be the most deadly weapon since the assassin's bullet. Or it can be the lotion of the heart...

– Norman Parkinson (1913-1990)

8

The shooting of *Unwelcome Children* took place in an old barn on the outskirts of Camden, New Jersey. Required to live within earshot of the "studio," Mildred drew an advance and rented an efficiency apartment above a drugstore.

Her moving from New York presented a problem. What if Max returned from Germany? How would he find her? She'd sent him her new address but, since he'd answered none of her letters, maybe he hadn't received them. Hoping to solve the dilemma, she invited her Hunter College friend, Harry Schwartz, to visit her in Camden.

Harry arrived on a Sunday afternoon, picked her up and spun her around. Remembering how she enjoyed Edna Ferber, he presented her with a copy of the author's latest work, *Showboat,* and a heart-shaped box of chocolates. He insisted on treating her to dinner at Camden's finest restaurant.

Over a second helping of crown roast of lamb and browned potatoes, she talked excitedly of Max's return to Hunter at summer's end.

Harry shook his head. "Don't get your hopes up, honey. It seems your heartthrob has a personal problem in der Vaterland. According to Schlecter, the new head of the German department, Hunter has extended Max's leave."

"Personal problem? What personal problem?"

"Bigelow is going to take over his classes."

"Answer me, what personal problem?"

Harry put down his fork and glanced at his watch. "Sweetheart, I gotta' go..."

"Wait!" She quickly reached into her purse and withdrew an envelope. "Harry, please, you're the only one at Hunter I can trust to give this to Max..."

"He isn't coming back, Mildred."

"Of course he is! Please, be a darling and see that he gets this the moment he returns. It contains my address in Camden and directions to where I'll be filming."

Harry pocketed the envelope. He planted a kiss on her cheek then held her at arm's length. "See ya' kid, don't take any wooden nickels."

A dairy farmer gave Mildred a lift from the drugstore to the city's outskirts. When a particularly run-down barn came into sight, he pointed to it. "That's the place, girlie. I should know... 'used work there milkin' Holsteins. Had me a heart attack birthin' a calf."

Mildred thanked him for the ride, climbed down from the truck, waded through knee-high weeds to the barn and ventured inside. The place reeked of manure, mildew and soured milk cans. Cecil Cerruti acknowledged her entrance. "The star has arrived!" He took her hand and led her to a bald man seated on a bail of hay. "Gorgeous, meet the film's director, my old friend Sid Platzner."

Greatly magnified, Sid's watery blue eyes stared into hers through thick, horn-rimmed lenses then swept down over her body, appraising her breasts, waist, hips and legs. "Not bad," he said to Cecil, "not bad–a tad *matronly*–but not bad."

Mildred glared at him. "Matronly?"

Sid rose. His hand encircled her upper arm and squeezed it. "Don't get hot—a tad 'matronly' is what we need considerin' yer about to become a mother."

It took Mildred less than a day's shooting to realize Sid was no director. What he was—a pervert, lecher and an oversexed, chauvinistic slave driver—became apparent all too soon.

He insisted on a fourteen-hour workday that started at dawn so as to "capture the right light." Only after sunset, when it became too dark inside the barn to see, did shooting stop.

Chores came with the starring role. Mildred was expected to run errands, serve as wardrobe seamstress and apply make-up to the hungry faces of dollar-a-day extras. On the rare occasion when Cecil could pay, she received twenty dollars for a seventy-hour week. In addition to supporting herself on this princely amount, she often had to cough up enough money to buy sack lunches for the entire crew.

Unwelcome Children seemed doomed from the start. Starring in the role of "Barbara Elliott," a pregnant whore about to give birth, Mildred anticipated her final scene with dread.

In the meantime, Sid ran amuck with "creative interpretation." Changing his take on the character "Barbara Elliot" more frequently than he changed his shirts, he saw her as every wayward woman from Mary Magdalene to Sadie Thompson.

Two days before shooting Mildred's scene, he took her aside to share his latest insight. "Look kid, yer vile. Yer mean spirited as hell. Yer so rotten yer gonna' cast off yer newborn twins like two dirty socks. Any questions?"

"Just one. Not having given birth on camera before, I'm at a loss as to what attire you would deem appropriate for this stellar performance."

"'Fer chrissakes, do I have to do all the thinking 'round

here? You figure out what to wear. But remember, the audience can't see your 'gina."

"My what?"

"You know, yer fuzz box—yer snatch—yer pussy."

"Sir, are you referring to a female's private parts?"

"Who calls it that?"

Mildred arrived on the set, looking like a giant, white-sheeted pumpkin. Sid scowled. "You call that a birthing costume?"

"They won't see my 'gina."

He signaled for two extras to help her up onto the gurney he'd rented from a hospital. A plumber from Camden would play the doctor and his wife, the nurse. They put on surgical masks and positioned themselves on either side of Mildred as she lay on the gurney. Sid called for quiet on the set and waited impatiently for the drone of a barnstormer to fade away.

The moment she heard "*Lights! Camera! Action!*" Mildred entered into the last stage of labor. Writhing, a clenched fist stuck into her mouth to keep from biting her tongue, her eyes flashing and tormented with pain, she made the cameraman shudder.

Sid, sweating with excitement, signaled for ever-closer close-ups of her contortions. Time after time he yelled "Cut!" He jumped to his feet, ordered a light adjusted, a microphone angled to catch her screams or a screen moved to achieve darker shadows.

His "*Roll 'em*" cued Mildred to resume her wild thrashing and fist gnawing. Convinced he should pace the action lest viewers faint, he repeatedly called for the cameraman to zero-in on the doctor's grim face and nurses' gaping mouth.

To simulate "heaven-sent thunder," Sid had a man off-camera pound on an oil drum. Although they seemed out of place in a delivery room, Sid called for bolt after bolt of lightening which, in spite of coming from the sweep of a Klieg light, seemed quite real.

After two-dozen takes and, at the height of the storm, Mildred gave birth. The camera moved in close as the doctor delivered her wailing twins—identical, naked, glass-eyed dolls. He held them up by their heels and slapped their bottoms. The wailing came from two off-stage babies rented for the afternoon and pinched on cue.

Mildred's final lines climaxed the action. To the crescendo of her newborns' wails she screamed, "No! I don't want them! Take them away! Take them away!"

"Cut!" Sid cried out. "That's a wrap!"

Mildred slumped back onto the gurney. Before she could summon enough strength to get up and join the exodus of her fellow actors, Sid stopped her. "Stay put, kid." They were alone in the barn. He thrust his hand up inside her birthing costume.

"You pig!" A kick to his chest sent him reeling backwards. He toppled over a stool and struck his head on a stake. As he lay stunned, she gathered the birthing costume around her, ran from the set, out of the barn and across the pasture.

A pair of strong hands caught her from behind just as she reached the road. Moist breath touched the back of her neck. Infuriated, she closed her eyes, wheeled around and let her fist fly.

"Ouch!" Max exclaimed, backing off.

She stared at him in open-mouthed silence.

They made love all night. When at last he raised the shade of her bedroom window, Mildred stretched in the sunlight and tried to coax him back to bed. Nothing would detract from this ecstasy. Her questions could wait.

He declined the invitation. "I'm starved! Look what you've done—you've turned a gentleman with no appetite into a ravenous ape."

He buttered toast and made coffee as she scrambled eggs with bits of bacon. He ate with gusto, polished his plate, rose and went to his briefcase. "Liebling! I have a surprise for you. Close your eyes!"

Her heart jumped. She knew what it was, she knew! Eyes pinched shut, she waited and, sensing him at her side, held up her left hand for him to slip the engagement ring on her finger.

He turned her hand over. "No peeking!" The instant she felt its weight on her palm her heart sank. "Now, no tears! No matter how moved you are, no tears! Open your eyes now—open them and behold my latest book!"

Her eyes remained closed.

"Look, Liebling—*Textbooks and Kulturkunde*! 'Kulturkunde,' if you remember, means 'cultured children.'"

Puzzled by her refusal to gaze upon his great work, he turned from her and walked to the window. He stood there gazing out as though enraptured by a rainbow. "Isn't it wonderful to think I've produced such a terribly important work! Thanks to this book students will come to comprehend not only the language and literature of Germany, but also the temperament of its people!"

Her eyes opened slowly. "That's nice, Max."

He seemed not to notice. "In this country there is such a strong reaction against Germany's positivism and naturalism. Writers alone do not give the American student the right information. Don't you agree? I intend to stir the impressionable minds of my students. You can't imagine what a thrill it is to regale them with German mythology or to introduce them to Spengler."

Oswald Spengler: Max's hero. No student ever successfully completed Max's course without memorizing the rudiments of Spengler's theories. Max completely subscribed to Spengler's thesis that civilizations underwent the same life histories as organisms and that Western culture had entered the twilight of its existence.

His monologue continued as she cleared the table. "What do you think gives credence to Spengler? Decadence! Look about you, Liebchen! Decadence abounds! Gone is the heroic world of Wolfram's *Parsifal*! Lost forever is Wagner's *Gotterdammerung*!"

Seeing his eyes cloud with hopelessness, Mildred forgot her disappointment and wondered at his dire pronouncement. Why was he always torturing himself with this strange longing for Germany's glorious past?

Despite her protests, Max returned to New York that very day. He'd resumed teaching at both Hunter and Columbia. Given no choice, Mildred stayed in Camden to wind-up *Unwelcome Children*.

His subsequent visits to Camden, always short and on weekends, were sporadic. The one thing she could count on was that, within moments of coming through her door, he'd sink into the overstuffed chair, exhausted.

Once, when he showed up pale and with huge dark circles under his eyes, Mildred protested. "You can't go on like this, Max. You have to get more sleep or you'll get sick! Surely you could cut down your workload..."

He threw up his hands. "You don't understand!" He began pacing, using his fingers to tick off his commitments. His writing required extensive research. He belonged to six professional organizations that looked to him to set their standard of excellence. The fall semester, with ever-larger classes, was shaping up to be his busiest yet.

"But Max, it's too much—teaching day classes at Hunter and night classes at Columbia..."

He seized her arms. "No! I love my work! It's the dunderheads—the fools in Hunter's administrative bureaucracy—they're the ones I hate! How dare they ask me for an accounting of my time!"

"Fools is a good name for them."

He withdrew his pocket watch, stared at it and shook his

head. "Never do I count the time I spend conferring with students. Would they have me punch a time clock to keep track of the hours I spend in libraries or at my desk preparing my lectures, correcting essays or reading books?"

"But sweetheart, don't they know your every waking moment is devoted to your work?"

"My lectures on the contemporary novel, on drama or even on German literature are to standing room only. They're aware of the hordes of students not even enrolled in my class that crowd in just to listen! Asking me to account for my time is just a smokescreen to hide their real reason for denying me a full-professorship."

"What *real* reason?"

"They're convinced I'm a Jew."

"Ridiculous! They've actually said such a thing?"

"I don't need their verbalizing."

She loosened his tie and, yearning to comfort him, led him to bed. With the exception of getting up for the necessaries, they remained there, lost in each other, for the remainder of the weekend. Before he left on Sunday afternoon she clung to him. "Promise Max? Promise to miss me terribly?"

"Have you forgotten? I am a man whose mind dwells always in the empyrean?"

Hoping his response was in some way a reply to her question, she looked up the definition of that strange word the moment he left.

> *Empyrean: n. The highest reaches of heaven; the sky, firmament; in the realm of epic visions from which petty practical affairs of the day-to-day world are excluded.*

During a subsequent visit Max reassured her he would try to see her more often. "But you must promise me, Liebling, that under no circumstance will you tire yourself by coming to see me in New York."

With the filming of *Unwanted Children* coming to an end, Cecil Cerruti took a break from his producer's duties to visit his star in her apartment. "Ya've done a fabulous job, Mildred. Take it from me, this film's gonna' be a hit!"

She folded her arms and gave him the fish eye. "You didn't come all the way over here to tell me that."

"We need yer help, kid. All ya' gotta' to do is show up next Friday night on the toll bridge in Philly."

"Philadelphia?"

"Ya'll be lookin' nine months knocked-up, got it?"

"I show up on a bridge in Philadelphia looking nine months pregnant..."

"Yeah, just strap a big pillow on yer belly and cover it with one of them maternity dresses. Arch yer back. Nothin' to it!"

"For God' sake, Cecil... *what?*"

"Don't worry, Sid will be there. All ya' gotta' do is wait for his signal and ya' climb up on the bridge's railing. Ya' shiver, maybe wail a little and pretend yer gonna' jump. That's all ya' gotta' do!!"

"That's *all??*"

"Guaranteed! Sid will see to everything else. Trust me, we'll make sure ya' get noticed!"

Dumfounded, Mildred walked to the table and sat down. Cecil came up behind her and placed his hands on her shoulders. "It's called publicity, baby. PUBLICITY–the life-blood of this business. Ya' can pull a little..."

"Suicide? No way!"

"Look, doll. It's not like we're talkin' the real thing here. Ya' just PRETEND yer gonna' jump."

"I won't do it."

Chewing on his cigar, he reached into his pocket and withdrew a rumpled sheet of paper. He placed it on the table in front of her, smoothed it out and tapped on the scrawled signature. "Oh, ya'll *do* it. Recognize yer John Hancock, Miss Mildred Gillars?"

She snatched up the paper and read the fine print above her signature:

> *In addition to the aforementioned terms of this contract I hereby agree to render whatever service the producer deems necessary to promote and publicize this film.*

Cecil buffed his fingernails on his sleeve. "Ya' know what happens to contract-breakers? They get blackballed, baby. Break yer contract and ya'll never work again—not even in the circus!"

He was right about one thing. She didn't have to jump. Along with the hoopla over Lindbergh's flying across the Atlantic, this article appeared in *The New York Times*:

> *ACTRESS ARRESTED*
> *FOR PUBLICITY HOAX*
>
> *Actress Mildred E. Gillars gave the name "Barbara Elliot" Friday night after threatening to jump to her death from a Philadelphia bridge. By her phony suicide attempt she hoped to publicize a sleazy movie about unwed mothers in which she stars. Miss Gillars was cited for disturbing the peace and given a stern reprimand.*

The article, buried with others in a section captioned, "Bizarre Tidbits" was not buried deep enough to escape Max's eyes. Infuriated by it, he sat down and wrote:

> My Dear Ridiculous Movie Star,
>
> Obviously you have lost your mind and all sense of decorum. I am embarrassed for both of us. Your conduct leaves me no choice but to question the continuance of our relationship. At this point I have serious doubts as to our future. It will take some time for me to get over this—if ever.
>
> Humiliated, (signed) Max

Telling lies is a fault in a boy,
an art in a lover,
an accomplishment in a bachelor,
and second-nature in a married man.

– Helen Rowland
(A Guide to Men, 1922)

9

It took the pawning of everything she owned and hitting up her friends for loans to raise enough to reserve the same bridal suite in the Waldorf Astoria that Max had, a year earlier, secured for their "night-of-nights."

It would be a reprise of that night. She overlooked no detail in its planning. Counting on nostalgia, surprise and the embers of banked love to rekindle her soulmate's passion, she arrived at the Waldorf hours ahead of time to set the scene. The room had a radio. She turned it on. Soft strains of Hindemith's *Das Marienleben* poured from the set filling the suite with an enchanting melody.

Max had treated her to hotel-prepared delicacies. With such a repast far beyond her budget, she had smuggled into the room a valise full of the best Schwartz Delicatessen had to offer. She arranged and rearranged sliced bread, cold cuts and cheese. The tin of liver pate she showcased by setting atop an upturned glass.

She unpacked the exquisite lingerie Max had given her.

There would be time enough for a bubble bath and to dress as a temptress after making the phone call.

Max had always, even during his recent visits to Camden, avoided giving her his home phone number. Forcing herself to forget an old promise, she placed a call to Columbia University's faculty club. It took quite a performance to feign an emergency of sufficient urgency to obtain the number at which Professor Koischwitz could be reached.

Her hand shaking, she dialed. The phone on the other end rang three times before someone picked up the receiver. "Hello my darling!" she said, "It's Mildred!"

"'Dis is Koischwitz residence. With whom you wish to speak?"

"Max?"

"Professor Koischwitz is not in. Who is calling?"

"Mildred Gillars... who is this?"

"Mrs. Koischwitz, Erna Koischwitz."

Mildred breathed a sigh of relief. "Erna! Of course! You're Max's sister-in-law!"

"Who? We've met?"

"Well, not actually, but Max has told me all about you!"

"He has?"

"I can't tell you how much I look forward to meeting you some day."

A long silence. "You wish to leave message?"

"Why... yes. Would you be so kind as to have Max call me the minute he gets in? I can be reached at the Waldorf Astoria... tell him I'll be waiting." A click followed by a dial tone caused Mildred to hold the receiver out from her ear. As though to deny being silenced, she completed the message. "Tell him to hurry!"

Dressed in the same filmy, crimson negligee she had worn to perform the Harem Dance for Max on their night-of-nights, Mildred paced the bridal suite waiting for his call. As the hours passed the food she'd laid out began to wilt; corners turned up on the slices of cheese, crackers lost their crisp and the cold cuts became tinged with gray. A wedge of ice chilling the one bottle of wine she could afford melted down to a sliver.

Convinced he hadn't gotten the message, she started for the phone. A vigorous knocking caused her to wheel around. "Max! Just a minute, sweetheart!" She raced to the door and, after a second's pause to fluff the marabou trimming her negligee, threw it open.

A woman stood there, her large bust, wasp waist and full hips encased in a long, snug-fitting coat that matched the midnight blue of her velvet tam. Her eyes sparked like emeralds. Without smiling, she pulled the tam from her head. Curls the color of copper cascaded about the beautiful face.

"Miss Gillars?"

"Yes?"

"I am Mrs. Koischwitz. May I come in?"

"Erna! Of course!"

Raising an eyebrow at the suggestiveness of Mildred's gown, the visitor entered. The eyebrow remained raised as she took in the burning candles, the tiny wisps of white smoke rising from sticks of burning incense and the food laid out on the table. She walked to the loveseat and sat down.

Mildred began to fidget. "May I offer you some wine, perhaps some crackers?"

"No, nothing."

Feeling somehow undressed by the woman's intense stare, Mildred shivered. "How are the children? Your husband?"

"My husband? Maybe *you* should tell *me*!"

"I beg your pardon?"

"You American women—so brazen, you are! You have no shame. You carry on with married men!"

"But Max isn't..."

"No? What tale he wove this time?"

"Please, we are not speaking of the same man."

"No?"

"Erna, you're married to Max's brother, Otto. I caught a glimpse of you shortly after you arrived from Constantinople to see your father—he was ailing, I believe. Yes, Max has told me all about you and Otto."

The woman snorted. "Rubbish! He has no such brother. And how could I visit my father? My father was dead already before my first birthday!"

"But... Max said..."

"Please. I am Erna, the wife of Max Otto Koischwitz, Professor of German literature at Hunter College. We are married. We have daughter."

Mildred's mouth flew open. "No!"

"Yes. I give birth to little Stella—Stellika we call her—in Germany this past summer." The gloved hand reached into the purse and withdrew a photo. "Look, we take picture."

Mildred stared into Max's face as he smiled up at her from the glossy surface, his one arm around Erna, his other holding an infant. The room beginning to spin. The photo fell to the carpet. With vomit rising in her throat she turned and reeled toward the bathroom.

Erna took off her coat and threw it over a chair. She walked slowly into the bathroom and sat on the edge of the tub to watch the negligee-gowned temptress with the luxuriant blonde hair wretch into the toilet. She remained silent until Mildred, reduced to dry heaves, began to weep. She helped her sobbing rival up from the floor and back to the loveseat.

"We need drink," Erna said as she strode to the ice bucket. She opened the bottle of wine and, while filling two goblets, noted the food spread out on the table. "It looks delicious. But the pate—not the kind Max favors. It is liver, yes? More he enjoys smoked salmon. Oh, forgive me, you went to much trouble..."

They drank in silence. Only after each finished a second

goblet did the awkward dialogue commence. "I swear to you, I didn't know, Mrs..." Mildred's throat froze around the name; the name she'd so often fantasized would be hers.

"Erna. You call me Erna."

"He told me you were his sister-in-law."

"I am his wife. I come from Germany in 1920 and find work as governess for wonderful family. You know Hartman family? They have mansion on Park Avenue. Philanthropists, yes, I believe that is the word. Mr. Hartman help me through Columbia where I study accounting until..."

Mildred cut to the quick. "When did you meet Max?"

Erna thought for but a moment before answering. "We meet August, 1924. Right away he ask me to marry. I answer 'yes,' but not for maybe one year or more. I wanted first return to American College for Women in Constantinople to complete Masters Degree."

"He was engaged to you when I met him? No! That can't be..."

"Please, I don't lie."

"No, of course not." Even if it killed her, she had to know. "Tell me, please, when did you marry?"

"Second Saturday of December, 1925."

Mildred's mind flew back through time until it snagged as though on a barb. December, 1925—the month she'd spent battling measles in Hunter's infirmary! She lowered her head and rubbed her eyes as though to erase a vision of Max on his honeymoon while she lay at death's door. "I was told he stayed away for fear of catching the measles and becoming sterile."

Erna rose. "Fraulein, I go now. My breasts fill with milk."

She put on her coat and placed the blue velvet tam back atop the mass of copper curls. "Such an appetite has little Stellika—always she wants to nurse!" Keeping up the nervous chatter, she edged toward the door. "She is very smart... very intelligent... already this is evident. Such beautiful eyes she has–like peeping stars. Her hair is shiny as coal but unfortunately, how you say... naughty... no, unruly, like..."

"Max?"

"Please, I go now."

Dazed, Mildred remained seated, staring at the door through which Erna disappeared. In time the numbness wore off. Rage took its place. Cursing Max with screamed obscenities, she caromed through the bridal suite smashing everything in her path. Envisioning the wine bottle to be Max's head, she smashed it against the fireplace. Seizing the fork she'd brought to spear the cold cuts, she stabbed the red satin pillow as though it were Max's heart.

Cornelissen, to try the gullibility of the public, reported in the papers that he had twenty ducks, one of which he cut up and threw to the nineteen, who devoured it greedily. He then cut up another, then a third, and so on till nineteen were cut up; and as the nineteenth was gobbled up by the surviving duck, it followed that this one duck actually ate nineteen ducks—a wonderful proof of duck voracity. This tale had the run of all the papers, and gave a new word to the language.

(French, *cane,* a duck.) Canard; more commonly: Hoax

– Cobham Brewer (1810–1897)
(Dictionary of Phrase and Fable, 1898)

10

Broke, in debt and convinced by Cecil Cerruti that *Unwanted Children* needed only a few of her scenes re-shot in order to be a blockbuster, Mildred returned to the barn-turned-movie studio. When it dawned on the crew that he intended to pay them with promises, the re-shooting ground to a halt and they took off. Cecil found Mildred a "temporary" job as a hat-check girl and magician's assistant at a nightclub in Cherry Hill. He then went looking for an "angel."

It took him a year to find the wealthy, stage-struck matron, Mrs. Terrence Wofford. Wooed by the guarantee of a leading role in Cecil's next movie, she eagerly agreed to advance the money he needed to complete the filming of *Unwanted Children*.

His pockets lined with the benefactor's money, Cecil tore Mildred away from her hats and disappearing act, reassembled the crew and returned to the Camden cow barn. Flush now, and certain he could tap Mrs. Wofford's wealth indefinitely, he took his sweet time in winding things up.

The re-shooting of Mildred's scenes dragged on for nine months. The fleecing of "angel Wofford" might have gone on forever had she not caught on, threatened Cerruti with arrest and demanded an accounting of every penny she'd advanced.

Film distributors laughed in his face. "Never heard of ya'."

"Whadda' ya' take me for, Cerruti?"

"You think I'm nuts? Only a moron would take a flyer on this flick. It's written by a nobody, stars a nobody and–no offense intended–it's directed by a nobody! These days ya' need big names to fill seats at two bits a ticket."

If grabbing the public's imagination was what it took, Cecil knew just how to grab it. "Believe me, Mildred, this time I'm handling it myself. I've got all the kinks ironed out."

She shook her head in disbelief. "That's what Sid said, remember? Or have you forgotten that fiasco that earned me a citation for disturbing the peace?"

"This is different, look." He handed her a copy of an advertisement he intended to place in newspapers:

URGENT MESSAGE!

Mrs. Barbara Elliott to her missing husband: About to give birth to your twins. Please come home. Don't let ours be Unwelcome Children.

"*Barbara Elliott*? My character in the movie is advertising in newspapers?"

"That's right, kiddo."

"I don't get it."

"Naturally ya' don't–my plan's brilliant!"

Timed to touch the million or so holiday-spirited readers, the ad would be placed in the Christmas Eve edition of both *The New York Times* and the *Camden Press Telegram*. Seconds after the papers hit the street, Mildred would start calling radio stations and reporters.

At Cecil's insistence, she stood before him and, pretending to speak into a telephone, rehearsed. "Hello, this is Barbara Elliot—the woman pregnant with twins who placed the ad in today's newspapers. I'm at the end of my rope! My husband has deserted me—he doesn't want these babies—they're unwanted children! I am desperate! Do you hear me? Desperate!"

"Still not enough emotion!" Cecil complained after the tenth run-through. "You're not talkin' to a bunch of dopes! These are hard-shelled news guys. Get their attention! Convince 'em this is a front page human interest story."

The brilliant Cerruti had, on the day he placed the ad, already doomed his "can't fail" plan, for when asked by the ad-taker for a phone number, he'd unwittingly, or more precisely "witlessly," given Mildred's. According to plan, just after newspapers containing the ad hit the street, Mildred began making her desperate calls. Not according to plan, the first reporter thought her suicidal and alerted police. A quick address trace from her phone number and they turned on their sirens and raced to her apartment.

The desk sergeant snorted at her excuse that the whole thing had been a publicity stunt. "Look, lady, the charge is perpetrating a hoax. Besides, this movie you're tryin' to promote sounds like a piece of trash."

"Oh, it is—it's awful! Please, I was tricked. None of this was my idea."

Her bail set at fifty dollars, she spent Christmas morning shivering in jail. The matron charged with overseeing the women prisoners sat just outside the cell reading aloud from *The New York Times*. In a thick Irish brogue she delivered a running commentary on various news items. "Well, would ya' look at this Walt Disney! The man's despicable! Imagine givin' a mouse a fine Irish name like Mickey!"

"Serves the damn mouse right!" retorted Mildred's cellmate.

The matron lowered the paper and looked over her glasses at the unrepentant, foul smelling Hannah Hardcastle. "Sure 'n what would you be knowin', Hannah? You must have the brains of a louse—gettin' yourself arrested on your sixtieth birthday for assaultin' a peace officer!"

A loud, whiskey-laced belch. "'Scuse me."

The matron turned the page and gaped at a photo. "'Me goodness, it's 'me brother Aloysius's submarine—the Argonaut! 'Sounds like what it is—the devil's work—a vessel made ta' run underwater like a snake. Imagine sneakin' up on poor unsuspectin' ships and blowin' them ta' bits with your nasty torpedoes."

Mildred shivered. "Please, may I have another blanket?"

The matron turned another page. Apparently finding an item of great interest, she got up to show it to Mildred. "Look here, 'tis the story of your shameful self and your poor, unwelcome children."

Mildred turned away. "I don't want to see it."

"Now what kind of a movie star are ya', not wantin' to see your name in print?"

"It's freezing in here. May I please have another blanket?"

"Don't be so glum, dearie, in a few hours you'll be free as a sparrow."

Mildred's eyes opened wide. "I will?"

"I'm told one of your rich gentlemen intends to post your bail."

"A gentleman? What *gentleman?*"

Released in late afternoon without having learned the identity of her benefactor, Mildred minced her way down ice-crusted steps, turned up her coat collar and started back to her apartment. Jammed the day before with last-minute Christmas shoppers, the streets were now deserted. A freezing wind blew from the north churning heavy, black clouds in a leaden sky. As she walked it began to sleet. A man blocked her path as she rounded the corner.

His blue eyes burned with indignation.

"Max!"

"You idiot! Jailbird! I..." Seized by a fit of coughing, he covered his mouth and wheeled toward the curb. His shoulders rose and fell, his head pitched forward and back. A convulsive gagging, a spit into the gutter's filth and relieved, he shuddered. Turning to face her, he took a deep breath and forced a smile. "Liebling?"

"Yes, Max?"

"What am I to do with you?"

She stared at him. Sunken cheeks, purple lips, skin as transparent and gray-white as the snow covering the ground. A fierce gust buffeted them. Store signs tore loose and windowpanes rattled. Afraid he'd be toppled, she grabbed onto his arm. "Come," she said, "we'll be blown away."

He reared back. "No! Don't touch me! I'm ill—a bad cold." He stuck his hands into his pockets. "I'll walk you home."

They leaned into the wind. The sky darkened. Snow whipped by the gale swirled around them. By the time they reached the stairs leading up to her apartment, Max's chest was heaving. He motioned for her to start up first.

Halfway to the top and not hearing the crunching of his feet on the steps behind her, she paused. "Sweetheart? Come on, in five minutes I'll have you warm and glowing."

He shook his head. "I can't..." His head pitched forward as he coughed into his handkerchief. Choking and gagging on phlegm, he spat, marring the snow with a streak of a bright red.

"Come! I have some brandy."

"I can't... I have to... I have to leave."

"No!" She raced down the steps only to have him back away. "Max... why?"

"Erna..."

"Erna? But I thought..."

Perspiration beaded on his forehead. His cheeks flushed, his eyes burned. "I... I love you."

"For God's sake Max..."

He lowered his eyes. "Erna's... there's another child on the way."

She slumped onto a stair. "You love me–hah! You love Erna!"

A tear started down his cheek. "I love you both." Leaning down, he kissed her forehead. "Good-bye." He turned and, head bowed, trudged back in the direction they'd just come. About to disappear around the corner he hesitated long enough for a parting glance and a tip of his hat. "Lebewohl..."

"Live well? You son-of-a-bitch!"

Born with the gift of laughter and the sense that the world was mad... and that was his only patrimony.

– Rafael Sabatini (1875-1950)

11

Cecil Cerruti's motion picture premiered at the Tower Theater in Poughkeepsie, New York on February 14, 1929. Two massacres occurred that Saint Valentine's Day: a bloody one at the hands of gangsters struggling for control of Chicago's bootleg liquor; and a bloodless, but equally merciless one perpetrated by film critics outraged by *Unwelcome Children* starring Mildred Gillars. Newspapers refused to advertise it. Not even Cecil's threats of Mafioso visits persuaded theater managers to display *Unwelcome Children* on their marquees. Owing everyone, Cecil hit upon yet another brilliant scheme. He skipped town.

Thinking the "roar" of the roaring twenties would grow even louder in the fast approaching thirties, Broadway worked overtime to keep theaters proliferating. Newer, brighter neon flashed across marquees to advertise such hits as *The Coconuts* with the Marx Brothers and *Coquette* staring Mary Pickford. Strains of popular songs poured from the music stores Mildred passed as she trudged from audition to audition. One such song, *Making Whoopee*, made her grimace for its lyrics, she thought, spoofed Max's return to Erna:

You'd better keep her... You'll find it's cheaper...
Than making whoopee...

Promised a speaking part just as soon as one became available, Mildred took a job sewing costumes and applying make-up to the cast of Eugene O'Neill's *Desire Under the Elms.* One evening, while standing in the wings, she spied in the audience Harry Horatio Schwartz. After the curtain rang down they set out to paint the town.

He showed her a swell time as they flitted from speakeasy to speakeasy. Anxious to share the juiciest tidbits of Hunter's latest gossip, he entertained her with madcap tales of scandalous affairs and improprieties.

He stopped smiling when she asked if he'd heard anything about Max. He took her hand. "Not a word."

"Did you ask in the German Department?"

"Look, honey, do yourself a favor–forget that goddamn fascist."

"Now, Harry..."

"Now? You're finally going to give me a tumble? Geez, babe, it's about time!"

She had to laugh at the clumsy segue. "I want to say 'yes' Harry–just so I can watch you run for the hills!"

A loud bang caused them both to gasp. The Phaeton, it's front tire blown, whipped wildly and glanced off a light standard. It jumped the curb and nosed a trashcan against a brick wall. "Shit!" Harry screamed. "You okay, Mildred?" Satisfied with her nod, he got out to assess the damage.

She got out and held the flashlight while he struggled to position the jack under the front axel. "Can I ask you something, Harry? Do you own a gold mine?"

"Hold the light a little more to the left."

"Let's face it, you spend money like it's water–fancy cars–

elegant dinners—fabulous vacations—speakeasies..."

A week later, the dented Phaeton replaced with the latest model, Harry treated her to the premier showing of *The Way of All Flesh* staring Emil Jennings. Later, over an elegant dinner, Harry made his off-handed proposal. "Honey, I don't suppose you'd care to accompany me to North Africa..."

"Au contraire! I love North Africa! Throw in Tasmania... a side trip to Timbuktu—and we're off!"

"Darling, they've given my aunt less than six months to live."

"Your aunt?"

"Actually, my great aunt, the Countess Freschot, grand dame of Algiers society. I'm her only living relative."

"Ah, so she's the gold mine!"

"A vacation in Algiers and it won't cost you a cent! Of course, it depends on how you prefer to spend the next six months—basking on the shores of the sunny Mediterranean or slathering grease paint on second-rate actors here in New York. I'll need your answer by month's end."

It was a month she would long remember. The New York Stock Market crashed. Wiped out, Hiram J. Hollingsworth, the financial backer of *Desire Under the Elms* rode his building's elevator to the twentieth floor. He wrote a note of farewell apologizing to everyone involved with the play. The note finished, he slugged down a pint of whiskey, threw open the window and jumped.

New York, stunned by Black Thursday, staggered. Theater after theater began to close. "Quitting Business" signs appeared in the finest shops. Gaunt-faced businessmen could be seen roaming the streets like so many sleepwalkers. Out of work and unable to pay the rent, Mildred called Harry and started packing.

"Sweetheart," Harry said as the ship put into the Bay of

Algiers, "there's something we have to go over before we get to Auntie's. Promise you'll hear me out before you scream."

"This better be good, Harry."

"As impossible as it seems, honey, my funds have run out."

"Go on."

"Auntie refuses to give me another cent. Clearly her illness has affected her mind. She thinks I've become something of a playboy."

"Hah!"

"Seriously, she's cut me off. That's why I've..."

Mildred's eyebrow shot up. "You've what? Stop this him-hawing and tell me what this is all about!"

"I... eh... well, I told her I've seen the error of my ways."

"Good. And?"

"And I also told her I've taken a wife—not just any wife, mind you—a beautiful, intelligent wife of course, one with whom I've completely settled down."

"You? A wife? Settled down? Hah!"

"Come on, Mildred, you're an actress. You can pull it off."

"You're kidding..."

"Look at it this way, honey. You masquerade as my wife. The old woman dies happy. I never have to worry about money again."

"Hooray for Harry."

"And hooray for Mildred, too! What would you say to ten thousand dollars?"

"Ten thous..."

"No more living at the YWCA, princess."

She took a deep breath and scanned the sky. "Forget it. I'm not about to trick a sick old lady."

Harry took a stab at her Achilles' heel. "Oh, well, it would take some really fine acting—you probably couldn't pull it off..."

"How dare you! I'm going back to New York!"

"To what? Soup lines? To home sweet home? To search for

a non-existent job? To a nice, cozy park bench for a long winter's nap?" He went for the kill. "And sweetie, don't count on seeing the professor when you get back. He's gonna' be where he is for a long, long time."

Her eyes flared. "What? Max? Where is he?"

Harry watched a tug ease the ship into its berth. "Erna–his wife–I ran into her a while back and she told me..."

Offered his hand, Mildred slapped it away. "She told you what?"

"The professor was doing a lot better during the summer but then he pushed it–became a visiting scholar at the University of Berlin. That's where their second daughter was born, in Berlin."

Mildred steadied herself against the ship's rail.

"He's in a sanitarium, Mildred–has been for months."

"Oh my God!"

"Incipient tuberculosis–so contagious they won't let her near him."

"I've got to go back. Harry, please, help me!"

"Sorry honey, I'm flat. There's not enough money in my wallet to pay your way home on a tramp steamer."

"You don't understand. He needs me."

"Look doll, it's a long swim from North Africa to New York–just a tad under four thousand miles." His eyes scanned sun-baked shops crowding the waterfront. They squinted at domes of distant mosques. At the sound of the gangplank being lowered, he took her arm and urged her toward the gate. "Come on, my little chickadee. Let's strut our stuff–let's give this pirate's Mecca a fling!"

He had that air of readiness for what would come to him, a kind of surety, an expectancy, the look of an inheritor...

– D.H. Lawrence (1885–1930)

12

North Africa – January, 1930

The ailing Countess Desiree Freschot had come to Algiers as the young bride of an ambitious Frenchman, Jules Freschot. She'd fallen in love with the city. Comprised of two distinct sections, Algiers had, she thought, a charming intrigue. The lower part, a modern, French-built city, offered wide boulevards, theaters, cathedrals, museums and an exquisite opera house. The upper part, a sixteenth century fortress built by the Turks, contained the Casbah—a mesmerizing mix of narrow, twisting streets, nightlife and mystery.

Jule's death, less than a year later, left her a childless widow. Desiree ignored her parent's entreaties to return to Paris and chose instead to try her hand at running the small boatworks her husband had started.

She delighted in telling Mildred and Harry of those early days. "The first thing I knew, I was one of the port's busiest traders. They called me 'Countess Moneybags.' Of course it didn't happen overnight. I'd come to Algiers knowing only two languages and I had to learn five more just so I wouldn't—how do you Americans say—*'lose my shirt?'*" A sudden sucking in of her breath belied a sharp pain. Her hand went for and rang a small bell sitting on the table. A servant appeared and, after a perfunctory bow of his turbaned head, stood at attention beside her chair. "You will excuse me now. Ahmed will help me to my room. I must rest."

On her good days, the countess, although frail and easily winded, enjoyed recalling her early days as an entrepreneur. "It took me less than five years to buy this place—the 'Taj.' Rather a stretch, wouldn't you say, naming one's home after the Taj Mahal?"

Mildred gazed out at the glittering white and red sandstone walls then lifted her eyes to the marble trimmed parapets. A breeze drew her attention to the stretch of white beach and to whitecaps dancing on the Mediterranean. "Why Countess, this place is... is..."

"Charming?" Harry interjected.

"*Charming* doesn't come close. It's exquisite—a pearl set on the shore of an endless sapphire!"

The countess smiled. "My! I can see my nephew has found himself both a poetess *and* a beautiful wife! My dear, I do so want you two lovebirds to be comfortable in my little nest!"

On days when her leukemia gained the upper hand, the countess would lie beside the reflecting pool like an exhausted butterfly, her paper-thin skin shielded from the sun by a servant-held umbrella, her emaciated body resting on a thick, goose down cushion. Near the end, Harry and Mildred took turns nursing and reading to her.

The old woman died with a smile on her face, holding their hands. Harry made a stab at stemming Mildred's tears. "She loved ya', kid. My aunt thought I'd chosen the perfect wife. Look at it this way, because of you she died happy—convinced her nephew wasn't a bum."

The countess's passing failed to bring Harry sudden

wealth. With the filing of her death certificate came the freezing of her assets subject to a maze of bureacratic red tape. Once inventoried, her estate would be appraised, legal notices placed, waiting periods observed and finally, a certificate of authorization to sell issued by the court.

Two weeks after the funeral, Harry and Mildred, although living in one of the city's most opulent residences, had less than fifty dollars between them. Harry dismissed the servants and took over their duties. Mildred volunteered to look for a job to tide them over.

It was while wandering through the garment district on the outskirts of the Casbah that she came upon the shop of Isaac Abrahms, Purveyor of Fine Custom Clothing. "Well, well, what causes a pretty dove to fly into my humble establishment? But come in, whatever you are looking for I have it—whether it be an Indian Sari for yourself or a tuxedo for your handsome husband!"

Mildred laughed. "I'm looking for a job."

Isaac Abrams clapped his hands. "Ester! Ester!" The whirring of a sewing machine in the back room stopped. A hand separated the doorway curtain and out stepped a plump, olive skinned woman.

Seeing Mildred, she threw up her hands as though embarrassed. "Thirty years I'm married to this man and still he keeps losing me!"

"This is my wife, Ester—the most sought after modiste in Algiers. My Ester caters only to matrons wanting exact duplicates of the latest Parisian gowns."

Ester nodded. "In size extra-large."

"How do you do. I'm Mildred... Mildred Gillars."

"Ah!" they exclaimed in unison. "An American!"

Anxious to know more about the land that had lured their son away to California, they peppered her with questions. Did she know this... this so-called *golden* state?

Mildred shook her head and explained that she had been

born in Maine and raised in Ohio. Ester eyes grew wide. "Ohio! My brother-in-law's sister lives in Ohio. She's a Fishburn. You perhaps know the Fishburns in Ohio?"

Isaac had heard of daredevils going over Niagara Falls in a barrel. Can such stories be true? And what of these tales of gangsters in Chicago? Was Mildred married? Did she have any children? Isaac had just recently purchased a piano for their ten-year-old daughter, Tamah. Did Mildred play the piano?

"Well yes, but I'm a bit rusty."

"What's a little rust? You sew, you play the piano—you're hired!" He made certain she understood what the job entailed. Working as Ester's assistant, she would do whatever needed doing. She would teach their daughter all about America, give her piano lessons and make sure she practiced no less than one hour each and every day.

"Harry! Guess what. I found a job!" Mildred shouted the instant she set foot back inside the Taj that afternoon. "Harry?" Maybe he was in his room, taking a nap. She ran toward it. "Harry? Did you hear me? We're in luck—I landed a job! A real, honest-to-God job!" Seeing his bed empty she pivoted and ran to the south wing. "Yoo-hoo! Mr. Schwartz, where are you? Stop hiding and come hear my good news!" She burst into the game room, certain she'd find him there. "Harry, I found a job as a..." Her mouth flew open and her eyes popped.

"Shit, shit, shit!" Harry moaned from atop the billiard table where, naked as was his partner, he writhed with the agony of interrupted sexual climax. His head, as though mounted on a periscope, shot up from the tangle of torsos, arms and legs. "You've found a... a... a... job... wonderful... peachy..."

Grimacing, he untangled himself. "Now, for Christ's sake, Millie, calm down." He climbed off the table and, pretending the nonchalance of a lord about to address parliament, cupped his hands over his penis. "I say. I'm forgetting my manners! Introductions are in order! Mildred, please meet my... er... friend."

Harry's lover raised himself up from the table, batted his eyelashes and extended his hand. "Charmed, I'm sure. Zachary... Zachary Millindar... rhymes with 'cylinder.'" Amused by her shocked expression, he winked. "Harry's told me ever so much about you, Mildred. Isn't he sweet? Now the three of us can be just like family."

Harry nodded. "For God's sake, Mildred. Close your mouth. Say something!"

"I don't believe it."

"Believe it."

"So that's why you never..."

"What?"

"Never made a single pass at me! And all the time I thought it was because you were... *shy*!"

Zachary snorted. He sat up and eased himself off the billiard table. "Heavens, he's not the least bit shy." He walked up to his newfound lover and kissed him on the mouth. "Harry's a *tiger*... rrrrrrr!"

Feeling queesy, Mildred made a break for the courtyard. Harry struggled to pull on his pants as he stumbled after her. "Mildred, please, if you don't mind, no one must know about this. Hunter doesn't exactly put out the welcome mat for..."

She turned around and glared. "Homosexuals? Really? I wasn't aware of that. Tell me, are you planning to return to Hunter?"

"Well... eventually. First though, Zachary wants to show me Paris."

With the blush of the moment faded, Millander "The Cylindar" went back to his apartment to pack, leaving Harry and Mildred to work out an agreement. During what Harry anticipated would be a one-month's sojourn, she would try out her new job while looking after the Taj. By the time he returned the government would surely have released the Taj for sale. Harry would sell everything immediately. "You'll see, Mildred, we will return to New York in style."

"Zachary too?"

"No, silly. Zachary is, unfortunately, a Piccadilly swallow. His wings are too fragile—he wouldn't last a day in New York. No, it'll be just you and me, kid—like old times."

Harry wrote her from a train. Zachary wanted to show him much more than Paris. The lovers traveled on, spent a month in Madrid, another in Majorca. In Portugal they co-wrote her a rhyming note: *Dear Mildred. In our continued search for the golden fleece, we next set sail for the Isle of Greece.* Another card told how in awe they were of Mount Athos and the Erechtheum. In Crete, Harry bought a vase depicting men enjoying men. From Ireland she received a rock guaranteed to have come from the Blarney Stone; from Rome came a relic of St. Vibiana, virgin and martyr.

Mildred might have been furious at Harry's failure to return to Algiers had she not lost her shoe in an anthill and met Charles Dunsworthy. "Rather smashing, all those ants," he said as he whisked her up into his arms and carried her shoeless to his car. "Fancy me rescuing such a beauty! I say!"

Charles, suntanned from years of serving his majesty in New Delhi, served with the British Consulate in Algiers. Impossibly English and irritatingly proper, he loved cheery talk and leisurely afternoons.

Isaac Abrahms, Charles' tailor, enjoyed altering dinner jackets and tuxedos to fit the handsome Englishman's broad shoulders and slim waist. Friends for many years, they shared an interest in American sports and debated endlessly over the merits and shortcomings of baseball.

Mildred, as she got to know him, tried to fall in love with Charles Dunsworthy. He would doubtless make an honest, loyal and considerate husband. And he was not without charm.

His marriage proposal, although not unexpected, caught her off guard. "You hesitate. Is there someone else, old girl? I'll be terribly broken hearted if there is—destroyed, actually."

Mildred looked away. "No, of course not. Charles please, won't you give me time to think it over? What with helping Ester and preparing for Tamah's piano recital I can't think straight. Perhaps when things quiet down..."

Harry, without returning to Algiers as promised, sold his aunt's estate to a Venetian—a wealthy importer of homosexual erotica. The notice to vacate the Taj arrived from Italy the same day Harry's letter arrived from New York:

> Hunter College – New York City
> My Dearest Mildred,
>
> Harry-the-Cad begs your forgiveness. Zachary proved untrue. He left me broke and stranded with pneumonia in a hospital on the Isle of Capri. I nearly died and would have had I not sold the Taj for a fraction of its worth. It was barely enough to get me home to an American pulmonary specialist. If you never forgive me I understand completely. I hate myself for leaving you in the lurch. I'll send you a ticket home soon—I promise!
>
> Fondly, (signed) Harry

You're an expatriate. You've lost touch with the soil.
You get precious. Fake European standards have ruined you.
You drink yourself to death. You become obsessed by sex.
You spend all your time talking, not working.
You are an expatriate, see? You hang around cafés...

– Ernest Hemingway (1899–1961)

13

"J'aime Paris!" Mildred wrote home to Edna Mae. "I have fallen in love with Paris!" She'd come to the City of Light at the invitation of the French fashion guru, Claude Maddalon.

In search of a tailor to mend his jacket during his vacation in Algiers, Maddalon had noticed Mildred the moment he stepped inside Isaac Abram's shop. Several more visits to the shop to observe her skill in assisting Ester with fittings and he invited the talented blonde American to Paris to help him stage an upcoming fashion show.

"Go!" Issac said. "Such an opportunity! Besides, you need a little vacation–a change of scenery."

The change did wonders. Her letters gushed with descriptions of brilliantly colored Tulerie tulips and of lawn bowlers, dressed in sparkling white, rolling silver "boules" across vast fields of green velvet. She wrote of poking along the broad, tree-lined Champs-Elysées. "And Edna Mae, you will be shocked to learn that Paris is a city overgrown with unabashedly demonstrative lovers. One sees them "carrying on" everywhere. They kiss like you wouldn't believe in the subway, embrace between every bite in restaurants and, I blush to write, go so far while reclining on the banks of the Seine as to invite arrest!"

To Momma she wrote: "You would love it here Momma! Montmarte is alive with artists! Sidewalks are crowded with them working at their easels, creating the most brilliant work! Yesterday, after visiting the Place du Tertre, I popped into a cozy restaurant, gorged myself on bouillabaisse and crusty bread then washed it all down with a cup of lavender tea!"

Her letters contained nothing of the exciting new friend who took her to cabarets throbbing with the Tango and then on to a Latin Quarter pulsing with after-hours eroticism. Most tellingly, she made no mention of her Sunday ritual of hiking up to the Sacre Cour to light a candle for Max.

Held captive by the city's charm, Mildred found it impossible, when her association with Monsieur Maddalon ended, to return to Algiers and to Charles. From her tiny garret off the Rue de Rivoli she wrote to him, weekly at first, then monthly.

In his replies, he invariably tried to pin her down as to the exact date of her return to Algiers. He expressed a half-hearted enthusiasm for her experiences as a part-time artists' model and for her involvement with the American Expatriates' Theater Group.

Unable to contain her excitement, she wrote: "Charles, did I ring in the New Year! The party was beyond avant-garde. It glittered! Imagine rubbing elbows with a White Russian Princess, a Maharaja and Zelda Fitzgerald all in the same evening!"

At one such shindig a German film director spoke excitedly of his film, *The Blue Angel*, but grew visibly angry at the mention of the film's star. "Star? She's impossible! If it were not for her legs, she would be completely worthless." The object of his derision was none other than Marlene Dietrich—the woman whose sexy voice Max had once urged Mildred to emulate.

Parties grew wilder. Guests came in severely cut black clothes, their faces powdered ghostly white. Lesbians, gays and transvestites cavorted freely. Men and women smoked thin black cigarettes. Intellectuals, eyes glassy with absinthe or other stimulants, held court on the "isms"—fauvism, cubism, futurism, constructivism, Dadaism and surrealism. At a Bastille Day bash held to celebrate the Counter-Culture Revolution, a fistfight erupted between two couples over whether the French government should abolished monogamy.

"Shocking" and "chic" were synonymous. Paris' most fashionable, to fly in the face of convention, stood in solidarity with the growing number of "liberal exhibitionists." A famous critic wrote a column on the trend, citing it as "a subterfuge to ignore the gathering clouds of financial and political upheaval." He drew readers' laughs with his warning, "Paris will pay a dear price for living the tune *Anything Goes.*"

At a reception for the French dramatist Jean Cocteau, Mildred met and became friends with German actor and producer Victor de Kowa and his Japanese wife, Michiko. Victor enjoyed great popularity in his homeland. Hoping to visit Hollywood, he engaged Mildred to tutor him in American protocol and to give Michiko diction lessons.

Wealthy, but always short of cash, Victor paid Mildred with pieces of jewelry from his vast collection. Each piece came with a printed certificate of authentication. The items she prized most were a jade bracelet once worn by Sarah Bernhardt, Lillie Langtry's amethyst earrings and opal cufflinks that Victor had bought from the great Caruso.

Edna Mae, enthralled by her sister's escapades, begged for naughty French postcards and for "the tiniest splash" of

French perfume. In another letter she described her latest beau, Herschel Hershberg. "Honestly Sis, he's the smartest fella on earth! Herschel says you should stay in Paris because President Hoover's rhetoric about prosperity being just around the corner is pure poppycock. I'm enclosing this clipping from *The New York Times*. As does Herschel, it claims the Depression will worsen with unemployment soaring to twenty-five percent!"

Any pangs of guilt Mildred had at living comfortably in France while those at home suffered were lost in the excitement of the drama surrounding her. France's economy seemed robust with everyone dressing well and throwing parties such as the latest one she'd been invited to—a spectacular bash to celebrate the rounding of the globe by Germany's great new airship, the Graf Zepplin.

French admiration of another beautiful blonde American, Amelia Earhart, opened doors for Mildred. At a party marking the one-hundredth staging of Bertolt Brecht's smash play, *The Three-Penny Opera,* the host plunked an aviator's cap atop Mildred's curls, draped a white silk scarf around her neck and, to cheers, proclaimed her "Earhart's Twin."

Paris, with the world's newspapers and magazines available on every corner, seemed the center of the universe. At a newsstand favored by American expatriates, Mildred met Yanks of every hue and political persuasion. She talked to a saxophone player who'd exchanged the clubs of New Orleans for the Place Pigale; an artist newly arrived from Buffalo—his portfolio stuffed with still-lifes; a Nevada-born biographer in search of a publisher for *Shackled–The Amazing Houdini*. And crackpots! They'd come from Savannah to Seattle, from San Diego to Syracuse. Standing atop French-made soapboxes, existentialists newly escaped from America's Christian-Judeoism baffled listeners with wild new takes on Dostoyevesky, Camus and Kafka; Communists preached and pleaded for the fulfillment of Lennin's dream;

Anarchists shouted down Socialists and an ever-present doomsdayer from Detroit wailed, "Repent! The end is near!"

Mildred spent more than she could afford at the newsstand, often dipping into rent money to buy *The New York Times*, *Vogue*, *Ladies Home Companion* and the bi-weekly *Expatriates Examiner*. That a column in the latter publication irked her, proved a godsend. Captioned "Hollywood's Heyday," and rife with misspelling, grammatical and factual errors, the shoddy writing prompted her to sit down and fire off a letter to the editor. In one paragraph she pointed out the article's inaccuracies, sloppy syntax and lack of focus.

The editor's reply came by return mail. Her writing impressed him. Perhaps she should write the column. Five-cents-a-word to start; ten cents should circulation double.

She got him up to seven-cents-a-word and started immediately. Certain it would meet with his approval, she changed the format and the column's name to "Ask Midge." Her first effort earned sacks of letters from readers interested in anything pertaining to the magical Hollywood:

> Dear Midge,
> What, in your opinion, are the two best American movies of 1930?
> (signed) Longing for Louisiana
>
> Dear Longing,
> I didn't even have to think. Number One: *All Quiet on the Western Front* with the handsome Lew Ayres. Number Two: *Hell's Angels* by Howard Hughes.
>
> Dear Midge:
> Please list the latest words to be banned from American movies.
> (signed) Burning Ears

> Dear Burning:
> Here goes, written on asbestos so as not to scorch the paper, the words recently banned from American movies are: *cripes, gawd, goose* (as in never goose a lady), *hell, damn, madam* (when relating to prostitution), *SOB, tart, whore* and *fanny.*

The column, although low paying, earned Mildred a certain celebrity status. To make ends meet, she took whatever other jobs came her way. Bartering English instruction for piano lessons, she quickly improved her keyboard technique while becoming acquainted with a surprising number of exceptionally talented musicians.

One evening, after favoring guests at a party with an etude by the French composer Charles Gounod, she looked up from the piano to see her friend, the German dramatist Josef von Sternberg. He cornered her just as she was about to leave. "Mildred, I may be able to help you. A certain American producer owes me a favor. He's going to produce a play in Washington, D.C. this spring. If I can get you a part, will you take it?"

The longest way round is the shortest way home.

– Bohn: Foreign Proverbs (Italian)

14

Washington, D.C. – February, 1932

Mildred came home to a changed America. Everywhere she looked, sober-faced citizens went about with heads hung and shoulders stooped. Unemployment stood at twenty percent. Those fortunate enough to have jobs lived in fear of losing them.

In the shadow of the nation's capitol, angry veterans congregated in a hobo jungle of sorts, determined to collect the bonuses the government had promised them for serving in the "war to end all wars." Headlines referred to these disenfranchised veterans as "The Army of Rabble." In a shameful act, the government ordered the men evicted and driven from the capitol. Under the command of General Douglas MacArthur, uniformed American soldiers fired on those veterans who refused to leave and set their shacks ablaze.

Throughout America, men from all walks of life rode the rails in search of work. A prolonged drought turned vast regions of the Oklahoma, Arkansas and Texas into a giant dust bowl. Farmers and farm towns went bust.

Mildred found America's pulse changed. Gone were the catchy phrases and lightheartedness of the roaring twenties. Everyone she met, whether dispossessed or struggling to stay solvent, showed increasing disenchantment with capitalism. Many expressed a deep-seated anger and distrust of the president who had promised "two chickens in every pot."

An actor invited her to his home for dinner, a home he shared with his large extended family. Following the modest meal, everyone huddled around the radio to hear the radical exhortations of popular fascist sympathizer Father Coughlin and to enjoy homespun witticisms of "America's Cowboy," Will Rogers. A break for sharing an apple pie cut in twenty pieces and the evening concluded with a radio visit to Fibber McGee and Molly's cluttered closet.

Five cents bought another great escape. Seven days a week, whether morning, afternoon or evening–people flocked to the movie theater. Their cares checked at the door for a nickel, their confidence bolstered by the sure thing unfolding on the screen, they felt–at least until reel's end–secure. Seated in the dark, they became Johnny "The Ape Man" Weissmuller, Lord of the Jungle, destined to romance Jane. Tom Mix and his Wonder Horse were certain to foil villains and catch cow rustlers. They could bet on singing cowboy Gene Autry to banish outlaws and ride into the sunset with the fair maiden.

In mid-March, with rent on the playhouse adding up and rehearsals cut short, the play opened much, much sooner than it should have. First nighters, their appetites whetted by a full-page ad in *The Washington Post*, packed the theater. The first act of *A Breath of Spring* ended with a burst of applause; the second with far less enthusiasm. A dull-eyed audience greeted the final curtain with a collective sigh of relief.

On the way to her dressing room, the stage manager beckoned to Mildred. "Hey kid, there's a gent waiting to see you."

"I don't know any gentleman."

"Who knows, he might be a big Hollywood talent scout. Could be your lucky night, sweetheart!"

At the sight of Max, Mildred's knees buckled. He held a florist's box decorated with a sprig of edelweiss atop a red bow. He flung the box aside and caught her. "Please Liebling, don't faint..."

"I... I..."

"Such a spectacular performance! Excellent! You stole the show!"

They dined by candlelight at an intimate restaurant overlooking the Potomac. He toasted her with champagne. "You look... *wunderbar*! More beautiful than ever."

She reached out a finger and touched the patch of gray at his temple. "Very distinguished." Aside from the tiny lines pulling at the corners of his eyes, she thought him surprisingly robust for someone who'd spent time in a tuberculosis sanitarium. "Shame on you, Max. How cruel you were to not tell me of your illness. I would have understood."

He poured more champagne and steered the conversation into a sea of memories he knew would make her smile. They dined on spring lamb, scalloped potatoes and a medley of truffles, asparagus and snow peas. They ate slowly, savoring each bite of food and sip of wine.

Sated, they snuggled in the back seat of a cab as it headed for her apartment. "Tell me the truth Max, how is your health? Are you taking it easier? Have you cut back on your work?"

He patted her hand. "Ah, well Liebling, except for an occasional bout of bronchitis, I'm fine. Of course I'm still holding down two jobs—teaching at both Hunter and Columbia. My career is going well. Fifteen of my articles have recently appeared in the German Encyclopedia *Sachwoerterbuch der Deutschkunde*."

"Gesundheit!"

He hugged her tighter. "And Saddler finally published my German language reader, *Deutsche Fibel.*"

"And Erna?" She gasped as though to suck the question back into her mouth. "I'm sorry..."

"Please... don't be. We have another child, you know."

"No, I didn't."

"Altogether now three little girls. Stella, Helene and last spring... Renata. Believe me, there will be no more."

"Believe you?" She pulled free of him and sat forward on the seat. "Three lovely daughters! You and Erna have my sincere congratulations!"

"Liebling, please..."

Tears stung her eyes. "You really must send me a picture of your wonderful family. Do you have something to write on? I'll give you my address in Paris."

"Paris?"

"Why of course. I'll be returning the minute the play closes—to prepare for my wedding! I didn't mention my engagement?"

"I don't see a ring."

"It's being... adjusted... set with a larger stone."

He lifted her face to his. "Stop it! Stop this farce at once! You know I can't exist without you. I'll divorce Erna. It's the only solution."

She leaned forward and ordered the cabbie to stop. He pulled to the curb. She grabbed Max by the lapels. "*Solution?*" she screamed, "You monster! You call leaving your wife—the mother of your babies a *solution?*"

"But you don't understand—it's for *us.*"

Her fists pounded his chest. "For *us*? You louse! You walked away from me last time, Herr Doctor Koischwitz, this time I do the walking... as far away from you as I can get!" She pushed him back against the seat, opened the door, stepped up onto the curb and, as he began to follow, slammed the door in his face. "Go home to your family, Max. It's over!"

The play earned poor reviews. In its third week, Mildred's mother, stepfather and sister somehow scraped enough money together to come to Washington for a Saturday afternoon performance. Afterward, hiding their disappointment, they invited Mildred to a cafeteria dinner.

Doctor Gillars, Mildred noted as they plunked their trays on the table, had aged. The maze of tiny red capillaries mapping his nose bore witness to his ongoing bout with the bottle. Years of peering into the mouths of dental patients had left its mark. Stooped shouldered and wearing thick bifocals, he seemed somehow smaller than she'd remembered him. His hands shook so that he gave up trying to eat his chowder. Massaging his yellow, nicotine-stained fingers he spoke his piece. "These are tough times, missy, there's no doubt about it. Nobody makes it in times like these, especially not these... theater people. Don't think you're any different. If you had half a brain you'd take the next boat back to gay 'Par-eeee!'"

Momma reached across the table and patted Mildred's arm. "Sweetheart, perhaps if you tried something a little more stable than acting... theaters are so... so drafty." Mildred glanced at Edna Mae, the one member of the family who'd improved with time. She'd become a beauty—a striking, curvaceous brunette who, at the moment, was rolling her gorgeous brown eyes in disbelief at her parent's remarks.

"I wish to make an announcement," Edna Mae said as a waiter laid the check on the table. "Edward Heron and I have agreed to marry. But, mind you, *not* without 'prospects.' Edward, I am delighted to say, has a promise of a job in Columbus!"

Momma changed the subject. "Mildred, you remember little Aaron Stern? Just imagine, he's a medical doctor specializing in kidney problems at some Jewish hospital in Los Angeles. His mother was Golda–Grandpa and Grandma's maid? Well, Aaron just bought her a home in California!"

Doctor Gillars gave his coffee an angry stir. "Beats me how a Jew servant's kid could afford such a highfalutin education."

"Edward wants to get married at Saint Stephan's, Millie. Will you be my maid of honor?"

"I wouldn't miss it for the world."

Momma sighed as though exhausted. "Mildred, would you consider coming home to Conneaut to help with the preparations?"

The good doctor shook his head. "She can't come home–at least not until this damn silly play of hers closes. Course that could happen tomorrow."

And it did. Newspapers gave little space to the play's demise. Mildred's one review came from *The Washington Post's* drama critic:

> *Miss Gillars rendered an adequate performance.*
> *Not inspired... adequate.*

> We have two or three great moving experiences in our lives—experiences so great and moving that it doesn't seem at the time that anyone else has been so caught up and pounded and dazzled and astonished and beaten and broken and rescued and illuminated and rewarded and humbled in just that way ever before.
>
> – F. Scott Fitzgerald (1896 -1940)

15

As her train approached Conneaut that late spring morning, Mildred looked out at shocking changes! What had happened to the old Pomeroy mansion? Its windows were broken out, its front door hanging open, its beautiful rose gardens a sea of weeds. The Merry Times Motor Court and the roller rink–where were they? And that blackened shell of a building over there used to be the Piggly Wiggly!

Twenty-five cents bought a cab ride home through streets of a ghost town. Comstocks department store stood boarded up, its windows plastered with notices of repossession. Lowry's Luncheonette used to be crowded to the rafters at this hour–where *was* everyone? The cab passed the Octagon barn. Had it shrunk? On the left, a white-haired man sat on the curb in front of Maloney's Tavern–a farmer judging from the plaid shirt and dungarees. The cab driver tooted his horn, waved and called out the window to the him. "Hey, Banker Ellingsworth!"

The pole from which the wooden tooth hung, Mildred

noticed as she walked toward the house, had fallen over. She found Edna Mae inside, weeping. The job promised the prospective bridegroom had gone poof. The wedding was off. "But you'll stay til he finds another one, won't you, Millie?" pleaded Edna Mae, "Please?"

Having lived in New York, Algiers, Paris and Washington D.C., Mildred couldn't believe how time dragged in Conneaut. The slowest turtle, she was convinced, moved and thought faster than Conneaut's brightest. And pessimism! This berg, she thought, should be named "Pessimism, U.S.A.–Hometown of Complainers."

At summer's end, she landed a job. As the Bijou's usherette, she had the opportunity to see not once, but on the same newsreel played nightly for a week, the victory speech of "The New Deal" candidate, Franklin Delano Roosevelt.

A howling snowstorm pounded Conneaut the day Edna Mae at last married Edward Heron. Momma cooked a wedding supper of fried chicken, mashed potatoes and creamed peas. Postman Si Jenkins played his fiddle. Septuagenarian Hilde Schnell, former diva of Germany's Dresden Opera, sang *Oh Promise Me.*

Father-of-the-Bride, Doctor Robert Gillars, kept disappearing, sneaking out to the garage for liquid fortification. He arrived back in time to see Mildred catch the bouquet. Garrulous, he staggered up to her, snatched the prized token and tossed it to one of Edna Mae's young friends. "Catch it!" he slurred, "Mildred's too old–way past her prime."

Anxious to set out for Dayton where he would take over his recently deceased uncle's repair shop, Edward took advantage of a lull in the storm to hustle Edna Mae out to his Model-A. Everyone poured out of the house to cheer the couple off. Doctor Gillars thumped the fender. "Damn crazy kids!" he snickered, "Write if ya' get work! Keep goin' if ya' don't!"

Momma would never be the same after that winter—not after Ira Rosen, her employer and secret love, suffered a fatal heart attack. She changed overnight. Light fled from her eyes, pride from her carriage, the smile and hint of seduction from her lips. Inconsolable, she stayed in her room with the shades lowered. At the reading of Ira's will she broke down completely. He'd left her everything: the debt-ridden Hidden Treasures Antique Shop, his old truck, an onyx ring and fifty dollars cash.

Unable to find a job since the Bijou's closing, Mildred tended Hidden Treasures alone until, after endless coaxing, she got Momma to return to the shop. In their struggle to keep the doors open, they could expect no help from the good doctor. These were the leanest of times—so lean his patients couldn't pay ten cents on the dollar owed. Washing down his troubles with ever more drink, he found himself forced to barter his services for haircuts, shoe repair, groceries and, in exchange for the extraction of a nun's impacted molar, a hand-knit sweater.

The letter arrived on the day of the summer solstice. Mildred had been sunning herself on the front porch when Si Jenkins lugged his mailbag up the steps. "Got somethin' unusual for ya' Mildred. Something from Algiers of all places! Lookee here—ain't this the *fanciest* stamp and seal ya' ever saw? Take a look at this fancy stamp and seal."

Mildred tore open the envelope. Charles Dunsworthy! Her eyes flew over his stiffly perfect handwriting. He wanted her back! "Please, Mildred, let's give it another go. Trusting that you will answer in the affirmative, I have enclosed a bank draft in the amount of one-hundred dollars and a steamship ticket for your passage from New York to Algiers."

Standing on the deck of the Bremen Star as it sailed out of New York Harbor, Mildred gazed at the Statue of Liberty and said a silent good-bye to her Depression-ravaged country.

A fellow passenger approached, doffed his hat and attempted to start a conversation. "You know, we Germans find you Americans most baffling."

Mildred didn't like the look of him. "Oh really? Then it's a good thing you're going home."

"It is indeed. Americans need to wake up. Only yesterday I saw New Yorkers standing in line to see the movie *Duck Soup.*"

"So?"

"*Duck Soup*, my dear, features the Marx brothers–Jews!"

"So?"

"Unfortunately, your entertainment industry is in a sorry state–run by and riddled with Jews."

She'd been invited, much to her delight, to dine at the captain's table that first night at sea. Wanting to look her absolute best, she spent an hour curling her hair and applying makeup. Edna Mae had given her, as a bon voyage gift, a pale yellow, silk chiffon gown. She put it on, dabbed perfume behind both ears and set off for the dining salon.

"Fraulein!" the captain said, taking her hand and escorting her to the seat next to his at the table. "How beautiful you look! No wonder a countrymen has pestered me so for the seat immediately to your left!"

The German who had so infuriated her earlier in the day, rose. The evening, she knew, would not go well. And she was right. Halfway through the first course, the German, distaining the more polite, innocuous conversation, began his needling. "You know, Fraulein Gillars, I found America a terribly depressed, sick place. Your President Roosevelt fills the airwaves with his optimistic Fireside Chats, while at the same time, in the very shadow of the capitol, the homeless shiver in cardboard-covered crates. Tell me, do you not find this deplorable?"

Mildred gave him a big smile and a pat on the arm. "No sir," she said, projecting her voice for every diner to hear, "what I find deplorable are your manners."

Mistress, know yourself, down on your knees,
And thank heaven for a good man's love.

– William Shakespeare (1564-1616)
(As You Like It)

16

Charles Dunsworthy waved a fistful of daisies and cheered as Mildred came down the gangplank. He handed her the flowers, kissed her and scooped her into his arms. "You slipped away from me once—we jolly well won't let *that* happen again!"

He led her to a shiny convertible. "Like it? Got it just last month."

"But Charles, it's a Rolls Royce!"

"Not just any Rolls Royce, sweetheart, it's a Phantom II Rolls Royce—top of the line!"

"I thought only kings and potentates drove such cars! You must be doing very well at the consulate, very well indeed!"

"Investments, my sweet—a series of smashing investments."

Anxious to demonstrate the car's superior maneuverability, he chose a roundabout way home. They crawled though the narrow winding streets of the old city and skirted the Casbah for a peek at the Great Mosque. Along the new city's European-style boulevards, well-dressed businessmen scurried about as though unscathed by the world's economic crisis. Charles patted her arm. "Not what you expected?"

"It seems Algiers hasn't heard about the Depression."

He chuckled. "You know how it is, the French are a little slow to catch on."

The Rolls purred along the harbor, past the yacht club and into an affluent neighborhood. It pulled into the driveway of a particularly nice home. "Why are we stopping here, Charles?"

"It's the home of a jolly good bloke—a handsome devil you won't be able to resist."

A dark-skinned butler opened the door. He bowed deeply to Mildred then delivered well-rehearsed words of welcome. "Greetings, miss. One trusts you had a pleasant journey. I am Jamal, the butler, and later you will meet my wife, Dauphine, the cook. We've been anxiously awaiting your arrival and will do our utmost to make you comfortable."

Mildred gaped at Charles. "Don't tell me this... this mansion is your place?"

His eyes twinkled. "Welcome home."

She went to visit her former employers. Isaac and Ester Abrahms greeted her with open arms and danced her around the tailor shop. Before she could catch her breath Isaac fired off a battery of questions about America. He had heard stories of soup lines—surely that couldn't be true—not in America! His son had written from California that he'd married and moved in with his bride's family—a custom perhaps?

"Well, yes. Things are rather bleak back home." Isaac's smile faded. "But don't worry, everyone says the Depression's almost over."

Having read the truth in her eyes, he faked a sigh of relief. "Good, good. America is a strong country. It will recover. Europe is another story. I tell you, my dear, those Nazis and their storm troopers mean my people no good. Next month I'm sending to Leipzig for my sister Sadie and her family."

"But surely..."

Ester interrupted. "Perhaps in America you've been shielded from Nazi rhetoric—you've not heard that we Jews are to blame for the world's problems. According to Hitler we control all the money, run all the banks and serve as roadblocks to progress. Oh yes, this Hitler will tell you *all* about us!"

"That's ridiculous. Why, Jews are creative and intelligent and..."

Isaac shook his head. "Hitler and his henchmen give no recognition to our brilliance, my dear. To him, Einstein is a myth and Moses a fictional character."

Mildred heard a great deal more talk of Hitler as she and Charles became caught up in the social whirlwind of Algiers. Controversy over the intentions of the Fuhrer and his Third Reich spilled into every gathering. Some lauded his leadership. Others considered him a crackpot and predicted he'd be nothing but a deflated balloon by year's end. Emotions ran high. An opinion offered at a bridge party could turn into an ugly debate. At a reception to celebrate the opening of his new corporate offices, a French entrepreneur scoffed at those who condemned Nazis tactics. "Why, Hitler is no more aggressive than the British!"

The comment, and the fact that many guests nodded agreement, outraged Charles. "How dare you, sir! I take grave exception to your scurrilous remark! When this beast bursts through the French border—just watch you come crying to the Brits!"

Afraid the two might come to blows, Mildred tugged at Charles's sleeve and, feigning a headache, steered him from the room. "Heavens, Charles, you're a diplomat!"

A Dutch dignitary interrupted them as Charles helped Mildred on with her wrap. "You have it all wrong, Mr.

Dunsworthy. Hindenberg made a smart move in naming Hitler 'Germany's Chancellor.' The last thing Hitler wants is war, why none of us will tolerate war. Thank God Europe has at last settled down to an eternal peace!"

Charles tried everything he could think of to persuade Mildred to marry him, including the oft-repeated direct approach. "Come on, old girl, let's do the right thing and tie the knot! Don't you like me?"

She did. And there was much about him to like. Handsome and blessed with a sunny disposition, he couldn't have been more sensitive or caring. He was wealthy, Eaton-educated and fiercely loyal. His strength and stamina never waned. In her heart Mildred found only one thing wrong with him—he wasn't Max.

Edna Mae sent a package. In addition to a long letter, it contained, at Mildred's request, everything she could find relating to Professor Max Otto Koischwitz. A publisher's flyer announced the simultaneous publication, in Berlin and New York, of Max's novel *Ellilenti* and his German language reader, *Bilderlesebuch*.

The package also contained past issues of Hunter's newspaper. One contained a letter from a disgruntled coed:

> Dear Editor,
>
> As a student of a certain professor who teaches German literature, I am writing to expose him for favoring his Jewish students to the point of obtaining for one of them a scholarship to the University of Berlin.
>
> (signed) Sarah Mullins, an indignant student

Max's reply appeared in the next issue:

> Dear Editor,
>
> In response to Miss Mullins' letter criticiz-

> ing me for showing favoritism: No, I did not obtain a scholarship to the University of Berlin for "one of my Jewish students." However, I am proud to say that I did try. If anything about me should be exposed it is the extreme distress I feel over Germany's refusal to allow this Jewish student, a brilliant young woman, to attend my alma mater.
>
> For the record: I am infuriated that my old fraternity at the University of Berlin now brags of purging its Jewish members. To this fraternity I submit my resignation! Also, I openly denounce National Socialism and anti-Semitism.
>
> Yours for universal enlightenment,
> (signed) Professor Max Otto Koischwitz

On the heels of Edna Mae's package, a letter arrived from Momma. It contained a wonderful surprise:

> My Dearest Daughter,
>
> You'll never, in a thousand years, believe this! Mr. Heckathorn, a collector of fine art, wandered into the shop last month and discovered what he is certain is a painting by the American Impressionist Mary Cassatt!
>
> Imagine, all this time the painting has been hanging on the wall–right in front of my nose! Thinking it worthless, my dear Mr. Rosen hung it there years ago. Wonder of wonders, Mr. Heckathorn wants to buy the painting for... hold onto your hat... TWENTY THOUSAND DOLLARS!
>
> Of course there are some wrinkles to be ironed out. Two of Mr. Heckathorn partners must confirm his appraisal and then he must

> solicit the consensus of his investors. Mr. Heckathorn seems most optimistic and says I might have my money by Christmas! Keep your fingers crossed!
>
> Yours 'til Niagara Falls!
> (signed) Momma

The letter temporarily lifted the gloom shrouding Mildred and Charles's relationship. He was becoming possessive, she more aloof. Their arrangement, as she saw it, was, although ostensibly one-sided, something of a trade off. He bought her lovely jewelry. To keep her from getting bored he paid for her piano and acting lessons, expensive clothes, trips to the beauty salon and weekly massages. Whenever she seemed down, he treated her to a holiday in Spain or the Greek Isles.

To reciprocate, Mildred became the perfect hostess and went all out to entertain and impress those capable of giving Charles' career a boost. The "who's who" of Algiers's upper crust vied for invitations to her opulent dinner parties.

He called her the "jewel in my crown." All too soon, however, she began to feel like nothing more than a well-kept bauble. The split came as they vacationed in Greece. Leaving Charles to a game of cribbage one evening, Mildred attended a play staged by a traveling theater company. She stayed after the performance to meet the director, the charming Sir Reginald Spencer.

"You're not!" Charles yelled at her later that night. "Either this is a joke or you're daft!"

"Please, try to understand."

"Understand? That you're going off with a bunch of traveling riff-raff?"

"They're not riff-raff, Charles. For your information, they're accomplished actors."

"Hah!"

"They've guaranteed me the best parts—parts that could lead to..."

We [actors] are indeed a strange lot! There are times we doubt that we have any emotions we can honestly call our own.

– Helen Hayes (1900–1993)

17

She caught up with the troupe in Majorca, Spain. Breathless from Sir Spencer's ebullient welcome, a bear hug and a flurry of wet kisses, she was then introduced to "the most talented company of actors to ever grace a stage."

Gloria, his Slavic wife bowed deeply. "I am 'Star Over-All', trained since childhood in the world's greatest theaters." Balding Shakespearean actors Arthur and Albert stepped forward, fell to their knees and kissed Mildred's hand. Marco, the black troubadour/magician produced an egg from behind the newcomer's ear.

Eleni curtsied and smiled broadly. "Last night, as Midea, I stole the show."

A pudgy hand shot out, its fingers heavy with gaudy rings. "Vivian Lehman, dear, 'Toast of London Music Halls.'"

Mildred's first speaking part, "Ariel" in a ruralized version of *The Tempest*, earned enthusiastic boot stomping from Albanian farmers. It took less than a fortnight, however, for her to admit to the awful truth. Sir Spencer and his brilliant troupe were simply a bizarre assortment of aging thespians solely gifted with fabricating past theatrical triumphs. Every night, after final bows to sparse applause, they'd congregate as for church in the lobby of their cheap hotel. A bottle, the actor's chalice of failed dreams, would be passed. A few moments for tongues to numb and it would start—the litany—the mantra of "has-beens who never-were," the slurred mumblings of "stars" stalled in their ascent or shot from the heavens by the slings and arrows of outrageous fortune.

Hardships aside, Mildred enjoyed the novelty of touring the countryside in Sir Spencer's battered bus. She mastered more roles as the company see-sawed north through Yugoslavia. She performed, relying on local translators, in such hamlets as Kragugevac, Tuzla and Sombor.

They crossed into Hungary and stopped for the night in Szeged. Sir Spencer's outburst woke the entire troupe before sunrise. "Bloody hell! My wife's left—run off with Marco! The whore! She's absconded with everything! My gold watch—the week's receipts!"

Agreeing that Sir Spencer should hang on to the small amount he had to fund one more performance, Arthur and Albert dropped their Shakespearian airs to spend the rest of that day as harvest hands to earn petrol for the bus. Eleni raised enough by singing on a street corner to buy sandwiches. The others cleaned hotel rooms to pay for the night's lodging.

On Christmas Eve, the troupe went bust in Budapest. Sir Spencer bade his thespians a dramatic farewell. "Fret not, noble bards and lovely ladies! We've shared a king's portion of romance and adventure! Take heart in the treasure trove of skills you've mastered—diction, discipline, dazzling entrances and don't forget those breathtaking exits!" He turned his pockets inside out. "Money is no indicator of talent, no gauge of one's true worth. That you are not mucked with gold means you are free—free to develop your great talent. Farewell, fair Portias and Iagos, my winter lions, my merry maids of May. Go with my blessing! Adieu!"

Adrift in a strange city and down to her last thousand forints, Mildred cabled Charles. He did not reply. She cabled her mother and quickly received a cabled response:

> Daughter,
> Sale of the Cassatt imminent. Will send money in thirty days. Hang on. Momma.

Mildred's outburst startled the delivery boy. "Thirty days? I don't have enough to hang on for thirty hours!"

She didn't panic. Charles had given her a lovely, gold filigree brooch. She bartered it for a month's stay in an old hotel. The deal struck, she resorted to tears to get the proprietor to accept her services as chambermaid in exchange for meals.

On the last day of her month's stay at the hotel, a letter arrived from Momma:

> Conneaut, Ohio – January 15, 1934
> Dear Millie,
>
> Brace yourself, darling. The sale of the Cassatt has run into trouble. Mr. Heckathorn's partners are insisting on yet another appraisal. Worried that I might sell the painting to someone else, he has advanced me one thousand dollars toward the purchase price.
>
> Your stepfather knows nothing of this advance. Please, when you write, don't mention it. I am enclosing a draft for three hundred dollars, which is all I can spare. Perhaps you can use it to fulfill your dream of studying music at the conservatory in

> Germany that Mrs. Schnell told you about. (I can't remember the name of the town.) Things are bad here. The Depression shows no sign of letting up.
>
> Love, (signed) Momma

A banker cashed the three-hundred-dollar draft and pointed Mildred toward a restaurant. After finishing two helpings of goulash, roast goose and chestnut stuffing, she returned to her room and packed. That afternoon, as a blizzard blew into Budapest, she boarded a train for Dresden.

Deep in my heart dear, I have a dream of you...

– Sigmund Romberg
(The Student Prince, 1924)

18

Hilde Schnell, the elderly woman who'd sung *Oh Promise Me* at Edna Mae's wedding, had been impressed with Mildred's piano accompaniment. "You've got great talent, Mildred. I've seen it since you were what, ten years old? Oh, if only you could study where I did—at the conservatory. In Dresden everyone is surrounded by music. The Student Prince pours from every door and window."

The day after Edna Mae's wedding, Mildred had scurried to Conneaut's library to learn more of the fabled city and to grow wistful over pictures of Linden-lined streets, quaint buildings and storybook churches.

Mildred found Dresden much different than the Dresden of Hilde's day. The Student Prince was long gone; the music supplanted by the blare of loudspeakers mounted on top of cars that continuously circled the streets. Metallic music came from them and stern voices speaking German too rapidly for a foreigner to translate.

"You hear that? They want us to think this Hitler is the messiah! All day and night they tell us of the glories of the NAZIS. They lie!" The protests, spoken to no one in particular, came from a street vendor selling roasted chestnuts.

As Mildred looked on in amazement, a well-dressed matron walked up to the old man and shook a furled umbrella in his face. "You damn Jews, always you put Germany last!" She poked at his chest. "Listen to the Fuhrer's message, Jew. Put Germany first!"

The retired archivist, a sharp-nosed, bespectacled bachelor who'd advertised for a lodger, opened the door to Mildred's knock and let her in. "From your voice on the phone I thought you were older." He raised his eyebrows. "You have no more luggage than this one small suitcase?"

"I require very little."

Ambivalence played on his face. This beautiful American who travels lightly and alone wishes to rent a room in my humble home? These were difficult times—one had to be careful. "You can pay a month's rent in advance?"

"Yes."

"Perhaps you would prefer more... more elegant accommodations. I furnish only tea and bread for breakfast, soup and crackers for dinner. You must wash, dry and put away your own dishes."

"Fine." She smiled coyly, reached out and touched his arm. "Herr Ewald, I assure you, I will be a model tenant."

As though enlightened with the reason for her coming to Germany, he softened. "Ah, you've come to Dresden to work as a model! Yes, of course, the newspaper speaks of our burgeoning fashion industry!"

"No sir. I've come to study piano at the Mendelssohn Conservatory."

His mouth flew open. "But, Fraulein! It has been torn down already twenty years!"

She took the room and enrolled instead in the Schlumweg Music Academy. The classrooms where Professor Igor Schlumweg and Frau Becker taught music theory, piano technique, harmonics and improvisation were well lit and warm. Practice rooms, located in the basement, were freezing, jail cell-sized cublicles.

Edna Mae wrote often. One letter contained a smaller, sealed envelope on which was written: "Don't open this until you read my letter."

> Conneaut, Ohio – February 24, 1934
> Dearest Sis,
>
> Momma has been dealt a brutal blow and can't bring herself to write. The Cassatt on which she has pinned all her hopes is a fake. The two experts called in to confirm the last appraisal all but laughed in her face and seemed to take glee in declaring the painting WORTHLESS! She hasn't spoken a word since and frankly, I'm worried. Edward has been laid off and we are now forced to live with his family here in Conneaut until things pick up. Keep your chin up. Things have to get better.
>
> Devotedly, (signed) Edna Mae
>
> P.S. Now you can open the other letter–it is from the one man I want you to FORGET!

Mildred tore off the tissue enclosing the letter and, recognizing the stiff, precise handwriting, gasped.

> New York City – February 1, 1934
> Liebling,
>
> Unable to live without you, I have filed for divorce from Erna. She agrees it is for the best–especially for the children. Fate is smiling on us at last, my beloved. The Trustees of

Hunter College have honored my request for a year's leave of absence.

I will be teaching at the University of Berlin this fall. The moment you meet me there we will be married!

Yours from and into eternity, (signed) Max

On April 1, 1934, a full six months before their scheduled reuniting, Mildred moved from Dresden to Berlin.

The capital of the Third Reich hummed like a well-oiled machine revving to ever-higher levels of performance. Massive construction projects sprouted everywhere. Huge monolithic structures were arising from the earth like erupting molars. Replacing buildings of old-world charm, they lined and guarded boulevards like giant soldiers—rigid, uniform, powerful, foreboding.

Somber-faced Berliners hurried along sidewalks. A man carrying two bulging shopping bags bumped into Mildred, knocked her hat askew and, without a sideward glance, hurried on. A woman, her shoulders ringed with the pelts and tiny heads of glassy-eyed foxes, pushed passed Mildred and hissed something that sounded like "Slow poke! Let me pass!"

As in Dresden, the Fuhrer's strident message spewed from a plethora of loudspeakers. It was as she stood waiting to cross the street, her ears ringing with his over-amplified promised Aryan Utopia, that she saw a dark-haired Asian girl running toward her. "Mildred! Mildred Gillars! Remember me? I'm Victor's wife, Michiko!"

Before Mildred knew it, Victor de Kowa, the German actor and director whom she'd met in Paris, had his arm around her shoulder. She squealed and hugged them both. "I can't believe it! What are you two doing here?"

Michiko's lovely almond-shaped eyes narrowed and darted about, surveiling the immediate area for eavesdroppers.

"Victor is directing again," she whispered nervously, "something for the Fuhrer..."

Victor forced a smile. "It pays the rent."

The rent must have been considerable for the de Kowa's tenth floor apartment boasted large, sunny rooms and had a sweeping view of the city. They insisted Mildred move into the spare bedroom. She accepted on one condition—that she earn her keep.

Victor nodded graciously. "Of course! You can resume teaching Michiko to speak better English. And you shall be my consultant—a sounding board for my brilliant ideas."

They got on well. Mildred enjoyed the camaraderie. Victor introduced her to members of the German film colony. Michiko pulled a few strings and got her a job teaching English at Berlitz of Berlin.

"But Michiko, two years of German in high school and some in college hardly qualifies me for..."

"You'll do fine."

The job offered good pay and flexible hours. Mildred started with two students: a vintner wanting enough English for basic communication with the increasing number of Americans visiting his winery; the other, a nursemaid hoping to acquire a basic vocabulary to facilitate travel to Wisconsin to visit relatives.

Heidi Heffner taught French and Italian at Berlitz. She quickly befriended Mildred and, upon learning of her interest in the theater, helped her land a bit part in Hitler's play, *The New Reich.* A staunch supporter of The New Order, Heidi also spent countless hours trying to convince Berlitz's newest employee of the Fuhrer's altruism. "Hitler is our hope for tomorrow, Mildred, he is for peace. You watch, he will see to it that all squabbles and misunderstandings get settled at bargaining tables, not on barbaric battlefields."

Every night before she drifted off to sleep, Mildred counted and recounted the days and hours until Max would arrive and claim her for his bride. She passed the summer without a word from him. With the start of the fall semester fast approaching, she went to the University of Berlin with hope of finding someone there who might have heard from him. Unable to answer the beautiful American's questions, a male clerk directed her to the dean.

Herr Zales sipped tea and listened patiently as she voiced concern over the whereabouts of her fiancé, Professor Koischwitz. Zales referred to a list on his desk. "No, my dear, I'm afraid Professor Koischwitz is not expected. Perhaps my senior administrator can shed some light on the matter."

The administrator directed her to Dr. Franz Six, Faculty Coordinator and Chairman of the Foreign Economics Department. Six took a batch of letters from a drawer and sorted through them. "Ah, here it is–Professor Max Otto Koischwitz. He scanned the letter, paraphrasing as his eyes flew over the typed message. "He says he is not coming to Berlin after all. The Board of Trustees of Hunter College has rescinded his leave of absence."

Mildred's eyes filled with tears. "Is there... is there any mention of me?"

"Of you?"

"I've come to Berlin at his request. I'm staying with friends. I've written him countless letters..."

Dr. Six's eyebrows shot up. "Ah! Fraulein Gillars! You are disappointed! Understandable, very understandable..." Obviously ill at ease, he began pinching withered leaves from the small potted plant on his desk. "I have heard a great deal about your Professor Koischwitz. He is well known in academic circles as an excellent teacher and as the author of many important books and articles. His lectures are..."

"Brilliant. Yes, I know–standing room only."

"Hmmm... one wonders then why his career stagnates and why he has not risen above the rank of assistant professor.

Tell me, my dear, could it be because of his lectures on Western decadence and his writings dealing with democracy as a failed, corrupt system?"

"Professor Koischwitz has no such beliefs."

"No?" Six fingered his moustache. "I understand your Professor Koischwitz has recently become an American citizen. Rather unusual, don't you think, for a confirmed Nazi to pursue American citizenship? Might not your famous defender of law and order, J. Edgar Hoover, interpret such a pursuit as a ploy to avoid deportation?"

"Professor Koischwitz has never been, is not and never will be a confirmed Nazi, Dr. Six. Good day."

Six watched her hips as she flounced to the door. "Perhaps we could discuss this further over dinner?" Interpreting the door slam as a definite "no," he spoke to the withered plant. "Sexy, was she not?"

With Max no longer headed for Berlin, Mildred pondered her next move. Her supervisor at Berlitz urged her to stay. "You would be foolish not to remain with us until your country weathers the storm. Your job with us is secure and you are being considered for a promotion. Tell me, Miss Gillars, what do you have to go home to?"

"Nothing."

Her promotion at Berlitz came as a reward for hard work and completion of intensive courses of both French and German. Better able to communicate, she came to befriend Berliners and to see them in a different light. Their awe of American celebrities amazed her. Stories of Charles Lindberg and Amelia Earhart captivated them. They cued up in lines three blocks long to see Fred Astaire and Ginger Rogers dance in the movie *Top Hat.* No actor was more imitated at parties than Boris Karloff in *The Bride of Frankenstein.*

Mildred continued to live with the de Kowas. Michiko,

concerned over Victor's depressed mental state, insisted she stay on. Victor had begun directing films for Doctor Josef Goebbels' Office of Propaganda and Enlightenment. "It's not a job," he complained, "it's a straight jacket! My every creative instinct is squelched–censored! Everyday they give me a new list of topics to avoid–imagine *verboten topics!*"

He took Mildred to see Leni Reifenstahl's latest motion picture, *Triumph of Will.* As they walked back home along Der Lindenstrasse he asked her opinion of Reifenstahl, Hitler's favorite filmmaker.

Mildred had been bowled over by the cinematography. "Leni Reifenstahl's a genius. Imagine having an elevator built to take her cameras up a hundred feet to get some of those spectacular angles! Her shots are sheer artistry."

Victor scowled. "Sheer artistry? They're calculated to brainwash! Did you see any shots of mutiny or civil insurrection? Of course you didn't. Leni's job is to make Germans look happy, fit, well fed and looked over by the one 'God of the universe'–the God Aryan!"

Edna Mae grudgingly sent her half-sister more news of Max. It came in bits and pieces, usually in the form of newspaper clippings. There came, from *The New York Times*, a blistering denouncement of his latest book, *A German-American Interprets Germany*:

> *Professor Koischwitz has, in this work, produced one of the most viciously clever pieces of Nazi propaganda circulated in the American classroom.*

The reviewer included a quote, lifted from the book's forward, and attributed it to Norwegian writer Knut Hamsun:

> *Germany, as she faces the head wind of the world's criticism, is cruising boldly ahead and will reach port. The day will come when nations great and small will change*

the tone they adopt with regard to this Reich in the heart of Europe. There is no night without dawn.

Mildred purchased a copy of the book and read it with disbelief. How could Max have written such tripe? He'd always defended Jews, now he was calling them "denizens of another land." The chapter entitled, "A Fight Against Death," written in defense of Germany's radicalism, so infuriated her that she hurled the book to the floor.

Berliners enjoyed unprecedented prosperity as Christmas approached. Everyone had a job, a comfortable lifestyle and great hope for the future. All Germans, at least on the surface, had unbounded faith in the Fuhrer, the "Savior."

Edna Mae's Christmas letter described a far different scene at home. "Things are bleak and getting bleaker. This year, Edward and I have gone without new clothes and cigarettes to buy Christmas presents for poor children. In case you're wondering, here's what American children are putting on their wish lists. Girls: Shirley Temple dolls, carriages and tea sets. Boys: Lone Ranger vests, Buck Rogers Solar Scout Badges, pocket watches, soldering irons and real telegraph sets."

During a long, lonely walk along the Kurfurstendamm, Mildred saw in a toy store window what Germany's children could expect from Father Christmas. There would be toys, but only those toys sanctioned by the Third Reich. All toys, whether tank, gun, soldier, helmet or dartboard with a Star of David as the target, would bear the official insignia of the New Order—the swastika.

Owens, James "Jesse" Cleveland (1913–1980)
At the 1936 Olympic games in Berlin, Owens astounded the world and upset Hitler's "Aryan" theories by equaling the world mark (10.3 sec) in the 100-meter race, by breaking world records in the 200-meter race (20.7 sec) and in the broad jump (26 ft 5 3/8 in/8.07 m) and by winning also (along with Ralph Metcalfe and others) the 400-meter relay race.

– The Columbia Encyclopedia (Sixth Edition, 2001)

19

Charged with hosting the Olympic Games, Berlin began, even before the spring of 1936, to fill with people from around the globe. The Office of German Tourism went out of its way to court this influx of impressionable minds. Visitors could, courtesy of Berlin Radio, listen to programs in their native tongue. American visitors had an added advantage. They could access, via Berlin Radio, President Roosevelt's latest Fireside Chat, and his lament that a full third of Americans were now "ill-housed, ill-clad and ill-nourished."

Berlin's newsstands carried *The Wall Street Journal* documenting America's staggering unemployment. Predictably, many visitors from the U.S. became so impressed with Germany's healthy economy, they joined the burgeoning number of expatriates living in Berlin.

Determined to court world attention and admiration, Berlin put on its best behavior. Anti-Semitic signs disappeared from shop windows, hotels, theaters and beer gardens. Known dissidents were rounded up. Store windows lavishly displayed the latest fashions and top-notch merchandise. The city added thousands to an already large staff of gardeners, custodians and security guards. Those wishing to help the Fuhrer strut his stuff put on lavish parties for blue bloods, politicians, sheiks, sultans, socialites and owners of foreign radio stations and newspapers.

At one grand ball an American guest approached Mildred. "Why, I can't believe it! Only a few short years ago, papers back home were filled with horror stories about Germany's bankrupt economy. Now I see only happy, healthy, prosperous citizens! No wonder Winston Churchill said, 'Every country would do well to have a Hitler!'"

Mildred's life took another of its quixotic turns on the day she, Victor and Michiko attended the Olympic track and field events. The program proceeded as predicted, with Germans doing exceedingly well–until the American runner Jesse Owens rocketed around the track to victory. A black man had trounced the Third Reich's best athletes, had beaten them soundly and had won the Gold!

An electrifying hush fell over the stadium. As though drawn by a magnet, every eye went to Hitler's box. He sat rigid, seemingly stunned. The general sitting beside him bent toward him and said something. The Fuhrer reacted vehemently, screamed something and pushed the general away. Owens mounted the pedestal to be knighted the world's fastest man. Gripped by silent tension, the crowd gasped in unison.

Hitler, decrier of blacks as 'sub-humans,' stood. He panned the sea of stricken faces. His eyes, like those of a hawk spotting carrion, came to rest on Owens. No Roman Emperor ever condemned a martyr with greater decisiveness. Hitler's fist shot out, extended its thumb and rotated it until the thumb pointed down.

An inebriated Frenchman occupied the seat in front of Mildred. Outraged by Hitler's condemnation of the black, he jumped to his feet and cheered Owens. Fighting off efforts of those near him to pull him back into his seat, he marked Hitler's exit with catcalls and screamed obscenities. Victor lurched forward, clamped his hand over the Frenchman's mouth and began pulling him toward the nearest exit tunnel. Michiko and Mildred followed close behind.

An usher ran up to them. "Come, this way. Get your drunk friend out of here before he gets torn to pieces."

When, after a harrowing ride through heavy traffic, they got the Frenchman to his hotel, Mildred made him a pot of strong coffee. It took three cups, an ice pack on his head and much forced walking before he came to his senses. "Sorry, I guess I made a fool of myself. My name is Andre DuPar. I probably owe you my life. Somehow I must make restitution for your kindness."

The next evening, after Victor and Michiko declined his offer of dinner, Andre treated Mildred to a sumptuous meal at the Hotel Kaiserhof. Over dessert he apologized again for his behavior at the Olympics. "Unfortunately, I have been drinking rather heavily since my wife left me last winter. I should have known better, marrying someone twenty years my junior. She was, understandably, easily seduced by her equally young fencing instructor."

A husky man of forty-five with brooding good looks, Andre owned an airplane manufacturing plant outside of Paris where he built and tested military aircraft prototypes. Mildred enjoyed several dates with him before he returned to France.

In November he invited her to his chalet in Provence. He met her train at the station and, jabbering a mixture of French and English, whisked her to his waiting Bugati roadster. Tires squealing, executing one hairpin turn after another, he raced up the steep road ascending from the station to his chalet.

Directed to an opulent bedroom, Mildred bathed, used an expensive formulation to cleanse her face and applied fresh make-up. She put on a new form-fitting gown and brushed her hair. Confident she looked her best, she joined Andre in the trophy room.

"Mildred—you're beautiful! Magnific! Tres chic!" He held out a tray of crackers topped with cream cheese and smoked salmon.

"Oh, Andre, this is such a beautiful place!"

He drew her to him and kissed her. "I was afraid you would... how do you say... '*stand me up*.'"

They dined on vichyssoise and roast quail with truffles. For dessert, served in front of a huge stone fireplace, they ate crepes-suzettes flamed with curacao. Then, warmed by the best wine Mildred had ever tasted, they sipped cognac and listened to a recording of George Gershwin's *Rhapsody in Blue*. Before the music stopped, he gathered her up into his arms and carried her upstairs to the master bedroom.

He insisted she see Paris through his eyes. They drove to his elegant townhouse in the fourth arrondissement, within walking distance of Notre Dame. Like honeymooners, they slept late, spent the day cruising the Seine, museum hopping and strolling through the Tuileries. Evenings began with a champagne toast to the sunset. A dinner on the town, a first-rate play or concert, then home for a nightcap and extended lovemaking.

She returned to Berlin intending to stay but a few days. Once she'd resigned from Berlitz, packed her belongings and said goodbye to Victor and Michiko, she'd hurry back to Paris—back to Andre.

"With no notice?" fumed Berlitz's supervisor. "Think, Fraulein Gillars! To resign with no notice is to burn your bridges behind you. And should someday, for whatever reason, you need your job back?"

Victor also begged her to stay. With his head hung he broke the news: Michiko had been diagnosed with breast cancer. A long period of recuperation would follow the surgery. They needed Mildred's help and moral support.

Andre understood. If she had to stay on in Berlin for a bit, they'd write daily letters and visit one another as often as possible. His new project would keep him so busy that the days would fly by until she returned to Paris for good.

His letters, the outpouring of a passionate Frenchman, also spoke of a France about to be pounced on by Germany. A letter, written on the day French Ministers of Defense rejected his tail-gun equipped pursuit plane, bristled:

> My Beloved, Precious Wife-to-Be,
>
> Forgive me, but at this moment there are no words to express my fury. The dunderheads have done it again, this time turning down my proposal. Mind you, I have repeatedly tested the prototype and found it flawless!
>
> And what do these fools do as Hitler defies the Treaty of Versailles? As he expands his Air Force and builds an army of thirty-six divisions? They sit on their thumbs! Doubtless, these dunderheads belong not in the French Ministry of Defense but in the only successful government division in all of France, Le Ministere des Loisirs—the Ministry of Idleness!"
>
> Oh dearest sweetheart, these are difficult times for romance. It's as if the world is experiencing an ominous time warp—an intermission of sorts. War hangs in the air like a menacing plague—I can taste it. We French must

wake up and stop deluding ourselves or we'll be visited not by the holidays but by goose-stepping hoards!

On a happy note, I have petitioned Rome for an annulment. It should, if all goes well, take less than a year.

My arms long to hold you,
(signed) Andre

During one of her visits, a French newspaper heralded the great zeppelin Hindenberg "a symbol of German progressiveness." Her eyes flew to lines describing the air ship as "a luxurious, flying palace." She turned to Andre. "Darling, I have a wonderful idea! For our honeymoon, let's take a trip to New York aboard the Hindenberg!"

"Who do you think you're marrying, my darling? Douglas Fairbanks? Max Schmeling?"

"But Andre, everybodys who's anybody travels on the Hindenberg. They say it's luxurious–plush staterooms, hot and cold showers, a bar, a dining salon, a theater..."

"Did *they* mention it would cost us a small fortune?"

"But, by the time we get married... we still have over a year..."

He took her in his arms. "An eternity, eh, mon ami? But you are right, let's consider the Hindenberg. Who knows, in time the dunderheads might give me the green light, fund my prototype and put a smile on the face of my accountant."

Their dreams of a honeymoon aboard the "Flying Palace" ended when, listening to the car radio as they motored through Normandy en route to visit Andre's family, they learned of the Hindenberg's fiery demise.

The glory of the French countryside dispelled their disappointment. May gave way to the kind of summer Vincent van Gogh might have painted. Starry nights held the fragrance of honeysuckle and freshly cut hay. The days, with the sun over-exposing every flower and field, were almost too bright to bear. Frolicking over Andre's beautiful estate, they romped through oceans of sunflowers, climbed green hills and bathed naked in the crystal pool of an abandoned limestone quarry.

But, as with all Edens, there came the serpent's hiss—in this case, the ever more saddening news of the day. A man with aviation in his blood, Andre grieved upon hearing of Amelia Earhart's disappearance during her flight over the Pacific. He kept his ear to the radio for hours hoping to hear her plane had been spotted. "A twin-engine Lockheed Electra? Why would she choose such a problem-riddled plane?"

Austria's Chancellor von Schuschnigg succumbed to Hitler's demands. The chancellor's resignation paved the way for the Anschluss, the new union of Germany and Austria.

"The swine!" Andre screamed upon hearing of it. "Twenty-five years ago Hitler was nothing but an impoverished vagrant. He slept in flophouses, ate in soup kitchens and had to leave Vienna because he couldn't sell his miserable watercolors. Now he returns as Vienna's liberator!"

In April 1938, Andre and Mildred vacationed in Czechoslovakia. He spent most of his time there sending warnings back to France's Premier Daladier that Czechoslovakia, now surrounded on three sides by Germany, was about to be devoured.

Upon his return to Paris, Andre received an envelope bearing the seal of the French Defense Ministry. "At last!" he exclaimed after reading the enclosed letter, "they're going to accept my prototypes! Let's hope it's not too late."

Official notification of the annulment of Andre and Emilie's marriage arrived. Consumed with work, Andre assigned Mildred the task of finalizing plans for their wedding. It would take place in a side chapel of the Sacre Cour on the tenth of June.

On June 1st, hours after Andre left for the airfield, his secretary, Nicole, appeared at Mildred's door. Nicole's eyes were red from crying, her face the color of alabaster. She threw her arms around Mildred and sobbed. "There's been a crash... Andre's plane..."

The next morning, news of Andre DuPar's death screamed from the front page of every newspaper in Paris. "The first half of the test was a complete success," Le Monde reported, "but the plane appeared to shudder during a critical dive. It went into a spin and exploded upon crashing to earth. Monsieur Andre DuPar, an accomplished pioneer in the field of aviation, will be buried in the DuPar family plot in St. Lo."

Mildred avoided the funeral. She spent the entire day at the Boulevard Theater on the Rue St. Germain watching James Cagney strut his stuff in *Angels With Dirty Faces*. Andre would have understood.

In July 1938 Mildred tuned in the BBC's *CBS World-News Roundup*. It featured live, on-the-spot reports from London-based American correspondent Edward R. Murrow and warned of the continent's "heating up." Simultaneously the German broadcasting network, Reichrundfunk, began its campaign against the British. Dr. Goebbels' English-speaking broadcasters lost no time in filling the airwaves with condemnations of the Crown.

Broadcasters on both sides interrupted their regularly scheduled programs to announce the signing of *The Munich Pact*. A supposed pact of non-aggression, it gave those with blinders on a sense of security.

It cannot be denied that for a society which has to create scarcity to save its members from starvation, to whom abundance spells disaster, and to whom unlimited energy means unlimited power for war and destruction, there is an ominous cloud in the distance though at present it be no bigger than a man's hand.

– Arthur Stanley Eddington (1882–1944)

20

Michiko lost her battle with cancer. The apartment unbearably vacant with the removal of her body to a mortuary, Victor and Mildred went for a walk along streets decorated for Octoberfest. "Mildred," he said, "I can't stay in Berlin. She's everywhere..."

"Where will you go?"

"Dieter... my brother... has a home in Brussels."

"Go there."

Opting to remain in Berlin and to keep her job with Berlitz, Mildred moved to Kudamm Strasse, to the apartment of her friend, Erica Trier. She soon found Erica's ebullience exhausting. "Look Mildred, if you think I'm going to let you sit home and mope, think again!" On Friday nights they attended the little theater on Unter Den Linden to watch newly released films such as *Bringing Up Baby* and *Jezebel.* On Saturdays, Erica invariably found someone eager to take them for a sail on the Wannsee and to treat them to dinner afterwards. On Sundays, they ventured out on foot as all traffic in Berlin ground to a stop for the monster rallies of the Third Reich.

A sea of people stretched as far as the eye could see. Corralled by walls of massive new buildings, proud Germans stood for hours watching Hitler's military might on parade. Convoys of armored tanks led banner-toting Aryan beauties and wave after wave of arm-banded youth. Whipped into frenzy by Nazis decrying Germany's God-given mandate to rule the world, individuals climbed lampposts to cheer "Deutschland uber alles! Long live the Fuhrer!"

The crowd, its passion primed by the foreplay of Nazi rhetoric to the brink of climax, became like an insatiable animal lusting for fulfillment. Hitler timed his entrance. The very sight of him pushed passionate followers over the edge. They blubbered, shed tears of joy, shook, grew rigid with orgasm and, emitting cries worthy of copulation, swooned.

The Fuhrer rewarded them with the smile of a stud who'd just satisfied a nymphomaniac. The smile prevailed as he endured the ear-splitting crescendo. Then, like the God of Genesis, he spread his arms and created silence.

His power to persuade manifested itself in hours-long speeches. Topics and slogans were limited. The mesmerizing came with the constant rhythmic repetition: Simple slogans, simply stated over and over again.

At the end of one particularly exuberant rally, Mildred pleaded, "Honestly Erica, can't we just go home and rest?"

"Not tonight. Tonight's our big chance to hob-knob with the German film colony. We've been invited to a soiree hosted by the head of Hitler's Foreign Ministry—Minister von Ribbentrop himself."

"Your brother's boss?"

"Adam is very influential."

The soiree, held in the home of the Dutch ambassador, turned out to be an enormous, dressy affair. A twenty-piece orchestra played catchy dance tunes. Champagne glasses tinkled. Mildred danced until the wee hours with puffed-up German officers, ambassadors, industrialists and German film celebrities.

Descriptions of these and other grand events she attended with Erica invariably found their way into letters Mildred wrote home. But, no matter how titillating the tale, she always wrote as a postscript, the all-telling question: "Any word of Max?"

Edna Mae reluctantly sent a copy of Hunter College's 1938 Yearbook. In it, Max's photograph appeared above the caption, "Voted Hunter's Most Popular Teacher of 1938." Inside the yearbook's cover, Edna Mae had pasted a clipping from Hunter's faculty bulletin. "Congratulations to Erna Koischwitz, the charming wife of our Professor Koischwitz," it began, "on being elected chairwoman of..."

Mildred tore the clipping from the cover and crumpled it in her fist. "His charming wife... damn him!"

The tone of German radio changed that spring. Broadcasts, beamed to Americans around the clock, urged the United States to stop wasting money by selling supplies to England and France on credit. "Demand that your politicians stick to America's policy of isolationism," advised broadcasters. "Don't allow yourselves to be pulled into the fracas. Stay isolated and insulated from the squabble on foreign soil."

Working collectively as The U.S.A. Zone of the Reichrundfunk, broadcasters introduced themselves as "fair-minded, patriotic Americans with only the best interests of the United States at heart." In reality they were American expatriates recruited by Doctor Goebbels solely to raise German credibility in the United States—at the expense of Great Britain.

The most effective broadcaster seeking to keep America from linking arms with England in the fight against Germany was Fred Kaltenbach, the first to take to the airwaves as "Lord Haw-Haw." Because of his tenure, Kaltenbach had earned the title "Dean of the U.S.A. Zone." He had a weakness for jingles and name-calling. His signature: offending the British.

Few of King George VI's subjects were spared Lord Haw-Haw's scorn. The gentry-class received his full verbal barrage. Lord Haw-Haw naughtily portrayed bumbling Englishmen as pious ministers supported by munitions profits, or as government officials turned warmongers. He also created a few "bright Brits." These characters, cast in many of Haw-Haw's scripts, urged parliament to apply England's wealth—not to building weapons—but to helping the commonwealth's poor.

On September 1, 1939 Germany invaded Poland. Britain and France, having signed a pact to protect Poland, half-heartily declared war on Germany. To Mildred's astonishment, her neighbors, rather than being outraged by the Wehrmacht's invasion of Poland, cheered. Corner loudspeakers crowed about the speed and superiority of German forces. Broadcasters came on the air to congratulate Hitler on the destruction caused by Panzer tanks, mechanized infantry and dive-bomber assisted blitzkriegs. Berlin rejoiced.

Erica and her brother Adam both worked for Hitler's Minister of Propaganda and Enlightenment, Doctor Josef Goebbels. They were expected to make the rounds of Foreign Ministry soirees. Erica insisted Mildred accompany her to one such party. "Close that book and put on your dancing shoes!"

The soiree sparkled. Champagne flowed. The orchestra set feet tapping. During the break, Adam introduced Goebbels' newest broadcasting recruit, William Joyce.

One look at the sharp-nosed newcomer and Mildred judged him a phony. He strengthened her conviction the moment he opened his mouth. For, in acknowledging the introduction, he tried to camouflage his panhandle twang and to pass himself off as a member of the English gentry. He didn't fool Mildred. A long-time student of both dialogue and diction, she knew that his high-pitched, "How dew you dew" had to come from either Texas or Louisiana. Small-headed, thin-lipped, pitted complexion and weasel-like, she thought William Joyce the ugliest man she'd ever seen.

A scrawny redhed stood beside him. "Oh yes, and this is the misses. Say hello, Maggie."

"Hello... charmed, I'm sure."

Several Gestapo-uniformed men and their satin-gowned women joined the group. The larger audience prompted Joyce to grandstand. "By jove, me and Maggie are here to stay! We've thrown away our British passports." He raised his champagne glass. "To Hitler's Germany–the cradle of the future!"

Adam challenged the newcomer. "You traveled on an British passport? But aren't you an American citizen?"

Joyce snarled like a Texas bobcat. "Don't mess with me, boy. Ah'll soon be a citizen of the Third Reich! Passports will be no damn good once the Fuhrer rules the world."

Goebbels thought Joyce a stellar fellow. Within a month of his arrival, the insufferable Joyce was promoted to "Professional Propagandist" and assigned Fred Kaltenbach's role of "Lord Haw-Haw" on Radio Berlin. As the new "Lord Haw-Haw," Joyce peppered England with broadcasts designed to irritate like a hair shirt. Relieved of his "Lord Haw-Haw" role, Kaltenbach took to the airwaves with ever more ludicrous programs.

"Who is this clod Kaltenbach?" Edna Mae asked in one of her letters to Mildred. "Have you heard his 'Dear Harry' broadcasts?"

Mildred had. Kaltenbach began these broadcasts with the salutation "Dear Harry." He would then read inflammatory propaganda as though it were part of a friendly letter to a boyhood friend in the United States. Whoever "Harry" was, he must have been mortified at being singled out on international radio.

Erica tried to make the Christmas of 1939 festive. She made presents, used a month's sugar ration to bake a Linzer torte and, for Christmas dinner served smoked cheese canapés, roast goose, mussels in wine sauce and French brandy.

Days before Christmas, the war's first dramatic confrontation had taken place. After a running battle, three British cruisers had bottled up the Graf Spee, Germany's pocket battleship, in Uruguay's Montevideo Harbor. The neutral government of Uruguay informed the Graf Spee's captain that he had seventy-two hours to get out. The whole world waited. Finally, with three hundred thousand people watching from the shore, the Graf Spee sailed out of the harbor and blew itself up.

As they tidied up from Christmas dinner, Adam commented, "It won't be easy for Goebbels to explain why we sank our own ship—not with the whole world watching."

Erica went to bed early on the night of January 19th, 1940. Not sleepy, Mildred wrapped herself in a blanket and sat in the kitchen listening to the debut of yet another new personality on the Reichrundfunk. "Good evening, lovely listeners," the newcomer said, his voice startlingly familiar. "This is Doctor Anders."

A chill went through her. No, it wasn't possible. She scooted her chair closer to the radio, adjusted the tuner and turned up the volume. Doctor Anders continued. "Confidentially, I must tell you how the American people are being duped..."

"Max!" Mildred screamed, "It's Max! He's on the radio! My God!"

The inevitable occurred at a ball held in the Chilean Embassy just off the Tiergarten. Eight years had passed, yet neither showed a scintilla of surprise or recognition when their host, assuming they'd never met, introduced them. "Fraulein Gillars, it is my pleasure to present Doctor Koischwitz, a man certain to become the brightest star of German radio. Doctor Koischwitz... the lovely and talented Fraulein Gillars."

Max took her hand, kissed it and stared into her eyes. "Ah yes! The beautiful American! I've heard so much about you."

Celebrity is a mask that eats into the face.

– John Updike (1932 -)

21

Former lovers re-introduced, they danced across a crowded floor oblivious to everyone around them. He held her so tight she could feel his heart racing. Forcing a note of nonchalance into her voice, her lips brushing his cheek, she whispered, "Is your wife here?"

He stiffened. "Erna? Why no, she's not. We separated a long time ago."

"Really."

"Please, Liebling, there's so much we must discuss." He spun her around, his eyes inventorying the room. "This is hardly the place. Perhaps we could get together..."

"No Max. I don't think so."

He touched his finger to her lips. "Don't. I can't bear it! Meet me later tonight... the Hotel Kaiserhof... I'll reserve a table."

The maitre d' ushered her to a secluded corner table in the hotel's elegantly appointed dining room. He pulled back her chair. "Herr Koischwitz sends a message,

Fraulein. He has been delayed. He requests that you wait."

Max arrived just before midnight. They ordered dinner and made small talk until the food arrived. Mildred warmed her hands over a bowl of steaming hot soup. "So, Max, what brings you to Berlin?"

He picked up the knife beside his plate. "They treat me like an outsider—like I don't belong."

"Who does?"

"Hunter's Board of Governors. Like this!" He thrust the knife into the butter. "They stab me in the back!"

"My, is that any way for Hunter College to treat its most popular professor of 1938?"

His face lit up. "Ah, you've followed my career, Liebling!"

"Not all of it."

He ate little and talked incessantly, expressing sadness at some memories, anger at others. He seemed genuinely baffled that, as a result of his admittedly pro-German lectures, some of America's patriotic societies denounced him for having "Hitlerite sympathies."

"You've become a thorn in Hunter's side."

His nostrils flared. "Hunter needs more than a thorn in its side—it needs a good kick in the ass! Imagine—them threatening to censure me for 'consorting with Nazi propagandists.' Hah! Just because I'm frequently asked to be guest of honor at the German-American Bund meetings." He lit another cigarette. "Liebling, its not just Hunter. I weep for America. Dark hordes overrun it—barbarians who would obliterate the light of learning and culture."

"Tell me about Erna and your daughters. Are they well? Still in New York?"

"They live in Denmark."

"Denmark! My, my..."

He didn't like to be toyed with. "I see my daughters when I can."

"And Erna? How often do you see your beloved?"

"You are my beloved. I see her only when absolutely necessary—only when one of my daughters falls ill or has a crisis requiring a father's presence."

"You know, Max, I'm really not interested in your marital situation. Tell me more about Hunter."

"Hunter? Where I've spent my entire teaching career only to have them spit in my face? I'll tell you about Hunter—where shall I start? With how they refuse to make me a full-professor because they think I'm a Jew? It's my name, 'Koischwitz'".

"You're not making a lot of sense."

He raised his voice. "Sense? They accused me of terrible things—they've threatened to prosecute me as a subversive!"

"Max..."

As though poking at the enemy's heart, he snuffed his cigarette in the mound of mashed potatoes left on his plate. "Ah, but I outsmarted them by resigning before they could carry out their threats. The idiots! May they rot in hell!"

Awakened by the outburst, the waiter quickly tabulated and brought the check. Without glancing at it, Max put down a large bill. "Sir," said the waiter, "have you nothing smaller?"

"Keep the change. Buy your girlfriend something nice. Now quickly, the lady's wrap. Summon a carriage!"

"A cab, sir?"

"Did I say *cab*? No, I said *carriage*!" Max lifted Mildred's hand, kissed it and, staring into her eyes, spoke again to the waiter. "If you value your job, by the time we reach the street you will have a horse-drawn carriage waiting at the curb—a carriage fit for a queen."

They dallied a bit over cognac-laced coffee then, bundled for the freezing temperature outside, exited the hotel. A very old carriage pulled by an even older horse stood waiting. The driver nodded and opened the carriage's door. "Come, there's a fur blanket inside."

"It's fine, Max," Mildred said, "let's get in before we freeze."

They drove around the Tiergarten. The inside of the carriage smelled like the inside of an old trunk. Max put his arm around her shoulder and, seeing her shiver, pulled the fur blanket around them.

"It's late, Max, I really should get home. I have to be at work before nine."

"Work?"

"I teach English and French at Berlitz."

His eyes left hers and studied the first wash of dawn on the horizon. "Liebling, I have a large and lovely apartment on Friederickstrasse. We could..."

"*We?*" She wiggled out from under his arm. "No, Max. *We* ended a very long time ago."

He threw up his hands. "But you must let me help you! I have influence. How would you like a job in radio?"

"Doing what?"

"Broadcasting."

"Oh, no, no, no! I'll not spew the kind of political hogwash one hears on Berlin radio."

He gripped her hand. "Trust me, you'll have nothing to do with politics—you will be a... social commentator broadcasting to American expatriates. It's perfect for you—playing recordings of American music. Think of it, Liebling, I can make you the star of Bremen Sender!"

Bremen Sender: the one German radio station she listened to, the only one that kept to a non-political, unbiased format. "Are you saying I could..."

Max nodded. "Yes, and to a huge audience!"

"I don't know..."

He cupped her chin and stared into her eyes. "It's a rare opportunity." He nuzzled her cheek.

"I'll... I'll consider it."

Max's broadcasts on the Reichrundfunk were winning ever-larger audiences. His voice came across loud and clear, his praise of the Vaterland and his Nazi rhetoric unwavering. Mildred listened at every chance, awestruck at how easily he transformed himself into different personalities. Mostly he broadcast as "Dr. Anders" or as "Mr. O.K." Occasionally he became "Fritz," a straight man to fellow-broadcaster Fred Kaltenbach on the lively program "Fritz and Fred, the Friendly Quarrelers."

She considered his offer for two weeks and might have considered it longer had he not grown impatient and summoned her to the lobby of Bremen Sender. He greeted her with a kiss on the cheek. "Brace yourself, Liebling, you're about to audition!"

He ushered her into a small studio. "Herr Director Johannes Schmidt-Hansen—Fraulein Gillars, the woman I've told you so much about."

"Ah, but you failed to mention how beautiful she is!" He handed her a script. "Please Fraulein Gillars, won't you step to the microphone and read the lines underlined in red?"

She rose to the occasion. "Good evening, my esteemed American expatriates, this is your fellow American Mildred Gillars, here to entertain you with up-to-the-minute state-side news and hit parade tunes."

"Wunderbar!" exclaimed Schmidt-Hansen. "You're hired!"

She started at a weekly salary of one hundred eighty marks, twice what she had been earning at Berlitz. The studio provided a special work permit and, as a bonus, an extra food-ration card.

On the eve of her first broadcast Max coached her on German Radio protocol. "It is very simple, Liebling. Do what you are told to do—no more, no less."

Her first broadcast went well. During the music-segment she played Ella Fitzgerald's *A-Tisket, A-Tasket*, Glen Miller's *In the Mood* and Bing Crosby's million-record seller, *San Antonio*

Rose. For her segment "Celebrity News" she announced that Henry Fonda, star of *The Grapes of Wrath*, had been nominated for an Academy Award.

Listeners flooded the station's switchboard after that broadcast. They requested favorite tunes, news of specific American cities and the latest on gangster/celebrity, Al Capone. Questions and requests poured in. Did she know the Lone Ranger's true identity? Where could they write for a list of the Brooklyn Dodgers? Did she have any idea where they could obtain a Buck Rogers' Solar Scout Badge for their children?

Impressed, Schmidt-Hansen doubled her salary. A more prestigious title followed on the heels of acclaim. "Mildred Gillars, Broadcaster of Expatriate News and Music" became "Mildred Gillars, Station Mistress of Ceremonies for the Entertainment Programs of the European Services of Reich Broadcasting."

One particularly colorful fan was Ezra Pound, the Idaho poet considered by Ernest Hemingway and Graham Greene to be the greatest American poet of the twentieth century. By the late 1930's Pound had a Rome-based radio program promoting Mussolini and urging Americans not to give any support to England or France.

Ezra wrote often to offer tips and advice based on his twenty years as an expatriate. In one such letter to Mildred, he included an autographed photo with the following ditty:

My dear lady, as you can well see,
my bushy beard is red.
Long hair of the same hue (and plentiful too!)
sprouts from my head.
Above my black cape, just below my pate,
please note a Byronic collar.
To learn from me of the great Mussolini,
please my dear–just holler.

A flamboyant, provocative and self-proclaimed political crusader, Ezra came across in some of his letters as an embittered opponent of democracy. He regarded Mussolini an apostle of law and order acting on a divine mandate to save Italy from the chaos of communism. Pound subscribed to the theory of German economist, Silvio Gesell—that "every country's economic troubles were caused by usurious interest rates extracted by Jewish money lenders."

"Dear girl," Ezra wrote in another letter, "war is horribly inevitable and tragically forgettable. You have a marvelous sensitivity in your voice. Use it to talk your country and mine out of getting involved in this rotten war. Enclosed please find another ditty, entitled 'War Is But a Jewish Plot' which you have my permission to read over the air to your listeners."

Momma, upon learning of Mildred's new career, wrote a long letter of congratulation. She'd received a note from Aaron Stern. "Can you believe he's a famous heart surgeon? And how time flies—our little Aaron will soon be thirty-two!"

Having read Momma's letter in the morning, Mildred reported for work that evening, her mind filled with memories of Greystone and Aaron. So distracted, she made a huge blunder. "Ladies and gentlemen, for your listening pleasure this evening, I will play a recording of *Summertime*, from Gershwin's *Porgy and Bess*. Oh yes, and wherever you are, Dr. Aaron Stern, I dedicate this song to you. Happy Birthday! Shalom!"

A great, communal gasp went up in the studio. Those present gaped at the microphone as though it might explode. Seconds later, all hell broke loose. Schmidt-Hansen came running and snatched the microphone from her. "'Shalom?' Are you crazy?" Beads of sweat glistened on his forehead as he clenched his fist and shook it in her face. "Mein Gott!"

dupe: n. A person deceived into functioning as the tool of another person or power.

– The American Heritage Dictionary

22

In May of 1940 the fighting between Germany, England and France erupted. Mildred, caught between warring countries, juxtaposed ideologies and loyalties that she could neither defend nor understand, spent her days, as did most people, ignoring the ever-vigilant Gestapo and getting on with life.

Doctor Joseph Goebbels went all out to win the sympathy of neutral countries. For starters he appointed Hans Klinger to the position of Director General of the Reich Broadcasting System. Klinger's job: to impose new standards of "patriotism" on the system's independent stations.

Surrounded by co-workers, Mildred listened with disbelief as Schmidt-Hansen read Klinger's ultimatums:

> *To eliminate any deviation from the truth, a Ministry officer shall approve all material, including music, to be broadcast. Broadcasters shall read verbatim and with the degree of emotion indicated in script margins. Anyone associated with a broad-*

cast station who defies or resists official directives shall be deemed a traitor to the Reich.

His reading of the material concluded, Schmidt-Hansen produced a stack of affidavits. "Ladies and gentlemen—please, before you go, each of you must sign one of these to affirm that you have been informed of and agree to Director Klinger's mandate."

Mildred refused. An hour later, she was summoned to Schmidt-Hansen's office. "I'm not signing it," she said. "Why should I? My job here at Bremen Sender has nothing to do with politics. Nothing I broadcast needs censoring."

"Please understand, Fraulein. We are at war."

"*You* are at war. I'm an American citizen."

He walked to the window and gazed at the distant hills as though longing to disappear into them. "The security of our nation is of critical importance."

Late in December of 1940 Mildred was ordered to the office of the Foreign Ministry's General Fussganger. He welcomed her with a click of his heels and a smile. He admired her dress, told her he hadn't expected such a beautiful woman and claimed to be an avid fan of her program.

"You sent for me?"

"What I don't understand, Fraulein, is why a woman of your considerable talent buries herself at a second rate station. Have you considered moving up—broadcasting for Zeesen?"

"The Reichrundfunk?"

"Of course, Zeesen... the Reichrundfunk... they're one and the same." He described the excellent career opportunities awaiting her at Europe's largest and most far-reaching broadcasting network. He assured her—she would not be expected to broadcast *anything* other than music and social commentary.

"I would be doing the same as I do at Bremen Sender?"

"Of course—but to a vast, international audience."

The thought set her heart racing. "I... I'm not sure. Can I sleep on it?" The confused look on his face made her smile. Clearly, she'd used an idiom he didn't understand. "No, General, '*Can I sleep on it?*' means I need more time to consider your proposal."

"Ah!" he winked. "I thought you wanted me to produce a bed! Very well, Fraulein Gillars, you may '*sleep on it.*' I will expect your answer tomorrow."

She returned to her apartment, changed into a satin gown and poured a glass of wine to quench the inner turmoil spawned by Fussganger's offer. What was she doing here in Germany? What kind of country pounces on its neighbors and ships Jews off to God-knows-where? But... just think of it, she'd be broadcasting to an international audience! Or should she go home... but home to what? The Depression? And to whom? Another glass of wine and she picked up the phone and dialed. "Max? Could you possibly meet me for dinner—Bitterman's restaurant, say seven-thirty?"

Foreign Minister Joachim von Ribbentrop welcomed her to Zeesen. "Fraulein Gillars! We are honored!" He took her hand, kissed it and insisted she sit. He stared at her legs as she crossed them. "You have a lovely figure, my dear. And such slender ankles! Cigarette?" His eyes strayed to her décolleté and lingered on her breasts.

"Max Koischwitz said something about orientation."

"Ah, yes, your... friend... Herr Koischwitz... an amazing man... though not very robust..."

"The orientation?"

"You are strong minded, Fraulein. I like that. Let's see, have I welcomed you to Zeesen and congratulated you on your promotion to The U.S.A. Zone of the Reichrundfunk?"

"You have."

"This is a splendid opportunity for you. Should you succeed—prove yourself an asset to our Fuhrer—your salary will be increased proportionately."

"I have been assured my broadcasts will have nothing to do with politics."

"Yes, yes, yes... of course. You can start today, immediately following your orientation."

She jumped to her feet. "Today? But..."

"We have no *buts* in Germany." His hand arced around her and came to rest on her derriere. "This butt is a lovely exception—a very nice butt... a very provocative one. I made an American joke, yes?"

She spun away from him. "Minister von Ribbentrop, could you possibly tell me where I might find Doctor Koischwitz? I have left countless messages for him."

von Ribbentrop raised an eyebrow. "And he doesn't respond? Why, it must be a matter of critical importance that causes him to neglect such a beautiful woman."

Introduction to Zeesen began with a film on the history, operation, scope and goals of German radio. Director of Orientation, Inge Doman, a husky, big-bosomed blonde, took over. Devoid of make-up and facial expression, she wore a tight-fitting black suit, dark stockings and sturdy shoes. Exuding a robot's cold efficiency, she escorted Mildred on a tour of the facility. Asked where she had learned to speak English so fluently, Doman snapped, "As you will be spending most of your waking hours here, Fraulein Gillars, you would do well to pay attention."

The Reichrundfunk, located just outside the small town of Zeesen, sprawled like a huge octopus. Tentacles housed office complexes and support facilities. The nerve center pulsed with state-of-the-art broadcast studios, broadcast-composing rooms, a control center and conference hall.

Fraulein Doman saw the question in Mildred's eyes as they stared at the glassed-in observation rooms overlooking broadcast studios. "They are used by visiting dignitaries–and, when we least expect him–by our Fuhrer."

She led Mildred into an annex housing windowless but well-furnished dressing rooms, each containing a shower and a bed. An elevator whisked them to the annex's top floor. Doman unlocked a door, ushered Mildred into a luxurious apartment and smiled smugly to see her charge gape at the huge swastika above the fireplace. "Impressive, isn't it?"

Mildred admired the beautiful oriental carpet and the rich, leather furniture. "How many of these apartments are there?"

"Twenty-five in all. But don't get your hopes up. These apartments are exclusively for those of value to the Reich. To live here one must be hand-picked by Doctor Goebbels."

Under the octopus lay a vast subterranean city. "As you can see, Fraulein Gillars, we offer far more than the mediocre broadcasting facilities of Bremen Sender." They toured the underground bakery, first-class restaurant, beauty salon, recreation room and fully equipped gymnasium. "The commissary is not for... not for you." She glanced at her watch. "Come, we have much more to see."

As they re-entered Zeesen's hub, Fraulein Doman picked up the pace and began to rattle off statistics which made Mildred's head swim. "Broadcasts from Zeesen are carried on 100,000 kilowatts to a world audience. Transmissions to the United States began in 1933; to South Africa, South America and East Asia in 1934; and to Central America and South Asia in 1938. Zeesen broadcasts in twelve languages at every minute of the day and night." They walked past a broadcast studio. Fraulein Doman nodded toward the wiry, white-haired man speaking into a microphone. "That one–he's Fred Kaltenbach–the best of our American broadcasters and that's not saying much."

The tour finished back at the reception desk. Doman snapped her fingers at the receptionist and received a clipboard. "You will fill this out, Fraulein Gillars," Doman said, tapping on the form, her voice as cold as her mud-colored eyes. "We here at Zeesen pride ourselves on efficiency. You will evaluate my performance as your guide."

Intimidated, Mildred checked all boxes indicating "excellent performance" and handed back the clipboard. "Very good," Doman said. "I will escort you to the broadcast studio and leave you with Herr Kaltenbach."

"Don't let my fancy title, scare ya'," Kaltenbach said as Doman beat a quick retreat. He put down his pipe and shook her hand. "I used to be denigrated by the handle 'Lord Haw-Haw' but my sidekick here fell heir to that moniker."

A giggle escaped the man standing at Kaltenbach's side. With the awkwardness of a schoolboy, he extended his hand. "William Joyce at yer service. I say, haven't we met before?"

"I've never been to Texas, Mr. Joyce," Mildred replied, again detecting the twang of the panhandle state in his fake British accent.

"Texas? Why I'm not from Texas—no siree! Why, I was born and raised in the shadow of Windsor Castle."

Kaltenbach pointed to the door. "Take a hike, your lordship, I'd like to converse with this lovely lady in private."

Joyce looked her up and down. "Not on your tintype, Herr Kaltenbach, I'm not moving an inch."

Kaltenbach took Mildred's arm and led her to the door. "Well then, since I'm starving, suppose I take you to lunch, my dear?"

Joyce cackled. "'*My dear*'? Ah hah! Say, beautiful, you'd bloody well watch out for this horny bastard—look at him—the rounder wants into your knickers."

"Thank you, Mr. Kaltenbach," Mildred replied, "That would be lovely."

Joyce emitted a high-pitched, tinny laugh. "By jove, she's ready!"

Over lunch, between bites of schnitzel and gulps of Pilsner, Kaltenbach touched on highlights of his life. "My parents emigrated from Germany to Dubuque, Iowa in 1884. I was born the following year." He finished his beer and called for another. While waiting for it he described a boyhood, uneventful except for several trouncings at the hands of a high school bully. "Then came 'the war to end all wars' and my stint as a second lieutenant in the Coast Artillery. Got a master's degree from the University of Chicago and ended up teaching high school back in Dubuque. Goddamn school board fired me."

"Why?"

"I'd started a hiking club for boys in the senior class. The idiots on the school board claimed it was a quasi-Hitler youth group."

"Was it?"

He shrugged. "Could have been. Anyway, after I got canned, I came to Berlin and the rest is history. Speaking of history, any idea how I landed this—the best goddamn job of my life?"

Hitler's first act upon coming to power in 1933, Kaltenbach explained, was to appoint Josef Goebbels Information Minister and give him the job of developing radio as a tool for international enlightenment. "I was working in Berlin at the time—making peanuts as a foreign correspondent for the *Tribune*. So, Goebbels offers to make me a high-paid broadcaster. You're looking at the first, and now the director, of American Broadcasters in Service to the Third Reich, or as it's more commonly known, The U.S.A. Zone of the Reichrundfunk."

"You have quite a following in the States, Mr. Kaltenbach. My family in Ohio started getting your broadcasts last year. Say, I have a question for you."

"Shoot."

"Well, my sister wrote and asked me about the 'Dear Harry' letters you read on your show. Who is this guy?"

"Harry Haggeman? He's an attorney in Waverly, Iowa. Back when I knew him in high school he was one goddamn, rotten bully. It gives me great pleasure to embarrass that son-of-a-bitch on international radio!"

Kaltenbach ordered another beer and downed a bowl of pretzels. "I suppose you know why Goebbels hired you."

"Goebbels didn't hire me."

"No? Who did, Charlie McCarthy? Trust me, sweetheart, Goebbels hired you—and for the same reason he hired all of us—to raise the credibility of Germany in the United States, to convince the folks back home of Hitler's neighborliness and good intentions."

Mildred finished her ham and cheese sandwich. Kaltenbach polished off another beer. En route back to his office he gave her a few pointers. "Don't trust anybody, watch what you say and make damn sure you attend every one of Goebbels' ministerial conferences. And pay attention. He wants all of us to come across as semi-detached, yet patriotic Americans. The pitch is that we want only the best for America and fair play for all. You wanna sound folksy during your broadcasts."

"As called for in the script's margins?"

Kaltenbach shook his head. "As the trusted director of this illustrious group I get a little leeway. Goebbels is smart, he encourages my corn."

"Doesn't he know your broadcasts are listened to for their humor and not for their content? Why, you're famous for your absurdities and wild exaggerations."

"Goebbels figures that the bigger ass an American makes of himself on the air, the more convinced listeners become of the Reich's tolerance of self-expression. Besides, without a little burlesque and ballyhoo, my listeners would turn me off."

Mildred later learned that Kaltenbach's Nazi censors could make neither heads nor tails of his ballyhoo. They were never quite sure what he meant by his name-calling, jingles and gag lines. During one of his broadcasts he launched into an hour-long explanation of what Americans mean when they say, "We eat what we can and can what we can't." Censors became so confused and wary upon hearing this mumbo-jumbo that they jammed the airwaves to prevent it from being heard.

"Funny Fred" Kaltenbach was considered by some to be a true Nazi. Mildred did not find him terribly funny—especially not when he spoke of his thorough disillusionment with the United States, nor when he predicted doom for all who failed to share the Fuhrer's vision. Near the end of her first week at Zeesen, she went to his office and tried to wheedle information out of him as to Max's whereabouts.

"Koischwitz? Haven't you heard? He's off covering the fall of Paris. His written reports from the field are first-rate. Yep, your friend does a cracker-jack job. He must be busier than a one-armed paper hanger with a dose of crabs."

"Any idea how I can get in touch with him? Or when he'll be back?"

"Nope."

The Battle of Britain began on June 22, 1940. Upon hearing the news, Mildred's co-worker, the insufferable William "Lord Haw-Haw" Joyce, took to the airwaves with a warning for the British. "See here Brits—you have only *one* chance of negotiating for peace in France. There will be no talking until you withdraw your war party. I repeat, it is up to you to take the first step. England, withdraw your war party!"

In addition to the simpering Lord Haw-Haw, the broadcasting crew crowned another "Lord." For his less-than-stimulating broadcasts, Edward Leopold Delaney, a once handsome, ex-actor from Chicago, became "Lord Ho-Hum."

Born to a poor Irish family in Olney, Illinois, Edward had spent his prime adding notches to his thespian's belt. At his theatrical zenith he'd been cast by Cecil B. de Mille to star opposite Blanche Sweet in *The Thousand Dollar Husband.*

Delaney shared Mildred's fear of Zeesen. "Don't listen to that crazy Kaltenbach. He'd have you believing Goebbels walks on water. Above all, watch out for Goebbels—he's a sadist with a rotten, violent temper. Stay out of his way, even if it means hiding under your desk. The son-of-a-bitch is the meanest viper you'll ever meet."

Mildred soon had a chance to observe Goebbels in action. Hysterical that one of his underlings had left a top-secret document in a public tearoom, Goebbels went berserk. Mildred and her colleagues looked on in horror as Goebbels, pulling the trembling young man by the hair, paraded him through the studios. Over and over, the young man's face received the full force of Goebbels' fist. No one made a move or uttered a sound, not even when the young man fell and tried to protect his stomach from kicks delivered by Goebbels' thick soled boots. As though throwing a rag doll, Goebbels hurled the poor fellow headlong into Mildred's office. The fine, aquiline nose struck the corner of her desk and began to spurt blood.

Two uniformed soldiers hoisted him to his feet. Whimpering like a puppy, the young man turned his mashed face toward her. His eyes beseeching hers, he shivered and lost control of himself. A dark wet splotch grew over the front of his trousers. Urine seeped over his shoes and onto the carpet.

Apoplectic with rage, Goebbels grabbed the desk ornament Kaltenbach had given Mildred. It was a swastika-decorated replica of a foot-long mortar shell. Goebbels' eyes danced with madness as he held the shell, its nose pointing slightly upward. He then charged and, with sickening force, thrust the missile upward into his victim's crotch. The young man's eyes blazed and from his throat came a sickening gurgle.

Breathing as though orgasmic, Goebbels set the shell down on Mildred's desk. He glanced at the young man writhing on the floor. "Forgive me, Fraulein, I'll have this vermin removed to the garbage dump."

On a warm summer night, Mildred and her friend Erica sat in Mildred's new apartment listening to Max broadcast from France. His tone serious, he described the defeat of the British at Dunkirk. The broadcast concluded with a long, pedantic commentary on the Franco-German Armistice.

"He sounds like he's lecturing to college students," Erica said. "Once a professor, always a..."

"Jerk!" remarked Mildred.

Max returned. "Dearest, I'm home! They're putting me in charge of the Reichrundfunk's educational programs. I'll be working night and day. How are you getting along?"

That night when Mildred reported for work at Zeesen, she discovered Max had taken the office next to hers. Wanting her constantly at his side, Max insisted she attend his series of broadcasts entitled, "The First Thousand Years of German History." He enlisted her aid in preparing his broadcast debut as "The Professor" in "The College Hour," a show he had written to attract American youth. At his urging she stayed late at Zeesen so he could use her as a sounding board for a lecture series entitled, "The Composition and Objectives of the U.S.A. Zone."

Conditions at Zeesen worsened. Goebbels' violent tantrums, bizarre mood changes and long periods of pouting detachment kept everyone in a perpetual state of low morale. Vengeful and fond of dishing out punishment, he relished on keeping civilian employees in line. Those who drew his ire received pay cuts and had their ration cards withheld.

Goebbels had a penchant for ministerial conferences. At one, Mildred met Constance Drexel. Sporting twenty or so gold bracelets and swathed in loose-hanging red and brown burlap, her first words to Mildred were, "Like my outfit? It's my own creation."

During lunch, the bubbly Constance sought Mildred out. "You're thirty-nine," she said. "I know because I peeked at your assignment papers. With me age is a personal matter—don't you dare try to guess my age."

"Your age? Why, I wouldn't..."

"Forty-six," she said, stroking her thin, salt-and-pepper hair. "You'd guess fifty-six, right? That's because I always have a cold. And please, don't believe all the pap they spew about me. Goebbels wants my listeners to think I'm a wealthy socialite from an old Philadelphia family. That's bullshit. Before my father became a U.S. citizen, he was a Frankforter... a wealthy one. Mother's people were well off too. She came from a long line of Swiss jewelers."

"Where precisely are you from?"

"Where am I from? Only a hick would ask such a provincial question! Wait a minute—I'm getting the sniffles." Her sniffles blown under control, Constance rambled on. "If you must know, the world is my home. I was born in Roslindale, Massachusetts, attended schools in four different countries and graduated from the Sorbonne. I was living in France at the outbreak of the so-called 'Great War.' And oh, lucky me! I became one of the first American women to volunteer as a Red Cross nurse. Got to serve in the French hospital at Domville."

"How wonderful!"

"Wonderful? Good gawd, girl, it was horrible!" She gazed out the window. "Mildred, it's up to us women to stop it—the carnage. We must stand up to the men—do whatever it takes to make them stop waging war. If only more women could witness the horror—see the blood pouring from shot-up peasant boys... the twisted tortures of tetanus. If more women were to change the filthy bandages... to wash what had once been a face..." Her eyes filled with tears. She blew her nose. A buzzer signaled the start of the conference's afternoon session.

Accepting an offer of a home-cooked meal, Constance arrived at Mildred's apartment just after dark. They had but tasted their soup when sirens started screaming. The lights went out. Mildred and her guest fell to the floor, deafened by the ear-splitting roar of planes flying low overhead. Explosions lit the room. Plaster rained from the ceiling. Windows shattered. The building rocked.

Mildred couldn't contain her fright. "My God! We're going to die!"

Constance opened one eye. "My dear, thousands of Londoners died last night. Did the Nazi's not expect the Brits to retaliate by bombing Berlin?" Turning her face toward the ceiling, she sighed at the gaping holes. "Don't worry about dying, Mildred. There are far, far worse things than dying. Do you think the plaster fell in our soup?"

The bombs kept dropping, shaking the building. During a lull Mildred crawled to the window and looked out. Everywhere smoke billowed up into the glowing sky. Light rays, as though cast from the eye of a tormented dragon, probed the heavens. One intense beam caught an R.A.F. bomber, impaled it and held it fast. A burst from an anti-aircraft gun, a ball of fire and the beam moved on.

The next wave of bombers flew even lower. Afraid their eardrums might burst, Mildred prodded Constance down to the cellar. They spent the rest of the night crouched under steam pipes.

With the last of the bombers turned back toward England,

Constance shared more of her past. She'd been the first female political correspondent on Capitol Hill and had championed Woodrow Wilson's presidential campaign. Between lending her voice to the support of world peace and a host of other international movements, she'd lobbied for the Equal Rights Clause in the Covenant of the League of Nations. Known as "A Woman's Woman," she'd enjoyed a long journalistic career with *The Chicago Tribune.*

The plaster, powdering down into the cellar from the floor above, added a note of irony. "Just imagine! I was once hailed as an authority on international arms control."

"Whatever brought you to Berlin?"

As though weighing a past folly, she permitted a tiny smile to lift the corners of her mouth. "I left America to care for my ailing mother in Wiesbaden. At least that's the *official* story."

"And the unofficial?"

"Unofficially, my departure had to do with my getting in hot water for writing what Roosevelt's henchmen termed 'Nazi Propaganda.' Actually, Roosevelt started gunning for me the minute I was declared Richard Waldo's favorite contributor."

"Richard Waldo?"

"He owned the newspaper Roosevelt hated."

The following day as Mildred walked down one of Zeesen's corridors, Inge Doman stopped her. Newly promoted from "Director of Orientation" to "English-speaking Broadcaster," Inge took it upon herself to warn Mildred against becoming too friendly with Constance. Ever the Nazi, Inge first, before speaking, checked the corridor for eavesdroppers. "Fraulein Gillars, you'd do well to keep your distance from that Drexel woman. She's a pest and a crackpot." Mildred let the advice go in one ear and out the other. Crackpot or not, the ailing, eccentric Constance had spunk.

Drexel's broadcasts aired in America every Sunday night and focused mostly on Berlin's social and cultural calendar. They were supposed to convince America's Depression-plagued of the pleasures of life in wartime Germany. Sounding like a grand dame with a stuffy nose, she described Germany as a cornucopia–a land of plenty destined for a glorious future. Her broadcasts concluded with titillating accounts of Germany's art exhibits, concerts, food surplus, haute couture and world-class entertainment.

Edward Delaney explained to Mildred the rationale of Constance's broadcasts. "It's basic economics. Banks issue loans to those who put up a convincing front. And believe me, with the way this war's going, Hitler will be asking for lots and lots of loans."

Few shared Mildred's regard for Constance. At a Ministry banquet, the young Nazi who introduced Constance's nightly broadcasts frowned at the mention of her name. "She's *wirklichy dumb* (just plain stupid). Such a pathetic, sick woman. Her work is *schrecklich* (terrible)."

Mildred came to think *herself* as just plain stupid. Nothing else could explain her believing Max when he swore that at Zeesen she would broadcast only non-political material. Within days of her orientation she was spending hours pouring over Nazi-prepared scripts. She'd been told in no uncertain terms–no matter how badly Goebbels' writers bungled English grammar or erred in syntax–she must read the material verbatim. They monitored her every word.

Had it not been for her training as an actress, she could have never projected the called-for anger, elation, sorrow and grief. In reading this script, she found it difficult to keep from laughing:

> *Shame on those who spread lies about the Vaterland!*
> *Do not believe here shortages exist! Stocked good are*
> *our stores! Germans eat three meals good every day*

> *while in England you for miles for one cup of tea line up! Shame on you Queen Wilhelmina, just because your Netherlands surrendered to the Fuhrer you did not have to England run off!*

Shortages gnawed at Germany's belly. Tremendous amounts of food, clothing and strategic materials were needed in ever larger quantities to keep Hitler's war machine moving. In Berlin, as throughout Germany, the lack of food and clothing became critical.

The war created fierce competition for radio listener sympathy and Germany's propaganda network constantly faced the problem of being tuned out. Although regarded treasonable, vast numbers of those under Hitler's boot were tuning in the BBC. Who could blame them? They were bored with shopworn propaganda and the Reichrundfunk's biased reporting. They hungered for a balanced perspective. Most of those who cowered in cellars or hid in barns listening to the BBC were never caught–however, by late 1940, more than 1,500 Germans had been sent to prisons and concentration camps for the crime of listening to London.

Goebbels, frantic to hold onto his declining audience, went through scriptwriters like pencil stubs. Only one of the replacements, sad-eyed Erwin Beckman, who became Mildred's friend, showed a writer's talent. Goebbels' other replacements were, for the most part, rabid Hitlerites.

Another American woman, Jane "The Georgia Peach" Anderson, joined the group. Jane was a weathered nomad with faded red hair. Large, protuberant amber-colored eyes gave her a fish-like aspect. Once a pro-fascist newspaperwoman, Jane had covered the Spanish Civil war as a spy for Franco and was proud of having served as a nurse in his army. She turned heads the day she arrived at Zeesen. Dressed in a Spanish Red Cross uniform complete with its heavy blue cape and Basque beret, the woman, soon to take to the airwaves, used a jeweled cigarette holder to chain smoke Turkish cigarettes.

Max had been away from Zeesen starting up new broadcast stations in France. He returned just in time to prepare Jane for her debut as a broadcaster with the U.S.A. Zone. On the night of Jane's debut, Fred Kaltenbach invited Mildred into his office to hear Max introduce Jane:

> *Dear listeners around the globe, it gives me great pleasure to present to you a world-famous Catholic laywoman and lecturer–one who has earned the praise of the archbishop of Washington, D.C. for her sacrifices in the cause of fascist Spain. Ladies and gentlemen, Georgia's fairest peach, Lady Jane Anderson!*

Kaltenbach got up abruptly, rifled though drawers until he found his bottle. He poured a drink and downed it in a single gulp. "Koischwitz gives the dumbest introductions! This Anderson babe's done a helluva' lot more than give Catholic lectures! Why, she's lived with H.G. Wells and Joseph Conrad. She's been a war correspondent. Hell, she's even done time in a rat-infested Spanish prison for spying for Franco. The Loyalists damned near killed her before the American State Department saved her ass."

He poured and slammed down another drink. Mellowing, he settled beside Mildred to listen to Lady Jane's first broadcast. She began:

> *Dear listeners, you have my heartfelt thanks for tuning in. Yours truly hails from the deep south, Atlanta to be exact. Although I generally go by my maiden name, Jane Anderson, I am in fact married to a Spanish nobleman. My correct title is "The Countess de Cienfuegos"... but heavens, y'all can call me "The Georgia Peach."*

It had been a long time since Mildred had heard such a sickeningly sweet delivery. As Jane Anderson's show became broadcast on a regular basis, Mildred could scarcely believe Max capable of directing such rot. Jane's programs began and ended with of all things, a ridiculous reference to Kellogg's Corn Flakes. "Thanks for listening," she cooed as her sign-off tune *Scatterbrain* played in the background. "Kindly remember y'all—*progressive* Americans eat Kellogg's Corn Flakes and listen to *both*—do y'all hear me—*both* sides of the story."

Shortly after "The Georgia Peach" hit the airwaves, another American expatriate arrived at Zeesen. Born in Chicago and raised in Baltimore, Douglas Chandler had graduated from Brown University before serving in the U.S. Navy during World War I. Thereafter he went from being a reporter on the *Sunday American* to founding a prosperous brokerage business. Chandler's wife, socialite Laura Jay Wurtz, claimed as her great-grandfather John Jay, America's first Chief Justice.

Kaltenbach stood by Mildred's side watching Max try to calm the newcomer seconds before airtime. "Chandler's just a poor bastard who got wiped out in the crash of twenty-nine," Kaltenbach said. "Mrs. Chandler is from Bar Harbor."

Mildred blinked. "Bar Harbor? My grandparents lived in Bar Harbor! Is she here in Berlin?"

"Mrs. Chandler? Yep, she is, with three or four kids. It's a good thing she's got money—Chandler hasn't made much since the crash. In the early thirties he worked here in Germany as a contributing correspondent for National Geographic. He also wrote some travel articles for American magazines. Of course, everyone dropped him the minute they heard of his working for the Nazis."

Max, using the fanfare of thumping horse hoofs and the tune *Yankee Doodle*, introduced the stage-frightened

Chandler as "Paul Revere." Chandler's hands shook so that he could scarcely read the script. He cleared his throat repeatedly and spoke in a monotone. "Fellow Americans... take courage and act now. Cast off the yoke of... of Roosevelt and his Jews."

When it came to reading prepared propaganda scripts, some had it and some didn't. Chandler didn't. No amount of coaching helped. He lacked the basics: diction, inflection, expression, sincerity and empathy. Colleagues placed wagers with odds at twenty to one that Paul Revere would be the flop of the year.

The frail Chandler quickly fell from Goebbels' grace and was made to feel an outcast. Mildred watched him become a frustrated, sad man who, perhaps to get attention one afternoon, began debating aloud with himself whether he should employ poison or a pistol to achieve suicide.

Goebbels overheard. "Quit talking about it and do it, Chandler! Either means will prove equally successful!"

Goebbels also grew displeased with Jane Anderson. Because of her bungled broadcasts, listeners had switched from calling her "The Georgia Peach" to "Lady Haw-Haw." Cultured, well-educated and proud, Jane was accustomed to getting her own way. Ever-lower ratings caused her to grow more eccentric and to step up her lambastes of Roosevelt's "New-Deal" socialism. She became obsessed with fear of communist world-takeover and convinced that only Hitler and Franco could contain Bolshevist hordes.

As Mildred's first year at Zeesen wore on and Max's dependence on her increased, she continued to rebuff his advances. She declined to attend the party given to celebrate his promotion to "Director General" of the U.S.A. Zone of the Reichrundfunk. She listened with seeming lack of empathy when he cried outrage at various articles in *The New York Times*–articles by his former colleagues at both Hunter and

Columbia that "slandered" him. But try as she might, she could not insulate herself from his pain nor from his increasingly fragile emotional state.

One afternoon Kaltenbach stuck his head into her office. "Your friend Koischwitz is fit to be tied. The New York Board of Education has ordered Lippencott to yank his textbooks. You should have heard him carry on when he got the news. 'My books are brilliant! They don't understand me!'"

"He's right, they don't."

Kaltenbach suddenly remembered something else he'd heard that day—jealous co-workers grumbling about Mildred's exorbitant salary. "By the way, did that son-of-a-bitch actually get you *more* money than I'm getting?"

Mildred didn't smile. "My salary is none of your business, Herr Kaltenbach. It's *streng geheim* (top secret)."

> Kafkaesque fantasies of the impassive interrogation, the false trial, the confiscated passport haunt her innocence.
>
> – New Yorker

23

The war escalated. Winston Churchill wired a plea to President Roosevelt: "Give us the tools and we will finish the job!" American legislators, going against the wishes of many of their constituents, passed a bill allowing the U.S. to sell military supplies to England. American warships escorting the supplyladen convoys came under German U-boat attack. Clearly, the Unites States could no longer pretend neutrality.

Goebbels ordered his U.S.A. Zone broadcasters to react with an air of nonchalance to the staggering turn of events. None came across more nonchalant than Mildred in her debut as "Midge at the Mike," the sexy-voiced "girl-next-door." As ordered, she broadcast verbatim what she was handed: Nazi-authored announcements and cheerful public relations blurbs meant to convince listeners of Germany's robust condition and to spread the news of Hitler's marvelous command.

Most Germans were kept in the dark and knew only what Hitler wanted them to know. The truth of German losses was kept from them. Goebbels' squad censored all world news, magazines, movies, books and letters. His Ministry of Public Information and Enlightenment intercepted, twisted and put a "New Order" spin on all world events.

Occasionally an incoming broadcast escaped the censors and squawked to life over the studio's wireless. One such BBC broadcast told of the mysterious flight of Hitler's deputy, confidant and second-in-command, Rudolf Hess. According to the BBC, Hess had flown a Messerschmitt on a "secret mission" to Britain only to crash on the Duke of Hamilton's estate in Scotland. Whatever the purpose of this "mission," and some insisted it was to negotiate a compromised peace, Hess had badly miscalculated his reception. Within minutes of his landing he was arrested and, to Hitler's mortification, labeled a deserter and imprisoned as a common prisoner of war.

Hearing Hess made a laughing stock on the BBC, Goebbels became enraged. He burst into a meeting at Zeesen and unleashed pandemonium. "Hess has lost his mind, do you hear?" Mildred and her fellow broadcasters cringed. "His was the flight of a madman. We Germans will not be made the butt of English jokes! You must convince your listeners of the insanity of Rudolf Hess!"

The attempt to paint Hess a madman backfired. It neither silenced jokesters nor mitigated the damage caused by his fiasco. In fact, the opposite happened. The alibi of Hess' madness prompted ever-more-humorous wisecracks including: "Hess not only flew a Messerschmitt—he flew the coop!"

Amidst the tumult of the Hess debacle, Adelbert Houben, a soft, watery-eyed Nazi whose boots shone like mirrors, became Mildred's immediate supervisor. On the day of his arrival he summoned her to his office. "Tell me, my dear, what do you think of this?" He fingered the large scar zigzagging across his forehead. "It is a memento of the crash of *my* Messerschmitt—the crash that landed me this desk job." He picked up a small mirror from his desk and studied the scar. "I am told that some women are aroused by such disfigurements."

"Not this woman."

"You are doing an admirable job, Fraulein!" He waved her toward a chair. "Of course we don't want to wear you out, do we?" He offered her a drink and a cigarette and smirked at the way she shook her head. "No indeed, it wouldn't do to have our highest-paid female broadcaster suffer exhaustion." He walked to a table near his desk. On the table stood a bronze statuette of a mermaid. He began to stroke the mermaid's breast.

"Please get to the point, Herr Houben."

His finger tapped the mermaid's right nipple. "Ah yes, the point."

"If you don't mind. I have work to do."

"My dear, how would you like a nice ten-day vacation in Athens?"

"Athens? You're joking."

"A working holiday! Professor Koischwitz will escort you to Athens, my dear. The two of you will, I'm sure, get in a little much-needed rest and relaxation."

She wanted to pick up the statue and bring it down on his head. "No! I refuse! Such an arrangement is out of the question."

Certain Max had finagled the trip, Mildred didn't speak to him once during the entire flight to Athens. Her silence continued after they settled into adjoining rooms in the International Hotel. She locked the connecting door. Frazzled by her behavior, he pleaded, "You are my heart's desire, the most beautiful, talented woman on earth! Liebling, please, I will die if you don't love me!" Rewarded with nothing more than silence, he resorted to a threat. "I swear Mildred, if you don't snap out of this funk, I will turn you in for insubordination!"

"Good, do it! I'd rather spend the rest of my life in a concentration camp than with you!"

She refused his invitation to his first broadcast from the heart of Athens and remained in her room during Greece's induction into the "New Order." In the wee hours of their eighth night in Athens, the door joining their rooms opened. "Liebling, please..."

She awoke with a start. "Get out! That door was locked. How did you open it? Get out or I'll..."

He slumped onto a chair. "You'll what? Call a Greek policeman?" He sighed and tossed the key onto the dresser. Tears stood in his eyes, pools of indigo refracting glints of light coming from neon signs down on the street. "I won't use the key again. I shouldn't have... forgive me. I am truly, grievously sorry."

"Fine, be sorry... and get out!" She held up a hand in protest as he came closer and, when he sat on the edge of the bed, she turned her face to the wall. "Get out of here, Max. Go back to Erna."

"For God's sake, don't crucify me. I love you. I want you forever by my side. You know ours is a great love..."

"Hah!"

"A predestined, passionate love... it consumes me. Please, I need you! Should you forsake me–I'll die!"

She turned toward him and, overcome by the tears streaming down his check, shivered. "Oh, Max..."

His kisses covered her face. The years fell away. They were for the moment discovering each other for the first time–a neophyte college professor and his adoring student.

"My dearest!" A sound, half groan, half purr came from him as he kissed her eyelids, neck and breasts. "Never, never shut yourself off from me again. I suffer such agony..." With the tenderness of a mother soothing a hurt child, she wrapped him in her arms and stroked his hair. "It's all right, Max, don't be sad."

Their return to Zeesen coincided with the sinking, by the British, of Hitler's greatest ship, the Bismarck. News of the epic chase and victory of His Majesty's Royal Navy crackled over the BBC as Max and Mildred entered the studio. Everyone sat gaping in disbelief at the wall-mounted speakers. Only one listener scoffed at the news, Mildred's nemesis, the insufferable James Joyce. "Bullshit! It's a bloody English trick! Come now, don't be fools! Don't swallow their hogwash!"

Events leading to Mildred's "passport nightmare" started with a script delivered fresh from Goebbels' scriptwriters. Max avoided her eyes as he dropped it on her desk.

She gave him a quizzical look then read the script's title: "A Message to Mr. Roosevelt–A Reply to the President's Declaration of the National Emergency." She glanced over the first few pages, skimming margins to see what vocal inflections censors wanted and noted the recording she was to play for background music.

Max lit a cigarette. "I'm off... I have an appointment."

The script's tone struck her as odd. "Wait a minute," she said, flipping through the pages to the payoff paragraph. "My God! Max, this is... I can't read this!!"

"You have to."

She stared at the offensive blurb. Laced with anti-Semitic pronouncements, it was to be read, according to the margined notation: With MAXIMUM emotion!!! The message:

> *Damn Roosevelt! Damn Churchill! Damn all the Jews who have made this war possible! I love America, but I do not love Roosevelt and all his Kike boyfriends. Roosevelt is pushing America into war, and all for capitalist profit!*

"No way, Max, I won't read this over the air."

"You must. *Tonight!*"

"*No!*"

He gripped her arm. "*Read it!*"

She wrested free. "Goebbels is nuts if he thinks I'll broadcast such rot. For God's sake, my grandfather's son is a Jew! I've told you about Aaron Stern, he's my... my half-uncle..."

Max clamped his hand over her mouth. "Don't!" His eyes darted around the studio. "Don't ever mention him again!"

Furious, she grabbed onto Max's tie and pulled his face close to hers. "How dare you! I am an American. I refuse..."

"You... we... have no choice. Read it or..."

"Or what? They'll hang me?"

"No, Liebling, it's me they'll hang."

Ashes filled her mouth as she read the awful script over the air. She returned to her apartment feeling defiled by the evening's dirty-work. As if the act of washing clothes could somehow cleanse her conscience, she attacked a mountain of soiled laundry. Real soap had been unobtainable for weeks. She poured a month's ration of the smelly synthetic substitute into the stopper sink. Hot water was another luxury usurped by shortages. The sink filled with cold water, she started in on her laundry. No matter that she scrubbed until her fingers bled, nothing came clean.

Late that night Berlin experienced a fierce air raid. The apartment shook with the ear-splitting noise of low-flying bombers. Alone in the dark, she opened a bottle of cognac, drank herself into a stupor and passed out.

When Max came to her apartment the next day to take her to lunch he frowned to find her in bed, puffy-eyed, moaning and with an ice pack on her head. "You look awful." He picked up the empty bottle and tossed it into the wastebasket.

"Go away."

He wrung out a washcloth and wiped her face and hands. Ignoring her profanity, he pulled her out of bed. "Come, get dressed, we're going out."

"Go away."

"You'll feel like new in an hour–I know how to put the color back in your cheeks." It was a cold, cloudy day. His plan included a brisk walk and a new hat. The frigid wind quickly cleared her head. When at last they reached the famous Kurfurstendamm, he propelled her from one millinery shop to another. Strangely enough, hats–the one article of women's apparel not rationed–had become quite popular. Max spotted one he liked. "Try on this one!" An oat-colored pillbox, trimmed with a large white feather, stood out from the others. He set it on her head. Its veil skimmed the tip of her nose. "It's perfect!" he said. "We'll take two!"

The summons for her to report to Vice-Consul Vaughn of the American Consulate arrived the next day. Mystified, Mildred dressed and went immediately.

The tall, rigid vice-consul ushered her into his marble-floored office and escorted her to the chair in front of his desk. She sat. A chilling dampness pervaded the room. He offered her a cigarette.

A man entered and stood silently behind Mildred's chair until Vaughn introduced him. "Miss Gillars, my attaché, Herbert Burgmann."

She turned to look at him. He wore wire-rimmed spectacles fitted with thick lenses. His poorly tailored, black suit needed pressing. A light dusting of snowy dandruff covered his shoulders. His nostrils sprouted disgusting wisps of hair.

Vice-Consul Vaughn picked up a long, sharp letter-opener and began slapping it against his palm. "So, Miss Gillars, I understand you don't like our President."

She gaped at him as though he had spoken Arabic. "I beg your pardon?"

"'Mr. Roosevelt and *his Kike boyfriends.*' That was the title of your latest broadcast, was it not?"

"The title of my broadcast? No... of course not. You see..."

"Yes, indeed I do see. I see that you derive great pleasure from portraying the President of the United States as a homosexual."

"A what?"

"*Kike boyfriends.* Your words, not mine, Miss Gillars. Were you not suggesting that F.D.R. relishes Jews as *boyfriends?*"

"No! That's not at all what I..."

"May I see your passport, my dear?"

"But you don't understand! Those weren't *my* words... why, I would *never...*"

Vaughn held out his hand. "Your passport..."

With Burgmann looking over her shoulder, Mildred rummaged through her purse. Finding the passport, she withdrew it and placed it on the vice-consul's outstretched hand.

He walked to his desk, opened a drawer and tossed the passport into it. He slammed the drawer shut. Then, as Mildred watched dumbstruck, he took a small key from his pocket and locked the drawer.

"What... what are you doing? You can't seize *my passport!*" Seeing Vaughn smile, she turned and pleaded with Burgmann. "Please, he can't do that!" She tried to rise.

Burgmann's hands clamped her shoulders and held her down. "Sit still. Don't make matters worse."

Mildred's eyes flared. "How dare you!"

The vice-consul smiled. "How dare I? Why very easily, Miss Gillars. One doesn't insult the President of the United States."

"Since when?" She wrested her shoulders free of Burgmann's grip and jumped to her feet. "Since when is it a crime for an American to insult *anyone?*"

Vaughn rounded his desk and extended his hand. "That will be all, Miss Gillars. Good day."

She slapped his hand away and shook her fist in his face. "You son-of-a bitch!"

"Why my dear, that's the name Hunter College professors now use to describe their former colleague, your lover Max Koischwitz. Ah, yes—we know all about you and Professor Koischwitz."

Burgmann grabbed onto her arm and began pulling her toward the door. Mildred flailed as her heels slid across the floor. "But my passport! How can I go home without a passport?"

The greatest danger of bombs is in the explosion of stupidity that they provoke.

– French Journalist Octave Mirbeau (1850-1917)

24

Panic set in. Surely, she thought, he'd come to his senses and send it back–her passport–her lifeline to home. She'd give him a day or two then go back to see him. She'd eat crow if she had to and apologize even though she'd had no choice when it came to broadcasting that garbage. She'd write a letter begging presidential forgiveness. She'd pour it on, beg, plead–get down on her knees to Vaughn if she had to–anything.

Nothing worked. Every time she made an appointment to discuss the matter, Vaughn stood her up. Persistence earned her nothing but the abuse of being kicked out of waiting rooms and hung up on by consulate secretaries. Going over Vaughn's head, she fired off a barrage of letters to Washington. It certainly didn't help her cause that, at the same time, she was being forced to broadcast ever more caustic bombasts against America's foreign policy. The word on "Hitler's mouthpiece" had gone out: all appeals for return of the passport of Mildred Gillars were to be ignored.

The harder she fought, the deeper she dug herself into a

hole. Stripped of her passport, her every avenue of appeal exhausted and getting out from German control made impossible by the very country of her birth, her panic escalated. Without a passport she had but two choices: she could obey her Nazi masters or suffer the consequences.

Edna Mae, unaware of her sister's predicament, sent a letter:

> Conneaut, Ohio – June 3, 1941
> Dearest Sister,
>
> You absolutely must come home! Quickly, while you still can! Everyone is predicting we will soon join England in its war against Germany. According to today's newspaper, the FBI just rounded-up thirty Nazi agents in a sweep of Boston, New York and the nation's capitol.
>
> It is difficult to remain calm when we are constantly warned to watch what we say. German spies are said to be on every corner, on trains and even working behind lunch counters!
>
> Momma is not well and is undergoing tests at the clinic. Si Jenkins, our mailman, passed away. Edward and I send you our best. Please, Sis, get on the next plane and come home before it's too late. We love you and pray every night that you will be sitting on our front porch by mid-summer.
>
> (signed) Edna Mae
>
> P.S. I clipped the enclosed article. Any idea whatever became of the subject louse?

Mildred read the article. Written by columnist Lillian

Ross, it contained a scathing denouncement of Ross's former professor, Max Koischwitz:

> *Koischwitz was different and unconventional. He hated the common people and had contempt for scholars. In his own field, literature, he was a phony and he clothed his phoniness in fantastic and subtle prejudices. He was dramatic and colorful, bombastic and unafraid. He was a good actor and an effective demagogue. He gave the impression of being highly emotional and sensitive, but actually he was cold and hard in the job he was trying to do at Hunter, namely, to get across his fascist rhetoric.*

One evening Max opened the cigarette drawer, found the article and read it. He turned livid. "I remember this *Ross* bitch!" Waving his arms, he paced the floor, shouting: "Such a pest she made of herself during my lectures—always raising her hand, always interrupting—rebutting everything I said!"

"That's water under the bridge, dear, calm down."

His hands clamped his temples. "They hounded me! Always, always I was hounded! Criticized! Persecuted!"

"Sweetheart, you're tired. Perhaps we should put off going to the opera."

He spun around and, eyes flaring, seized her by the arms. "Liebling, please! Never lose faith in me. I couldn't bear it."

Star of Berlin Opera soprano, Hildegard von Wilheit, waited for the applause to die down then strode to center stage. High pitched, staccato notes like the chirping of an exotic bird poured from her lips as she launched into the third act's aria. At first she seemed not to hear it, the sudden wailing in unison of a dozen or more air-raid sirens. The audience's gasp silenced her and sent her scurrying into the wings. Mesmerized, the audience remained seated, staring up at swaying crystal chandeliers. A loud thud reverberated through the building. Smoke-filled air issued in, eliciting a chorus of coughs. All lights went out. A voice sounded through the darkness. "Lutgefahr 15! Lutgefahr 15!"

Through the blackness Max reached for Mildred's hand. "It's going to get bad, Liebling "

"What are they saying? What's *Lutgefahr 15*?"

"It's coming–an imminent bombing of maximum intensity."

"Silence! Everyone is ordered to remain seated! It is forbidden to leave before the 'all-clear.'"

The macabre symphony of war began. Wave after wave of planes thundered overhead creating the percussion of a million kettledrums. And, with each wave, as though played by a mad violinist, came the high-pitched screams of falling bombs. Resigned to having to wait it out, Mildred settled back in her seat. Her breathing controlled by sheer will, she tracked each scream to its death and, tightening her grip on Max's hand, counted the seconds of silence before each earth-shaking explosion.

On the fourteenth of August 1941, the United States and Great Britain signed *The Atlantic Charter*, a pact to supply weapons to the Soviet Union. The Third Reich reeled.

A knee-jerk reactionary, Goebbels forced his propaganda machine into high gear. His conferences with Zeesen staff took on the aura of pep rallies. "Throw everything you have into your broadcasts! Pull out all stops to convince the United States that it is on a course destined for disaster!"

William "Lord Haw-Haw" Joyce enjoyed these staff meetings. They provided him an opportunity to denigrate the United States and to goad Mildred. Whenever she objected to his traitorous remarks, he laughed in her face. Once he sent her a note that concluded:

And another thing, you talentless trilby, you're daft to be servicing Koischwitz when you could be bedding a man like me.

When shown the note, Max merely laughed. "Pay no attention to him, Liebling. Poor Lord Haw-Haw is sure to hang himself."

At another of Goebbels' rallies, Joyce jumped to his feet and, in his high, tinny voice made an announcement. "Here, here, there is wonderful news! The Fuhrer, in his benevolence, has granted me German nationality!"

Fred Kaltenbach turned to Mildred. "Speaking of citizenship, any progress in getting your passport back?"

"It's hopeless."

Having overheard, Joyce sidled up to Mildred and spoke for all to hear. "The goddamn Yankee bastards! Keeping your fucking passport, are they?" He gave her a coy, yellow-toothed smile. "But then, my dear, you've been around–you don't need a passport to fuck."

December 7, 1941. Word of the Japanese attack on Pearl Harbor struck Zeesen like a thunderbolt. Had it grounded itself in Mildred's heart, she could not have been more stunned. Throughout the day horrifying details trickled in. Numb with grief, she listened to accounts of Hawaiian civilians being slaughtered. On-the-spot coverage painted a gruesome picture of the hysteria enveloping Honolulu.

Over the BBC came the voice of an American reporter. Fighting back sobs, he described a fleet of ships sinking to the bottom of Pearl Harbor and lamented the slow, agonizing death certain to befall an estimated 2,000 trapped sailors.

Mildred's anger flashed. She jumped up shaking her fists. "Sons of bitches! The dirty, yellow, slant-eyed bastards! Goddamn Hitler! Goddamn him! He's behind this, I know he is!"

Max ran to her. "Stop it! We're being watched!" He tried to hustle her out of the crowded broadcast studio.

"Who cares? Let them watch!" She broke from him, bolted into an unoccupied control room and locked the door. With Max pounding on the door she activated a microphone and yelled into it. "Are you listening, Herr goddamn Hitler? Tell me, how many deutsche marks did you pay the Japs to bomb Pearl Harbor? What did they charge you for crippling my country's navy?"

Kaltenbach and Delaney came running to help Max. Strong and sinewy, Delaney used his shoulder like a battering ram to defeat the door's lock. The three charged in, their faces taut.

Mildred tore the microphone loose from its wire and, holding it over her head, held them at bay. "Don't worry, fellas, I'll tell Goebbels you arrived too late to retrieve my words and push them back down my throat."

They overpowered her. As Delaney carried her, kicking and screaming from the booth, another news bulletin came over the airwaves:

> *"The death toll here on Oahu is rising by the minute. Eighteen ships have been sunk. Thousands and thousands of American sailors are drowning like rats. Women and children have been cut down. Burning hulks of planes dot the island. Hospitals are in flames..."*

Mildred clawed Delaney's face. He let out a yell and dropped her. She slithered away from him and got to her feet. Outdistancing her pursuers, she threw books and cleared desks with a swipe of her arm. Inge Doman ducked to miss the vase Mildred hurled at her. The vase missed Inge's head and struck a typewriter. Mildred ended the rampage by upsetting a rack of foreign newspapers and hurling a telephone at Hitler's portrait.

Her fury spent, Max pulled away those who surrounded

her. She collapsed onto the floor. He helped her to her feet and led her back to her desk. Her fur coat lay on her chair. He snatched it up and placed it over shoulders. "Come, Liebling. Let's go home."

The next day, December 8, Franklin Delano Roosevelt signed the Declaration of War on Japan and Germany. His act sealed Mildred's fate. Any hope she had of retrieving her passport or of returning home to America died that day.

On the heels of Roosevelt's Declaration of War, Goebbels ordered Mildred brought to his office. Two black-booted goons flanked her and snapped to attention as Goebbels entered.

His eyes had the luster of ice. "Fraulein Gillars. You are a very, very stupid woman to have thrown such a fit."

Mildred stood mute, eyes cast on the floor, her heart pounding visibly through her blouse. Goebbels stepped forward and clamped a hand around her throat. He squeezed hard and cut off her breath. Her eyes flared and rolled in their sockets. "My, my, have I made you dizzy? Perhaps some water?" His hand went from her throat to her chin and held it as though in a vise. "Yesterday, Miss Gillars, you vilified the Reich's eastern ally, Japan. I am told you also said some very nasty things about our Fuhrer."

There came a knock at the door. It opened and, without looking at Mildred, Max shuffled in. He clicked his heels and stood at attention in front of Goebbels.

Goebbels smiled broadly. "My dear Professor Koischwitz, how good of you to come! I was just informing Fraulein Gillars that for her outburst yesterday she is to be executed."

Max stepped forward. "No! You can't!"

As if on cue, Goebbles released her chin. "Compassion however, prompts me to give her a choice. Yes, Professor, she has a *choice*—the executioner's axe *or* the hangman's piano wire. We prefer the latter of course. Hanging is so elegantly slow when done with piano wire."

A look passed between the two men. Max hesitated, then began to wail. "My God, my God, my God... Oh no... Oh, my God."

Goebbels roared with laughter. His goons glanced at each other and then smirked to see Max reach out and touch Mildred's cheek.

"Behold the sweethearts!" Goebbels cackled. "See how they yearn for one last fuck! Go on, Professor, take her, now–right here on the floor–right here in front of me! How I'll enjoy watching my two favorite broadcasters fuck!"

Max squared his chin and looked Goebbels squarely in the eye. "Please don't execute her. I promise you with my life... there will be no more... episodes. Please, she can be of great value to our beloved Fuhrer."

Goebbels, visibly aroused, his eyes dancing, rubbed his genitals. Prolonging his pleasure, he took a knife from his desk. His hand trembling with excitement, he brought the blade's sharp edge up to Mildred's neck. "Like it?" A sporatic laugh and he spun around and impaled an apple sitting on his desk. He took a bite. Apple juice trickled from his lips. "So, Professor, you think she can be of use to our Fuhrer? I shouldn't execute her?"

"No, please, I beg of you..."

"Very well."

Max bolted forward and clasped his boss in an embrace. "Thank you!"

Goebbels grunted and pushed him away. "How long would she like to stay in prison? Fifty... sixty years?"

"Oh, Doctor Goebbels! Not prison! She will do anything... anything!"

"Very well, I'll give her one more chance." He whipped a one-page document from his desk. "Consider this her stay of execution," he said, handing the page to Max. "Read it to her."

Max cleared his throat. "A Pledge of Allegiance to

Germany." His eyes riveted on the page, he read off the commitments, duties and sacrifices incumbent on those loyal to the Third Reich. A quick, agonized glance at Mildred and he read the page's final sentence, the acknowledgment: "This pledge has been taken by Mildred E. Gillars and, by her signature below, made official on this, the ninth day of December, 1941."

Goebbels smiled and handed Max a pen. "Have her sign it."

Max held the pen out to her. "Please, Liebling."

She remained rigid, hands at her side, her eyes staring at him as though at an actor taking part in an unbelievably bad melodrama. For she knew. Amidst the horror of this scene it had come to her—the note of falseness in an under-rehearsed line, the cat's rush to toy, the mouse's too perfect dodges.

He, her beloved who'd become one of them, wrapped her hand around the pen.

She signed.

The American Embassy in Berlin closed on December 11, 1941, the same day Max received orders to go to Italy. Mildred accompanied him to the station. "Take care of yourself, Max. Wear two undershirts and remember to keep your vest buttoned. Try not to get your feet wet and if you do, take an aspirin. Any idea when you'll return?"

He touched her cheek. "Liebling, since when do they tell me such things? It could be a month. It could be a year."

Stranded, alone, battling depression—her every move watched by the Gestapo—Mildred saw no way out of the trap. Her world began to spin out of control. On Christmas Eve, certain she had no future, she decided to end her life. Ten sleeping pills remained in the bottle on the nightstand. One by one, each launched with a sip of cognac, she let them slip down her throat.

She took a leisurely bath. As though expecting the Angel

of Death to be a handsome lothario, she blotted her body dry and sprayed it generously with perfume. Tipsy, but not yet groggy, she poured another drink and raised the goblet in a toast. "To Germany, a hell-hole awash in cognac but devoid of hot water, soap, sugar, coffee and toilet paper!"

For her birthday, Max had given her an expensive turquoise negligee. Crossing naked to her dresser, she put it on. She brushed her hair and put on lipstick.

Fearing the ten sleeping pills might not do the job, she picked up Max's straight razor, walked to the bed and reclined on the black satin sheets. Without hesitation she drew the razor's edge firmly and slowly across the inside of her left wrist. The line, fine and insignificant at first, slowly widened. Satisfied to see blood seep from the slit, she similarly, with the same smooth stroke, slit her right wrist.

As blood seeped into the satin she began to pray. "Dear God, please watch over Max. Bless Momma and Edna Mae. Put and end to war and suffering." Spots of blood on the sheet grew larger and darker. "And God, please, if you can... forgive me." Groggy now, she closed her eyes and began to drift.

Many died on that war-torn Christmas Eve. Bombs fell, burning houses collapsed on entire families and shrapnel tore bodies apart. On the eastern front "General Winter" came to Russia's aid, leaving thousands of frozen German corpses to stand sentry. Countless merchant marines, their vessels ripped open by torpedoes, drowned in icy waters of the North Sea.

Mildred's name would have also appeared on St. Peter's list that night had Max not arrived home unexpectedly. He found her unconscious, lying in her own blood.

A glass of cold water hurled in her face failed to bring her around. His heart racing, he wrapped dishtowels tightly around her wrists. Knowing he had to get help, he stared at the phone. He would have to be careful. He picked up the receiver and dialed. Hearing a male voice on the other end, he infused his voice with matter-of-factness. "Hello, Dr. Grossman? Carl Schmidt, here. Say, did I tell you about the little girl who claimed her doll tried to commit suicide?"

Mildred picked that inopportune moment to come around. "Oh, poor me," she babbled. "Wait until Goebbels hears what the naughty Fraulein Gillars..."

Max cupped his hand over the receiver. "Quiet!"

"Sorry... sorry... sorry... sorry."

"As I was saying Doctor, this silly child claims her little doll lives at four-eight-eight Streiholtz Strasse, number fifty-two. Come see my happy family at your earliest convenience. Good bye."

It worked. The doctor arrived within the hour and began stitching and bandaging Mildred's wrists. Paid handsomely, he left Max with a pledge of confidentiality. "Don't worry, there will be no record of this unfortunate incident. You have my word I will tell no one." He handed Max a vial of pills. "She should start taking at least three of these each day."

"Pills? How can pills help?"

"They will put her on 'cloud nine' as her fellow Americans say. These pills are new and are still considered experimental. The literature claims they tranquilize."

Fearful she might make another attempt on her life that night, Max sat by her bed until dawn. "Liebling," he said when at last she awoke, "you must promise me something."

"What... what Max, that I won't try it again?"

He brought his face close to hers. "That you'll let *me* be the first to leave this dark, cooling star."

This swamp is a monument to death.
Snakes, alligators, quicksand, all bent
on one thing: destruction.

– Edward D. Wood, Jr. (1922-1978)

25

She sank deeper into the quagmire of Zeesen. Late one evening as Mildred worked alone in her office, Claude, a French architect turned German janitor, shuffled in and leaned on his broom. She knew him to be one of the thousands of military-age Frenchmen who had volunteered to work in Germany in exchange for the release of German-held French POW's.

"Hi, Claude, what's up?"

He looked around to make sure he would not be overheard. "According to the grapevine, Hitler's top men are meeting at Wansee to concoct newer, faster methods."

"Methods for what?"

"Hitler wants it speeded up—the elimination... the slaughter of Jews, gypsies, homosexuals and defectives."

She shook her head. "Come on, Claude, they can't be that depraved..."

"No? Fraulein Gillars, every last one of them, from Hitler on down is a depraved, maniacal..." A sudden sound silenced him. Like a hare catching scent of a fox, he froze. The sound, discernable now as that of boots striking tile, came closer. Claude bolted for the door.

Two husky, uniformed Gestapo blocked his exit. They seized him, twisted his arms behind his back and held him fast. "He is molesting you with his little 'stories,' Fraulein?"

"No, of course not. Let him be, he's done nothing wrong."

A knowing glance went between the Gestapo. "Come," the taller one said, dragging the prisoner Mildred would never see again toward the door, "it's past your bedtime."

Burgmann was the last person she ever expected to see at Zeesen. He strolled into her office late one night as casually as a delivery boy, gaped at her through his thick, wire-rimmed glasses, flashed a smile and tweaked his straggly moustache.

She closed her eyes and shook her head as though to dispel a mirage. "It's not possible..."

He thrust out his hand. "That's right, Miss Gillars, 'Joe Scanlon,' we meet again. Looks like I'll be your 'partner in crime.'"

She refused his hand. "That's *not* your name! You're Herbert Burgmann!"

"Nah, that's who I used to be–Herbert Burgmann, Assistant Toad to the American puppet, Vice-Consul Theodore Vaughn. Sorry I had to restrain you with such force. That was quite a battle you gave us over seizing your passport."

"Get out!" She reached for the telephone.

"Calling a bouncer? Try Goebbels, he just hired me and approved my new name."

She slammed down the phone. "He *what?*"

Once more the visitor stuck out his hand. "Joe Scanlon, at your service, my dear, Joseph P. Scanlon, 'Broadcaster-in-Training' for the Third Reich."

When it came to creativity in broadcasting, Max led the pack. He experimented with formats and tried on a mix of personas in order to reach his listeners. On weeknights he used the name "Dr. Koischwitz" to host two different, consecutive broadcasts. Saturday nights he became "Fritz" to play opposite Kaltenbach's "Fred" in the radio comedy, "Fritz and Fred, the Friendly Quarrelers." On Sunday nights he broadcast as "Dr. O.K." to answer made-up questions on the show "America Asks—Germany Answers." Immediately following this program, he came on as "O.K. Speaking" for a program with yet another format. Ever the professor, Max enjoyed most broadcasting as "Dr. Otto Koischwitz—Host of the College Hour," to beam Hitler's dreams to America's youth.

He became so cocky over his success that when higher-ups at Zeesen reneged on their promise to increase Mildred's salary, he went after them. "Liebling!" he exclaimed bursting into her apartment to tell her of his victory. "I made them grovel! They've agreed to start paying you what you deserve! Seven hundred marks per week!"

"My, my, seven-hundred marks—*that* should be enough to numb me. Gee, Max, think of all the filthy Nazi lucre you stand to inherit when I'm shipped off to a concentration camp... or beheaded!"

He sank onto the sofa and covered his face. "Don't say such things."

"What should I say... *thank you?* Wake up, Max! They don't take Deutsche marks in hell!"

"Perhaps we can take some of the money and..."

"And what? Exchange it for passage home?"

"I *am* home. Germany is my home."

"Well, it's sure as hell not *mine*. I want nothing to do with a country that silences dissenters—a country whose henchmen strike in the night. Go ahead, Max, explain it to me—the burning of synagogues, the disappearance of Jews—the slaughter of innocents!"

"Hitler has restored order."

"Order! Ah yes, the God of the German psyche! You agree, don't you, my darling, that no price is too high, no sacrifice too great, no measures too extreme as long as Germany gets back its precious *order*?"

Max lit a cigarette and sucked the smoke deep into his lungs. "Liebling, what is it you want? To leave me? To never see me again?"

"No, dammit! I want a life. Jesus, Max! I want to be young again! I want to be your wife! I want to bear your children!"

"Impossible! We can't turn back time."

"All right then, goddammit! I want us out from under Hitler's boot!"

In the two years since Max and Mildred had reunited, he had rarely mentioned Erna or his daughters. She knew they lived in Denmark, in the village of Nykbling. She lauded the faithfulness with which he sent money for his daughters' food, shelter and education. That the girls wrote to him often pleased her. She loved to see the happy glint in his eye when he opened their letters.

He never let her read them but commented aloud should something excite or provoke him. "Ah! Beautiful, golden-haired Stella! She writes of receiving a high mark in mathematics!" or "Helene, the shy one, writes of learning to ski!" or "Renata will not do well in life—she always makes excuses for her failures. She writes that her low grade in history can be blamed on the teacher. Nonsense!"

After reading them, Max always tore the letters into tiny pieces and flushed them down the toilet. Mildred invariably took this as a slap in the face. "Afraid I might get my hands on them? Something in them I shouldn't see? Something about Erna?"

Max picked up a bar of soap and hurled it against the wall. "Stop it! Are you trying to drive me mad? In their letters my daughters beg me to take them back to America. Shall I leave their precious letters lying around for the Gestapo? Would you like to see my girls thrown into a concentration camp?"

Should he—on rare occasion—travel to Nykbling, he would always return to Berlin late evening of the same day. When, after one such visit, he failed to return, Mildred imagined the worst. Perhaps he'd been caught in a raid and blown to pieces. She'd read of a major fire in the area, maybe he'd been trapped in a burning building or run down by a speeding ambulance.

He returned, safe and sound, ten days later. Stunned to see him walk through the door, she broke down. He moved to embrace her. She pushed him away. "I thought you were *dead*! And *don't* tell me the trains weren't running—they were—I checked!"

"Did I say the trains weren't running?"

"You slept with her, didn't you... you slept with Erna."

"I haven't touched Erna in years."

"You said it was over... you gave me your solemn word!"

"I have to go *back*."

"What?"

"Erna is gravely ill and in the hospital. She is to be operated on tomorrow. My daughters are alone. I've only come back because Goebbels insists I meet with him this afternoon."

Mildred slumped onto the sofa. "Shit."

Max turned and headed for the door. "Liebling, watch your step while I'm gone."

Constance Drexel was a sight to behold when she arrived at the Hotel Kaiserhof restaurant. An hour late and a bit tipsy, she teetered in on four-inch heels. Askew, her hat looked like a birds nest atop her mop of thinning, red-dyed hair. A loose-fitting dress hung on her angular body as though on a scarecrow. "Like this get-up? Don't I look just a tad like Mata Hari? Just a tad?" It had been a long time since Mildred had laughed.

The Hotel Kaiserhof had changed drastically. Most windows had been blown out in recent bombings. It was poorly lit and chilly inside. A sour smell pervaded the dining room. The patrons were mostly elderly and there was but one waiter. He seated them promptly but took forever to return for their order. Constance smiled up at him and asked what he would recommend.

"Madam, as we have but one item on our menu, may I suggest the cabbage soup?"

Constance took a taste of the lukewarm gray-green broth and put down her spoon. "Guess what, Midge..."

"'Mildred'–'Midge' is just a broadcast name."

"Very well, guess what Mildred."

"What?"

"I've been promoted from 'Culture Critic' to 'Mistress of Political Enlightenment.'"

Mildred shook her head. "We've gotten ourselves into an awful *mess*, haven't we?"

Constance bit her lower lip and nodded. "Worse than awful. Be careful, dear. You're pushing them too far–they're watching you now more than ever."

"I could care less."

"Listen Mildred, if you value that gorgeous neck of yours, keep your opinions to yourself and your temper in check! Just go along–read whatever they hand you. And for God's sake, smile!"

Mildred asked if she'd seen the *Time Magazine* article accusing the "once-prominent Constance Drexel" of being a "pro-Hitlerite."

"Sure, I've seen it."

As the waiter arrived with the check, two flies lit on the tablecloth. He grabbed a newspaper from an adjacent table, rolled it up and smashed them with a single swat. Constance used her knife to scoot away the tiny carcasses. "You know, Mildred, we're just like these two varmints—in the wrong place at the wrong time."

That evening Mildred thought it ironic that the first tune she had to play over the air was *Shoo-Fly-Pie*. Censors ordered that she introduce the song with "soothing sexiness."

> *Hello my sweetheart soldiers—from Africa to Italy. Your first love song from Midge at the Mike will be hah... hah... pardon my laugh, boys, but its Shoo-Fly-Pie. Stay tuned for sentimental tunes straight from Tin Pan Ally—all selected to make you home-sick for your two-timing wives and sweethearts. And keep your ears cocked for my sign-off song tonight. Calculated to nauseate you with nostalgia, it will be the wonderful German tune you've made your favorite, Lilly Marlene.*

Did her listeners *buy* this drivel? Had her broadcasts destroyed morale? Hardly. If anything, "Midge at the Mike" backfired in Goebbels' face. He glowered at reports from the Nazi spy network in America that evaluated her effectiveness. To Goebbels' chagrin, these reports showed that most American servicemen expressed a certain fondness for the daffy, sexy-sounding American girl whom they nick-named 'Axis Sally.'" Goebbels became even more upset when told American soldiers thought her broadcasts "too ridiculous to take seriously," and "more hilarious than disturbing."

Goebbels had only his scriptwriters to blame for making her so "lovable." They might have had their heads lopped off had Goebbels not been distracted by the R.A.F.'s sudden commencement of systematic and concentrated bombings. Night after night for weeks on end, waves of R.A.F. bombers pierced the skies, often dropping thousands of new 'high-capacity' bombs on a single German city. It fell to Goebbels, as Minister of Public Information and Enlightenment, to convince listeners that these bombings were ineffective.

Determined to produce more potent broadcasts, Goebbels pressed Max into service as a consultant for the Foreign Ministry's top brass at Zeesen's Station ZDZ. It took two Nazis to fill the spot left vacant by Max's promotion: Adelbert Houben would direct the station's English-speaking broadcasters. Hans von Richter would supervise Houben.

von Richter was a stiff-backed Prussian with all the spit and polish of a formidable military figure. Oddly, however, he had acquired a bizarre addiction to American-made "Black Jack" chewing gum during his service with the German Consular Service in Cleveland, Ohio.

His mania for the tarry substance spawned endless wisecracks behind his back. "Stay clear of 'Black Jack,'" Kaltenbach warned Mildred, coming up with a pun that would be endlessly repeated, "or he'll gum your works."

von Richter liked to pop into her office to practice his somewhat rusty English. He introduced her to Heidi, his American-born wife. The attractive and spoiled daughter of a wealthy Ohio businessman, Heidi thought highly of herself. Confident, although she had no experience, that she could be more effective than the women she saw manning microphones, she had charmed Goebbels into giving her a job as propaganda broadcaster and, in record time, wheedled her way into a prime-time spot.

Late January 1942, a U.S. Army pilot, the olive-skinned, gaunt-faced, Lieutenant Martin J. Monti, stole a fighter plane from his base in Italy and flew it behind German lines to join Hitler's Luftwaffe. Born in Missouri and raised by fiercely Catholic Italian immigrant parents, Monti harbored a fanatical allegiance to his Italian roots and a great fear of communism. What better way to fight it, he reasoned, than to help Hitler help Mussolini–communism's archrival.

Unbelievably, Monti was accepted into the Luftwaffe as a probationary pilot. He failed miserably. What to do with this American renegade so eager to serve the Fuhrer? Transfer him to Zeesen, make him an American broadcaster in service to the Third Reich—hand him a script and a microphone.

Kaltenbach broke the news to Mildred that Monti was coming aboard. "Now don't go getting upset."

"But he's a... a deserter!"

"Nobody's going to force you to talk to him or to work with him. Oh, by the way, he's not 'Monti' anymore. His name's been changed to 'Weithaupt' (White Hope)."

"I wouldn't spit on him."

Hitler controlled the most powerful and efficient propaganda machine. Roosevelt, Churchill, Stalin and Mussolini ran a close second. Competition for public opinion became frenzied. It eclipsed the competition for war materials. Sent to cover major encounters, Max wrote Mildred of battlefields littered with "something for soldiers to read as they lie dying"—German, English and American propaganda pamphlets. Fired into the air by artillery or dropped from bombers, these pamphlets urged soldiers to desert. Max brought home one of the Nazi brochures he'd found in Italy. Meant for American G.I.'s, it asked:

> *Who is cashing in on huge war profits at home while Americans shed their blood over here?*

Goebbels got his hands on some propaganda photographs being distributed by Americans—photographs showing German prisoners eating enormous meals. Each photo bore the caption: "Surrender, don't starve." Goebbels became enraged. "Surrender? I'll teach these traitors to be a tool of the enemy! I'll give them something to eat! I'll chop off their cocks and stuff them down their throats."

The war raged on. Throughout Germany, people suffered horrendous deprivation. In ravaged fields, battle weary soldiers chaffed under a daily ration of hardship, hunger and suffering.

Despite this climate, Jane "The Georgia Peach" Anderson took it upon herself to write a script painting for the allies a rosy picture of life under Hitler. Goebbels and his censors were delighted with it!

Spurred to greater embellishment when she took to the airwaves, she marveled at the champagne being served in Berlin's cabarets and gave a mouth watering account of the delicious meals obtainable at Berlin's restaurants:

> *"In a tea shop on the Unter den Linden, waitresses went from table to table carrying silver platters laden with sweets and pastries. We were served Turkish cakes with marzipan, of which I am very fond. My friend ordered a goblet of champagne—one with a liberal shot of cognac added to make it livelier. Sweets! Cookies! Champagne! Not Bad!"*

"Not bad?" Mildred demanded aloud of the small radio that brought her Jane's broadcast. "Not Berlin!"

Working in America's Office of War Information, Captain Wendell Hutton caught Lady Jane's broadcast via short wave radio. Hutton had a brainstorm. He taped the broadcast, translated it into German and beamed it back to Germany. His plan worked! Hearing how well Berlin's businessmen and bureaucrats were faring, German soldiers on front lines as well as hordes of hungry Germans civilians, became infuriated.

Hitler never screamed louder than he screamed at Goebbels for the boomerang of Lady Jane's broadcast. Goebbels, humiliated and apoplectic with rage from the reprimand, burst into the broadcast studio just as Jane opened her mouth to begin yet another "Beautiful, Bountiful

Berlin" broadcast. "Lady Haw-Haw?" he screamed, snatching the microphone from her hand. "No! You are Lady *Idiot*... Lady *Fool*!" He hurled the script at the pitiful, cowering woman. "You are not a Georgia peach, you are a... rotten apple! Get out! Get out! If I see you here again, you will be shot—your carcass dipped in acid!"

The thaw of winter 1942 saw German troop losses in Russia rise to more than one million. Afraid Hitler's staggering losses would cause resource-supplying countries to doubt the Third Reich's ultimate success, Goebbels again increased the use of radio as a major weapon in the fierce global competition for public opinion.

To bolster the ratings of Station ZDZ, he instituted "on-the-spot" news broadcasts. He then dispatched Max to canvass France, Holland and Portugal as "The Traveling Correspondent."

Whenever possible Mildred went along, broadcasting her "Home Sweet Home" programs from Nazi-run studios in Chartes, Paris and Amsterdam. Her sweet, sexy voice became increasingly familiar to G.I.'s from North Africa to Italy. Intelligence reports told of American soldiers listening to "Axis Sally" over short-wave radios in barracks, foxholes and latrines.

Aware of her popularity, Goebbles moved to increase her effectiveness. He brought in a new slate of writers. They set to work. From *Billboard Magazine's* latest list of "hits," they selected more torchy songs for her to play and, unwittingly, even cornier material for her to spew on newly formatted programs.

First came the priming—the section to set a soldier's "juices" flowing. To achieve this, scripts called for nostalgic ballads and her "girl-next-door" voice. Next, lonely listeners were to be fed seeds of doubt—doubt as to the faithfulness of wives and sweethearts, and doubt as to the value of capitalism with its penchant for profit at the cost of battlefield butchery. All scripts concluded with a call to action, usually along the lines of:

> *"War is folly, boys. Get smart! Put down your arms and go home!"*

On assignment in Holland, Max and Mildred tuned in Station ZDZ to listen to the debut of Goebbels newest recruit. Sounding both clever and mentally disturbed, Robert Best read what he claimed was his "own composition." It was a parody of Rudyard Kipling:

> *"Ship me somewhere east of Suez*
> *Where the worst is like the best,*
> *Where John Bull broke all commandments*
> *And British is the word for pest.*
> *Hark! The Jappy boys are marching*
> *And out there soon boss will be,*
> *While from the old Moulmein Pagoda*
> *The Brits are running for the sea."*

Best concluded the broadcast by urging listeners to "sing it occasionally to your friends."

Max switched off the radio. "No wonder listeners by the thousands are tuning us out! Goebbels' sagging ratings won't be helped by *this* idiot!"

Mildred returned to Zeesen alone. Kaltenbach greeted her. "You're back from Holland minus Herr Direcktor Koischwitz? Good! Welcome back!"

"Max is off covering another battle."

Kaltenbach took her arm and led her down the corridor. "Come on, I want you to meet someone. He's our latest recruit, one we've christened 'Mr. Guess Who.' During his first broadcast he read a nutty parody of Kipling."

"I heard it."

"He's a real character. Not only is his German wretched–

brace yourself Mildred, he wears a broad-brimmed, half-cocked Stetson and saunters around in high-lace shoes."

Mildred laughed and rolled her eyes. "Where did he come from?"

"Werner Plack recruited him." Seeing Mildred make a face he added, "So, you *know* Plack?"

"Ugh... *I do*, unfortunately."

Werner "The Operator" Plack had returned to his native Germany in 1940 and, because of his supposed connections within Hollywood's movie industry, had flimflammed his way to the top of the Nazi Foreign Office's Radio Division. Truth be known, Plack's sole connection to filmdom had been as a wine merchant. "I sold wine to the biggest stars!" he liked to crow.

To reinforce his claim, Plack would reach into his desk drawer and withdraw a bottle of Moselle wine. On the label was a small sticker that read: "Personally Selected by Werner Plack"—an endorsement he insisted carried "some weight" in Hollywood.

Kaltenbach took Mildred to meet Robert Best. They found him sorting through a pile of memorabilia he had brought from his post at Vienna Radio. "Robert Henry Best, at your service, ma'am." He whipped off his Stetson. Six-foot-two and two hundred twenty pounds, he towered over them. With the flamboyance of a destitute Rhett Butler he took Mildred's hand and pressed it to his lips. "Darlin', you see before you the son of a Methodist minister—a native of Sumter, South Carolina. Yours truly attended Columbia, served a hitch with doughboys in France and spent umpteen years in Vienna working as a correspondent for United Press. The dogs... they up and fire me." He took a deep breath and twirled his Stetson on his finger.

"And?" Mildred said, thoroughly amused.

He winked at her and grinned. "And that, my beautiful lady, is all I'll say about myself. Course, should you invite me to your apartment for a home cooked meal, it would be mah' pure pleasure to tell you mah' whole life story."

Robert Best came to be known around the studio as a generous, modest, self-effacing and perpetually-broke eccentric. He amused Mildred with tales of his days in Vienna and with descriptions of his mistress, a mysterious Russian countess. He claimed as former friends—Dorothy Thompson, Sinclair Lewis and Vincent Sheehan. He was a gold mine of information about Austria, Central Europe and the Balkans and eagerly shared his knowledge with anyone who would listen.

At the start of the war, Best—and a host of other American newsmen—had been interned at Germany's Bad Nauheim Spa. Of his decision not to return to America with them when given the chance, he said in his soft, southern way, "'Ah couldn't leave Countess Anika behind. It would have killed me."

Anyone who saw Robert Best and the countess together believed that. "Please, just call me 'Anika'" she said when introduced to Mildred. "The New Order frowns on royalty."

Although misguided and often taken advantage of, Robert Best exhibited the grandiloquence of southern gentlemen. He had no deep political beliefs, no aspirations to become rich or famous—no hidden agendas. Although his job included spewing denouncements of Jews over the air, Best hated anti-Semitism. "Hell," he told Mildred, "more than half of my old European newspaper friends were Jews. Why, we spent a thousand nights together chewing the fat in Vienna's Cafe Louvre. God, how 'Moishe the Jew' and 'Best the Methodist' used to regale them with our brilliant plans for world peace!"

"Moishe?"

"The greatest friend I ever had. Moishe worked his way up to editor of the biggest newspaper in Vienna. And then came the Anschluss, Germany's brutal annexation of Austria. Poor Moishe, he came apart that night—that gawd-awful night

Austria caved in to Hitler. They stripped him of everything. The next morning I gave him all I had—a month's salary—enough to get him the hell out of there before the Nazi's could have a go at him."

Robert Best broadcast some of the most repugnant scripts ever written by Hitler's henchmen, scripts constructed to belittle U.S. news stories about Russian successes. "Tune them out," Robert read over the air as censors monitored his delivery. "Don't listen to such poolroom reporting by Roosevelt's mouthpieces—they're jackasses. And as for Roosevelt, why everyone *knows* he's a tool of the Jews."

The narratives grew more strident, the message more vicious. Renaming the New Deal the "Jew" Deal, scripts became laced with praise of the German New Order. One script, Best first refused to read, and then verbatim after being forcefully convinced to do so:

> *"This is 'Guess Who' bringing you the BBB... Berlin's Best Broadcast."*

The next words stuck in his throat:

> *"I never knew real freedom until I came to Germany!"*

Then, looking up from the script, he gave Mildred a wink. His face paled:

> *"I see no reason why Europe will not demand the life of one Jew for every European who died in the present war, and personally I must say that I firmly hope that such will be the case."*

Then, possibly thinking of Moishe, Robert swallowed hard and forced his voice to obey the script's commands for emphasis.

> *"Down with Judocrats! Down with Kikes! On with the crusade—day after day after day!"*

The danger of the past was that men became slaves.
The danger of the future is that men may become robots.
True enough, robots do not rebel. But...

– Erich Fromm (1900-1980)

26

Mildred's special "Fourth of July" broadcast came from pens of scriptwriters growing more hip: "Happy Glorious Fourth to all my G.I. sweethearts! Too bad the only fireworks you'll see tonight will be the real thing. To show you my heart is in the right place, I'm signing off with a special treat. It's RCA Victor's first million-dollar seller. By the way, if you like *Chattanooga Choo-Choo* by Glen Miller, why don't you think of choo-chooing yourselves home? Go ahead, choo-choo home boys and send back in your place all of Washington's profit-mongers."

As early as mid-1942, plotters were at work scheming to assassinate Hitler and to negotiate a peace with the Allies that would allow Germany to rise from the ashes as a democracy. One evening, never guessing that she was in their midst, Mildred attended an intimate party. Adam Strautman, his face shining with honor, certitude and too much brandy, lifted yet another glass to make a toast: "To my brave German brothers ready to put their life on the line to save our beloved Vaterland from Hitler... from extinction!"

Cautioned to be silent, he grumbled and slumped onto the sofa next to Mildred. "Tell me Miss America, why does your President turn his back on us? Does he not care that millions of people will die needlessly? Americans too!" His friend, an intense, bespectacled youth, grabbed Adam's hand, pulled him up from the sofa and tugged him toward the door. Chastised for his loose tongue, Adam yelled back over his shoulder, "Forgive me, shatze! When I drink I spew bullshit."

August 19, 1942–11:45 P.M. Summoned back to Zeesen by a late-night phone call, Mildred sat in the broadcaster's briefing room listening to Goebbels crow over the latest Axis victory–the thwarting of the Allied invasion of Dieppe, a French port city for channel steamers. "The idiots! We knew they were coming! They didn't stand a chance! This is the best proof yet of Allied ineptness!" Goebbels crowed. "A horrific blunder–one we'll turn into a propaganda triumph."

The invaders–British and Canadian soldiers–had clearly been the victims of woefully incomplete Allied reconnaissance. Allied Intelligence had mapped out most German defenses, but not guns located on headland cliffs–guns ultimately responsible for the greatest slaughter. Additionally, an encounter with a small German convoy had cost the first-in Allied comando unit the element of surprise. Alerted by the exchange of fire, German garrisons in the area had caused subsequent units to meet with unsurmountable resistance. Allied troups had beat a bloody retreat.

Days later, Mildred sat viewing film footage of the carnage and watching wave after wave of young Brits and Canadians die. She broke down. Sound engineer Paul Noback helped her from the room. Once outside he held her and stroked her hair. "Go on, it is permissible to weep, Fraulein. Hearts are not made of iron.

All legal restraints on Hitler's reign of terror ended on August 26, 1942 when the Reichstag conferred on him discretionary power in the administration of justice. German newspapers front-paged the decree's preamble:

> *At present in Germany there are no more rights, only duties...*

Both sides concentrated on developing new, more powerful weapons. In Peenemunde, far from public view, scientists held the first successful test of a German V-2 rocket. At the same time in America, scientists secretly achieved the first controlled nuclear chain reaction, enabling the U.S. to begin production of atomic weapons.

While waiting in block-long lines to buy bread and meat, Mildred heard all sorts of comments and gossip based on news which could only have been gleaned from the BBC. Expressions of outrage crackled down the line the day London confirmed the execution in America of six German saboteurs who had been brought by U-boat to Long Island and the Florida coast.

"I have two sisters living on Long Island!" one woman volunteered.

An old man nodded. "My sons live in Florida... no, I didn't say that... Elvie told me not to..."

One of the women in line, a neighbor, recognized Mildred. "You are such beasts, you Americans! Imagine executing eight fine, young men!"

In spite of Nazi censorship of radio, newspapers and incoming mail, snippets of "verboten" information reached Mildred from a variety of sources. One such informant was Gerdt Wagner, a close friend of co-broadcaster, Douglas Chandler. Wagner, an English-speaking, naturalized U.S. citizen, had become involved with the Oberkommando Der Wehrmacht (OKW), an offshoot of the German High

Command—and, ultimately part of the July 20, 1944 plot to kill Hitler. Wagner's OKW assignments took him to Germany, Italy, Yugoslavia, Turkey, Austria, the Baltic and Mexico on a regular basis. Traveling so broadly, he heard news kept from most Germans.

On one trip Wagner learned that SS Colonel Karl Jaeger's squad had carried out a series of massacres in the Lithuanian towns of Kovno, Ukmerge and Vilna. The toll: 137,346 Jewish men, women and children annihilated. Once back in Berlin, he stunned his friend Chandler by advocating Hitler's incarceration. Chandler became enraged and, believing German soldiers incapable of such slaughter, turned his friend Wagner over to the Gestapo.

The Argentine diplomatic mission was the last bastion of social life in the capital. At the conclusion of a reception given at the embassy, Mildred ran into a beloved friend. "Victor, Victor de Kowa!" She hugged him and planted a kiss on his cheek. "What brings the most popular actor and producer in Germany to this shindig?"

Avoiding the question, he winked and slipped her two tickets to a theater showing his latest film—tickets impossible for a civilian to buy. He then walked her toward the street fronting the embassy. "Forgive me for not offering you a lift home. I lost everything, including my car, during last week's raids. I now ride the subway... when it is working, of course."

An air-raid's urgent wailing cut short the farewell. Mildred, determined to get back to her apartment, ran down the deserted street toward the subway station. Lights sputtered and went black. Bombs began to fall. The night sky became blanketed with dense, choking smoke. More and more bombs screamed toward earth. Their exploding fury tore up streets, torched homes and sent rivers of flames coursing down gutters. The night, pierced with rocketing shrapnel and cinders, took on a smoldering, orange glow.

Super-heated winds whipped the conflagration, causing it to devour everything in its path. Mildred lost her way. As she rounded a corner, a woman clutching a little girl beckoned from the ledge of a burning home. The ledge collapsed, dropping mother and child into the flames. Mildred raced on. The next street was littered with bodies ripped apart. Steel shards of "window" bombs jutted from heads, torsos and limbs.

A hand grabbed Mildred's and pulled her into a hot, smoky, pitch-black cellar. The flash from an explosion showed the cellar's interior to be crowded with terrified old people and a few children. The cellar smelled of burnt flesh and vomit. A child screamed with pain.

A woman's voice came through the darkness. "Don't cry little angel. God will chase away the bombers, He will..."

A huge explosion shattered her words. The building shook and collapsed. People screamed. "We're trapped! We'll die!" "God help us!" Torrents of water from burst water pipes rained down. "I can't swim!"

Caught in a pocket close to the cellar's entrance, Mildred and two others managed to claw their way out. Once outside, they could do nothing but listen in horror to the screams of the trapped. The rescue team, comprised of teenaged boys and old men, arrived too late. "All of them drowned like rats," an on-looker muttered, "like poor, helpless rats."

War distorts the mind. Like a caged animal, not knowing whom to trust, Mildred lived on through the nightmare of a great city grinding to a halt. Pulverized night after night by saturation bombing, Berlin's transportation system and utilities became crippled. The city's finest homes and businesses were laid to waste.

The surrender of Field Marshall Rommel's famed Afrika Korps in late October 1942 devastated the German people.

Goebbels' Ministry of Information and Enlightenment went into high gear to keep from them the fact that their Fuhrer, by failing to supply critical fuel and ammunition, had rendered Rommel's army impotent.

A second major defeat came on the heels of the first. Berliners wandered about in a daze upon hearing of the loss of the battle of Stalingrad. It seemed impossible. In three short months, the Soviets had killed or captured twenty-two German divisions and turned the tide of war in the East.

Max worked long and hard preparing his next broadcast:

> *"Happy Thanksgiving Americans! Or are you thankful? Thankful for the disaster of Pearl Harbor? Thankful for the heavy ongoing losses of the U. S. Navy in the Pacific? Thankful that your sons and brothers are dying by the tens of thousands, their bodies lying unburied on beaches, farmyard battlefields and baking desert sands? Thankful for America's rising prices, higher taxes and lower standard of living? Did you give thanks today for increased working hours, oil restrictions, rationing, limitations of individual freedom and the muzzling of American liberty? Are you thankful for the way your government embraces Communists?*
>
> *"Well, take heart! There is one thing for which you can indeed be thankful! Raise your eyes to heaven and thank God that between you and Stalin stands the German Army!"*

Whether on the Atlantic coast interviewing U-boat crews or sampling French cuisine in Paris, Max always found time to broadcast as "Fritz" opposite "Fred" Kaltenbach on Saturday night's "Fritz and Fred, the Friendly Quarrelers." The sole purpose for this ridiculous show was to convince listeners of Germany's relaxed hilarity, amid rumors of military defeats and predictions of a second front.

Another program, authored and delivered by ace broadcaster Hans Fritsche, Head of the Radio Chamber of the Reich Foreign Office, was "Hans Fritsche Speaks." Fritsche's program enjoyed an impressive following in America. Belittling enemy struggles, he praised Axis defeats as heroic encounters fraught with tough resistance, adversity and faith. Germany's miracle weapons, he claimed, would ultimately make the Third Reich victorious.

By January 1943, according to German Intelligence, nine out of ten Allied soldiers fighting in the European theater knew Mildred's voice. The same source kept tabs on which "Axis Sally" broadcasts G.I.'s liked best. Certain that life back home was passing them by, they preferred the movie-review/hit parade format. To keep her supplied with fresh material, censors worked overtime writing thumbnail reviews of movies like *For Whom the Bell Tolls*, *Heaven Can Wait* and *Girl Crazy*.

Approving Hit Parade tunes for airing, however, was a censor's nightmare. Always on guard, they ran every lyric past Zeesen's decoding experts who, upon hearing *Jeepers Creepers*, scratched their heads. The tune censors felt most comfortable with, and had Mildred play most often, was Harry James' *Sleepy Lagoon*.

Goebbles ordered his English-speaking broadcasters to hone their "believability quotients" by keeping abreast of happenings on the American home front. He had them peruse American newspapers, movie magazines, radio programs, sports reports and almanacs. All such materials came censored–with numerous pages, paragraphs, pictures and even advertisements blacked out. Broadcasters also received so-called intelligence reports from the German spy-network operating in the U.S.–reports so persuasive that few questioned their accuracy.

Mildred often wondered how Americans were coping with limited supplies of butter, shortening and meat. She envisioned Edna Mae growing vegetables in a "victory garden." Was Momma saving kitchen fat in tin cans—fat from which glycerin could be extracted for the manufacture of TNT, nitroglycerin and machine gun bullets?

In February 1943, a student uprising took place at the University of Munich. "How can this be?" a dumfounded and embarrassed Hitler reportedly demanded of Goebbels. "These young people have been reared under National Socialism and drilled to be perfect examples of Aryan youth!" Humiliated for his Fuhrer, Goebbels immediately declared all information relative to the uprising "top secret" and imposed a press and radio blackout. Much to his frustration and rage, Goebbels could not black out the BBC.

News of the student uprising spread like wildfire. Germans by the tens of thousands turned to their wireless to hear BBC coverage of the event and its tragic aftermath. In a eulogy to the slain students, the BBC praised ringleaders Hans Scholl, Maria Scholl and Adrian Probst. Started with unrest in university corridors and ugly whisperings in nearby beer halls, the uprising's point-of-no-return had come during a high Nazi official's address to the student body. Instead of listening, students stamped their feet in a chorus of disapproval and shouted "genug" (enough). They then walked out en masse.

The ringleaders, students who had authored and distributed a protest pamphlet, were arrested and brutally executed. In the week following the massacre, the BBC concluded all of its broadcasts:

> *"So that the world might hear these brave young heroes' exhortation from the grave, we offer here the crux of the pamphlet for which they laid down their lives:*

> *'Fellow students, the eyes of even the most stupid Germans have been opened by the terrible blood bath in which Hitler and his confederates are trying to drown all Europe in the name of the freedom of the German nation. Germany's name will remain forever dishonored. Our nation looks to us in 1943 to break the National Socialist terror even as in 1814 the Napoleonic terror was broken. The dead of Stalingrad exhort us. Arise, ye people, the time has come.'"*

Responding to German outcries of "cover-up," Goebbels ordered Max to write and broadcast a statement to counter BBC accounts of the uprising and to debunk rumors of Hitler's ever-growing penchant for keeping Germans in the dark. After working on it for hours, Max stepped up to the microphone, cleared his throat and read the statement:

> *"It is with great sadness that I inform you of a recent uprising at the University of Munich by a few misguided 'typische Einzelganger' (typical individual cranks). Rest assured, our Fuhrer deprived these scoundrels of headlines until after they were found guilty. And, thanks to our efficient justice system, found guilty they were! Guilty of inciting fellow students to show grave disrespect to one of our most decorated heros! Guilty of distributing their scurrilous, unpatriotic pamphlet—a pamphlet written to spread defeatism and encourage sabotage! You may breathe a sigh of relief tonight, my beloved fellow Germans—Hans Scholl, Maria Scholl and Adrian Probst have been beheaded!"*

More disclaimers, appropriate for both individual and group beheadings, poured from Max's pen. As spring wore on, a dozen more victims followed the ringleaders' path, each crying out a denouncement of Hitler before laying his or her head on the block of the white-gloved axe man.

Her flower, her piece of being, doomed dragon's food.

– Gerard Manley Hopkins (1844-1889)

27

Britain's improved sonar and depth charges began to turn the tide against German U-boats. Germany's heartland also felt the shift as day and night bombings leveled more and more cities, power plants, radar stations and railroads. At sunset on May 16, 1943, the R.A.F. blew up the Mohne dam on which four million Germans and the Ruhr industrial complex depended for water and energy.

Whispers swirled of an Allied invasion. The sour taste of defeat lay on the tongue. In Berlin, Lieutenant Colonel Baron van Gersdorf came close to assassinating Hitler.

Goebbels promoted Max to oversee Radio Political's Subsection IX of the Foreign Office. The former head had been deemed guilty of shoddy editorial work and shipped off to a concentration camp. The increased workload took its toll. Max's bronchitis returned. He lost weight, smoked more and slept less.

On the second anniversary of "Midge at the Mike," Mildred did something she had never done before. She traveled by streetcar to an old residential area on the outskirts of the city, entered a Catholic church and furtively slipped into a confessional.

The tiny door separating penitent from priest slid open leaving in its place an opaque screen. "Yes, my child?"

"I'm not sure how to start. You see, I was baptized a Catholic, but I've never... you see, my father was a Catholic but then he abandoned me and Momma and we never..."

"Go on."

"Well, I... I'm an American..."

"Yes."

"They seized my passport... I can't go home... I'm being forced to do bad things... I..."

"You are contrite?"

"What?"

"Do you have sorrow... are you sorry for your sins?'

She drew in her breath. "I am."

That she left off "and I seek the Lord's forgiveness," the usual penitents response, caused the priest to prompt, "Yes, my dear, and what is it you seek?"

"What?"

"You have sorrow for your sins, and you seek..."

"Why, I seek an end to this beastly war!"

"I see. Hmmmm. Is there anything else?"

"Yes, dammit. I want to go home."

"Ahh, you want to go home to America! So..." The urgent ringing of a bell interrupted the priest. "Forgive me, I must go. I absolve you of your sins."

Mildred heard him rise. "But... what shall I do?"

"Do good, help others... sin no more."

Word of her visit to the confessional reached Max even before she set foot back in her apartment. "Well, *now* you've done it!" he roared, following on her heels as she walked to the closet to hang up her coat. "So now you're a church-goer! A penitent, I hear!"

"But, how did you..."

He glared at her. "Since you've become so *religious*, may I suggest that you *pray* for your poor confessor? You realize of course that he is at this moment undergoing interrogation by the Gestapo."

It was as though he'd punched her in the stomach. "Nothing we spoke of would interest the Gestapo. The priest just listened. He just..."

"He just what? Gave you advice?"

"Yes, he did. We spoke of peace. He urged me to do good... to help others."

Max's eyes danced as they always did when a solution suddenly presented itself. "Ah! So *that's* what you want—to do good, to help others!" He embraced her. "Providence speaks, my dear... I can help you in this noble quest!" He withdrew a paper from his vest pocket and handed it to her.

"What's this?"

"A list of interview questions."

"I don't do interviews."

"But Liebling, does not your salvation *depend* upon doing good and helping others? What greater good can you *possibly* do than to record interviews with American prisoners of war?"

"I don't understand."

He led her to the sofa. "Liebling, you and I will travel to camps. You will conduct and record interviews. The recordings will be broadcast back home to their loved ones. Think of it! Can there be *any* greater good than to fill an American mother's ears with the sound of her son's voice? To soothe her heartbreak? Oh yes, Liebling, each interview will bring you one step closer to salvation!"

Mildred turned suspicious. "What's in this for Goebbels? Has our beloved boss gone soft in the head? Oh, I can just see the headlines, 'Viper Becomes Ambassador of Good Will!'"

"Goebbels will do what it takes to convince America that its true enemy is not Germany but Russia. Besides, these interviews will prove a humanitarian gesture–one certain to garner admiration."

"Admiration? For whom, Goebbels? For your beloved Fuhrer? What are you getting us into?" She rubbed her forehead. "I haven't been sleeping... my head hurts. No, Max, no way."

He drew her closer and began stroking her hair, nuzzling her neck. "Don't fret, Liebling, I'll just ask Inge Doman."

Her eyes narrowing and nostrils flarring, Mildred gritted her teeth. "That Nazi bitch? You're taking her on the road to do the interviews?"

"She has a nice figure, don't you think?"

"Midge's Medical Reports," recorded interviews with American prisoners of war, would not be edited. She had Max's word on that. Once recorded, they would be broadcast completely uninterrupted and untouched.

With their itinerary approved by Goebbles, they set off in a roadster driven by Emil Christiani, a crack radio engineer and recording technician. They motored from camp to camp in search of American POW's who'd cooperate. Most imprisoned G.I.'s greeted them with suspicion and contempt. Should they find a prisoner willing to record a 25-word message to his father, mother or sweetheart, they went to work.

"What's a nice kid like you doing in a place like this?" a black infantry sergeant asked Mildred before his interview. He had heard scuttlebutt that "Axis Sally" was making the rounds. "You know somethin'? You saved my life once."

"No, I *did?*"

"Yep, one day I had decided to pull the plug. I couldn't take their shit another minute. My plan was to rush the gate and make a run for it and let the fuckin' bastards...'scuse me... the guards... shoot me in the back. That was when you..."

"Me?"

"Yep, you. Just as I started to run I heard *Blue Skies*, and I stopped on a dime."

She scowled. "I see, you saw blue skies and you..."

"No! *Blue Skies*... the song... it was pourin' from the loudspeaker... your opening song!"

Another soldier, his feet swathed in bandages, greeted Mildred. "Well, if it ain't 'My old gal... Axis Sal!' Baby, I've spent many a night in a foxhole with you! Yep, many a night I snuggled down in my foxhole with your voice purring in my ears. There we were–you, me and the stars. Ah! The sound of your sweet, sexy voice and those bombs exploding all around!"

Every prisoner she approached greeted her differently. Many turned their backs on her. One turned his back, bent over and let out a loud fart. Some made obscene gestures and yelled profanities.

At one camp a young POW came almost nose-to-nose with her and screamed, "You lousy, Hitler-fucking whore!" A guard came running and seized the screamer.

Thinking fast, Mildred stamped her foot on the floor and ground something underfoot. She squared her chin and, like a German officer, spoke to the guard. "Let him go this instant!" She directed his gaze to the floor. "There was a spider on my arm, he shouted a warning."

The guard unhanded the prisoner and stepped back, uncertain of what to do next, his eyes troubled with indecision. She placed her hand on the guard's sleeve and, giving him a seductive smile, let her fingertips gently knead his forceps. "My, you're strong! What is your name?"

"Klemperer... Sergeant Gunther Klemperer."

"Well, Sergeant Klemperer, I will mention your name to our Fuhrer, when next I see him and tell him of your splendid service. Our beloved leader will be most pleased to hear of your sensitivity to a lady's fear of spiders."

The threesome motored on to Stalag 11-13 near Hammerstein. The camp commandant welcomed them, escorted them to a large group of prisoners assembled in a mess hall and introduced them. "Attention prisoners! Our benevolent Fuhrer sends you these special visitors! He is compassionate, our Fuhrer, he does not seek the suffering of your loved ones back home in America. He has sympathy for their not knowing where you are–whether you are dead or alive. And so he sends you this angel, this gifted sister of yours to interview you individually. These interviews will be recorded and broadcast to your homes throughout America to comfort your parents... wives... sweethearts... children. I present Miss Mildred Gillars, radio star and Red Cross representative who has..."

"Red Cross representative my ass!" yelled an American lieutenant. "Let's see her authorization." A chorus of vile taunts and jeers arose. Guards, like a pack of dogs, set on the throng, pushing, punching and jerking them apart.

Max hustled Mildred to the door. "Come on, you don't have to take this."

The commandant chased after them. "Please!"

Max spun around. "Our Fuhrer will not be pleased. He expects his commandants to exercise better control over prisoners..."

The commandant paled. "Please, this is most unusual. Come, let me escort you to my personal dining room. I've arranged a marvelous lunch."

The finest wines complimented the feast of sausage, schnitzel, potato dumplings and red cabbage. The commandant, while serving Mildred a second helping of dessert, a sherry-laced apfelkuchen, begged her not to leave without getting the interviews. "On my word of honor, Fraulein, I guarantee you will find the prisoners more receptive than they were this morning."

Persuaded, Mildred, with Max at her side and Emil Christiani tending the recording equipment, went back to work. She found her subjects strangely subdued. "Look fellas, I know how you feel. I'm an American just like you. Forgive me if I upset you this morning. I'm here solely to record whatever messages you want sent back home to your loved ones."

"Yeah? If you're an American like us how come you're free to travel around Germany?"

Max chewed his lip. "That does it. We're leaving."

A prisoner stepped forward. He handed Mildred an unopened carton of Chesterfield cigarettes. "Here, babe, a little going away present." He grinned at her stunned expression and at the way her eyes filled with tears as she hugged the carton to her chest.

The threesome was halfway to the next camp before Mildred opened the carton. A strong odor of excrement suddenly filled the roadster. Max squeezed his nostrils shut. "Phew! What have you got there?"

She closed the carton, lifted it and, her eyes glued straight ahead, let it fall onto the asphalt streaking past. "Horse shit. He gave me a carton of horse shit..."

The guard who ushered them into Stalag 7A pointed to an emaciated prisoner. "Recognize that fellow? He's Mickey Gressell of the Chicago White Sox."

Max had, during his tenure at Hunter, often listened to broadcasts of American baseball games. Gressell he remembered as a star player. As though greeting an old friend, Max felt compelled, as he offered his hand, to josh with the prisoner. "My, my, the famous Mickey Gressell!" Max paused, his forefinger pointed heavenward as his mind strained for a witticism. "Once a White Sox now an *A-W-C-R-F-E!*"

Gressell kept his hands at his side and stood mute.

"Get it? 'American Who Can't Run Fast Enough!'"

Gressell hawked up a wad of phlegm and spat it at Max's feet "Asshole. You'll be the one running in a few months."

As they toured from stalag to stalag, Max wrote his "Field Reports" and sent them back to Zeesen for broadcast. The reports, laced with ridiculous imaginings of a prison utopia, were supposed to entice listening American soldiers to surrender. "Listen to this one, Mildred, I'm becoming quite a fiction writer:

> *"Stalag 7A reports sunny days for prospective tans. A few gaudy umbrellas and some Frauleins, and the area would resemble a beach; but no frauleins are allowed. The art exhibit in Barracks 18, sponsoring the works of Joe Demarre and Bert Green, is attracting a crowd.*
>
> *"Last week Camp Marlock Moor complained that parcels sent to prisoners from home had failed to arrive for some weeks. Those boys are getting tired of American Red Cross parcel No. 8 with its monotonous sardines and corned beef.*
>
> *"Another camp reports spectacular progress in cooking research. The most startling discoveries made in that camp are these: a piece of clove candy will remove the scorched tasted from a pudding and, eggshells added to a pot of water produces a delicious brewed coffee. How about an American housewife trying the clove candy idea? If it works in the U.S., it seems to me that 'Good Housekeeping' should send the camp a prize for the recipe."*

To busy himself while Mildred and Christiani obtained interviews, Max produced charcoal sketches of the prisoners. Once, when beyond the guard's hearing, he attempted to reach out to a gaunt-faced captive. "Say, soldier, is there anything I can do? Anything to make you more comfortable?"

"Yeah, send me home!"

All interviews were voluntary and obtained without offers of money, food, medicine, cigarettes, liquor, more comfortable quarters or better treatment. As to those who declined to make a recording, Mildred respected their wishes. Whenever possible she provided paper and pencil to those who preferred to write a letter and promised to get such letters mailed home via a neutral country.

Emil Christiani, driving them one afternoon toward yet another stalag, expressed concern that Russian troops were advancing on Germany's eastern border. Max's eyes flashed with anger. "Stop the car this instant!" The car skidded to a stop. "Stay here!" Max commanded. He scampered up the embankment. As he neared the top, Mildred saw him tire, gasp for breath, stagger and begin to cough. Alarmed, she raced after him.

He was sitting on the ground when she reached him, staring out over the fields. "Look at how my beloved country suffers! This monstrous new alliance between America and the Soviets will put another nail in Germany's coffin!" Tears started down his cheeks. "Oh, if only Americans would read Spengler's *Decline of the West...*"

Goebbels ordered Max back to Berlin. Mildred and Christiani remained on the road to complete the last of the interviews. Two weeks later, their work finished, Mildred returned to her apartment and to Max.

They were about to turn off the radio and go to bed when she heard the first of her POW interviews. She stared at the radio in disbelief. "What? No! He never said that!" As Max beat a retreat to the bathroom she ran to the radio and turned up the volume. Thinking she'd detected the almost imperceptible click of a splice, she put her ear to the receiver. *Click*—there it was again. The prisoner's voice took on a strange inflection as he continued his message to his mother back in Cheyenne:

> *"They're treating me well, Momma. Don't believe Roosevelt's propaganda–once Hitler wins this damn war, we'll all be better off."*

Mildred jumped to her feet screaming. "It's dubbed! Distorted!" She ran to the bathroom door and began pounding on it. "You bastard! You..."

He waited for the pounding and cursing to stop before reappearing. His hands shook as he poured a drink. She took the glass and flung it against the wall. "You son-of-a-bitch! You swore they wouldn't..."

"Believe me, I..."

"You *liar*! You *knew* this would happen!"

Max hung his head and tiredly rubbed his eyes. "Always, always you doubt me. Liebling, I had no way of knowing."

It was done–a despicable deception made possible by her gullibility. Max, Eden's serpent, had held out the apple of salvation. But it was a rotten apple crawling with worms of deception. She'd led American prisoners into a trap. Because of her, American families would think the worst–that their beloved son, husband, sweetheart or father had been "won over" by the enemy–had come to praise Hitler and all he stood for.

The first person she encountered upon her return to Zeesen was Goebbels' pet rat, William "Lord Haw-Haw" Joyce. "Mildred, dearie! Hi-ho hello! I say, old girl, congratulations on the recordings! One thing's for sure–you'll never go home again! You'd be stoned!" His greeting concluded with an unwitting slip of idiom borrowed from his Texas roots. "A necktie party, that's what they'll give ya'!"

She wanted to scream that she was through, that she'd never have to see his ugly face or listen to his high, whiny voice again. But no one quit Zeesen; no one walked away from any job in war-torn Germany.

Early in the summer of 1943, Max, using the name "Fritz,"

hosted the "Home Sweet Home" program on which Mildred starred as "Midge at the Mike." Designed to dishearten U.S. troops in North Africa, these broadcasts were well received.

The Chicago Tribune ran a piece on "Axis Sally." It included a letter from a G.I., which read in part:

> *Midge sounds like the girl next door. Me and my buddies want to know her last name so we can look her up when we get home!*

The piece concluded with this more scholarly appraisal of her impact:

> *The heavy-handed blandishments of Hitler's "Axis Sally" have such a high entertainment value that they actually strengthen the morale of our American fighting men. "Sally" sounds like a comic combination of Marlene Dietrich and Mae West.*

In July, 1943, the Federal Grand Jury of the United States of America indicted, in absentia, for treason: Robert Best, Douglas Chandler, Constance Drexel, Fred Kaltenbach, Jane Anderson, Ezra Pound, Edward Leo Delaney and Max Otto Koischwitz.

News of his indictment caused Max to throw back his head and laugh. "Liebling," he said, taking Mildred into his arms to dispel her fears, "don't worry, you are all that matters to me–you and nothing else."

"Don't worry? My God, Max! You've been indicted for treason! They might send you to prison–or to the electric chair!"

"Might they? Won't they have to catch me first?"

"Why did you bother becoming an American citizen in the first place?"

"Becoming a citizen of your country was a matter of expediency. Please, don't throw stones at me... I live, in case you haven't noticed, in a house of glass."

Robert Best's reaction to this turn of events belied the eccentric's tortured soul. Pale and trembling, he read Mildred an article on his indictment that he'd found in *Time Magazine*. Cleverly captioned, "Worst is Best," it alluded to his "fall from grace" and quoted the opinions of his former friends as to where Best had gone wrong. His voice broke as he read what the noted journalist Dorothy Thompson had to say:

> *"I can't imagine what happened to Bob Best, but I believe he turned traitor because he is intellectually lazy and ignorant."*

"Get this, William Shirer really lambastes me!" he said, his eyes troubled.

> *"Robert Best has stayed away from his own country so long that he has lost touch with American thinking. He's become infected with the Nazi virus."*

Best threw back a shot of vodka. "Why would they ask Shirer? We worked in Vienna at the same time, but he hardly knew me. He always struck me as a queer bird with a fanatical religious bent." He tapped a finger on Shirer's printed words. "But I never thought he was a son-of-a-bitch!'"

Living is strife and torment,
disappointment and love and sacrifice,
golden sunsets and black storms.

– Laurence Olivier (1907-1989)

28

The air war heated up with the Allies obliterating two and a half German cities per month. Berlin experienced ever more horror from "windows"—bomb-sized bundles of thin, razor-sharp metallic strips dropped from Allied planes. Once expelled from a plane, a "window" would fall a few hundred feet and rupture. The resultant mid-air storm of whirling metallic strips confused German radar. When whipped by super-heated winds, the strips formed a cyclone that assaulted those on the ground like a blizzard of guillotine blades.

It was a quiet, intimate conversation, one blanketed by the tram's clattering and not likely to be overheard. They spoke in French, Mildred and the young man who sat next to her on the crowded tram headed for Potsdam. He was one of the many French boys forced to work in Germany. Had she heard that Mussolini had resigned? Did she think the war would end soon?

Mildred avoided the political. Had he ever visited Mount Saint Michelle? The French Riviera?

Yes, he had, with his mother who'd gotten out of France just in time and now lived with her sister in Atlantic City. As the tram neared the station, he quickly took a piece of paper from his pocket, wrote something on it and handed it to Mildred. "This is my mother's name and phone number in the States. When you get home to America would you give her a call and tell her you saw me here in Berlin? Tell her I'm fine?"

His smile kept her from begging off, from telling him she'd given up all hope of ever going home. "Certainly. And shall I tell you're mother you'll be visiting her at war's end?"

He gave Mildred's hand a parting squeeze. "I doubt I'll survive, Fraulein. Please, just give her my love... tell her I looked well."

When her seatmate exited, a large, sweating man took his place and, when she got off at the next station, followed her. She ducked into and used a public toilet only to find him waiting for her when she came out. Pretending not to notice, she attempted to walk past him. He blocked her path.

"Fraulein! You spoke French to that young man on the tram."

"So?"

His fist angrily hammered the air. "The French direct the Allied bombers to our cities–they wiped out my family. Never speak French again–do you understand?

"Ja," Mildred replied, again uttering but a single syllable lest he detect her American accent. She put up with his babbling for two blocks then gave him the slip by suddenly jumping onto the steps of the train headed for Alstadt Hospital.

A line of sick and injured waiting to be treated at the hospital snaked around the building. Seeing Mildred hugging an exterior wall to pass the line, a security guard warned her away. "Last night's raid destroyed most of the east wing. Stand away from the building–shards of glass come crashing down when you least expect it."

Mildred entered the hospital by an alternate route. Inside, frantic medical workers hurried about. She spoke to the frazzled matron manning the reception desk. "Dafne Bredow. Please, where can I find patient Dafne Bredow?"

The matron shrugged. "They gave me this job only this morning. All records have been destroyed. I do not know what to tell you."

Starting in the hospital's cellar, steeling herself against horrific sights, Mildred began a bed-by-bed search. Not finding Dafne there amidst the unattended comatose, she searched the badly burned on the next level and those awaiting triage and emergency surgery on the next. At last, on the fourth level, she found her friend.

Assigned to a corner cot in an overcrowded room with a dreadful stench, Dafne lay on her back, partially covered by a blood-spattered sheet. A huge, dome-shaped apparatus covered her feet. Her skin glistened with perspiration. Her blue eyes stared vacantly from large, dark pockets.

Mildred bent and kissed her forehead. "Hello, dear friend."

She looked up as though studying a speck on the moon. "Mildred?"

"Yes, dear, it's Mildred. I've found you at last. No one knew which hospital you'd been taken to."

"It is awful here." Dafne's eyes drifted to a floor-stacked pile of bloody compresses. "It smells." A table near the window held six or eight foul-smelling, fly-covered bedpans.

"I'll call someone to empty those."

Dafne nodded toward a still figure lying on the floor beneath the next cot. "Gerti died two days ago."

The old woman lying on the cot above the corpse inserted herself into the conversation. "There are no coffins—no one to do the burying. I'm fortunate; my daughter will make my coffin with her own hands. She will dig the hole and bury me beside my husband."

"Please, Mildred," Dafne said, "can you get me some water?"

Mildred looked about. There was no water in the room, not a pitcher—not a cup. She hurried out into the hall. "Water! We need water in here!"

A nurse raced past. "Two floors below—a spigot near the nursery."

"Pitchers? Cups?"

The nurse's reply trailed after her as she disappeared around a corner. "Make do..."

Mildred spotted a small, empty bottle standing on a windowsill. She grabbed it, hurried down two flights, filled it and raced back up to her friend.

Dafne's lips quivered as she drank. Suddenly she pushed the bottle away and sucked in her breath. "Ohhh... ohhh God!"

Mildred glanced at the dome over Dafne's feet. "Do they hurt horribly?"

Dafne's eyes burned into the inquisitor's. "They're gone—amputated... cut off..."

A jagged cry interrupted. It came from the farthest, darkest part of the room. The old woman in the cot next to Dafne spoke. "Her cries are becoming weaker. I do not know her name. Two days ago she gave birth. Her baby lived but a short time. Please, give her a drink of water..."

Mildred crossed the cot-crowded room. Another jagged outcry led her to the woman. She lay on sheets wet with perspiration—a woman with matted hair the color of frosted copper.

"Here," Mildred said, holding out the bottle. "Water. Take a sip." The woman's eyes, two emeralds blazing with fever, bore into Mildred as into an apparition. Mildred slid a hand under her head and gently propped it. She held the bottle to the parched lips and let a tiny stream of water trickle down her throat.

The following week, thousands of leaflets from Allied planes floated down on Berlin. "Leave now!" they warned, "Leave or die!" Ignoring the warning, many mothers filled baskets with the valuable paper and rushed home with it. On the blank side their children could draw pictures or practice writing. Others used the paper to kindle a fire to cook on. All welcomed the leaflets as heaven-sent toilet paper. When at last the Nazis ordered the women and children to vacate Berlin, the leaflets went uncollected and clogged gutters.

Max, covering Allied attempts to get a foothold in Italy, phoned Mildred. "Get a permit and leave Berlin now! Liebling, do whatever it takes. For God's sake, get out!"

The woman officer at the Ministry of Travel sighed when she saw Mildred for the third time in as many days. "The answer, Fraulein, will be the same on your hundredth visit," she snapped. "Permits are reserved for brave Germans, not for cowardly Americans. Request denied!"

Mildred's job became more abhorrent with each broadcast. She was handed a long list of the names and hometowns of American G.I.'s killed or wounded in action and ordered to read the list over the air.

The next day, perhaps in response to that broadcast, the Allies pounded Berlin with the greatest intensity ever. U.S. planes carpet-bombed the city from dawn to dusk, then, with no intermission, the R.A.F. continued dropping death and destruction from dusk to dawn.

Mildred found sanctuary from the pummeling in a dark shelter near her apartment. Someone turned on a short-wave radio. There in the dark, Max's voice reached her. "Hang on, Berliners!" he broadcast from Italy. "Hang on, my dear ones! And as for you, America—shame! You are obliterating innocent civilians. Horrible, horrible, horrible will be your day of reckoning!"

The bombing continued ceaselessly for a week. When it ended Mildred bolted from the shelter and ran along the sidewalk of a collapsed street. Passing the pulverized shop of the neighborhood druggist she saw, amidst the rubble, several packets of bandages and medicines. She stuffed the precious goods into the pockets of her jacket and started for Altstadt Hospital.

The driver of a license-less Mercedes gave her a lift. "Hell could not look worse," he said as he drove through streets pitted with gaping chasms. Several times, at his bidding, Mildred got out and pushed obstacles out of the way—part of a bed, a smoldering rocker, a car fender.

"You'll have a rough go from here, Fraulein," he said when the Mercedes, still miles short of the hospital, died for want of petrol. Mildred got out and climbed over a fallen theater marquee advertising Leni Reifenstahl's latest Hitler-pleasing film.

Before walking away in the opposite direction, the Mercedes driver handed Mildred two bottles of water. "Good luck in finding your friend. But, don't get your hopes up. I doubt there's anyone still alive in that part of the city!"

The queue of patients had grown longer. It now snaked around the hospital and off toward a once tree-shaded suburb. Patients in all manner of distress waited stoically in the sweltering heat. Some advanced by stepping over the bodies of those who had fallen in line.

Anxious to deliver bandages, medicine and water to Dafne, Mildred entered the hospital and climbed to Dafne's fourth floor room. It held even more occupants than before and cots were now wedged so close together in the stinking, dimly lit space that Mildred could barely squeeze by.

In Dafne's cot lay a young girl, her hands blackened and burned, her hair scorched, her scalp bald in spots. Mildred wheeled around, her eyes sweeping from patient to patient. "Dafne?"

"She's gone," said an old woman occupying a cot by the window.

"Gone? She... died? When?"

"Yes, they're all gone. All dead."

"No," came a whisper from the far side of the room, "No."

Mildred worked her way through the cots to the whisper's source. She found the emerald-eyed woman burning with fever. Matted coils of coppery hair cascaded about her face. Mildred propped the woman's head and gave her a drink of water.

The woman, in English, muttered, "Thank you."

"Dafne, did my friend Dafne–the girl who lost her feet... did she die?"

"No."

Mildred wet a handkerchief, folded it and attempted to lay the wet compress across the woman's forehead. The emeralds filled with torment. "Tell Max... tell him... his son..."

Mildred's heart stopped. As though dealt a blow to the head, she squeezed her eyes shut against slivers of light flashing through her brain. With a wail of torment, she slowly sank to her knees beside the cot and buried her face in its blood stained sheet.

Erna's hand slowly came to rest on the blonde hair. "Tell him... for one hour he had a son... a son..." A ragged gasp and the breathing ceased. The light in them extinguished, the glistening emeralds turned to weathered jade.

A siren screamed. Windows reverberated the thunder of approaching aircraft. Mildred let out a cry as she bolted from the room. The crush of others making for the exit swept her along the corridor. Bedlam reigned in the jammed staircase. Orderlies, bandaged patients, confused old people and wailing children stampeded, trampling those who fell.

She reached the street and, deafened by a roar, looked up. Overhead, a monstrous bird flew low. Its under-belly opened. Out fell dozens of whining, death-delivering eggs. The first hit shook the earth. Shock waves slammed her against the pavement. Debris rained down on her head. Smoke and dust obliterated the sun. The sky flashed with explosions and began to glow with the light of wind-swept fires. Afraid to get to her feet, she slithered across the sidewalk and down into a stairwell.

A crazed woman, her nurse's uniform in charred tatters, appeared like a ghost through the smoke. She staggered past a mad town crier shouting the news at an equally mad world. "Gone, the hospital's gone. All inside incinerated. All inside incinerated."

Running, stumbling, falling and at times cursing, Mildred hurled herself at the mercy of the rubble-stoppered streets. The air raid intensified. Phosphorus bombs rained down, each molten banshee screaming, "Heeee! Heeee!"

There was no grief left in him. Was he glad?
Yet how could he be glad, or reconciled,
Or anything but wretched and undone?

– Edward Arlington Robinson, (1869-1935)

29

Robert Best found her days later, badly beaten, covered with plaster dust and lying in the ruins of a building that had but two walls standing. Startled awake by his approach, then mistaking him for the soldier or devil that had raped her, she growled, grabbed a brick and hurled it.

Best ducked. "Jesus Christ, hold your fire!"

She seized another brick.

He picked up a garbage can lid and, using it as a shield, slowly advanced. "Now calm down, Mildred. Everything's gonna' be okay."

Her eyes, blackened and swollen almost shut, had trouble focusing.

"Harry?"

"No, it's Bob... Bob Best. I've been searching for you all week. Hell, who else do you know who wears a Stetson hat and high-laced shoes?" Her arm relaxed. The brick tumbled from her hand. He caught her as she collapsed and carried her to the street.

Near an alley, an old man with a handcart rummaged

through the ruins. Best carried Mildred to him. "Kind fellow, can you help? My wife is injured. Please, let me lay her atop your cart and give me a hand wheeling her home."

The old man shook his head. "I have work to do."

"Please, for a bottle of cognac?"

The old man stroked his beard. "Two bottles... two bottles and some goat cheese."

Best bathed her and washed the blood, grit and ash from her hair. He dressed her in his pajama top, rolled up the sleeves and put her to bed. While she slept, he washed and mended her clothes. She slept fitfully at first, moaning and crying out. Tremors, at times so strong as to rock the bed, wracked her body. As dawn approached the fitfulness subsided and she began to sleep so soundly that he got up often to check to see that she was still breathing.

She awoke at midmorning with a start. She sat up, hugged herself and, rocking back and forth, began to weep. Robert understood women better than he understood men. He remained perfectly still and let her grieve.

When at last she lay her head back on the pillow, he went into the kitchen and opened a can of vegetable soup. His back turned, she slipped out of bed and sat at the table. "Good girl!" he said, setting the soup in front of her, "Sorry it's cold but the stove's not working." She had yet to speak but the way she consumed the soup, like a starved animal, was a good sign. He noted a slight tick in her right eye, the wariness, the fearful expression. It would take time.

When, two weeks later, Best and Mildred returned to Zeesen, they were immediately flanked by two guards and marched to the main office. William Joyce taunted them as they passed. "I wouldn't want to be you two!"

The doors of the main office opened. Horst Cleinow, Hans von Richter and Adelbert Houben stood waiting.

Houben spoke. "Well, well, well... the lovely, absent-without-leave Fraulein has condescended to return—to grace us with her presence!"

Best had been preparing for this moment. He took off his Stetson. "Why gentlemen, y'all should be jumping for joy to get her back! Just look at her, why this woman is a national hero!"

Adelbert smirked. "My, my, a national hero? Not a deserter?"

"No way a '*deserter*!' Why, Hitler's sure to decorate her for bravery once he hears how many German children she saved before that bomb struck..."

It was von Richter's turn to poke holes in the alibi.

"Any *particular* bomb?"

Best wasn't backing down. "Well, hell yes, it was a *particular* bomb, it collapsed the building and trapped her—Goebbels' most valuable English-speaking broadcaster—for nearly two whole weeks."

"A most creative excuse, indeed!" said Houben dryly. "Herr Best, return to your office at once and get back to work. You will be fined a month's salary, of course."

With Best gone, the monocled Host Cleinow, fixed his good eye on her. "Fraulein, until we decide on a punishment appropriate for your 'little vacation,' you will go on broadcasting to your precious G.I.'s. Be warned, however, one more disappearance—for whatever reason—and your pretty neck will immediately feel the axe."

Hans von Richter nodded. "I will be most interested in Herr Koischwitz' reaction to your behavior, Fraulein. You know, of course, that he returns from Italy next week."

During the week prior to Max's return, the toll of suffering and death rose exponentially. Mildred's elderly friend, Carl Langbehn was cruelly tortured and finally executed. A Frenchman charged with repairing gas lines in Mildred's neighborhood took the full force of an exploding shell. A bridge she frequently crossed over collapsed, sending seven children to their deaths in a debris-dammed river.

"He exaggerates!" Goebbels exclaimed, listening to a BBC broadcaster give an account of the damage caused in Berlin by the latest R.A.F. bombings. To prove his point, he insisted that his American broadcasters, Mildred included, tour Berlin's suburbs with him. They came upon an entire city block that, still burning, had been obliterated. Goebbels slammed on the brakes, jumped out and began screaming obscenities. "The fuckers! The filthy British bastards! This is my neighborhood—I grew up here!"

He raced over to the large group of civilians who had been displaced by the conflagration. "Thirty! I need thirty volunteers to fight this fire. Step forward!"

The civilians, some in bed clothes, others draped in blankets, stood soot-covered, shoulders sagging with exhaustion, eyes dull from lack of sleep. Expressionless, they stared hard at the wild-eyed, black-suited recruiter.

"I say step *forward*, thirty of you! This is an *order*!"

En masse, the civilians turned and walked away.

Goebbels' first act, upon returning to Zeesen after that tour of neighborhood devastation, was to order all pictures of war damage and civilian suffering censored.

Those with political clout, social connections or reputations as intellectuals fared far better than the city's poor. Ironically, the upper strata clung to their station despite gaping holes in the ceilings of their mansions. They attended concerts, promoted plays and hosted social soirees. They served tiny watercress sandwiches and poured French champagne.

A member of Germany's nobility, the Baroness Maria von Gersdorf turned her opulent Berlin home in the Wayrschstrasse into a political and intellectual salon. Here,

Germany's landed aristocracy could ignore air raids while hobnobbing with industrial giants, stars of the academic world, military generals, diplomats and the creative elite.

Several days past the date of Max's expected return from Italy, Mildred, as the guest of her old friend Victor de Kowa, attended a reception hosted by the baroness. "Mildred," Victor said as he handed her a drink, "I'm afraid you're wrong about Max's not having returned. Isn't that him over there surrounded by those girls?"

The instant she spotted him, he looked her way. The smile left his lips. With a quick, nervous bow, he excused himself from his admirers. He rushed to Mildred's side and steered her toward a quiet corner. "Liebling, I know I should have called you, but my train arrived only a few hours ago. Before coming here, I had to go straight to von Ribbentrop with my report." He attempted to kiss her.

She pushed him away. "No."

Suddenly cocky, he put his hands on his hips. "Very well, my cold one, I know what you need. Go home and put on something seductive. I'll join you within the hour."

He arrived at her apartment late the next day, strolled in and pulled her to him. "At last, Liebling! These past two months have been hell! Oh, how I hate Italy! Come... let's go to bed. I'm starved for you!"

Mildred twisted free. "I must be out of my mind." She lit a cigarette, inhaled the smoke deep into her lungs and, holding it, stared at him. "You really are a louse, you know, a totally worthless pile of shit."

"Why, wha... what's happened?"

She crossed to her dresser and began to brush her hair. "I don't know Max, suppose *you* tell me. How many women besides Erna have you impregnated lately?"

"What are you talking about? Other women? Erna?"

"I was with her Max, in the hospital following the death of your son."

"But I..."

"Oh, *yes*, you had a son—a premature baby boy who lived but an hour—she wanted you to know that before she..."

"Before she what?"

"She's dead, Max, blown to smithereens."

He did not wail, fall apart or collapse. He stood there, as stoic as a soldier slapped in the face by a commanding officer. It was more than she could bear. Ignoring her tears, he walked out the door and, without a word, disappeared into the night.

His eventual return, she thought inevitable. Like two candles leaning on one another, melting together in the eternal flame of Erna's fiery death, they could no longer stand alone. "I am so ashamed," he said when, a week later, he trudged back into the apartment and sank onto a chair. "I've deceived you so terribly. Will you ever find it in your heart to forgive me?" He read her expression. "No, of course you can't. I'll rot in hell."

"*We* will rot in hell! What happened to Erna guarantees it. She'll haunt us, Max. Your son's last cries will ring in our ears through eternity."

He hung his head. "I beg of you, don't leave me."

"Leave you? So they can lop off my head with their medieval axe? Leave you and let you do penance at Oranienburg?"

The mere mention of the place, the most dreaded of Hitler's torture prisons, caused him to shudder. "I deserve Oranienburg..."

"Oh no, neither of us deserves such an *easy* out. The beast has swallowed us, my dear. We're not going anywhere until he's through with us—until he excretes and buries us like the shit we are!"

"Don't..."

"We have no choice but to get on with our worthless lives... however..."

"Anything, anything."

"Hear my vow, Max. Never... *never* again, for as long as I live, will you touch me."

Showcased in the September, 1943 issue of America's *Atlantic Magazine* as Goebbels' "Awkward Squad," American broadcasters in service to the Third Reich were dubbed "the laughing stock of the airways." The absurdity of Hitler's broadcasters, however, paled in comparison to the long diatribe Hitler delivered that month. His voice thundered over every radio and public address system. "The cowardly Italians have stabbed us in the back! They will pay! These despicable cowards will pay for their shameful surrender!"

Berlin's entire Italian colony clung together like whipped dogs as, pelted with stones hurled by jeering German patriots, they awaited transport to the train station.

Murmurings abounded of a plot to assassinate Hitler. One heard more and more rumors of dissension in the ranks. Risking imprisonment, Berliners huddled near short-wave radios to listen to the pleadings of German officers broadcast from Moscow. Identifying themselves as members of "The Union of German Officers Captured at Stalingrad" these captive officers begged for peace. Goebbels, upon learning the identities of the group's founders, ordered their names added to his ever-lengthening list of traitors to be shot on sight.

Goebbels despised the Russians and considered them Germany's greatest threat. He personally generated an anti-Soviet propaganda campaign using photographs of the remains of 4,400 Polish officers murdered by the Soviets. One of Mildred's friends, a young woman who worked at the Foreign Office, was given the job of captioning these grisly pictures.

Max, privy to all sorts of intelligence by virtue of his war-correspondent status, saw an ominous undercurrent in the slaughter. Was Hitler blind? Did he not know what Russia was up to? The slaughtered were not just Polish *officers*—they were four thousand of Poland's top intelligencia—university professors, doctors, lawyers, engineers, schoolteachers, journalists, writers and industrialists. By obliterating these non-communists, Russia was eliminating much future resistance to its take-over of Poland at war's end.

Mildred felt more comfortable discussing the war with Donald Day, the latest American recruited to broadcast from Zeesen. She shared with him her hope that Roosevelt, upon hearing of the latest atrocities in Poland, would change his war posture and re-think America's alliance with Russia.

Day shook his head. "Roosevelt hears *only* what those around him want him to hear. Henry Morgenthau heads FDR's advisors—and nobody gets past him. Morgenthau's one of them, kid, he shields the President from all news unfavorable to Russia or communism."

On the afternoon of November 22, 1943, Max and Mildred went for a stroll in the Woyrschstrasse. They'd walked but a block when sirens started. It began to rain. Max, scheduled to broadcast that evening, proceeded to Zeesen. Mildred returned to her apartment. His phone call came just as the lights went out in her apartment. "Liebling, get to a shelter now! Spotters say the formations are the largest yet!"

"Sure, Max, I'm on my way." She lied. The memory of having nearly drowned in a shelter still haunted her. She remained in the apartment. As a precaution, she filled a bathtub with water and placed a flashlight on the floor next to it. She then lit a cigarette, sat on her fourth-floor windowsill and scanned the night sky. Searchlights came on and began to probe the mist.

A devil's confetti of incendiary flares poured from the heavens. With the brightest flare came a sudden, violent barrage of flak. The sound of a million, low-flying, monster-bees filled the smoky aftermath.

Expecting a direct hit, Mildred dropped to the floor and lay face down, arms folded over and hugging her head. She heard a whine and a deafening blast. Doors and windows blew in. The sudden change in air pressure made her cry out with pain in her ears. Hot air blasted in. As she gasped for breath the apartment filled with smoke and red-hot cinders. Choking, she crawled to the bathroom.

Max found her hours later, after the "all clear." She was up to her neck in a bathtub full of ash-black water, her head wrapped in a wet towel. She smiled up at him. "How do I look?"

"Wunderbar! Like you've been mining coal for the last eight hours! He helped her out of the tub, cleaned and applied salve to her scorched forehead. As she changed into dry clothes he told her the heart of the city had been destroyed and Zeesen severely damaged.

Four days later they were ordered to return to work. Getting there was not easy. Fires raged around Berlin, shrouding the city in thick, hot, noxious smoke. They set out holding wet handkerchiefs over their faces. Carcasses of trams, burned, crumpled and blown off their tracks, lay about the streets. Amid the mud and ashes of the Tiergarten, people of every class and description wandered aimlessly. Some wore expensive, scorched furs. Others resembled bandage-swathed zombies.

They came to the zoo. Max gawked in disbelief at the damage then spoke to an old man struggling to lift the felled, front gate. "How terribly sad!"

The old man shook his head. "Last night's raid. Early this morning they shot all the caged animals."

"And the aquarium?"

"A bomb landed on it and killed all the fish and snakes... but not the crocodiles..."

"Not the crocodiles..."

"They had to shoot them too, the crocodiles..."

After many failed attempts to flag down a ride, they reached Zeesen hours later, on foot. Horst Cleinow greeted Max with a slap on the back. He scowled at Mildred. "Heavens, my dear, you look terrible! I should have sent a car."

She smirked. "You should have sent a tank. Look Horst, I'm hungry. I need to wash up and get something in my stomach."

"There's no time. You'll start broadcasting when I give the signal. There's a stack of records next to your microphone. Play them as ordered in your script. And Fraulein, *tonight* you pour it on like never before!"

She went on the air almost immediately and, as ordered in the script, played the first record, *Somebody Stole My Gal.*

The notation "Purr like a kitten" appeared in the margin to the left of her opening line. She purred:

> *"Well boys, how are my sweethearts tonight? Comfy? Feeling like cuddling up with that special, soft and sweet someone? Dying to hold her in your big, powerful arms? You may dislike my repeating this to you, but let's face it, you may get mutilated and not return home in one piece. Now, you know how your girl wants her man. Suppose she'll settle for damaged goods?"*

von Ribbentrop returned to Zeesen late that night, disheveled from visiting the smoldering remains of the Foreign Ministry complex. Brushing ash from his uniform, his face taut and streaked with soot, he rushed into the studio, a man in shock. "I can't believe it! Everything, everything is in ruins! Everything! All gone! Smashed! Burned!

Everything pulverized! They've even leveled the diplomatic quarter!"

"Not quite!" Kaltenbach whispered to Mildred, "Damn poor bombardiers if you ask me. They missed the biggest targets of all—the Japanese and Italian embassies are still standing!"

von Ribbentrop misread Mildred's laugh. "What? You think it's funny? I tell you, Army Command Headquarters is a smoldering skeleton! The Ministry of the Navy is a heap of cinders! Mein gott!" Eyes darting, his hand clamped on his forehead, he hurried for the door. "I have to speak to our Fuhrer! We must re-think our position!"

Had Father Christmas visited Berlin that winter, he would have found the city's "Bombengeschadigte" (bomb victims) shivering in long lines leading to emergency field kitchens. There were thousands upon thousands of them, queued for hours, desperate for rations of soup, strong coffee and cigarettes.

The walls of gutted buildings became outdoor bulletin boards. They bore messages scrawled with cinders, crayons, mud-daubed brushes, paint and lipstick:

> *Ellen, Sopie hides GL4B2.*
>
> *Children of Rolf and Rose Krug sent to SW orphanage.*
>
> *To the mother, wife and children of Josef Henning: I live—love Josef.*

In clogged train stations, mobs of frantic people pushed and shoved to board trains leaving the city. Those resigned to their fate or unable to travel stayed on. Although their sacrifices went unheralded, the German people showed great courage and resilience. Heroism and great acts of kindness abounded. Young and old alike helped firemen get air to those trapped in cellars. Thousands froze in window-blown residences, cooked meals on up-turned irons and melted snow for water.

When the street outside Mildred's apartment building was cleared, a veteran who had lost both an eye and a leg, went from door to door distributing pine saplings he'd cut in a bomb-ravaged city park. The one he brought to Mildred's door had just two straggly branches.

"What is this?"

"It's a Christmas tree. Decorate it. It will lighten your heart."

Christmas eve, during a freezing snowstorm, Gretl Fischer arrived at Mildred's door. An English-speaking clerk, Gretl worked in the Foreign Ministry's photo archives. "I've come to say good-bye. Everyone in my section is being evacuated to Krummhubel tonight. Our office took a direct hit yesterday. Every desk in the place has been blown to bits and all files burned."

At Mildred's insistence, she stepped inside and sat at the table. Served cold soup and a heel of stale bread, she thanked her hostess profusely then ate slowly, savoring every spoonful, every bite. The farewell feast consumed, the friends joined hands and, in voices often cracking with emotion, sang *Silent Night*.

A glance at her watch caused Gretl to frown. She rose to leave. "Mildred, my friend, there's a favor..."

"Name it."

"Well, you see, I've survived one train's derailing... perhaps next time I will not be so lucky. Here, please take this—mother's address in Leipzig. I have a strange sense about this journey to Krummhubel."

"Nonsense!"

"Perhaps, but if you hear of my luck running out... you have mother's address."

Mildred shivered. "Yes... of course."

"Auf Wiedersehen, my good, good friend."

The next day Mildred dressed warmly and set out to hear Christmas Mass at a nearby Greek Orthodox Church. While waiting to enter, another churchgoer turned to her with the latest news. "Have you heard? There's no way out of Berlin... last night... the train to Krummhubel..."

"What about the train to Krummhubel?"

"Bombed to pieces! Tracks in both directions are kaput... gone!"

Christmas afternoon hosted a thousand-bomber raid. Mildred spent those hideous hours at home, composing draft after draft of a letter to Gretl's mother. "Dear Mrs. Fischer, it is with utmost grief..."

As she continued to broadcast from Zeesen, specific details were added to Mildred's scripts. From one such script, beamed at American soldiers about to storm a German-occupied village in Italy, she read:

> *"Hi, fellas. I see you synchronizing your watches against the clock in the village square. Yes, you heard me right, Private Howard Hagerstrom from Idyllwild, California. You are the son of Holly Hagerstrom–how is her oil painting coming along? And I see you synchronizing your watch, Sergeant Stanley Ochefsky, brother of the former linebacker for the Fighting Irish. Well, enough chitchat sweethearts. Here's a big tip: That clock on the steeple–yes, the one you're staring at–it's two minutes fast."*

Mildred shut off her microphone and turned to Max. "This is crazy! Why am I reading all this gibberish?"

"Gibberish nothing! Hearing their names and details about their relatives gives them the jitters! I can see them now, asking their buddies, how you can possibly know these things."

"And the clock?"

"It's a fact—that clock *is* two minutes fast! Your knowing it spooks them. You're an unseen presence in their midst. Its like you're looking over their shoulder."

That Hitler would not win the war did not dawn on her overnight. It was a conclusion annealed over time in the searing evidence of Germany's ultimate defeat. The statistics, gleaned either from the BBC or while pouring over Zeesen's supply of foreign newspapers, were horrific. In the first eight months of 1943 alone, the R.A.F. had dropped more than 11,000 tons of bombs on Hamburg, 8,000 tons on Essen, 6,000 tons each on Duisburg and Berlin, and 5,000 tons each on Dusseldorf and Nuremberg. Then, prompted by Air Marshal Hamm's resolve to "wreck Berlin from end to end," came the most fierce onslaught to date. His R.A.F. went all out in their next thirty-two attacks, dropping 25,000 tons of bombs, destroying nine square kilometers of the city, damaging 315 factories, leaving 6,166 people dead, 18,431 badly injured and 1.5 million homeless.

Painfully aware of Max's inability to accept the situation, Mildred tried only once to force him to face reality and to come to grips with the fact that his country was on its knees and breathing its last breath.

He stared at her as though she was fabricating what they both already knew—that Germany was finished, its major cities obliterated, its citizens maimed and starving, its children trained with wooden guns and waved into battle to replace fallen fathers. Having heard enough of her outpouring, he reached out and clapped a palm over her mouth. "No more! Do you hear me? No more! If you want to kill me, do it with a gun, not with your tongue!"

rampart: A fortification consisting of an embankment, often with a parapet built on top; A means of protection or defense; a bulwark.

– The American Heritage Dictionary

30

Given the common names "rape," "rape seed," "colz" and "oil-seed rape," and the botanical nomenclature "brassica napus," the European relative of the mustard family grows in great profusion above the beaches of Normandy. The English consider it a pest, a noxious weed and a dreaded, garden-destroying invader. The French cultivate the plant as fodder, press valuable oil from its seed and marvel at how in springtime its blossoms burst forth to turn the countryside into an endless sea of pure gold.

The beauty of the rape fields above Normandy's beaches, when she saw them for the first time that spring, took Mildred's breath away. Delighted by the look of wonder on her face, Max made a sweeping gesture with his arm as though to make her a gift of the dazzling scene. "It's so good to see you smile, Liebling. If I had the money, I'd buy you every single bloom!"

She left the footpath and waded into a field until knee-deep in blossoms. There were millions of them—bright yellow florets blooming in tight-packed profusion. They extended from bluff's edge inland as far as the eye could see. A gentle onshore breeze billowed her skirt and stirred the blossoms, sending a shimmering current of gold rippling to the horizon. A bee buzzed her ear. A meadowlark, perched on an outcropping of rock, trilled a tune to the Dutch-blue sky.

As they neared the fortifications, Max—ever the teacher—led her into a quiz on the region's history. "Don't be fooled by the seeming tranquility of this beautiful spot. For centuries the blood of a dozen conquerors has fertilized this ground beneath our feet. Can you name any of Normandy's conquerors?"

"Sure. Hannibal, Caesar and Alexander the Great."

He sighed. "No, not even close. Normandy began as part of ancient Gaul. The Romans, Franks and Norse then successively conquered it. After the Norman Conquest it belonged to England. The Hundred Years' War restored it to France." He smiled, inhaled the crisp air and rubbed his hands together. "Now, as we know, it belongs to Germany."

He seemed healthier than he had in weeks; there was color in his cheeks, a hint of energy in his stride. Being this close to the Atlantic Wall excited him. "Ten thousand fortified positions stretching more than three thousand miles! Think of it! All built by Operation Todt. Gun batteries, bunkers, observation towers and radar posts. Great, impenetrable fortresses built by a workforce of 500,000 men and manned by 300,000 of our Fuhrer's finest!"

They came to the first of many enormous concrete fortifications. Like the others, it stood menacingly atop the bluff, it's cannon thrusting out toward the Channel, its smaller guns flanking the cannon, jutting from horizontal slits in six-foot-thick concrete and scanning the beach below.

Max showed identification and spoke to the bunker's commander. "The Fuhrer's Minister of Public Information and Enlightenment, Doctor Josef Goebbels, has asked me to commend you on the fine job you're doing here. He's sent me to inspect our fortifications."

"For the purpose of public information and enlightenment?"

"Not quite. Let's just say for the purpose of research before the storm."

The commander smiled. "Alas, it is projected the storm will strike further to the south and my cannons will remain silent. Calais is certain to get all the action. But, come, come step inside." The commander turned toward Mildred and, without Max's seeing it, gave her a quick, suggestive wink. "Perhaps the lady would also like to inspect my big gun?"

"No, thank you, they are always so vastly overrated. I prefer to stay out here in the fresh air."

Max entered and shook hands with the dozen or so men on duty inside the bunker and began his inspection. He patted the cold iron barrel of the monster sixteen-inch coastal cannon. "Tell me, Commander, how far can this beauty shoot?"

"The maximum range is twenty-five miles."

"Depending on the visibility, correct?"

A look of strained patience crossed the commander's face. Did this civilian with the pasty complexion, this expensive-suited representative of Goebbels himself, know nothing of telemetry? "Obviously, Herr Koischwitz, you have not visited the telemetry room of the Riva Bella Fire Direction Tower. Its stereoscopic range finder scans the horizon for us."

"Of course! A powerful telescope!"

The commander pretended not to hear the groan of one of his eavesdropping crew. "Not exactly. The way it works is that an observer looking into the sight initially sees two identical images of the target. To determine the target's distance he turns the instrument's dials until the two images merge into one picture. The distance is then entered into fire control calculation to determine our firing coordinates, which are relayed to us by telephone. With such precise information, we will be able to fire on Allied ships long before they reach the coast."

"And if some of them get through?"

"My, they must be keeping your boss in the dark. We have coastal cannons such as this one mounted on railway cars so they can be moved to optimal firing positions at a moment's notice." He walked the visitor over to one of the bunker's observation slits and pointed first to beach obstacles and then to rafts floating near shore. "Everything you see is mined. If the invaders don't blow themselves up, we'll detonate the mines and do it for them."

Max emerged from the bunker ecstatic. Mildred stood gazing at the Channel's high, choppy waves. He rushed to her. "Liebling, you should have come inside! Now I am convinced—the coastline is absolutely, positively impenetrable! Such foresight and preparedness! When our people realize we've turned back the greatest assault of all time, they'll rise up from their suffering and stand tall! Invigorated! Oh, Liebling, we will fight on to victory!"

It all but crucified her, knowing for certain that on the coast of France, a slaughter of epic proportions awaited American soldiers. Unable to sleep, she sat up nights chain smoking. She lost her appetite, drank more and, whenever she thought of the impending invasion, burst into tears.

Every evening she reported to Zeesen. It was abuzz with predictions of how many Allied soldiers would attempt the landing. Estimates ranged from fifty to two-hundred thousand. Gripping the microphone with shaking hands, her voice unsteady, she envisioned the young men listening to her—their loved ones back home in England, Australia, Canada and the United States. How could she be doing this—playing records and joking with boys she knew positively were about to die should they challenge those fortified beaches? She prayed for courage to veer from the script, to shout into the microphone what she believed with all her heart—that Germany couldn't last another year—that this slaughter didn't have to happen.

Her prayer unanswered and, convinced of her cowardice, she began, during one night's raid, to beg the Almighty for an end to her life. "Please, let it happen tonight! Let me be bombed to pieces!" She curled up on the floor and waited. Wave after wave of R.A.F. planes roared overhead. The caghophany at its zenith, the idea came to her. Like a whisper—unexpectedly, gently and with absolute clarity. There *was* something she could do to save those boys lives! She spent the morning transfixed, her mind weighing the idea, trying to pit holes in its logic. Whether an inspiration from the God to whom she prayed, or an idea spawned in the sheer desperation of her own tormented brain, she knew, with absolute certainty, that she must act on it.

"A play? You want me to write a play? What about?" They were weekending at a mountain retreat outside of Eberswalde. Max glowed as she kissed him and playfully ran her fingers through his hair. He breathed heavier as she led him to the sofa, sat him down and curled up on his lap.

Snuggled against him, she outlined the play she wanted him to write. It would be about an American mother who, in a nightmare, sees her soldier son crossing the English Channel about to participate in the invasion at Normandy. The nightmare jumps ahead. The son storms the beach. A bullet rips his face away as several others riddle his chest. He falls dying onto the surf. The mother suddenly awakens from her nightmare. She calls out to her son. She begs him not to approach Normandy. She pleads with him to turn back, to save himself and his comrades.

Max jumped up, his eyes clouded with confusion. "Turn back? What an idiotic idea! Hitler is counting on the assault.

The German people have had enough defeat. Are you mad? We *need* this victory!"

She coaxed him back to the sofa and again sat on his lap. Kissing and caressing him, she at last felt him grow hard. She loosened the top buttons of her blouse and fluffed her hair. Moistening her lips, she led his hand to her breast. "Darling Max, what if it turns out to be an Allied victory?"

His eyes sparked with anger. "Nonsense!"

Her hand found his penis. "After all, sweetheart, they *too* have been preparing. What if by some miracle..."

"Impossible!"

"Well, yes, of course it will be *impossible...* in a few months... when Hitler's new arsenal is ready. Oh, look about you, darling. We need more time! Trust me, someday the Fuhrer will thank you, maybe even promote you to work at his side—and all because your play caused the Allies to turn back—to run away—until another day—the day Germany smashes them once and for all. Face it, my dearest, Germany needs just a few months more to prepare—to refine the new weapons."

He took several days to consider the idea—days in which Mildred stayed by his side. She walked with him, cooked for him and, breaking the vow she made following Erna's fiery death, bedded him. His decision came late one evening, after his being exhausted by her lovemaking. He raised up on one elbow. "Liebling, I think you're right! I'll write the play."

"Good." She ran a finger over his lips. "And the starring role?"

He gazed at her and, seeing the same eagerness in her eyes that had attracted him to her some twenty years earlier, nodded. "Yes, you may play the mother."

With great trepidation he approached Horst Cleinow. Contrary to what Max expected, the head of Zeesen's propaganda crew did not blow a fuse. He listened with interest to the entire proposal.

Horst was a depressed, but a very intelligent Nazi. Privy to a host of grim statistics, he suspected that German troops sorely needed on the eastern front would be pulled and sent to help repel the invasion of Normandy. And, if by some miracle the invasion should succeed? If only Hitler's miracle weapons, those being developed at Peenemunde, were ready. But they were not. The new super-speed jet planes and unmanned guided missiles—which would guarantee the repulsion of the Allies—might not be ready for months. Cleinow decided quickly. "You're premise seems sound—forestalling the invasion makes sense. However..."

Max had come prepared. Repeating Mildred's exact words, he spoke glowingly of how the Fuhrer's great gratitude would, in time, be lavished on those responsible for the play.

Cleinow's eyes lit up. "Let's do it! You write it, Fraulein Gillars stars in it, and I get credit for producing it!"

"You won't be sorry!"

"One condition—top secrecy. One word about this play before it's broadcast—and I'll have you shot!"

Given the go-ahead, Max began to write "Vision of the Invasion." Sitting for long hours caused his circulation to worsen. His feet and ankles swelled so big that he could scarcely tie his shoes.

On occasion Mildred tore him away from his work long enough to get some fresh air. Their walks took them through the newly destroyed Kurfurstendamm, past Berliners living in tents like Bedouins and over the snow-covered remains of the city's heart. Once they came upon several bloated, rat-ravaged bodies awaiting burial. It snowed often, adding white powder to the frozen pack already nearly a meter high.

As they rounded the corner of Nettlebeckstrasse, Max's breathing became labored. They ducked into a restaurant and sat at a bare, scratched table. He loosened his tie, grimaced and rubbed his chest. Beads of perspiration formed on his forehead. He clenched and unclenched his left hand.

Mildred became alarmed. "What's wrong?"

He gave her a dismissive wave and spoke with great effort. "Whatever happens, Liebling... you are... my love... my beacon..."

The waiter filled a glass with cognac and came on the run. Max swallowed the thick, amber liquid in one gulp. When at last his color returned, he took Mildred's arm and hobbled outside. "Don't worry, Liebling..."

"Worry? You nearly died in there."

As work on the play progressed, Mildred's routine remained unaltered. What few hours she had left after her broadcast schedule at Zeesen were spent waiting in food lines or scavenging for such luxuries as soap, cigarettes and toilet paper. When a raid spelled an end to the neighborhood's power supply, she became obsessed with finding candles so that Max could write into the wee hours of the night.

With supply lines cut off and food more severely rationed, their diet became bizarre. At times they subsisted on toast soaked in fat. At a rare celebration they fared much better. Behind closed drapes the Countess Alfreda Schonkranz served hoarded oysters, roast hare and cognac. Donald Day, Mildred's Irish-American fellow broadcaster, hosted a small St. Patrick's Day party. Lacking corn beef and cabbage, he offered nuts, raisins and dried figs saved from his last trip to Turkey.

Max began experiencing more frequent and severe bouts of chest pain. "Don't worry, Liebling, it's nothing more than dyspepsia caused by overly-watered soup." He slept fitfully, sitting up in a large overstuffed chair only to wake often, his shirt soaked through from debilitating night sweats.

She spent every free moment sitting beside him as he slept, reaching for his hand when it began to tremble and trying to hush fragmented outcries for a dead wife and missing daughters.

One night she returned from Zeesen to find him smiling from ear to ear. He opened a bottle of scavenged wine, poured them each a glass and offered a toast. "To the play! Finally, finally it's finished!" He lifted the loose-leaf binder from the table. "Here, my inspiring angel, read it!"

She sat on the sofa, pulled a shawl around her shoulders and poured over the handwritten sheets. Tears rolled down her cheeks as she read the ending. At first she was too moved to speak, then, after several moments of silence: "Bravo! Max, it's a masterpiece!"

"It's what you wanted?"

"Exactly! Hard hitting! Convincing! Moving!"

He smiled. "Might it really turn them back?"

"Oh, absolutely! I know it will. It's certain to convince them of the horror awaiting them. They're not stupid, Max—they don't want to die. Trust me, this play will make them turn back."

"If only it can buy us enough time to develop our super-weapons."

Her expression gave no hint of what she was thinking: *Please, God, let this play cause those boys to turn around—to choose life instead of death—to wait until Germany crumbles!*

Cleinow read the play and liked it. "Perfect! Doctor Koischwitz, I salute you! You're a genius!"

"You can get it broadcast? Tell me the truth, Horst."

"Don't worry, I have my ways, Professor Playwright. Leave Goebbels to me." Horst had reason to be smug. While Max had been busy writing the play, Cleinow had learned of the change in the thinking from Hitler on down the chain of command. Setbacks, both along the eastern front and in the development of the super-weapons, had altered the outlook. There was dissension in the ranks. A plot was in the offing, one said to be of such cunning that it would finish the Fuhrer and paralyze the Wehrmacht. Faced with these grave problems, Hitler had his hands full. The last thing he now wanted was an Allied invasion.

Cleinow came through. "Goebbels gave us the go ahead! He wants your play broadcast from Paris. Max, you and your troupe are to go there and start rehearsals at once."

Max was confused. "Just like that, Goebbels gives us the green light? He wants the Allies to turn back? He doesn't want the invasion to take place?"

"I said I could handle Goebbels. Get going."

The troupe, with Max as director and Mildred cast in the starring role, began rehearsals right away. A week later the play had its live premier broadcast from Paris's Reichrundfunk station to Allied troops preparing for the invasion of Normandy.

Ulrich Haupt played the part of "Alan," the American mother's G.I. son. A seasoned German actor before the war, and before the firestorm that had melted the left side of his handsome face, Ulrich had, in the thirties, starred in Fritz Lang's great science fiction film, the stunningly futuristic *Metropolis*. Five-foot tall George Heinrich Schnell, an aging Thespian with a penchant for hamming-it-up, played the role of "Alan's father."

Mildred gave the performance of a lifetime. Choking with emotion and with tears streaming down her cheeks, she cradled the microphone. "Please, please, my son, I beg of you... your mother is on her knees begging you... please Alan, do not take part in this invasion–this trap. Please don't, I can't bear it! Don't pierce my heart with the grief of losing you. To challenge those German fortifications above those beaches is to die a horrible death." Her voice began to quiver. "It will be a slaughter, my darling—the worst slaughter in history." Her tone turned ominous. "Alan, my brave, intelligent son, I've had a vision."

Ulrich didn't miss a beat as he continued his portrayal of the son. "A vision Mother? You've had a vision?"

Schnell came in right on cue. "This is your father, Alan. Yes, Mother's had a vision of the invasion. It's destroying her, knowing how you'll be slaughtered if you participate in this folly—you won't stand a chance! Don't listen to the generals, they never die because of their mistakes—it's you innocent young boys who get ripped apart. Don't do it, son, your father begs you—turn back!"

Caught up in her role, Mildred interjected a cry of agony and began to weep. "Alan, listen to Mother. In my vision I see the bodies of your comrades tossing and pitching in the waves, some have had their heads shot off, others have been cut in half. I can hear them, Alan, the bells of Europe's bombed cathedrals tolling your death knell. Please, while there's still time, please my precious son, lay down your arms... lay down your arms, and come home!"

Acting is a form of confession.

– Actress Tallulah Bankhead (1903-1968)

31

Pleased with the play, Goebbels ordered recordings of it broadcast around the clock. Beamed primarily to Allied troops massing in England, "Vision of the Invasion," starring Mildred Gillars, traveled airwaves around the world. Goebbels was especially pleased when, on May 18, 1944, Foreign Ministry Intelligence sources confirmed monitoring of the play by Station KGZQ in Silver Hill, Maryland.

Also delighted with such far reaching exposure, Horst Cleinow phoned Paris. "Congratulations, Fraulein! You are at last famous in America! A stellar performance, my dear, absolutely stellar!"

In the early hours of June 6, 1944–it happened. Short wave radios, manned by members of the French resistance, crackled with the news. The Allies had struck, pounding before dawn the beaches of Normandy with more than five thousand artillery rounds and ten thousand tons of bombs. An estimated one hundred fifty thousand Allied soldiers had crossed the Channel and come out of the mist over the sea. Weighted down with heavy packs and uniforms, their landing craft blown out from under them by German artillery, thousands had drowned. Many more thousands, as they lumbered to the beach, were cut down by accurate and well-directed small-arms fire.

Mildred sat in the Paris studio listening to the BBC, numbed by accounts of the slaughter and horrified by descriptions of the seesawing battle. The mid-morning report astonished her. Landed the night before, north of the Vire, an Allied airborne division had taken and was holding Sainte Mere-Eglise, a town on the main road between Cherbourg and Carentan. The battle seemed to be turning. Shellfire and rockets from the Allied fleet were blasting the shore, destroying minefields, pulverizing bunkers and eliminating many of the German defensive positions.

Despite their gains, it was not going well for the invaders. They had taken only one beach. On the beach further south everything was going wrong. The reporter described as "thousands of corks"—the corpses of Allied soldiers tossing in a sea, red and churning with blood. "It is a scene from hell! Tanks too numerous to count are sinking or being blown out of the water. Wave after wave of young men stream ashore. They don't have a chance. Most gain only a few yards before being shot or—should they step on a mine—blasted to bits!"

The 1 P.M. BBC report made Mildred sit up. Germany's artillery units were beginning to run out of ammunition. As the afternoon wore on, U.S. divisions were able to get off the beach, capture coastal defense positions and get their armor past anti-tank obstacles. At nightfall, Mildred could hear strains of the Marseilles softly playing background to the speaker's choked-up voice. "I can now report to you that the Allies hold the coastal perimeter. May God, in his infinite mercy, bless our Allies and take unto His bosom the thousands upon thousands of brave young men who today, in the cause of freedom, died on our beaches."

Mildred lowered her head. "If only they had listened..."

The darkest pit of the profoundest hell, chaos, night...

– William Wordsworth (1770-1850)

32

Clearly, "Vision of the Invasion" was of no further value to the Third Reich. Goebbels quickly found another use for Max's creative talents. Ordered to go immediately to French towns and villages within earshot of advancing Allied artillery, Max would help to quell the growing hysteria of the German people. His "on-the-scene" reports from the front would detail only German successes.

As ordered, Mildred remained in Paris to broadcast propaganda to Allied soldiers fighting a slow, steady, bloody advance. Knowing that mail censors had been called to fill more critical roles, she felt comfortable writing to her friend Kira Sonntag in Berlin a factual description of post D-Day Paris:

> *On the surface, Kira, you would think it's a city doing business as usual. Underneath you see a cauldron of turmoil, a city of split allegiance–a city in chaos and terror spawned by grizzly prophesy of rape, pillage and plunder.*

The chaos, both in Paris and in Zeesen's radio substation, reached its zenith in the hours following the July 20th assassination attempt on Hitler. News of his death hit the studio like the bomb that had allegedly gone off under Hitler's table.

Learning, later that afternoon, that all radio and telephone communication with Germany had been cut off, Mildred sat stunned. The shift manager raced into the room. "What in God's name is going on? The SS and the Gestapo are being rounded up and taken into custody!"

"What? By *whom?*"

He pulled at his hair. "By whom? Why, by the swine who are taking over—traitors in league with the murderer of our beloved Fuhrer!"

Before she could leave for her apartment, where she intended to celebrate with a large glass of brandy, another messenger entered. "He's alive! They failed! Hitler lives!"

Hours later, radio contact with Germany restored, a military fanfare blasted from studio receivers. A pause and Hitler began to speak in a slow, grave voice, of the attempt on his life that regrettably took the life of a colleague near and dear to him. Then, with great elation, he described his miraculous escape:

> *"I was spared a fate—which held no horror for me—but would have had terrible consequences for the German people! I see in it, a sign from providence that I must, and therefore shall, continue my work. Let no one doubt that the tiny band of traitors who tried to take me from you will be promptly and ruthlessly exterminated!"*

Max arrived back in Paris at month's end looking more dead than alive. Exhausted, his bronchitis turning to pneumonia, he could scarcely breathe. Seemingly endless spells of coughing and choking wracked his body, causing him to bring up wads of bloody phlegm.

Mildred nursed him as best she could, and sat by his bedside through the night, wiping his clammy, sweat-drenched forehead. "Max, you're scaring me. No more work—you're killing yourself."

His eyes burned with fever. "Really, Liebling, one more death—what possible difference?"

She rose and changed from her satin robe to the faded housedress she always wore when venturing out into the neighborhood to shop. He watched as she covered her blonde curls with a scarf, picked up a battered handbag and put on sunglasses. "Where are you going?"

"To get you some medicine."

The moment she set foot on the street she sensed the impending Allied take-over. Frenchmen, their loyalties sharply divided, pushed and shoved, hissing angrily and exchanging insults. A Frenchwoman spotted her. "There she is—the bitch who broadcasts for Hitler! May you rot in hell, you no-good German whore!"

Mildred lowered her head and hurried on. Reaching the druggist's she bolted inside. He looked up and recognized her. She'd come in before to have Max's prescriptions filled. A huge report of Allied artillery shook the shop. "Ah, Fraulein! How is it they say in your country—'*the worm is turning!*'"

She nodded and asked for medicine to bring down Max's fever. Shaking his head, he handed her a bottle of elixir. "This might ease his cough. Five dollars, if you please, Fraulein." He cocked an ear toward the south. "The value of the Deutsh mark is dropping with each boom."

She reached inside her dress, unfastened a small gold pin attached to her brassiere and placed it on his upturned palm. Something about her—perhaps the look of tired resignation in her eyes or the aura of defeat—made him hand it back. "It's beautiful, Fraulein, but you keep it. You will need it far more than I in the days that lie ahead." He handed her the small bottle of elixir. "Put this in your pocket lest they snatch your purse. Tell Herr Koischwitz I have put it on his account."

Max grew worse. Unable to work, he asked Mildred to go to the radio station and try to get through to Zeesen. "Tell Goebbels something's come up... Perhaps in a week..."

It took an entire day of trying before someone at the mother station finally picked up the phone. "Hello, this is Fraulein Gillars. I have an urgent message from Herr Koischwitz for Doctor Goebbels."

"You're out of luck, kid—we're all out of luck—one hundred percent out of luck—finished—washed up—bloody well fucking done for."

She whipped the receiver from her ear and stared at it as though a snake had sprung from it. William "Lord Haw-Haw" Joyce began to blubber. "What shall I do, Mildred? Where shall I go? How could the invasion have succeeded? Everything's turned to shit." How she hated that high, tinny voice with its pathetically fake British accent!

"Please, is there someone else I can speak to?"

"No, no one. The Fuhrer promised I could return to Britain as his deputy. Oh, girl, y'all don't know how I've dreamed of rubbing those blue-noses in the mud for the way they snubbed me!"

"And you, the Earl of Lunacy—a dirt poor Texan passing yourself off as born next door to Windsor Castle. Why the King..."

"He was once going to knight me."

"For making an ass of yourself?"

"I'll have you know, Maggie and I were well received by the Royal Family."

"Bullshit. You and your dumb wife wouldn't be well

received by vultures on the Kalahari Desert. Now quit taking up my time and put me through to Goebbels."

Goebbles ordered Max back to work. Every broadcaster would, by Hitler's expressed order, commence immediately to broadcast reports written to minimize the attempt on his life, and to warn those foolhardy enough to be contemplating another such attack.

The streets of Paris had become rivers of pushing, desperate pedestrians who, in the blink of an eye might coalesce into an angry, jeering mob. "You're not going out there Max, not in your condition. If they want you back in the studio broadcasting their nonsense, they'll have to send a car.

She had her way. Arriving at the Paris station by car, they were met by Werner Plack, wine merchant to the stars during his former life in California. He and Mildred had been at each other's throats ever since their first meeting at Zeesen. "Fraulein! Still seducing G.I.'s?"

"Still hustling Moselle?"

Max stepped between them. "Werner–you must have fabricated quite an excuse to be permitted to leave Berlin! We hear the city is reeling. I still can't believe it–the plotters nearly succeeded!"

Plack straightened. "I don't fabricate excuses–it was imperative I come to Paris. As you know, Doctor Goebbels has great faith in me. He has charged me with reinforcing trust in Hitler's ultimate victory."

Mildred's hand went to her mouth to stifle a laugh. Angered by her impudence, Werner went toe-to-toe with her. "Fraulein Gillars, for your information–I am here to pump-up those Paris-based broadcasters whom Doctor Goebbels considers ineffective and less than enthusiastic. He suggests I start with you and Herr Koischwitz."

Max slumped down onto a chair. "Really, Werner, you're being ridiculous."

"Here," Plack said, handing Max a sheaf of papers. "Dr. Goebbels himself has authored these. You are, without delay, to read his every word over the air."

Max took to the microphone. In a bronchitis-weakened voice he read Goebbels' claim of "the world's rising sympathy for Germany." Then, after a fit of coughing, he turned the page and spewed into the microphone his boss's take on "Germany's wonderful new flying bomb." The treatise ended with Goebbels' prophesy of the ultimate doom awaiting Eisenhower's forces:

> *"The advancing Allied soldiers are like mindless insects being drawn into the Wehrmacht's web. They will be cut to ribbons, pulverized... devoured."*

That night, returning to their Paris flat, Max attempted to give Mildred the one possession he valued above all—his gold pocket watch. A family heirloom, the timepiece had passed from father to son for generations.

"No, Max," she said, clenching her fists, resisting his efforts to pry them open. "It should go to your..."

"To my son?" He fought back tears. "My son is dead—dead before he had a chance to live."

"But surely then, to your..."

"Daughters? They're gone too. I didn't tell you..."

"You've had news of them?"

His shoulders sagged. "Gone—all three of them." She threw her arms around him. "Oh Max, I'm so, so sorry."

He pulled back, his face pale, his eyes tired, the pocket watch in his outstretched hand. "Please, now that you know—take this. It's time, Liebling. Time to put my affairs in order."

His expression caused her to panic. "There's something you're not telling me. What is it?"

"Liebling, please..."

"You're scaring me, damn it. I don't want your watch. You keep it and stay alive, do you hear me? Christ, Max, I love you. I'll always love you."

He nodded. "And I you—longer than always. Liebling, why fret? Nothing can ever separate us—neither distance, nor time." He looked away and sighed, "...nor death."

She clasped his shoulders and made him look at her. "Death? We're not talking *death* here, are we Max? Are we?"

He wrenched free of her grasp and again held out the watch. "I command you to take it. Keep it as you keep my heart. Please, Liebling, I will have it no other way."

She extended her palm.

"Thank you."

"It's beautiful." Then, staring down and seeing in the fine gold the intricately carved coat of arms, she began to weep.

"Liebling, I have to be on the next train back to Berlin."

She gaped at him. "So *that's* what this is all about! No, Max, you're *not* going—not without me!"

"I can't take you with me."

"Why not?"

"It's not possible. Werner has given me his word. He will get you out of Paris in a few days and personally escort you back to Berlin."

"But..." A touch of his finger to her lips silenced her. Dazed, she felt his kisses on her forehead, cheeks and eyelids. There came a knock at the door.

Werner Plack entered and gave Max a solemn nod. "The car is waiting. We must hurry."

Mildred reached for a sweater. "I'm going too."

"No, Liebling. I told you, it is not possible."

Plack walked to the door. "I'll be outside. You have less than two minutes."

Her mind churned a course of action. Somehow she'd get into that car and be driven to the station. At the last minute, she'd charge up the steps. She'd find Max and cling to him so tightly that he would be forced to take her along.

As though he could read her thoughts, Max smiled and took her into his arms. "I want us to say good-bye here, Liebling—here where we are not jostled by the desperate crowd. I want to remember you standing here. Please, let me go with a smile—with the sound of my name on your lips."

"Max..."

There is, however, this consolation to the most way-worn traveler, upon the dustiest road, that the path his feet describe is so perfectly symbolical of human life.

– Henry David Thoreau (1817-1862)

33

Werner Plack had no intention of keeping his word. "Get this, you're *not* going anywhere!" His index finger poked her shoulder. "As Herr Koischwitz is no longer here to keep an eye on you, you will be closely watched. And don't get any ideas about running after him. You will stay here in Paris until terminated." He handed her the day's script. "Now turn on your microphone and start reading."

> *"Good evening, my sweet, sweet fighting men. This is your dear friend Midge, here to tell you that they're lying to you. Don't believe that baloney your officers are spewing. Take it from me—you know I have your best interests at heart. It's a lie that the Allies are making inroads into France. The truth is just the opposite. The Wehrmacht has repulsed your tired, half-dead comrades. Did you hear me? Hitler's Wehrmacht has successfully repulsed the aggression of all enemy forces in France."*

Ironically, the Allies were—at that very moment—using wavelengths formerly under German control to broadcast the same type of material—material meant to demoralize those still hanging on in the Vaterland. Originating in England, BBC-authored German language programs entitled, "Soldatensender Eins" and "Soldatensender Calais," gave gruesome accounts of Wehrmacht casualties and assurances that Allied forces would, within weeks, be knocking on Hitler's door.

Paris entered August of 1944 with one ear cocked toward the distant thuds of a slowly advancing American Army. Throughout those long days and nights, Mildred kept her ears pressed to the Rundfunk, hoping to hear Max's broadcasts. But their were none. Hadn't Max said he would be on the air non-stop to put Goebbels' spin on the latest developments and to assuage the fast-spreading angst of disillusioned Germans?

"Where is he?" she demanded of Plack.

"You don't like the current programming?" he replied, referring to the station's perpetual airing of old, scratchy recordings of both the Berlin Symphony and Hitler's speeches. "Don't you find it stimulating?"

That evening, as she was about to turn off the radio, the music stopped. Fred Kaltenbach came on the air. Horrified, she listened to his chilling description of the round up and torture of those immediately involved in the July 20th plot to assassinate Hitler. Kaltenbach spared no adjectives in detailing the torture: finger-screws, spiked leggings, branding irons and the mediaeval rack.

Overhearing a conversation between Plack and the station manager, she learned just how bad things were back at the mother station. Sixty percent of Zeesen's German staff had been mobilized; the men dispatched to the front, the women to ammunition factories or hospitals. Goebbels, they said, was growing more unstable, taking to the airwaves himself with frantic pleas for "total war and general mobilization."

On a Wednesday riddled with cloud bursts, Werner Plack skipped out of Paris alone. Left to fend for herself in a city about to be shelled by American artillery, Mildred stayed locked in her flat. No one came to force her back to work. No one phoned. No one knocked at her door. To hold her terror at bay as howitzers thundered ever closer, she wrote countless letters to Max. Meanwhile, Paris—like a woman about to be raped—held her breath.

At mid-month, the Allies staged more amphibious landings on French beaches between Nice and Marseilles. Prompted by Allied successes to switch sides, Mildred's landlady turned on her. "Now you'll get it, Mata Hari!" she shouted through the door. "You'll see! The Americans will be here any minute. They're animals—*all of them*—they have the same appetites their fathers had in the last war!"

Somehow, Mildred had to get back to Berlin. It would be a brutal, hot journey. For weeks, transportation corridors had bulged with Germans fleeing France for the chaos of the Vaterland and with French collaborators trying to escape to anywhere. Only the most desperate women traveled alone—and did so at great risk of being attacked, violated... or worse.

She'd travel light—a dress, a sweater—sensible shoes. A pocket sewn into her brassiere would hold her money. She'd wear three pairs of panties, layered one over the other. A pocket sewn in each pair should accomodate a washcloth, a supply of tightly wadded toilet paper and perhaps three sanitary napkins. Into a pocket sewn into her garter belt, she'd put a card imprinted with Edna Mae's address in Ohio. The backside of the card would bear the message: "To the finder of my corpse: Please, at war's end, notify person listed over."

Max's pocketwatch lay on Mildred's dresser, its engraved gold cover glistening in a beam of light seeping into the flat through a hole in the roof. She picked it up, touched it to her cheek and kissed it. No way would it fall into a thief's hands. She put on the dress best suited for the journey—her faded housedress. Once more she picked up her needle. Taking the utmost care to make it secure and undetectable, she stitched the beloved timepiece into the dress's hem.

Before dawn, looking like a common, war-weary peasant, she set off for the train station. From her arm hung a canvas bag containing dry salami, a wedge of cheese, crackers, raisins, nuts and two bottles of water. The streets were already crowded and, when at last she reached it, the station mobbed.

Everywhere she looked, wild-eyed people shoved and cursed, all frantic to board a train leaving Paris, leaving the onslaught of the American Army. Overwhelming ticket agents, angry would-be travelers crowded the counter, their fists clinching and thrusting forward Deutsche marks, French francs and all manner of other currencies.

Out-pushing and out-maneuvering those around her, she at last made it to the counter. "Please, a ticket to Berlin. I'll pay double... triple."

"Impossible! The train to Berlin is full... overloaded."

"I don't need a seat—I can stand. Please, I can pay well...." A flick of her eye drew his attention to her clenched fist. It's finger's opened then closed quickly, just long enough to flash the money, just long enough for him to glimpse, sandwiched in the wad of German marks, several U.S. tens and twenties.

The agent opened his drawer, pulled out a ticket and slipped it into his pocket. He turned to a fellow agent. "Henri, take over for me. I have a personal emergency. I'll be right back." Then, to Mildred: "Follow me."

The surreptitious exchange of U.S. currency for the ticket to Berlin took place behind a kiosk. Ticket in hand, she raced for the gate. "Mind you, miss—the ticket does not guarantee you'll get aboard!"

She flew through the gates and ran with a pack until she saw the train begin to move. She charged ahead, determined to grasp onto the handrail leading up the last car's crowded steps. A sharp elbow to her ribs knocked her off balance. Her knee hit the platform first, then her right shoulder. The train snorted a puff of black smoke and, picking up speed, charged down the track away from her and into the arch made brilliant by the morning's sun.

In tears, she returned to the agent. "This ticket is worthless."

"I warned you."

"Please, I must get to Berlin. When is the next train?"

"To Berlin?" He shrugged his shoulders.

"To *anywhere*, damn it!"

A sigh and he scanned the schedule. "The train to Holland is supposed to leave at ten. Then again, it may not leave at all. But it will do you no good—already it is sold out three times what it can hold."

Embarrassed at teasingly being called "Sir Galahad" by the older, rougher men with whom he shared the train's steps, the German boy-soldier blushed the color of the fresh blood seeping through his bandaged arm. He'd done nothing more than reach down and pull her up. He could feel the fullness of her breasts now as, with the train's rocking, their bodies swayed together as one. He looked down upon her babushka and smiled. It felt good. Sixteen and fresh from participation in the front's slaughter, he was still capable of kindness.

She wormed her way into the rear passenger car. An old Belgian with a patch over his eye pushed forward to make room. When a sign announcing the next small village flew past he cried out, "Thank God! No harm will come to us now! We are almost to..." A sudden roar and the sound of bullets ripping into the train's roof silenced him. He shook his fist at them, the American fighter planes swooping down from the sky like an angry swarm of hornets.

They made pass after pass, strafing the train and laying waste to tracks both fore and aft. Like a trapped and helpless lamb, the train bleated its whistle and screeched its brakes. Mildred lost her footing. Welded to those packing the aisle, she flew forward. A hard list to the right and the train derailed. She pitched onto her side. Her head hit the roof.

Her vision dimming, she had the sensation of being a drop of water whirled in a bucket. Only slowly did she stop hearing it—the endless roll of thunder, the snapping of metal, the hissing of steam, the shattering of glass, the splintering of wood and, last to fade... the screams.

A Belgian farmer's rough hands on her skin brought her around. "I'll have you untangled here in a moment." She rubbed her eyes and looked around. A dozen or so bloody, limping men were being loaded onto a hay wagon. A woman, her legs grotesquely twisted from her torso, lay screaming at an advancing line of small, crackling straw-fed fires.

Ignoring the throbbing in her head, Mildred wriggled free of the farmer's grasp. "See to her. My injuries are slight—I can fend for myself."

He took a large, dirty-looking handkerchief from his pocket. "Very well, miss. But at least take this to stem the bleeding of that gash on your leg."

"How far to the next village?"

"An hour by wagon... two on foot."

Just before midnight, having hid until she could follow the tracks under cover of night, she limped into the small village. She knocked on the door of the first house she came to. Inside, a candle flickered to life. The door cracked open. "It is midnight, what do you want?" Hearing a moan, he threw open the door and, pulling his bathrobe around him, gaped at her. "You need help?" She collapsed sobbing into his arms.

A short, slight bespetacled man with a friar's fringe of hair, he dragged her inside. A glance back outside to make sure no one was about and he quickly closed the door. He helped her to a seat on the couch then went to set on the tea kettle. "You can't stay here of course," he said from the kitchen, "a few hours at the most. I am Herr Franzen, village schoolmaster. As you know, people tend to gossip..."

For a moment she thought she was hallucinating—hearing Max as she'd heard him on that first night when, under the pretense of tutoring her, he'd first visited her apartment. "Certainly, I understand," she'd replied, "...gossips."

The schoolmaster laid out a meager repast of toast and tea. "Thank you," she said, "you are most kind."

He squinted at her. "I believe I detect an accent... you're American?"

Her mind raced. Should she say *yes*, he could do one of two things: turn her in or risk execution for harboring her. "What I am doesn't matter. I have to get to Berlin. It's urgent!"

He returned to the kitchen and, as she cleaned and bandaged the gash on her leg, filled a sack with a bottle of water, several slices of dried salami and a jar of apple juice. "Here," he said, holding out the sack to her. "But I must tell you that Hitler's Ministry of Transportation had decreed all trains off limits to civilians. Henceforth all trains will be used exclusively for transporting soldiers and critical supplies. In short, my dear, getting to Berlin is impossible."

Carrying the sack, she left the schoolmaster's house at dawn. By sun up she came to the road he'd described that funneled army tanks and vehicles back to Germany. She took a deep breath, positioned herself by the side of the highway to thumb a ride and waited.

At mid-morning, from far down the road, came the first of a long convoy of soldier-loaded trucks. One by one they passed her, as passing a cow in a field. The soldiers stared through her. Not a single catcall or whistle. Not one licked his lips, beckoned to her or scratched his crotch. The day wore on. Tanks and cars loaded with officers passed. Her arm grew numb.

If flagging wouldn't stop them she'd try something else. She ventured into the middle of the road and stood there, her arms spread wide. A truck squealed to a stop. Loaded with grim-faced boy-soldiers, it was driven by a disheveled German officer who, irritated at being blocked, honked incessantly. "Bitch! Get out of the way!"

"I must get to Berlin. Please, I beg of you, give me a lift. You're going back to Germany, aren't you?"

His eyes shone with madness. "Me? I'm going to hell! We're *all* going to hell!" Laughing like a loon, he shoved the truck into gear and, forcing Mildred to jump aside, sped off.

The next vehicle, a camoflaged sedan, stopped. "Colonel Fritz Nieman, at your service, Madam. How can I help you?"

Recognizing him as an officer she'd danced with at an embassy party, she rubbed her eyes as if hallucinating. "Colonel Nieman! Thank God! I have to get to Berlin. It's urgent!"

"Do I know you?"

Gambling, she identified herself.

"Ah yes, you broadcast for Doctor Goebbels. I am a fan of yours—an avid fan. Certainly, I'll give you a lift. Please, step in. Unfortunately, I'm going no further than Maastricht to take over for a colonel who has, unfortunately, gone mad."

Maastricht's train station throbbed with stranded travelers. Along one wall of the waiting room, queued in long lines leading to a dozen phone booths, stood an assortment of civilians and bedraggled soldiers. Some waited patiently, others pushed and snarled at those attempting to break into the line.

Frantic to get in touch with Max, Mildred took her place at the end of a line and patiently inched forward. In time she got to a phone and dialed Zeesen. All circuits were busy. Many tries later she got through... to Inge Doman.

"Inge? This is Mildred... Gillars. I have to get a message to Max." There was a long, cold silence. "Inge?"

"What you ask is impossible. Professor Koischwitz is dead... dead by his own hand."

Let us embrace, and from this very moment
vow an eternal misery together.

– Thomas Otway (1652-1685)
(The Orphan)

34

The news of Max's death struck her like a blow from a giant's club. A scream froze in her throat. Reeling, her vision dimming, she sank to the floor of the booth. Fists pounded on the glass. A soldier forced the door in against her body. He grabbed her, pulled her out and deposited her on the floor. With a grunt he then stepped over her to use the phone.

"Get up, you crazy woman!" someone growled. "You're blocking the way."

"Let her be! Shame!" The priest stood over her, his long, mud-streaked cassock touching her knee, his eyes peering down through bent wire glasses.

Her hand grabbed for his ankle. "Please! I have to get to Max! I have to bury him... to kiss him good-bye!"

The cleric bent down and, gently freeing his foot, whispered, "Pray to Saint Christopher."

"No, help me!"

He looked around cautiously. "I must be on my way. God be with you."

The station's lavatory attendant, a stocky peasant woman with a missing front tooth, cackled at the sight of Mildred pleading with yet another conductor. When Mildred gave up and walked toward the toilet, the woman followed behind giving advice. "Trainmen like a little gift–a bit of chocolate, a packet of coffee. My brother, Yuri, sells such things."

Alone and minus the exorbitantly priced, black-market coffee she'd paid for with money freed from the hem of her dress, Mildred sat locked in the boxcar of a supply train headed for Berlin. It moved at a snail's pace then switched onto a siding and stopped for hours. The only sound: the thunder of passing trains she envisioned loaded with soldiers being rushed by frantic generals from one front to another.

Stopped again she knew not where, during the hottest hours of the third day, the boxcar became an oven. Her head throbbing, her water bottle empty, she chewed on her tongue for saliva. A thin ray of light shown through the sliding door's junction with the floor. She lay with her nose close to the slit.

At first she did not hear it–the sound of gravel crunching under boots. She cocked an ear. Footsteps–coming closer, closer... closer. They stopped. A loud bang reverberated through her cell. The butt of a rifle stricking the door? It came once more, followed by the metallic yawn of a latch opening its jaws. The huge door rolled open, pulling a curtain of blinding sunlight.

The huge door, as it rolled open, pulled a curtain of blinding sunlight. "What's this? What's this?" sputtered a male voice.

"I don't know! It's... a woman!" retorted another.

Unable to see her captors, she lay tensed, expecting to be probed by the barrel of a rifle, seized by the hair and yanked from the boxcar. Several seconds passed. She blinked and rubbed her eyes. A black image, contoured by the sun's glare, separated into two silhouettes that slowly took on features. They stood gawking at her—two old men, armed only with flashlights. She raised her head. "I can't move... my legs..." she lied.

"Bitte, Fraulein, hang on, we will go for help!" They started for a building at the far end of the yard.

"Where am I?" she called out.

The older of the two stopped for a moment to reply. "Why, you're in Berlin—the railroad yard of Berlin."

"My gawd!" Robert Best exclaimed, recognizing the grimy face of the woman who'd fallen against his apartment's door. "You look like the Angel of Death!"

"Water! Please, I need water!"

He pulled her inside, laid her on the couch and brought her a glassful. "Don't gulp. There, that's good, take very small sips. Come on, a little more—take your time."

Her eyes filled with fear. "Am I too late? Oh God, I can't be too late..."

"Too late for what?"

"To bury Max."

Best shook his head. "You're not too late. If anything, you're too early. He isn't dead, Mildred... not yet."

Dismissing his urging that she need more rest, she insisted he take her to Spandau Hospital. Once there, she waved him off to Zeesen for his evening broadcast. She entered the hospital alone, identified herself to the clerk as "Frau Koischwitz" and demanded to see her husband.

"As you must know," the doctor said before allowing her to enter the cubicle, "Herr Koischwitz has for years suffered tuberculosis and a bad heart. Unfortunately, he will not survive this pneumonia. You have but a short time to bid him farewell."

Max lay sleeping on a narrow cot, his face partially covered with an oxygen mask. His eyes, slits sunken in dark discs, were slightly open. His hair limp and soaked with perspiration. Mildred bent over him. With a feeble wave of his hand he motioned for her to remove the oxygen mask. She started to object. His eyes insisted.

"Thank you," he whispered.

His fever burned her lips as she kissed his forehead. She took his hand. "Oh, Max, *please* don't leave me."

"Liebling... I... have... no choice." His eyes, faded to pale blue from years of ill health, welled with tears. She watched them overflow, course down his cheeks and disappear into thick, gray whisker stubble.

She pulled up a chair and sat beside him. As he dozed and the night tumbled toward its darkest depth, her fingers picked at the hem of her dress to free the gold timepiece.

His breathing grew more labored. His face and arms twitched. Air raid sirens wailed in the distance. The sound of a tank navigating the street below caused him to stir. "Lieb..."

"Oh, Max. Whatever became of us?"

He opened his eyes and gazed at her. Then, managing a sad smile, he gave her hand a slight squeeze. "I'll... come... for you... I'll..."

Her arms flew open and gathered him to her. "No—*please*, take me with you..."

His heart stopped just before dawn. Her hand continued to hold his. After a few moments she took the gold timepiece he'd entrusted to her, pressed it to her lips and then to his. The anointing complete, she felt his spirit take leave.

And after all, what is a lie?
'Tis but the truth in masquerade.

– Lord Byron (1788-1824)

35

Best didn't mind Mildred staying on in his apartment and sleeping on the spare cot. And he wanted no credit for what he'd gone through to get the casket. With the help of a few friends they buried Max in a blackened apple orchard. He'd held her up throughout the reading of the twenty-third psalm and carried her all the way back to his apartment after she'd collapsed over the grave. But two weeks had passed–two weeks of the deepest mourning he'd ever seen. She had to snap out of it.

"No amount of grieving will bring him back."

The vehemence of her reply startled him. "*Back*? Back to the rubble of his beloved Germany? Back to being a slave at Zeesen? Back to America to face his indictment?"

He took her hand. "Speaking of work at Zeesen, it's stacking up. When ya' coming back?"

"Never!"

"They'll hunt you down."

"Let 'um."

. . .

A squeak came from under Kira Sonntag as she sat down on a corner of the mattress. "It's about time, sleepy head!" she said as Mildred's eyes slowly opened. "You've slept for days."

Mildred squinted up at her "Kira?"

"Of course–Kira Sonntag–you've forgotten your old friend from Berlitz? Some guest you are! I open my door to your knock and, without a word, you walk in, curl up on my sofa and go to sleep. Anyway, I'm glad you're here. You must be starved! I'll heat some soup then you can tell me what's going on."

A description of Max's death concluded Mildred's tale. "He's free at last, thank God. Ironic, isn't it? All these years I've spewed Nazi propaganda over the air knowing they'd kill him if I refused–and he dies of pneumonia."

"But wouldn't they also have killed you–if you'd refused?"

"Kira, I'm not going back. With God as my witness, I'll never broadcast another word."

Kira went to the window and looked out. "My mother–she also left us this month. Melted... melted to nothing in a firestorm..."

"No..."

Kira turned from the window. "It's for the best. Her mind had slipped..."

"I'm so sorry."

Kira went to the bedroom. "I have an idea." She returned with a purse. "Here! Take this–it contains Mother's identity and food cards."

"But why on earth..."

"It's simple! *You* become my mother!"

"What?"

"The Ministry of Records has been bombed and burned a dozen times."

"Yes, but..."

"I never reported Mother missing."
"What if I'm caught? You'd be..."
"Trust me, no one will check."

Mildred liked to think it was her theatrical training, and not middle age, that allowed her to pass for a woman twenty years her senior. Olga's matronly dresses fit her with room to spare as did the long, granny-style cotton stockings. She managed to walk in the deceased's low-heeled oxfords only by padding them with wads of newspaper. The heavy-duty hairnet worked well to hide the fugitive's graying blonde curls.

Mildred had always been too vain to wear glasses. She had but to put on Olga's horn-rimmed spectacles, while on an errand for Kira to buy bread, to see what she'd been missing. Street signs suddenly became legible, objects emerged from the fuzzy distance and flags flying over the Reichstag bore distinct, sharp-angled swastikas.

Hugging Olga's shabby black purse, she took a place at the end of the long queue. The stench of putrefying flesh hung in the air. The man ahead of her spoke fearfully of Germany's latest reversals: the liberation of Paris, the fall of Bucharest to the Russians and the routing of Nazi troops from Brussels.

A hausfrau countered the doomsayer. "Wait until we drop the Fuhrer's new bomb on America! You'll see–the war will end in one day! Listen to our Fuhrer, trust him!"

Angry mutterings against Hitler swept along the queue. Most had heard the Fuhrer's radio address following last July's attempt on his life. He had assured the world that the "tiny band of traitors" responsible would be rounded up and exterminated. The people in this line, as well as people throughout Germany, were dumbfounded by the rounding up and extermination that followed. Every day the number executed for taking part in the plot grew. Now, halfway through October, the number had swollen past ten thousand. Just to make sure they got them all, Gestapo were executing not only suspected plotters but their parents, spouses, children and, in many cases, aunts, uncles and even cousins.

A loaf of bread tucked into her purse, Mildred hurried home to check out a rumor. Switching on the BBC she learned the truth: Hitler's favorite general, Field Marshall Rommel, had committed suicide rather than face execution for taking part in the July 20th plot. She found Kira sitting in the kitchen, listening to Robert Best on Station ZDZ. Revealing himself a master of deception, Best described Rommel's "brave death at the hands of the enemy." Days later Hitler, intent on convincing the world of Rommel's allegiance, gave him a state funeral.

Mildred heard from Robert Best again when he surprised her with a visit. How he'd found her, she couldn't figure out—but he had. "Just thought I'd drop in to tell you I'm running for President of the United States."

"Don't be silly."

Clowning, he spun his Stetson and faked a southern accent. "Ah'll announce, duh-ring my broadcast to America, mah candidacy for both the United States Congress and for the presidency. Then ah'll make speeches and ask listeners to write-in mah name on their ballots."

Mildred laughed. "Oh, sure."

He gave his Stetson another spin. "Go ahead, laugh, Scarlet. It's Goebbels' brainstorm, not mine." He held up his hand as to take an oath. "Honest to God, Goebbels thought this up—he even wrote my campaign slogan: 'A vote for Robert Best is a vote to save the American people from Kikes.'"

"I don't believe it!"

"I swear it on my mother's grave. He's convinced his brilliant scheme can actually throw a wrench into the U.S. electoral system."

The wail of air-raid sirens cut the visit short. Determined to get home, Robert took off. Mildred and Kira would, as usual, sit out the raid in the cellar of the building next door. "You go ahead," Kira said, "I have to use the toilet first. Go on, I'll be right down."

Mildred barely made it to the cellar before the biggest explosion she'd ever felt rocked the earth. Boards, plaster, bricks and mortar rained down. All lights went out. Smelling gas, someone moved through the suffocating dust to snuff a candle. Others felt their way toward the exit only to find it sealed off by tons of rubble. A woman screamed hysterically then fell silent. Sobs. The whimpers of children. A mother's hushing.

It took until late the next afternoon for Mildred and her shelter-mates to be rescued. As the outside world came into focus, her worst fear was confirmed. In place of Kira's apartment building stood a blackened skeleton rising from a smoldering mound. Like mother, like daughter—Kira's body would never be found.

Homeless and continuing to masquerade as Olga Sonntag, Mildred wandered about Berlin as October drew to a chilly close. Some nights she managed to sleep in quarters abandoned by fleeing Berliners, other nights she shivered under a bridge or in the ruins.

Everywhere, war-worn Berliners spoke of V-2 rocket attacks against Great Britain and wondered at reports that Roosevelt had been elected for a fourth term. Contradicting German and Allied propaganda abounded. What was this *Battle of the Bulge?* Who was winning it? Hearing of Russia's unchecked advance, Berliners lost their last remnant of hope.

The snowstorm that ushered in 1945 brought Mildred pneumonia. Stabbing chest pains brought her to the brink of jumping in front of a train. Or would it be easier to burrow into a snow bank and fall asleep? And why not? She'd kept her promise to Max–she'd let him be the first to leave this dark, cooling star. But something, either conscience or instinct, caused her to trudge instead toward Robert Best's flat.

Poor Robert. Half-crazed by the chaos engulfing Zeesen, he talked constantly of his fellow-workers and superiors. "That goddamn von Richter!" he exclaimed, feeding her a bowl of soup. "He lectures us on 'staying with the ship' while he hides out in Fusl with his wife and kids! Jesus, Mildred, die grosse Entsheidung (the great climax) is at hand–the Allies are about to crush us!"

"Robert..."

"Ya' I know... get some rest."

On the eve of the Yalta Conference, the Allies resumed massive air strikes against Germany's civilian population. The misery of Berliners grew more staggering. All services ceased. Utilities broke down. More lines formed–long, snaking lines in which people stood for hours to pump their allotted two pails of water. The city reeked with sewage spewed from broken lines. Toilets hadn't flushed for weeks. Showers and baths were impossible to come by. It turned bitterly cold. During the long, terror-filled nights entire families, having supped solely on a few potatoes, hovered for warmth around candles stuck in bottles.

Food cards were honored only at the shop of registry of the cardholder. As soon as Mildred felt well enough to venture out of Robert's flat, she again disguised herself as Olga Sonntag and returned to the shop of Olga's registry. She had no trouble with the disguise, for all German women had come to look alike–cheeks sunken from malnutrition, hair no longer colored or styled, faces minus make-up and skin smudged with the ever-swirling soot. Using Robert's money, she bought the only food available—potatoes. The vendor sold her three—each bruised, turning green and starting to sprout.

As she walked back to the apartment, a badly burned child, a girl of nine or ten, ran up to her. "Mutte!" Her hair and eyebrows were singed. Fresh, oozing blisters covered the eager face. "Mutte!"

Afraid to touch her, Mildred screamed for help. An old man appeared out of nowhere. "Quickly, we must get your child to the hospital! Here, let me help you!"

Mildred was wearing Robert's coat. She took it off and spread it on the sidewalk. The old man gently lifted the child and lay her atop the coat. Then, working fast, he covered her with snow.

Using the coat as a sling, they carried the girl to nearby Arminius hospital. A nurse glanced at the blackened skin. "Sorry, Mother—your little girl will not make it."

"She is not my child."

"Mutte!" the little girl cried out, her eyes alive with pain. "Mutte!"

Mildred grabbed the nurse's hand. "Give her something!"

"What? We are out of everything—morphine, salves, bandages." She pried her hand free. "We are desperately shorthanded. If you like, you may comfort the child, perhaps ease her passing."

The old man seized a bedpan and hurried outside. He returned moments later, the bedpan heaped with snow. "This will numb the pain." He gently placed the snow over the child's torso. "Spread it over her arms and legs—I'll get more."

Just before midnight the child died. The old man made a sign of the cross on her forehead, kissed her cheek and, fighting back tears, left.

When the nurse returned, she found Mildred still sitting there, holding the dead child's hand. "We could use your help," she said, touching Mildred's shoulder. "Have you any nursing experience?"

"Nothing more than bandaging burns and wounds."

"You won't be required to perform brain surgery," the nurse replied and, for the first time, smiled. "Go to the office and sign up to be a nurse's aide. The pay is almost nothing but the hospital provides meals–such as they are. Please, we are in dire need of help."

The next day, her blonde curls contained by a white babushka, Mildred reported for work as "Olga Sonntag, Nurse Aide Class Two."

She'd left Robert's apartment to live in the attic of a partially destroyed house near the hospital. He visited her there. She was distraught. "They brought two American airmen to the hospital today. Their plane was shot down over Potsdam."

Robert removed his Stetson. "What kind of shape were they in?"

"Mangled–horrible."

"I don't suppose you were allowed to speak to them."

"They were put in the cellar ward, with the worst cases."

He listened. She told him how her chance to speak to the wounded Americans had come with the day's first air-raid warning. When all ambulatory patients, doctors and nurses fled to the shelter of a nearby railway tunnel, she'd slipped into the hospital cellar. The lieutenant from Dallas had a foot blown off. He'd held her hand as he died. The other one, a boy from Milwaukee, suffered terrible burns. They talked until he, too, died. She'd dropped her guard and told him who she was. He'd heard her broadcasts.

Robert squirmed. "So?"

"Do you know what he said?"

"What?"

"He said I was an idiot to have worked for Hitler. His last words were: 'It's okay, lady. Have a safe trip home!'"

Robert had to get back to work. "Dear heart, I just stopped by to tell you I'm thinking of jumping the good ship Zeesen and letting our die-hard colleagues go down in flames."

"A mixed metaphor if I ever heard one. Does Kaltenbach know?"

"Ah, yes... Kaltenbach dreams of dying at the microphone while delivering a brilliant broadcast!"

"And the others? Chandler? Delaney? Day? They're still on the air?"

He shook his head. "'Recordings mostly. Hell, they even play recordings of you and Max..." He bit his lip. "Sorry..."

"Don't be."

"We've sure managed to screw up, huh, old girl? Maybe we shoulda'..."

"I'm a great believer in destiny, Mr. Best."

"You still think that's what Max was–your *destiny*?"

A sad smile crossed her face.

"How the hell can you think that and still believe in a merciful God?"

"Robert..."

"Gotta' run. See ya' soon, sweetheart! Save me a dance!"

In its last days as capitol of the Third Reich, Berlin writhed and bellowed like a mutilated beast. It's heart lay in ashes. Tens of thousands of tons of Allied bombs had reduced its great churches, museums, art galleries, theaters, stores, office buildings and treasured opera house to smoldering heaps. Carpets of glass littered streets. Gone were water and sewage systems. Electricity cut off, a million candles flickered in the night before the final darkness.

Mildred sat by her window watching bombs scream down and flak bark at the night sky. She heard a lone accordionist playing *The Blue Danube Waltz*. Midway through the second stanza an explosion rocked the building. The accordion gave a sudden wheeze as though shot through its bellows and, in mid-stanza, fell silent.

Promoted on April 1st to Nurse Assistant First Class, she became, due to the dire shortage of nurses and doctors, sole caregiver for an entire ward filled with burn victims. There was little she could do for them except give them sips of water and whisper encouragement to those who begged to die.

One morning, as she wiped the face of a dying young soldier whose burns bubbled with gangrene, a German officer swaggered into the ward. "Phew!" he said to her, his nostrils flaring, "It stinks in here! Open the windows!"

"They *are* open."

"Private Hollenbeck? I have come to decorate Private Hollenbeck!" Led by Mildred to the boy's bedside, the officer scowled. "Here," he said, holding out to her a quarter-sized swastika, "pin this on his sleeve while I recite the Proclamation of Bravery."

Like a mother bear protecting her cub, Mildred's hand shot out and swiped the swastika from the officer's palm onto the floor. "Shove it up Hitler's ass!"

The startled officer did an about face and marched out of the room. Minutes later the director of nurses entered. "Frau Sonntag, you've lost your mind? Such insolence to a German officer–it's a wonder he didn't draw his revolver and shoot you between the eyes! You're lucky that all he has demanded is that we get rid of you. You're employment here is terminated. Please, leave at once."

Deciding to risk a visit to Robert Best's apartment, Mildred descended the steps from her attic room and walked out into the smoke-hazed sunlight. As she started down the street she caught the scent of narcissus. Further on a crocus pushed its head up through a fallen fence. A detour took her past a plundered cottage in whose shell-pocked yard bloomed a bed of lilies. She picked one. It would be Robert's birthday present.

Forced by heat to walk down the center of a street lined with buildings still ablaze from the last bombing, she merged with a fleeing throng. Gaunt-faced women pushed past her, their backs straining to pull wagons stacked high with all manner of possessions. A young boy pushed a pram sagging under the weight of his pregnant mother. Children, their backs stooped under strapped-on bundles, bedrolls, pots—and in some cases, chairs and lamps—struggled to keep up. An old man, a garden hose wrapped around his neck, his wheelbarrow balancing a giant, empty birdcage, blew a whistle to pass.

As she drew nearer the city's escape portal, the stream of fleeing Berliners widened. Overhead, hysterical Nazi rhetoric poured from pole-mounted speakers. "Long live our Fuhrer! The war is not lost! Vaterland uber alles! Do not flee! Stand and defend to the death the land of your ancestors!"

Sensing a pain in her side after she'd walked nearly a mile, she paused to rest. Two city workers argued nearby. "I tell you, it *is* the end! At this very minute, the Russians are encircling Vienna!"

"Bullshit!"

"No bullshit! They're raping every woman in sight—from little girls to old grandmothers! The same they'll do to every woman in Germany!"

The way to Robert's apartment looked different. Guessing, she walked southwesterly. A hard right at Liepziger Platz to Potsdammer Strasse, and then left. Five blocks south after Lutzow Strasse and she should be there.

Liepsiger Platz had always been surrounded by upper-class homes. Passing them now, she wondered at fate's tendency to favor the rich. All of these homes were badly damaged but, unlike most homes in poorer sections, they were still standing. Passing a particularly elegant home, albeit one with a caved in roof, she marveled at several perfectly intact stained glass windows.

A block further a dog's sudden, fierce barking stopped her in her tracks. Without seeing him, she knew what kind of a dog he was. With the city starving, only soldiers had dogs—vicious, snarling search dogs used for flushing out deserters.

Envisioning his sharp fangs, her eyes darted to both sides of the street. Suddenly—with a loud, spitting hiss—a cat bounded out of the next house, streaked across the street and disappeared into a cellar. In fast pursuit, the dog charged into view. Behind him, pulling back on the leash, a soldier cursed. A brutal yank on the leash whipped the dog's head around. Another yank brought a whine of pain. Heeling, the dog lowered his nose to the ground. In the next second his nose twitched. He'd caught her scent. A staccato whelp preceded the long, low growl. Fangs bared, the canine sprang forward, broke from his master and charged. Terrified, Mildred pivoted and took off running.

"Halt!"

The dog, snarling and intent on devouring her, had her by the skirt. She stopped. Cursing, the soldier came on the run. He gripped the dog's collar and, with a rough pull on her shoulder, spun Mildred around. "Papers!" The dog pawed her leg, his sharp nails raking and catching on her cotton stockings. Shaking, she rummaged through her purse.

"Sheiss! I don't have all day!" He snatched the purse from her and riffling through it, tossed out her comb, handkerchief and sanitary pad. Upon finding her identity card, he let the purse fall to the ground.

He squinted at the information on the card. "Olga Sonntag?" His eyes followed her finger to the nametag pinned to her dress. "So, Olga, you work at the hospital?"

Her nod aroused the dog. Growling, he began to nose butt her crotch. Her expression amused the soldier. "He wants a date. Where are you going Olga?" He watched her carefully as she raised her arm and pointed in the direction of Lutzow Strasse. With a sigh he handed her back the card. "Pick up your things and be on your way. Don't loiter or you'll lose more than your voice."

Where Robert's apartment house had stood, she found a smoldering crater–a giant, glowing cavity. She walked as close to the rim as the intense heat would permit and peered down into it as though she might find him there. "Robert?" she shivered, "Robert? Oh God, Robert..."

"Roosevelt Dead! America Dead!" proclaimed graffiti, scrawled overnight on a wall in Mildred's neighborhood. Word of the confusing message brought the curious out to read it for themselves.

Mildred's landlady read it and shook her head. "Surely this can't be how it works, the death of one spells the death of the other?"

A baker who lived in the room below Mildred's attic stepped forward with the answer. "No, Frau Snabel, the country does not die. Upon the death of an American president, his son takes over."

A legless veteran put an end to the discussion. "No! Dummkopfs! The Americans have a new president. His name is Truman. Like Roosevelt, he is in bed with the Russians–Russians about to *destroy* us!"

The conquerors drew their ring tighter. Fighting could now be heard on the outskirts of the city. Beat-up cars plied the streets, their roof-mounted loudspeakers urging, "Stand to the last man! Women and children will not be evacuated! There is no escape!"

Goebbels' voice blared from the few remaining pole-mounted loudspeakers. "Happy Birthday to our beloved Fuhrer! He is in us and we are in him!"

An old woman, perhaps the only one listening, stopped and shook her fist at the loudspeaker. "Happy Birthday? You idiot! Our armies are decimated! Our homes are gone. We are starving! Pity the womb that bore the monster!"

The loudspeaker droned on. "We will rebuild the Third Reich to its rightful place in the sun. What greater birthday gift can we give our Fuhrer than..."

Blaring like banshees, air-raid sirens drowned him out. All day and all night they blared, marking Hitler's birthday, deafening celebrants as Allies advanced on all sides.

Mildred watched from her attic as wave after wave of planes filled the sky, their bomb doors opening, discharging clusters of eggs. Explosions came so closely together they sounded like a roll played on a giant kettledrum. A shroud of suffocating smoke cut visibility to zero. Glowing embers whirled in and, striking her face and arms, caused her to cry out. She sank to the floor and, whimpering Max's name, waited for the world to end.

World, do not ask those snatched from death where they are going, they are always going to their graves. The pavements of the foreign city were not laid for the music of fugitive footsteps...

– Nelly Sachs (1891-1970)

36

May 1, 1945. Following Hitler's suicide and days before Berlin fell to the Allies, Mildred joined the throngs of Germans fleeing the city–Germans half-mad with fear of the atrocities certain to befall them should the Russians reach Berlin first.

The river of hungry, foot-sore travelers coursed through the countryside, widening dramatically as it absorbed streams of weary vagabonds–dispossessed villagers, unemployed factory workers, widows, orphans, the maimed, the sick and the demented.

Before the ink dried on German surrender documents, more than half a million of these refugees died, tens of thousands felled by starvation, diphtheria and cholera. Instinct told Mildred to leave the disease-ravaged procession. She did so ambiguously, heading ever so slightly away from the masses until she found herself walking alone.

In Wittenberg, she passed a convoy of horse-drawn ambulances carting victims of scarlet fever. Following the Elbe to the hamlet of Torgau, she washed at a centuries-old cistern as starving young girls lined up outside houses requisitioned as brothels by American officers.

She moved on, the search for food consuming her every waking moment. Always a finicky eater, she discovered she could chew and swallow insects by closing her eyes and pinching her nostrils shut. She gleaned fields, searched forests for mushrooms and stripped bushes of overlooked berries. On a good day she might steal a bottle of milk. From a farmhouse outside the village of Chemnitz, she stole hot bread from a baker careless enough to trust the cooling loaf to an unwatched windowsill.

The countryside lay scarred and desolate. In Hof, the window-shattered eyes of a cottage watched disapprovingly as she shook plums from a front yard tree. Digging potatoes in a patch behind a silo, she slipped and sliced her foot on the shovel. Infection set in. A high fever followed. There appeared, in her delerium, the ghost of a pitchfork-wielding farmer demanding, with outstretched hand, the return of his potatoes.

Improved, but slowed by the oozing, bandaged foot, she took to begging on the streets of Regensberg—a town teaming with boisterous G.I.'s careening about in jeeps. "Out of the way, old hag!" a young soldier yelled as she jumped back to avoid being hit.

News of the war in the Pacific and accounts of the Allied thrust toward Japan reached her in bits and pieces. To get out of wind whipping a nearly destroyed section of Saarbrucken, she took refuge in a Catholic church. A Mass was being said, the priest reading an epistle from Timothy: "...for there will come a time when the faithful will not endure the sound doctrine; but having itching ears, will heap up to themselves teachers according to their own lusts, and they will turn away their hearing from the truth and turn aside rather to fables." He paused and, seeing in the passage a description of how eagerly his parishioners had embraced Hitler, began to rail against the Third Reich. He concluded his scathing denouncements with a reading from the Gradual: "The mouth of the just tells of wisdom and his tongue utters what is right."

A woman in the back pew grew agitated. "Hypocrite!" she cried out.

An old man hurried to the woman's side and began pulling on her arm. "Please, you go outside."

The woman resisted. "The church said nothing... *nothing*!"

Hunger honed the scavenger's skill. Crossing the Mosel to Aachen, she scavenged from ruins a charred, but edible salami and a small crock of moldy cheese. Her finger dipped into the cheese then went into her mouth. She smiled. What luck! Rationed carefully she might be able to feast on it for an entire week! As she carried her precious find to the street, she suddenly felt the assault on her back of small fists. The urchins were all over her in a second. A curley-haired waif kicked her in the shin. Another, a thin-faced child with huge, dark eyes grabbed her by the hair. A dozen hands at the ends of flailing, skinny arms seized the salami. Squealing like a rabid squirrel, the biggest of the lot wrested away the crock of cheese.

"Stop it, you bastards! Don't! Give it back!"

A flurry of shoeless feet took off, running through debris to the street. A lame youngster wearing a single, built-up shoe took up the rear. Before disappearing with his cohorts, he turned and smiled. "Danke grossmutte!"

Backtracking to Duisburg, she settled into the three-sided ruins of a once elegant home. Sitting one night in the massive, roofless living room, she saw, through holes in the floor, the glimmer of a half-buried object. An hour spent extricating and opening the badly dented metal box and she held in her palm a diamond earring, an amethyst studded pin and a ruby bracelet. Having learned a lesson from Aachen's band of marauding waifs, she set out immediately to find, or to steal, needle and thread. Her mission accomplished, she returned to the living room and, by moonlight, sewed the jewelry into the hem of her dress next to the section holding Max's watch.

Hunger, illness and exposure proved thieves of a different, more brutal sort. Too weak from hunger by the time she reached Nijmegen to go on, she bartered away the amethyst pin for a sack of food. A bout with dysentery after reaching Osnabruck decreed the earring go for a bottle of paregoric. Frostbitten toes suffered in Oldenburg and the specter of starvation forced the trade of the ruby bracelet for a week's lodging in a widower's cottage, his oldest pair of boots and a German officer's torn, bullet-pierced, winter coat.

Expelled from the widower's on the fifth day for pilfering a tin of sardines, she returned to the road and, half-starved and with nothing left to trade, trudged into the maws of winter.

She'd left Berlin on the first of May. By the time she staggered into Schwerin, villagers were decorating a Christmas tree in the town square. Her trek had approximated the greater part of a circle. Covering nearly eight hundred miles on foot, she had journeyed from the heart of chaos to a town preparing for a visit from Saint Nicolas.

But for a hand held up in feeble desperation, history might have recorded Mildred Gillars, a.k.a. "Axis Sally," never seen again after the fall of Berlin—a casualty of war. But, while driving through Schwerin during a snowstorm, a truck driver saw the hand and took pity on the shivering wretch waving it. He gave her a lift. The date: December 20, 1945. His next stop: Berlin.

As a ship aground is battered by the waves,
so man, imprisoned in mortal life,
lies open to the mercy of coming events.

– Ralph Waldo Emerson (1803-1882)

37

"Military Police!" barked the U.S. Army corporal. He advanced slowly. Light from a fire pit's glowing embers reflected off his helmet, his weight crunching rubble beneath his boots. His flashlight, like the eye of a cyclops, probed the cellar. Its beam stopped on Gustav's surprised face, paused and moved on. It swept over the woman, did a double take and then caught her in its full, blinding glare.

"Hey, Sarge!" the corporal called back over his shoulder. "Come see who I've found! Rita Hayworth! And, Kilroy!"

Alarmed, Gustav jumped to his feet. "Kilroy? Oh no, my corporal!" He thumped his chest. "I no Kilroy. Bitte... please!" He struggled to speak English. "Du... you have me wrong. Ich bin...sick–I am but a sick, unemployed vagrant!"

"Yeah? And I suppose this gorgeous dame's your girlfriend?"

"Oh, no Corporal. She ist but eine schrecklica–an old wreck of a woman... sie hat alles vergessen... eh, everything, she has everything forgotten! Not even her namen–her name can she remember!"

The sergeant, aroused at the prospect of seeing a female who might even slightly resemble Rita Hayworth, came on the run. Raw boned, chin squared, a rifle held loosely in his right hand, he stopped next to the corporal. "Okay, so *where* is she?"

"There." The corporal pointed.

Hunched over, she sat on a blackened concrete block. Wisps of matted hair escaped the babushka covering her head. She wore the German officer's overcoat. The right sleeve hung by a thread. Standing out from mud spatters, a stain the color of dried blood drew attention to the breast pocket's three bullet holes. She sat motionless, her face emaciated and showing the ravages of exposure, her eyes cast down on rag-wrapped feet.

The sergeant's face fell. "You fuckin' need glasses, Fogarty."

"Okay, okay, maybe not Rita Hayworth–maybe Betty Grable."

The sergeant delivered a light, but stinging punch to his subordinate's shoulder. "You horny, pussy-hungry bastard. Leave it to you to sniff out a good lookin' dame!" His attention switched back to the woman, the sergeant's grin faded. He hawked a thin stream of tobacco juice at the fire pit, watched it hiss and send up a wavering ribbon of white smoke. He shook his head; the mental image he'd formed from the "most wanted" circular in no way fit this wretch.

"You want I should search her?"

"And bring lice back to the barracks? Hell, no... Uh... well... maybe you should..."

"Oh no you don't!" The corporal lunged for Gustav. "Get back here, damn it!" He seized his arm and dragged the cowering suspect back toward the fire pit. "Where the fuck you think you're going?"

"Forgive me, my corporal. Bitte, I need to relieve myself."

"Sarge? Is it okay for Old Kilroy here to go take a leak? He claims Rita-baby's just some old granny who can't remember nothin'."

The sergeant stroked his chin and studied the woman. She had yet to move or to acknowledge him. He bent over and tapped her shoulder. "That right, babe? You got amnesia?"

She gave no sign of hearing—no sign of being in the presence of others.

"Maybe she's deaf, Sarge."

"Or faking."

Her eyes, unblinking as a mannequin's, remained cast down. Only two slight movements set her apart from a statue—the feeble rising of her shoulders when she breathed and, the flaring of her nostrils, the age-old and involuntary female response to male musk.

The sergeant squatted, reached out his hand and lifted her chin until their eyes met. Suddenly his face contorted and he reared back as though stung by a wasp. "Shit! Shit! Shit!" His thumb and forefinger clamped his nose. "Jee-sus H. Christ!" he said, his voice pinched and comically nasal. "Lady, you stink!"

The corporal laughed. "Don't go pukin' on us Sarge."

A quick, long stride and the sergeant stood face-to-face with his subordinate. "Don't just stand there, asshole. Do your duty!"

The corporal turned toward the cellar's entrance and, using two fingers to stretch his lower lip, emitted a loud whistle. "Casey! Smith! Get in here! On the double!"

Two privates came running. Reading their expressions as they approached, Gustav shuddered. He knew all soldiers to be brutal, why should Americans be any different. He'd served as a cook, an ambulance driver and finally as an artilleryman. He'd worn the uniform of three different armies. In the heat of summer he'd sweated, marched and plundered; in the depths of two winters he'd starved, suffered frostbite and fought. Like these young marauders, he'd known the frenzy of the hunt, the lust for corner and capture. His hands tensed into fists as the four, uniformed American's encircled the woman.

"Come on, momma, get to your feet," commanded the sergeant. Ignored, he tried again. "Look, sweetie, we don't have all day. Why don't ya'make it easy on yourself. Come with us and before ya' know it you'll be sleeping in a nice, warm bed."

Again, no response. The sergeant rubbed his eyes and sighed. "Okay, be a dumb broad. If that's the way you want it–shit, that's the way you get it. Casey, Smith... drag her out."

"Ya' want old Kilroy too?" asked the corporal.

"Christ no, he's fought his last battle. Let him be."

The privates supporting the woman, the sergeant led the way out of the cellar. They continued to the street and then stopped before a warmly dressed gentleman. A well-tailored cashmere coat covered his fine wool suit. An expensive black fur cap hid all but a few wisps of graying hair. Older and softer than the soldiers, he held in his gloved hands a manila folder bulging with papers.

"Well, Mr. Whitmer, sir," the sergeant said as the soldiers brought the woman before him, "whadda' ya' think? She the one?"

Whitmer studied the woman. Catching a whiff of her, he scowled and stepped back. His went to her spindly, mud-caked legs and her rag-wrapped feet. His sigh suggested both disgust and pity.

Large, wet snowflakes fell from the leaden sky. A chill wind blew from the north. Whitmer drew his coat collar up around his neck. He rummaged though the folder, taking his time, glancing at one page and then another. He assessed the woman's height. For the first time he looked into her eyes and noted that they were brown. Shaking his head, he turned to the sergeant. "Damn, I *don't* know. Maybe she's the dame, maybe she's not." He withdrew a large photograph from the folder. "Take a look, Sergeant, what do you think?

The sergeant, his eyes often glancing at the captive, studied the photograph. His deliberation concluded, he scratched his head and shrugged. "Beats me."

Whitmer saw that her lips were turning blue. He held the photograph up next to her cheek to compare her features with those of the beauty caught on film. "Hell, Miss Gillars," he said, "you look more like a dead skeleton than the dish in this picture." He showed her the photo. "Recognize yourself?"

She stared at the photograph and, showing no emotion while biting into the soft flesh of her inner cheek, tasted blood.

"Do you? Do you *recognize* yourself?"

Unable to elicit a response, Whitmer heaved a sigh. "Okay, honey, I'll play your game."

The sergeant remembered Gustav. "Mr. Whitmer, sir, would you like to talk to the old guy she was with down in that cellar? He claims she don't remember nothin', claims she's just a nutty old German grandma."

Whitmer closed his eyes and, with two gloved fingers, massaged the bridge of his nose. The snow stopped. A hush filled the twilight. Suddenly he turned on her and angrily pressed the photo against her face. "Erkennen Sie sich?" he screamed. "Erkennen Sie sich?"

That he asked the question in German made her heart pound. Perhaps...

The sergeant touched Whitmer's sleeve. "I'd suggest you don't stand too close to her, sir. She's probably teaming with all kinds of vermin. Needs a good de-lousing."

"Shame on you Sergeant, saying such nasty things about this lovely lady." He stepped back and studied the photograph. "She looked real happy back then... *real* happy..."

The sergeant caught on. From now on it would be the old "bait and switch." "Mr. Whitmer, sir, didn't you say this Gillars dame you're looking for would be about forty-five? Christ, this old hag is seventy if she's a day."

"Now, Sergeant, there you go again insulting this beautiful lady. Besides, I don't see how anyone this pretty could be a traitor. But then, 'Axis Sally' wore lots of disguises. Heck, some guys called her 'My Gal Sal'—others, 'The Bitch of Berlin'!"

"That she was, a Hitler-lovin' whore."

The two men, whispering and nodding, circled her. "Okay," Whitmer said at last, "So, we agree on one thing—that she's *at least* sixty?"

With the woman standing between them, they entered into a protracted argument over her age. Whitmer backed up his estimate by pointing out that she still had her teeth and a glint in her eye.

The sergeant shone his flashlight into her eyes and appraised them. "A *glint*? Looks more like the beginning of a cataract to me. Nah, she's way past sixty. Get a load of those lines around her eyes and the way her shoulders sag. Why, ya' could practically plant potatoes in those creases around her mouth. Course, she's been on the run for a long time."

"So," Whitmer said, "'sixty-five?'"

The sergeant chewed his lip to keep from laughing. "I have to stick with seventy."

Her head began to reel.

Whitmer scowled. "Damn it, Sarge, we need a consensus. Poll your men to see what they think."

The sergeant complied. "Fogarty?"

"Seventy if she's a day."

"Private Casey?"

"I'd say closer to sixty, sir."

"Smith?"

"Yes, sir. Seventy, sir."

The wind picked up. It sent icy blasts howling through the skeletons of buildings and set shards of glass tinkling in window frames. The dog she had listened to the night before resumed it's lonesome, anguished barking.

"Forty-five," she heard herself say in English, her tone that of an indignant schoolmarm. "I am neither sixty nor seventy. I am forty-five."

Like an athlete at the moment of victory, Whitmer shot his fist into the air. "Ah-hah!"

"Well, I'll be goddamned!" the sergeant yelled. He let out a whoop, danced around and delivered a solid slap to Whitmer's back. "Son of a bitch, Mr. Whitmer, sir—we nailed her!"

Suspicion is the companion of mean souls,
and the bane of all good society.

– Thomas Paine (1737-1809)

38

Stripped and sprayed with cloud after cloud of yellow powder from a flit gun, she was left alone in a holding cell until morning. In time, two hard-faced German women came for her. The heftier one took charge. "So, by now your lice are dead, yes?"

"Where *am* I?"

"You did not see my husband Carl's sign out front? So many letters–he painted every one himself: 'U.S. Army of Occupation Stockade,' that's what it says. Come, they've hired us to clean you up."

The other woman scowled. "*Phew*, hot soapy water and a good scrubbing, that's what you need."

Her skin and scalp still burning from the harsh soap, Mildred sat on a stool in an interrogation room encircled by Agent Whitmer, the sergeant, a captain and two lieutenants. In the corner, a corporal sat at a desk poised to take notes.

Whitmer looked her up and down. "She cleaned up pretty good, eh, Sergeant?"

"Yes, sir—she looks two shades lighter and a good ten years younger than she did last night."

Gazing at her, the captain shook his head. "I find it hard to believe she was once the highest paid performer on German radio. You sure that's all she had on her, Sergeant—one mark and eighty-five pfennigs?"

"Yes sir, that and four cigarette butts."

The captain quickly withdrew a pack of Lucky Strikes from his pocket. "Ah, so you smoke, Miss Gillars!" He offered her the pack. "Please, take as many as you like." He received but a long, wary stare. "Well, maybe later, after you've answered a few questions." He lit a cigarette. "Tell me, dear, on the day you fled Berlin, where did you go?"

Her eyes dulled at the memory of being swept along in the ever-widening river of starving refugees. It had been so cold in Schwerin... so ungodly hot in Augsburg. Potatoes... she'd dug but two potatoes before the farmer came running. His dog... she rubbed her thigh as though it still hurt from his bite. Crickets... last night she'd not heard a single cricket.

The youngest interrogator, a freckle-faced lieutenant, took over. "Okay, so we figure you roamed all over Germany for almost a year. Can you tell me, Miss Gillars, how you got back to Berlin?"

"A truck."

Not to be outdone by his underling's success, the captain took Mildred's hand and began stroking it. "Yes! Of course! A good-hearted truck driver sees you shivering by the side of the road and gives you a lift back to Berlin." He touched her cheek. "Tell me dear, when was that?"

"Christmas."

"Christmas? You've spent three months hiding in that cellar? But you *had* to go out. When you left the cellar, where did you go? To visit your fellow traitors? Fred Kaltenbach? John Delaney? How about Robert Best? Did you have a little rendezvous with Robert Best?"

The youngest interrogator interrupted. "She couldn't have, sir—Best got hauled back to the States last summer."

Mildred's couldn't hide her shock. "But that's not possible... he..."

A short, balding colonel presided over the formal military tribunal. He began by pounding a gavel on the mahogany table to get the attention of his seven stone-faced cohorts. "Okay, let's get this over with." He glanced at the prisoner. "Let the record show that Miss Mildred Elizabeth Gillars has been apprehended at the behest of the United States Justice Department, acting on the orders of the Attorney General."

Whitmer stepped forward. "Let the record also show that, on orders issued by the U.S. Justice Department, I hereby command this military tribunal to hold without bail one Mildred E. Gillars, a caucasian American female... Also known as 'Axis Sally.'"

"Also known as the 'Bitch of Berlin,' came a jibe from a member of the tribunal.

"The charge, Mr. Whitmer?"

Put on the spot, Whitmer scratched his head. "Oh crap, Colonel! That's up to the big shots back home. For now, let's just say... 'held on suspicion.'"

"Suspicion of what?"

Another pause. "How about... eh, okay, I've got it..." Whitmer's hand made an arc as though pointing to a title printed on a marquee. "Suspicion of treasonable activities on behalf of the German propaganda agency."

"But that's not true," Mildred mumbled. "They made me..."

Whitmer cut her off. "Save it for the jury, Miss Gillars. Until we fly you home to stand trial, you'll be incarcerated at the U.S. Army prison in Frankfort."

The colonel had a last question. "Let's get this straight,

Agent Whitmer. You want her held on suspicion but not formally charged?"

"Right."

"For how long?"

Whitmer shrugged. "For as long as it takes."

As WAC Lieutenant Catherine Smaha escorted her charge through Templehof airport en route to the plane that would take them to Frankfort, a grizzled G.I. spotted Mildred and pointed her out to his comrade. "Look! There goes 'Axis Sally'–the babe they're gonna' hang for playing the hit parade!"

His comrade bristled with indignation. "That's horse shit! She played the sweetest music... and had the *sexiest* voice!" He jumped up onto a seat to wave and yell at his favorite disc jockey. "Don't let 'em get ya' down, Sally. I loved ya'!"

The Army prison in Frankfort brooded over the city. Four guards were assigned to watch the suspect around the clock. One of them, knowing that his charge had lived outdoors for more than a year prior to being captured, likened her to a newly caged animal. During his graveyard shift he watched her closely. She'd hug her knees, rock for hours and scratch herself as though covered with lice. That she ate almost nothing concerned him. "You've got quite an ordeal ahead of you, if you don't mind my saying so, ma'am. You'd best eat and get some meat on your bones–you'll be needing your strength." No answer. She turned her back. He continued, "They say you tried to sweet-talk G.I.'s into putting down their guns and going home. Is that so, is that what you done?"

She turned and appraised his boyish face. "Did."

"Huh?"

"Is that what you *did*. 'Done' is a weak verb–it needs a helper."

"Oh."

Her friendship with Sergeant Ridgeway Ryan of Foley, Alabama developed slowly. It started with his proposal: "You teach me to talk good and I'll learn you Casino." His grammar, vocabulary and diction began to improve almost immediately. At a much slower pace, Mildred came to master the tricky card game.

Although sure he wanted out of the Army, and the sooner the better, he'd given little thought to a career. When Mildred suggested journalism, he jumped at the idea. A newspaper reporter! That's what he'd become.

She described courses he should one day take in college. But there was a journalistic tool he could learn right now, during his off hours. Frankfort's huge army base must have a decent library. He could learn to use it. She'd start him out searching for specific bits of information such as what had become of her former colleagues at Zeesen.

At the start of his next shift he handed her typed results of his first assignment. Robert Best did not die in the bombing of his apartment building. He'd lived on only to be captured when American forces overran Berlin. Now, sitting in a jail cell in Washington D.C., he would soon be tried for treason.

Constance Drexel, described by reporter Harry W. Flannery as "Goebbels' diminutive blueblood from Philadelphia," had fared better. Arrested following V-E Day, she'd spent a year in jail and internment camps only to have the treason indictment against her dropped for lack of evidence.

Jane "Lady Haw-Haw" Anderson, aka "The Georgia Peach," former confidant and mistress of authors H.G. Wells and Joseph Conrad–had also managed to wiggle her way free. Although the Department of Justice had declared her a traitor, Jane's brief fiasco as Nazi propagandist with Goebbels' Awkward Squad had been quietly deemed "not worth prosecuting."

Mildred's nemesis, William "Lord Haw-Haw" Joyce, the Texan who had masqueraded as a Brit, and his wife Margaret, had—while hiding in a woods near the Danish frontier—been captured by British forces. On the first of February 1946, reasoning that since Joyce had traveled on a British passport, they had the right to treat him like one of their own, the British hanged him for treason.

After reading Ridgeway's report, Mildred praised it. Amazed by the last paragraph, she shook her head. "Now *there's* a first—the British hanging an American for treason..."

Ridgeway's subsequent research turned up more. Two of the men with whom her name had been linked were also incarcerated at Frankfort. One was Herbert Burgmann, a.k.a. Joe Scanlon, who had helped his boss, Vice Consul Vaughn, confiscate her passport. Donald Day, Goebbels last recruit and a former *Chicago Tribune* correspondent occupied the cell next to Burgmann.

Ridgeway also learned that although only a handful of American's shared Mildred's situation, tens of thousands of Europeans were being added to the list of suspected traitors. Postwar courts were springing up throughout Europe solely to try those charged with crimes against their country. The French were rounding up thousands of suspected collaborators, shaving their heads and parading them through the streets to be severely beaten by angry mobs. Shorn men were being shot vigilante-style.

Reporting back to Mildred regarding one article, Ridgeway became enraged. "If this ain't a crock, I don't know what is!" he fumed. "Get this, while you're sitting here doing time for what they forced you to do, ex-members of the SS and former Gestapo are being appointed 'consultants' to the U.S. Advisory Committee! Just think of it! I read it with my own eyes! Hitler's goons will be drawing up plans for the new German Federal Republic."

In mid-December 1946, the U.S. Justice Department authorized a Christmas amnesty for certain prisoners incarcerated at the U.S. Army Prison in Frankfort. The names "Burgmann," "Day" and "Gillars" appeared on the list.

"An amnesty! Who'd a thunk it?" Ridgeway teased as he carried her small suitcase down the front stairs. "How much mustering out pay did they give ya'?"

"The princely sum of fifty dollars." Seeing his hand go for his wallet, she shook her head. "No, please. It's plenty. I'll manage."

They passed through the front gates and walked to a waiting car. He tossed her suitcase onto the back seat, turned and gave her a quick kiss on the cheek. "Guess this means I'll be playing Casino by myself."

"You just keep studying–you hear?"

"Sure will miss ya', Mildred."

She looked away. "We'll be in touch."

amnesty: in law, exemption from prosecution for criminal action. It signifies forgiveness and the forgetting of past actions.

– The Columbia Encyclopedia

39

Haggled down to less than the amount he'd printed on his sign, the shoemaker showed her to the small room above his shop. "If you climb up on the chair, you get a good view of Frankfort, Fraulein Gillars." With the prison so close, it was his custom to learn the names of the newly released. "The only heat this room gets seeps up from below, but I expect you are accustomed to worse. Doubtless you'll fare better when you get home to America."

The word "home" rang in her ears long after he descended the stairs. She hadn't set foot on American soil in more than fourteen years. Memories of that 1932 return to her Depression-ravaged homeland crowded in. Max had surprised her on the play's opening night—they'd strolled along the Potomac, she could almost feel his hand now, squeezing hers. A shiver dispelled the thought.

She kept to herself and seldom ventured out; nonetheless, her presence in Frankfort caused Thomas Hartney, a correspondent for *The Washington Post* to come knocking. "I saw your name on the amnesty list, Miss Gillars, and bingo!"

"I don't play bingo, Mr. Harney."

"Awe, come on, just a few questions?" He whipped out pencil and notebook. "You got your start in German radio as a broadcaster, right?"

She sighed. "I started as Mistress of Ceremonies of a radio program exclusively for American expatriates. My job had nothing to do with Hitler, his policies or his propaganda. I was assured it would remain that way."

"Rather naive, weren't you?"

"*Trusting* would be a better word. I trusted the man who got me the job and made the assurances."

"What of your returning to the States? Scared?" Reading the answer in her silence and in the subtle tightening of her hand into a fist, he pushed harder. "How do you think the folks back home will welcome an American woman who's behaved like Hitler's girlfriend? You're not exactly the average U.S. citizen, you know!"

"The fact that my passport's been confiscated rather brings into question the status of my citizenship, wouldn't you say?"

"You're claiming German citizenship?"

"I was forced to sign an oath of allegiance to Germany. I have no papers, no job and no income. Clearly, the magistrate of Frankfort with whom I spoke this morning doesn't consider me German. He refused to grant me a food card. It would seem that as a 'woman without a country' I'm allowed to do but one thing–starve."

On to her scent, a dozen other reporters sought her out, always asking the same questions, always managing to twist the answers they scribbled down.

> Question: *"Why did you serve as Hitler's mouthpiece?"*

> Answer: "*I never, of my own free will, broadcast a single word of propaganda. Only under threat of a horrific death did I air those vile, Nazi-written scripts.*"
>
> Question: "*What about that play, 'Vision of the Invasion?' Was that your sweetheart's idea?*"
>
> Answer: "*No, actually it was mine–an idea instilled in me by a 'higher power.' In my heart of hearts I knew that Germany couldn't last another year–therefore the invasion of Normandy was unnecessary. Convinced of the needless slaughter about to take place, I promoted the play and starred in it in hopes of saving lives.*"

A publisher, a man with strong anti-war sentiments borne of having lost two sons at Normandy, came to call. He'd heard her play broadcast and, after the fact, had come to appreciate what she'd tried to do. He asked her to write a pamphlet, her account of why she'd taken part in the play. He'd publish and promote it.

"My Vision of the Invasion–How I Tried to Save Thousands of Young Men from Dying in America's Worst Blunder" by Mildred E. Gillars was well received–and, surprisingly so by Germans chafing under curfews and other restraints imposed upon them by the U. S. Army of Occupation. The pamphlet immediately drew her into the cross hairs of two big guns: The American public still smarting from D-Day losses and, the cadre of America's politicians and military pundits who had urged the invasion.

The pamphlet sold out quickly. The publisher's effort to have more printed mysteriously blocked, she was re-arrested and returned to the Frankfort prison. As though awakened by the banging close of her cell door, the U. S. Justice Department did an about-face and, citing her "political views," decided she should stand trial for treason.

With Ridgeway gone home to civilian life, her second incarceration at Frankfort dragged on. He wrote a newsy letter detailing both the good and bad of post-war America. Another, more ebullient epistle told of his being accepted by the University of South Carolina. His last correspondence described an after-hours job as janitor for the *Columbus Herald.*

August 20, 1948 dawned warm and humid. By mid-morning the heat turned Mildred's cell into an oven. Lying on her cot, she imagined herself baking to ash and blowing through the bars to freedom. Her fantasy evaporated at the sound of a key turning the lock. "Come along," said the stouter of the two prison matrons. "It's time for your debut."

"My *what?*"

Tight lipped, they escorted her down the corridor, through a series of doors and out to a waiting sedan. They ordered her into the back seat then, after climbing in from either side, sat squashing her. Two U.S. Army military police occupied the front seat.

They drove to a two-story brick residence situated on a tree-studded knoll within sight of the prison. They were greeted and ushered into the foyer by the warden's plump wife, Leona Crabtree. She mopped her brow then tucked the lacey handkerchief into the décolleté of her ample bosom. "Let's see," she said, nervously flexing dimpled fingers, "the colonel told me just how this is to be done..." She stared at the prisoner. "Miss Gillars? The beauticians from that nice salon on Dortmund Street are waiting upstairs for you."

"Where do you want us, ma'am?" asked the driver.

The protuberant eyes blinked. "If I remember correctly, the colonel wants one of you soldiers at the front door and the other at the back—just in case she tries to escape. Go now, *shoo...*"

Mildred scratched at the bead of sweat stinging its way past hairs held taught by her long, graying ponytail. The two matrons led her to the staircase. Leona Crabtree's eyes fixed on the back of the drab, loose-fitting prison dress. Then, as she watched legs encased in heavy cotton stockings and feet shod in men's oxfords bear the prisoner up the stairs, she remembered another of her husband's directives. "Oh... and after you turn her over to the beauticians, you matrons are to come back down here and wait."

Four hours passed. Mildred reappeared at the top of the stairs. Her skin glowed with professionally applied makeup—mascara, eye shadow, powder, rouge and bright red lipstick. Gone was the lank, gray hair. Waves of shimmering platinum hugged her head then gave way to a luxuriant cascade of bouncy, stylish curls. Befitting a glamour queen about to audition for a starring role, a tight fitting, knee-skimming black dress hugged her every curve.

Colonel Crabtree had come home during the makeover to see that orders had been followed to the letter. A look up at the beauty and his eyes nearly popped. "My God! I don't believe it! She looks like Mata Hari!"

Playing to her audience, Mildred paused and, with a provocative tilt of her torso leaned back to check the seams of sheer stockings caressing her long, shapely legs. She started her descent tenuously—it had been a long time since she'd worn three-inch high heels, the kind that cause breasts to bounce and hips to sway.

Awed by the theatrical descent, the squared shoulders and the proudly held head, no one made a sound. Reality set back in the instant her foot touched the marble floor. The heftier matron reached out, seized her charge's hand and gaped at the long, scarlet-lacquered nails. "Look, they drip blood!"

The way the driver and the guard gawked at the prisoner amused the colonel. "Well, boys, what do you think?"

A long, low whistle poured from the driver's mouth. "Hubba-hubba. Oh yes, sir, I'd say she's ready!"

"Take her then. This is as far as the matrons go with her."

"Come on, sweetheart, you heard the colonel. Say goodbye to these nice people. From here on, it's just you, me and the open road."

The colonel brought him up short. "Sergeant!"

"Yes, sir! Sorry, sir."

Holding onto his arm for support, her stride hobbled by the tight-fitting dress, Mildred minced her way to the waiting car. Two additional armed guards waited inside. "Okay," one of them said to the driver as the car sped out the driveway, "Now to the... how do you say *airport* in German?"

"Flughafen," the captive muttered.

He squeezed her knee. "Right, baby. Next stop Flughafen!"

A deafening roar came from engines straining for altitude. Her forehead against the window, she watched Frankford swim past under the silver wing and disappear into the dusk. The plane climbed higher until, upon reaching the divide between the earth's warmth and cold upper strata, it shuddered and bobbed like a cork. Once above the turbulence and headed toward the setting sun, she leaned back and closed her eyes.

Treason doth never prosper: what's the reason?
Why, if it prosper, none dare call it treason.

– John Bartlett (1820-1905)

40

A crush of reporters and photographers greeted the C-54 when it landed in the nation's capital. Police held back jeering crowds. An FBI agent escorted the shapely blonde from the plane. An onlooker held up *The Washington Post*. Hot off the press, its headline blared: "Two Sirens Return!"

Mildred's guard glanced at the headline. "Uh, oh... it looks like they're lumping you with Tokyo Rose." He strengthened his grip on her elbow and started hustling her through the catcalling throng.

"That's her, that's 'Axis Sally!'" a man yelled, angrily waving the hook at the end of his arm.

A woman spat. Another laughed at the way the spittle hit its mark and cascaded down the front of Mildred's dress. "Serves ya' right, hussy!" An old man held his hands high and made an obscene gesture. "Hey, Berlin Bait! How was der Fuhrer in bed?"

U.S. Justice officials waved the entourage through customs. In the terminal's main lobby they pushed against a larger, meaner crowd. Someone yanked Mildred's hair. "Steady," her guard said above the taunts, "there's a car waiting at the curb."

Sirens from the motorcycle escort blared in the fast drive to the office of United States Commissioner, Cyril Lawrence. Seated at his throne-like desk and pouring over documents, he took one look at Mildred and quickly pushed the papers aside. He cleared his throat, straightened his tie and slicked back his hair. "Ah, Miss Gillars... yes, yes, yes, I've been expecting you. You've had a comfortable journey? Good! Hmmm, well... I guess we'd best get down to business." He picked up a document and scanned it. "I see you've been held in U.S. Military prisons in Germany for the past two and a half years. Held all this time without being formally charged, is that correct?"

"Yes, that is correct."

"Well, we'll certainly have to change that!" He sighed, gave her a sorrowful look then, riveted his gaze on the print. "I hereby charge you with giving 'aid and comfort' to the enemy from December 11, 1941 through May 6, 1945." His duty done, Commissioner Lawrence informed Mildred that her half-sister, Edna Mae Heron, was waiting in his chambers. He'd grant the reunion, but only for ten minutes. The women clung to eachother and wept.

The ten minutes up, Edna Mae pleaded to post bond. "The answer is *no*, Mrs. Heron," Lawrence decreed. He held up his hand to stem her protest. "Yes, I know, I have read every one of your letters. Unfortunately, given the likelihood of the accused's flight from prosecution, she shall be held without bail." He picked up a pen and signed an order for Mildred to be jailed in Washington D.C. pending outcome of a preliminary hearing to be held on a date set by a Federal magistrate.

Another crush of reporters and photographers awaited her arrival at the jail. She was allowed to answer a few of their questions while her guards busied themselves signing her in.

"Heard you were once in a stage play here in D.C.–is that *true?*"

"Yes it is," she answered, smiling as though being interviewed for *Vanity Fair*. "But you're talking ancient history. That was years ago."

"What's it like coming home?"

She drew in her breath and took a moment. "What's it *like*? It saddens me to return under such circumstances, of course. I've been living in a country subject to a great deal of tragedy." That night, she collapsed on her narrow prison cot. Tomorrow, with its desolate dawn, would come soon enough.

News of "Axis Sally's" return and speculation on her upcoming trial continued to make headlines. Her photo graced the front page of *The New York Times*. An old friend saw it and made a beeline for her cell. "Fifty-two skidoo, kid! Harry Horatio Schwartz is once again at your service!"

The sight of him brought a happy smile. If ever she needed Harry's corny, upbeat humor, it was now. "Harry! I don't believe it!"

"Wow, honey, you sure got yourself into a pickle this time!"

"Tell me, are you still at Hunter?"

He nodded. "Yep, I single-handedly kept the war from the gates!"

"You look great! Handsome as ever! Meet any more guy's whose names rhyme with *cylinder*?"

He blushed. "Mildred, honey, is there anything I can do for you?"

"You're a savvy, betting man. Tell me, what are the odds on my getting out of here?"

"You mean on bail?"

"I mean permanently."

He heaved a sigh. "Nil. You're their scapegoat, kid. Christ, you couldn't have come home at a worse time!" They talked for an hour. He explained how President Truman, accused by his detractors of "political softness," sat uncertain in the White House, counseled and comforted by a constant stream of advisors. "Truman is being crucified in the press. They're calling him 'a communist sympathizer' and 'Stalin's sweetheart.' Monikers like those are sure to cost him big-time in the next election. His advisors, naturally, are having fits. They're telling him: 'Harry, if ya' wanna save your political ass, ya' better get tough—tough on traitors—tough on commies.'"

A letter arrived from Ridgeway. Using flawless grammar, he told of his leaving Columbus and moving to California. He now had a job as a cub reporter with the *San Francisco Chronicle*. He promised he'd get to Washington to see her and included an article he'd just written for the Chronicle:

INNOCENT UNTIL PROVEN GUILTY?
Not in the U.S.A.!!!

Without regard for reputation or careers, members of the newly appointed U.S. Congressional Committee—charged with purging America of Russian sympathizers—ferret out Hollywood's celluloid commies. Stunned by the accusations, actors, directors, producers and screenwriters call upon the Fifth Amendment for protection. Protection? Taking the Fifth is the surest, swiftest route to Hollywood's blacklist. Innocent until proven guilty? Not according to Senator Joe McCarthy. Anyone McCarthy points his finger at and who takes the Fifth is automatically sentenced to career oblivion.

She didn't answer his letter. The last thing he needed was to be put in the position of defending a friendship with a woman touted in the press as "the American Jew-hating traitor who slept with Hitler."

Rarely, and then only after careful scrutiny of a reporter's background, did she grant personal interviews such as she granted to Neil Meyer, a writer for the *Christian Science Monitor*. "Tell me, Miss Gillars... why, after detaining you for so long, has the Justice Department suddenly decided to put you on trial?"

"Good question, Mr. Meyer. You've heard that the pen is mightier than the sword?"

"Of course."

"Well my being put on trial is sort of a contortion of that old adage. I used my pen to write a pamphlet and they unsheathed their swords."

The Los Angeles Times sent Hal Emory, who seemed to know more about Mildred's upcoming trial than she did. "I understand they'll be playing recordings of your broadcasts at the trial. What do you think this German woman Inge Doman and your old Nazi superiors have against you?"

"Against me?"

"They're listed as witnesses for the prosecution. I hear this Doman woman hates your guts."

"Did you come to interview me or to chat?"

"Sorry, just trying for the human interest angle."

The matron's announcement of "ten more minutes" caused Emory to go for the kill. "Throughout the war you constantly referred to yourself as 'a one-hundred-percent American girl,' yet you told soldiers over the air—and I'm quoting you: 'This is a Jewish war and good honest-to-God American blood is being shed for it.' Tell me, Miss Gillars, how will such a statement set with the jury?"

"Goebbels' goons wrote those words, Mr. Emory, just as they wrote every word of propaganda I broadcast—the sexy innuendos, names and addresses of imprisoned G.I.'s, the anti-Semitic pap..."

"But surely, you had a choice..."

"Why, yes, I did—a very clear-cut choice. I could follow their orders and broadcast everything they handed me verbatim or... *die*!"

"I see." He'd stopped writing and, as though bored, was examining his fingernails.

"Your pencil, has it run out of lead? Not interested in what really happened?"

"It's not that."

"No? Then write this down in big, bold letters. 'Mildred Gillars did what she did, said what she said, and read what she read only because she was forced to do so. If she refused she would have met with Hitler's favorite means of execution—the exquisitely slow and tortuous process of being hanged with a piano wire."

On September 6, 1948 a guard ushered into Mildred's cell a white-haired, flush-faced gentleman. "Good day, Miss Gillars. I'm John Holzworth of Gladding and Holzworth, New York and Washington. I've been engaged to defend you."

"By whom?"

Furrows on Holzworth's forehead came together in one deep crease. A finger to his lips and a roll of his eyes toward the corridor let her know their conversation was being monitored. He began to whisper. "By an interested party—I'm not at liberty to divulge his identity."

"What interested party?"

"That, madam, I cannot answer."

"Well *that,* Mr. Holzworth, doesn't set right with me. No dice. You can leave. Now!"

"He said you might react in this manner."

"He?"

"Believe me, my dear—this all makes no sense to me either. He said that to set your mind at ease, I should say this phrase: 'Beware of the destroying angel.'"

Stunned, Mildred sank down onto her cot. "Beware of the destroying angel?" It was a phrase her grandfather had used to warn children away from the deadly "Destroying Angel" mushroom. She hadn't heard the phrase since her sixteenth summer when she and Aaron Stern had adopted the ominous sounding phrase as their "secret code." Nor had she thought of Aaron Stern for years. Aaron—Grandfather's "little secret," the product of his extra-marital affair with Golda, the young Jewish maid.

Holzworth smiled. "I see the phrase means something to you. Shall I tell our 'interested party' that you accept my representation?"

"But it will cost..." Her eyes fixed on the attorney's diamond stickpin.

"Good, I take it your answer is '*yes*'—a wise decision!" The next day, without consulting her, he filed a Writ of Habeas Corpus in which he declared: "*Miss Gillars is a German citizen being held unlawfully in the district court of the United States of America.*" Based on the same argument, he then filed a petition for her release.

The New York Times kept her name in headlines:

SALLY SPY WITNESSES
PROTEST $5 DAILY FEE

The accompanying article alluded to a demonstration staged on Capitol Hill by American vets who had been prisoners of war in the camps Mildred and Max had visited. These men had been subpoenaed to testify against her before the grand jury.

"Five bucks a day ain't nowhere near enough," their spokesman said of the amount the government would pay them. "Five bucks a day is less than prisoner of war pay. We're crowded into boarding houses, cutting down on our meals and doing our own laundry trying to make ends meet, but it won't work. At this rate we'll all be broke before long."

Knowing how much they'd been through, Mildred couldn't bear the thought that she was causing these veterans more grief. Who else might she hurt? Aaron... Aaron Stern, the financier of her defense. Now chief-of-staff at a major medical center, he would face the outrage of his colleagues. The press would crucify him for coming to the aid of a "Hitler-loving traitor" and "a rabid anti-Semite."

Determined to put an end to Aaron's jeopardy, she sat on her cot and wrote, in duplicate, a letter that would, by dismissing Holzworth, sever Aaron's connection to her:

> *To Whom It May Concern: I, Mildred Elizabeth Gillars, hereby reject the legal services of John M. Holzworth. As of this date, Mr. Holzworth is no longer my attorney.*

One copy went to Holzworth, the other to the judge who had officiated at her arraignment.

For dinner that evening, the prison's cook whipped up what the matron who brought Mildred's tray described as "Hangman's Stew." Swimming in greasy gravy, chunks of stringy, gray-brown beef pushed against gummy noodles, mushy carrots and shriveled peas. Mildred ate several spoonfuls before noticing the strange taste. An hour later, sweating and doubled over with gut-wrenching cramps, her tongue swelling and the cell starting to blur, she cried out.

The next morning she awoke in Washington's General Hospital. Her stomach had been pumped. The doctor stood at the foot of the bed. "She's presenting signs of poisoning—I'd guess strychnine," he informed interns flanking him. "Whoever gave it to her didn't give her enough."

On September 14, 1948 guards escorted her, weak from her bout with strychnine, to the federal courthouse. The jury foreman began to read the indictment: "Your honor, we members of the Grand Jury charge Mildred E. Gillars, born Mildred E. Sisk and also known as 'Axis Sally,' on eight counts of aiding the German government in its psychological warfare against the United States. We further charge that she did this in order to weaken both the resistance of Americans at home and the fighting power and morale of United States troops overseas."

A hush fell over the room. Every eye stared at the accused. He read on: "Mildred Gillars has violated the allegiance to the country of her birth by knowingly, intentionally, willfully, unlawfully, feloniously and treasonably adhering to the enemies of the United States."

"Miss Gillars," the judge said, staring down at her over the top of his reading glasses, "your trial date is tentatively set for November fifteenth. Who will represent you?"

A hawk-nosed, balding gentleman rose and removed his wire-rimmed spectacles. "I will, your honor. I've been retained to represent the defendant."

Mildred turned and leveled a quizzical look at Edna Mae. The judge, apparently acquainted with the lawyer, turned towards the court stenographer's desk. "Let the record show that the defendant is represented by Attorney James J. Laughlin."

A reporter let out a whistle. "Laughlin? Man, he's expensive!"

"How does your client plead, Mr. Laughlin?"

"Innocent!" Mildred exclaimed. "Completely innocent! I have never willingly done anything to hurt my country! Not willingly! You see, they forced me... they..."

The judge brought down his gavel. "You're out of order, Miss Gillars. Another such outburst and I'll have you ejected."

Laughlin raised his voice. "Innocent, your honor! My client pleads innocent!"

"Innocent," said the judge disgustedly, making no attempt to hide his distain as he looked at the shapely blonde in the snug fitting black dress. "Innocent."

"And may it please your honor, the defense requests that the court issue a special subpoena."

"Really, Mr. Laughlin, for whom?"

"For whom? Why, for Harry S. Truman, President of the United States! Let the record show, that in order to properly represent my client, I hereby request the court to subpoena President Harry S. Truman!"

The courtroom erupted. "What? What did he say?"

"The President? He wants to subpoena the President?"

"He's a nut!"

"Her lawyer's crazy!"

"Order! Order! Order, or I will clear this court!" His ultimatum unheeded, the judge signaled for bailiffs to take action as reporters, like fish in a feeding frenzy, pushed and shoved to take flash pictures of an attorney who'd gone so over the edge as to attempt to subpoena the nation's president.

"Mildred, honey, you did just fine today," Edna Mae said in a late afternoon visit to her sister's cell. "Just fine."

"Who is he, this Laughlin, this lunatic? Better yet, who's the lunatic paying him to represent a penniless wretch accused of treason?"

Edna Mae lowered her eyes. "Please, Sis, try and understand. Edward and I can't just sit by and do nothing. We have to help you."

"You and Edward? Oh, no... oh, no... What have you done? Mortgaged your house? Emptied your bank account?"

A criminal trial is like a Russian novel: it starts with exasperating slowness as the characters are introduced to a jury, then there are complications in the form of minor witnesses, the protagonist finally appears and contradictions arise to produce drama, and finally as both jury and spectators grow weary and confused the pace quickens, reaching its climax in passionate final argument.

– Clifford Irving (1930 -)

41

The term "The Red Scourge" crept into print. Newspapers warned of it. The "cold war" was said to be "heating up" to pose a threat to the very existence of man on the planet. Political cartoons depicted "The Red Tide" engulfing the globe and Stalin's hands dripping blood as he shut "The Iron Curtain."

Those awaiting trial for treasonous activities during the "hot war" (WWII) were lumped together with the newly indicted "cold war" traitors, Alger Hiss and Whittaker Chambers. In someone's well calculated attempt to liken her to these two, *The New York Times* ran Mildred's photo adjacent to an article on how Hiss and Chambers had aided the spread of world communism by selling top U.S. secrets to the Russians.

No one championed witch-hunts for communists and traitors with greater disregard for due process than Wisconsin Senator Joseph McCarthy. A master at publicizing accusations of political disloyalty or subversion with insufficient regard to evidence, McCarthy played the media like a harp.

The dread of being featured on the front page—"accused of being a national security risk"—silenced most who opposed the senator's slanderous tactics.

For an American to be convicted of treason, there must be at least two "essential witnesses" to each overt act. The two essential witnesses used to obtain the convictions of Robert Best and Douglas Chandler were ex-Nazi imports Hans von Richter and Adelbert Houben. Former officials of Goebbels' short-wave radio propaganda service, they had been the superiors of the American broadcasters at Zeesen.

"Rest assured," Mildred's attorney said, "these old Nazis are well paid for their testimony. Most likely they will be kept on and used as essential witnesses against you and Monti."

Martin J. Monti. The name still gave Mildred the shudders. The former U.S. Army pilot now sat in a Brooklyn jail charged with flying his fighter across German lines to join Hitler's Elite Guard. A Luftwaffe washout, Monti had been reassigned to work as a broadcaster at Zeesen. Monti's trial was scheduled to start before hers.

Joining Hans von Richter as an essential witness against Monti would be Gunther D'Alquen and Herman Rockmann, former officers in Hitler's Elite Guard. Doubtless the trio would testify that Monti asked for membership in the SS Corps and was actually issued the uniform and equipment of a German officer.

On January 24, 1949 bailiffs brought Mildred to the federal court in Washington D.C. to stand trial. Judge Edward M. Curran would preside. The jury selection process took her back to a very crowded audition for the play, "Wheels of Justice." The twelve who would share the spotlight with her, and decide her fate, would be chosen from a pool of ninety-two prospective jurors.

A bailiff read off twelve names. The twelve took seats in

the jury box. Challenged on their ability to be objective in judging the accused, many stepped down. At mid-morning the selection concluded with an equal mix of men and women, negroes and whites.

The last woman chosen had second thoughts and raised her hand. "Your honor, I'm not sure if I should be here. Yes, I believe traitors should be harshly punished but I don't hold with putting anybody to death. Not even Hitler-loving riff-raff like this 'Axis Sally' here. Killing people violates God's commandment."

"You may step down, Mrs. Tigbee." A stern-faced white man replaced her.

The judge then adjourned the proceedings pending the installation of an amplification system for the anticipated replay of Mildred's recorded broadcasts. It took a crew of sound engineers and technicians several days to fill the order. A second delay came on the heels of the first when the judge ordered a bank of seats installed for members of the press.

Attorney Laughlin kept her informed. "The courtroom will be jammed with reporters and photographers from all major broadcasting stations, magazines and newspapers. Factor in law students, witnesses and the morbidly curious 'John Q. Public' and there'll be standing room only. Let's face it, Miss Gillars, you are the news of the day. I'm sorry to say this, my dear, but it will be a witch-hunt."

After a dramatic reading to the court of the charges against her, Prosecutor Kelly began his opening statement. "Ladies and gentlemen of the jury, in the case of the United States versus Mildred Gillars, the prosecution will prove beyond a reasonable doubt that Mildred Gillars is guilty of treason..."

Laughlin began his response with an appeal to the compassion of the stoic-faced jurors. "I beg of you, when listening to prosecution witnesses malign Miss Gillars, as they will doubtless do, you must consider the wartime plight of this poor, unfortunate woman. Imagine yourselves being in Berlin on the eve of Pearl Harbor and having your American passport taken from you—not by a pickpocket, but by an official of your own country! Imagine—stripped of your passport! Stranded! You have no means of going home! Bombs explode and blow your apartment and your neighbors to bits! You have no money! No food card! No job!"

He walked to Mildred and placed a hand on her shoulder. "Is it any wonder that she turned for survival to the one man she loved and trusted? Ladies and gentleman of the jury, Mildred Gillars was not, is not—and never will be a traitor! Young and innocent, she made a tragic mistake—she fell hopelessly, inextricably in love with her Hunter College professor. Imagine how wonderful this man's love must have seemed to one who, at an early age, had been abused and abandoned by her own father!

"Professor Koischwitz mesmerized her! Alas, but for him, Mildred Gillars would not be sitting in this courtroom today, charged with treason. Picture if you will, this suave academician. Using the charm of Svengali, the trickery and deceit of Lucifer, he led her, blinded by her love for him, down the primrose path! 'I have found you a job with Radio Berlin!' he tells her. 'At last your dreams of becoming a great dramatic actress can come true! Come, follow me and I will make you a star!' Naturally she responded with apprehension. Who wouldn't have reservations about taking a radio job in prewar Germany? 'Don't worry' he reassures her, 'your broadcasts will be solely for the entertainment of the burgeoning number of ex-patriots. You will not have to utter a whisper of propaganda, I promise, not a whisper!'"

With each rise and fall of Laughlin's deep, resonating voice, tension escalated. The enthralled jury leaned forward and, as though anticipating the climax of a great Shakespearian tragedy, paid strict attention. Keeping them hanging from a precipice, he paused to buff the lens of his glasses. Then, like a panther, he took three, slow, soundless strides toward them and pounced forward, his arms spread like the rising Christ. "HE LIED!" Startled, jurors reared back in their seats, wide-eyed. Laughlin's voice grew louder, angrier. "Max Otto Koischwitz lied! He deceived and hypnotized this poor woman! Capitalizing on her love for him, this German-born Svengali lured Mildred Gillars into the bowels of Hitler's propaganda machine! She tried to escape! Too late! The doors of the Nazi dungeon snapped shut!"

Hearing Max so maligned, Mildred lowered her head. Memories of him—a collage of him lecturing from a podium, talking to students, sketching with charcoal, dressing for dinner and laughing at a joke, whirled through her brain. Thank God he's not here, she thought. He'd die of shame! Seeing him in her mind's eye, she covered her face with her hands, shuddered and began to weep.

The press had a picnic chronicling her first day in court. Richard Rover, a renowned journalist covering her trial, ended his column in *The New Yorker*:

> *By dressing like a siren out of a B-movie, the defendant shoots herself in the heel. Mildred Gillars has the hair of Mother McCree but she wears it like Veronica Lake!*

Time Magazine followed suite:

> *It's easy to picture this sexy-gaited seductress in Hitler's den, broadcasting sugarcoated pills of propaganda to American troops. No wonder the American public wants this glamour puss drawn and quartered.*

Attorney Laughlin resume where he had left off the previous day. "Jurors! Let us return with this poor woman to wartime Berlin! Let us put ourselves in her place! Nazi bosses close in. Oh, what a despicable lot they are—Joseph Goebbels, Joachim von Ribbentrop, Adelbert Houben, Hans von Richter... Werner Plack! Horst Cleinow—Hitler's henchmen all!

"These scoundrels made themselves perfectly clear. 'Read our Nazi-prepared scripts over the air,' they demand, 'or we will decapitate you!' They taunt her. 'Decapitation is not pretty, my dear. Imagine your beautiful head falling into a basket... lopped-off by Hitler's medieval axe!'" A juror shivered. Laughlin had cast his spell.

A late night broadcast summed up his performance.

> *"Is this fiasco the trial of 'Axis Sally' or the Perils of Pauline? Tune in tomorrow for another of James Laughlin's theatricals."*

Prosecutor Kelly charged into court determined to cast a spell of his own. "Ladies and gentlemen of the jury, Mildred Gillars is on trial for the crime of treason. She gave aid and comfort to the enemy. And why? For pure PROFIT! If you want proof of this fact, you have but to listen to the testimonies of her former Radio Berlin superiors and associates."

Laughlin jumped to his feet. "Your honor! In the name of justice surely you won't allow Nazis to testify against an American citizen! Not hand-picked-by-Hitler NAZIS!"

"*Former* Nazis," the judge said, visibly irked. "The war is over, Mr. Laughlin. Hitler is dead—the Third Reich is no more. These gentlemen now serve the German Federal Republic."

Laughlin's eyes rolled in disbelief. "Gentlemen? These blood-thirsty Nazis who forced this poor woman to do what she did?"

Judge Curran's lips pursed. "You, sir, are a hair away from being cited for contempt."

Laughlin, his face flushed to scarlet, took a handkerchief from his pocket and mopped his brow. "Your honor, unlike these 'former' Nazis, my client has never committed a single violent act. Mildred Gillars has never harmed anyone—she has never shot a gun, never dropped a bomb, never torpedoed a ship. Not one—not one person has she ever imprisoned or tortured. Nor has she prodded countless thousands into ovens to be gassed!"

He paused, turned and, as though looking at Hitler in triplicate, stared at the prosecution witnesses. "Unlike these 'former' Nazis, this innocent woman has not a single drop of blood on her hands!" He then pointed to Houben, von Richter and Plack. "Which of you—you 'former' Nazis!—can say as much?"

All three squirmed. Houben stared straight ahead. Plack's nose twitched. von Richter worked his chin from side to side as though his collar had suddenly become too tight. Laughlin swiveled toward the bench and, with out-stretched hands, pleaded. "Have these 'former' Nazis stood trial for their crimes against humanity? No! They've not served a day—not a single day in prison!" Pivoting, facing the jury: "Imagine, ladies and gentlemen, we have sitting here free in our midst, Hitler's 'former' henchmen! Yes, they're FREE! *Free* to walk our streets! After forcing her to commit the acts she's accused of, they are free to come into this courtroom in the shadow of our nation's capitol, free to testify against this poor woman, this innocent American citizen!"

The jurors gaped at the threesome. Houben, frowning as though viewing the wreckage of his Messerchmidt, massaged his forehead's zigzagging scar. Plack swallowed then giggled nervously at von Richter's squirming.

Laughlin seized the moment. "Yes, ladies and gentlemen, study them closely. Who do you suppose paid them their thirty pieces of silver? He bounded toward the jurors, finger pointed. "You did!" He pointed to them individually. "Yes!

You—you and you and you! You the American taxpayer—you supplied the filthy lucre!"

The large clock above the door ticked like a time bomb as, playing to the silence, Laughlin cupped a hand behind his ear. "Listen, it's the jingling of your money in the pockets of these 'former' Nazis—these Judases paid to do their best to send Mildred Gillars—American Citizen Mildred Gillars—to the electric chair!"

Everyone in the courtroom seemed turned to stone as the four strangely syncopated syllables echoed through the heavy air. Then, as though switched back on, the courtroom surged with an explosion of excited chatter.

"*Electric chair?*"

"She's going to the *electric chair?*"

"Could be."

"Great!"

"We're paying them Nazis?"

"Nah, not me!"

"Her mouthpiece is a nut!"

"She oughta' fry up real good!"

"Serves her right!"

The judge brought his gavel down again and again as if smashing a cockroach. "Mr. Laughlin!" he bellowed. "This is preposterous! You've gone too far!" He turned to the jury. "I order you to disregard Mr. Laughlin's remarks—all of them—they are—inflammatory! Completely out of order!"

The prosecution started its parade of witnesses with Adelbert Houben. As he took the stand, Mildred thought of the first time she was called to his office. After making her nervous by locking his door against "interruptions," he'd done his best to seduce her. Failing, he'd rubbed the scar zigzagging across his forehead and asked, "But why, Fraulein? Most women are aroused by disfigurements such as mine."

She thought it a ploy that Houben prefaced his reply to

the prosecutor's first question with a denouncement of what he called "the United States Government's terrible treatment of Miss Gillars." His "opinion" stricken from the record, he gave a truthful account of having seen Mildred shun and refuse to work with Martin J. Monti, the turncoat American pilot.

However, when asked questions critical to her exoneration, Houben lied. "Yes," he said, without once looking at her, "I served as Miss Gillars' superior during part of her tenure at Radio Berlin. Yes, she ad-libbed Nazi propaganda on the air. No, she was not forced. No one was forced to work for Radio Berlin."

Hans von Richter took the stand. Everyone in the courtroom, except Mildred, was shocked at what they saw—the stiff-backed Prussian was, with great, exaggerated movement of his lower jaw, chewing gum!

Mildred covered her mouth to keep from laughing. Black Jack! Her last encounter with Hans had taken place in a shelter during the air raid that destroyed the Tiergarten. "Damn! I'm out," he had complained while frantically rummaging through his pockets. "Don't snicker—it's because of you Americans that I'm addicted to Black Jack!"

The judge gaped at von Richter; then, turning to Kelly, exploded. "Prosecutor! Unless your witness is a cow, have him get rid of that cud! Have him get rid of it this instant!"

Awash in a wave of tittering, Hans, like an embarrassed schoolboy, squirmed. Like an ostrich trying to swallow a baseball, he attempted to swallow the wad. The audience gawked, fascinated. His eyes bulged, his Adam's apple bobbed, but in vain—he couldn't swallow it. Mortified, his Nazi-general's demeanor hopelessly ruined, he stiffened. "Very sorry, your honor," he said with considerable difficulty. "Forgive... bitte."

"Bailiff!"

von Richter's brow knit as the bailiff came up and stood

before him. A glance at the judge and Hans knew what he must do. Shamed, as though being stripped of a medal, he pulled the black, tarry wad from his mouth and deposited it on the bailiff's upturned palm.

The episode left him visibly shaken and ill-prepared for Kelly's questions. He answered too quickly, his response striking Mildred as the rat-a-tat of a machine gun. "Yes. That is right. Yes. I have spent some time in the United States. Yes—as a member of the German Consular Service I was stationed in Cleveland, Ohio. When? 1935 to 1940. Yes, that is right, 1935 to 1940."

"Do you know the defendant?"

"Yes, I do. I served as Miss Gillars' superior while she worked for Radio Berlin." Before answering the last question von Richter took a deep breath then shot Mildred a quick, sad smile. "I saw Miss Gillars at the microphone many times. She was... she *is* a very lovely woman."

Allowed then to cross examine the witness, Attorney Laughlin smiled. "Yes, Mr. von Richter, she is a very lovely woman. And speaking of lovely women, is it true that while in Ohio you married the daughter of a wealthy Ohio businessman?"

"Yes, that is true."

"You returned to Germany shortly after the wedding and took your bride with you, I believe. Once in Berlin, your new American wife soon began broadcasting for German radio. She continued broadcasting for Joseph Goebbels all during the war?"

"Well, off and on."

"And when the war ended your wife returned to this country on an American passport—a free woman?"

"Yes."

"Tell us, for her work on behalf of Hitler's propaganda machine, has your wife, the daughter of this wealthy Ohio businessman, ever been arrested or prosecuted?"

von Richter squirmed. "Well... eh... no."

"NO? Why not?"

The prosecutor jumped to his feet. "Objection! Immaterial!"

"Sustained. Members of the jury, you are to disregard all questions put to this witness by Mr. Laughlin. Also disregard Herr... Mr. von Richter's answers. Court is adjourned until tomorrow."

The day's proceedings over, Mildred stood flanked by guards awaiting transport back to jail. Hans von Richter hurried up to her. "Fraulein Gillars, I am so very sorry. Please, please forgive me." Then, before the guards could shoo him, he planted a kiss on her cheek, pressed something into her palm, and darted away. It was a pack of Black Jack gum.

The following day, Werner Plack, the prosecution's third witness, took the stand. Mildred thought the expensive pin-stripped suit and pretentious manner a poor disguise for the rat. She'd never forgive him for having broken his promise to Max by skipping out of Paris and leaving her stranded.

"Mr. Plack," Kelly asked, "during your pre-war days as a Hollywood wine-merchant, you also worked for Hitler as a spy?"

"A spy? NO! Of course not!" Werner snorted. "Ridiculous! Why should I, a successful businessman, get mixed up with spying?"

"Well then, Mr. Plack, were you ever a member of the Nazi party?"

Kelly's dog and pony show so infuriated Mildred that she jumped to her feet. "You ass! Was Werner Plack ever a Nazi? Good God! He was Goebbels' right-hand man!"

Laughlin grabbed her arm and hissed, "For God's sake! Sit down!"

Not wanting to be manhandled by the fast-approaching

bailiff, she obeyed. Besides, she could feel Werner Plack smirking at her. When she glanced at him, he winked.

Kelly re-asked the question.

"NO! Absolutely not! Never have I been member of the Nazi Party!"

Attorney Laughlin took his turn. "Mr. Plack, you must be a very, very clever businessman! I imagine you made a small fortune selling wine to movie stars before you joined Hitler's Foreign Office. How very clever of you to decorate bottles of Moselle with stickers bearing your handwritten endorsement, 'Personally Selected by Werner Plack!'"

A nod and a nervous giggle came from Plack.

"Mr. Plack," Laughlin snapped, "you recently testified in another United States Federal Court, did you not?"

"Yes."

"You testified against former United States newspapermen Robert Best and Douglas Chandler?"

"That is correct."

"Isn't it true that your testimony helped put these two Americans in prison for life?"

Hollywood's unknown wine merchant paled. "Eh... yes, I believe it helped."

"As a matter of fact, haven't you and your 'former' Nazi friends Adelbert Houben, Hans von Richter and Inge Doman—haven't all of you been making postwar careers of testifying against American citizens accused of treason?

"Eh... er... I don't know if you could call it a 'career.'"

"No? Well Mr. Plack, how do you and your 'former' Nazi friends support yourselves? Tell us, where do you get your money?"

"Objection!" screamed the prosecution.

"Over-ruled."

As though choking down balls of cotton, Plack swallowed several times. He motioned to a water pitcher on the prosecutor's table and Laughlin brought him a glass of water from it. He sipped slowly.

Laughlin snatched the glass. "Once again, Mr. Plack. How do you support yourselves?"

"From witness fees."

"Louder, Mr. Plack–the jury did not hear your answer."

Plack's nostrils flared and his chin jutted out. "From witness fees... we have expenses... you know..."

"Witness fees! Well, well! Imagine that, from witness fees! Do you mean to tell me, Mr. Plack, that American taxpayers are footing the bill? Can it be that American taxpayers are paying you 'former' Nazis to testify against this American citizen, Mildred Gillars?"

"Yes, that is the case."

Kelly had the last of Mildred's "former" Nazi detractors take the stand. Inge Doman looked older and heavier, but even more buxom than when, as Goebbels' Director of Orientation, she'd shown Mildred around Zeesen's broadcasting complex. Except for the rigid posture and matronly shoes, she showed no sign of her former stark, German fastidiousness. Her hand on the Bible, she made cow-eyes at the clerk who swore her in. "I do, I swear to tell the truth, the whole truth and nothing but the truth, so help me God."

"Liar," muttered Mildred, fighting an urge to get up and throttle the big-titted Nazi robot.

Asked about her wartime experience, Inge fluttered fake eyelashes and spoke with the breathy softness of a southern belle. "Why, yes. I did, I did a long time ago serve as an announcer for The U.S.A. Zone of the Reichrundfunk."

"And, while working in that capacity, Miss Doman, did you know the defendant, Mildred Gillars?"

"Fraulein Gillars?" She turned and stared long and hard at the accused.

Kelly, possibly afraid his witness might forget her lines, prompted, "Miss Doman, you knew Mildred Gillars quite well. You often watched her broadcast Hitler's propaganda. Isn't that so?"

"Yes, of course I knew Fraulein Gillars. I frequently announced her programs. Of course, she was well paid. Her salary greatly exceeded mine."

"Did anyone force her to broadcast?"

"Force her? Hah! Of course not!" Pleased at thrusting the dagger deeper, Inge gave her freshly bleached, shoulder length hair a flip. With a sensuousness not lost on male jurors, she fingered her neck. "Fraulein Gillars always had free reign. She took great pride in flavoring her voice with emotion. You know... she talked sexy... very sexy to arouse American soldiers listening to her."

Mildred's attorney cross-examined. "Tell me, Miss Doman, didn't you, a loyal and efficient member of Hitler's Wehrmacht, resent your competition–the beautiful, talented, immensely popular Mildred Gillars? Didn't you resent the fact that they gave you a lesser position–you a loyal, hard-working German? Didn't it anger you to be paid less than an American woman whose accomplishments were not nearly as impressive as yours? Wasn't that unfair? Weren't you just a little jealous of Miss Gillars?"

Inge inhaled deeply causing her huge breasts to rise and hover beneath her gold necklace. Every eye on them, her breasts then fell only to rise again with the next breath. "Me? Jealous of her? Don't be ridiculous!"

The final witnesses for the prosecution included eleven former prisoners of war–ten Americans and one Canadian, all former interns of Hitler's prisoner of war camps. Each told of his outrage at Mildred's visits, as if reading from the same script:

> *"No sir, I didn't believe a thing she said. The minute she arrived at our camp, I knew she wasn't legit."*
>
> *"Did I believe she was a Red Cross worker? Absolutely not! The Red Cross wouldn't send an*

> *American woman to tape a message from me to my folks back home."*
>
> *"Yeah, I recognize her. She vowed my message would be sent without any propaganda, but I knew that was bullshit–excuse me, I didn't believe her."*

Another veteran gave his profession as an unemployed plumber. Asked if Miss Gillars' visit to his camp lowered his morale, he jumped to his feet and shouted at her. "Shame on you! It made us mad as hell to see an American woman traveling free as a bird with them Nazis!"

"She disgusted me," said the veteran from Colorado. "It was awful the way she tried to seduce me in order to get her interview. First she tried to ply me with cognac and cigarettes. When that didn't work she sat across from me with her legs spread apart." Feigning altar-boy innocence, the ex-POW cast wide blue eyes at the judge. "I swear your honor, I could see everything... she wasn't wearing panties."

The preposterous tale caused her to laugh out loud, a response that earned her a barb in the press:

> *Mildred Gillars is beyond the pale. Instead of being shamed by these veterans' accounts of her treasonous acts, this wanton woman threw back her head and laughed! Making a further mockery of the court, she posed with her chin cupped in her hands, passed notes to her half-sister and, playing the temptress, winked at the very veterans who testified against her!*

From *The Washington Post*:

> *Hopeful of swaying the male jurors, Miss Gillars walked out of the courtroom swinging her hips with considerable movement!*

Newspapers had a field day reporting the prosecution's playback of Mildred's broadcasts.

From *The Chicago Tribune*:

> A BLOODCURDLING PERFORMANCE!
>
> *Today, we heard the most telling evidence so far presented against Miss Gillars. Shocked, we listened to the Office of War Information recording of her radio drama, "Vision of the Invasion"—a drama Nazi's repeatedly broadcast in the weeks preceding D-day. In dramatizing what might happen if the Allied forces crossed the Channel and invaded the Nazi-fortified coast, Miss Gillars gave a bloodcurdling performance. At the insistence of Prosecutor Kelly, the recording was played over and over until the defendant began to squirm.*

The once prominent German actor Ullrich Haupt, who played the role of Mildred's soldier-son, Alan, in "Vision of the Invasion," came forth. Although called by the prosecution, Ullrich gave testimony that he had been forced to broadcast propaganda. The press ignored Haupt's testimony.

George Heinrich Schnell, the petite German actor who portrayed the soldier's father, took the stand. Before Schnell could utter a word, Mildred's attorney objected. "Your honor, Herr Schnell is an atheist! As such, he cannot be sworn-in. Atheists cannot take an oath!"

The attorney's contention sent reporters racing to typewriters. This was news! Next-day headlines blared: "Atheist on Spot," and "Schnell Can't Swear!"

The New Yorker's Richard Rover, moved by the trial's "fine bits of low-keyed tragedy and comedy," wrote:

> *George Heinrich Schnell is an aging German thespian, a battered ham with fake romantic gestures and long hair, a man who looks as though he asks nothing from life but an occasional beer and an occasional bar maid. Schnell believes in*

> *an existence after death, but not in our God whom he terms "a small-minded deity who goes in for punishment and rewards."*

Court adjourned in order for lawyers and judges to privately weigh the merits of Attorney Laughlin's argument. Judge Curran, in response to the objection to Herr Schnell's taking oath, ordered Schnell to write an essay to explain his personal beliefs. While lawyers combed law books for precedents, Schnell wrote his essay.

The minute court resumed, Attorney Kelly read an excerpt:

> *"As to religion, when I recollect what I have seen and experienced of men, Christianity seems almost blasphemous. Oh, how infinitely greater would I wish to see the deity!"*

Silence fell over the courtroom. A few heads nodded in agreement. Apparently moved by Schnell's sentiment, the judge turned to the prosecutor. "If your witness agrees to take the Quaker Affirmation in lieu of the oath, the court will allow his testimony."

Schnell's performance on the stand did not altogether please the prosecution. "Yes, I know this woman, Mildred Gillars. She performed with me in the radio drama 'Vision of the Invasion.' But she did so solely in hopes of warding off the quickly approaching mass slaughter of men on the beaches of Normandy."

Kelly winced. "Now just a moment, Mr. Schnell, just a moment. You have testified that you performed with Miss Gillars in that play, but surely your last comment is supposition, surely you couldn't see into the mind of Miss Gillars. You *supposed* that her reason for making those broadcasts was humanitarian, did you not? You couldn't read her mind, could you?"

"No... no, of course not."

"Might not her motive have been to delay the invasion a few months in order to give Hitler's scientists at Pennemunde the time they needed to develop new monster weapons—weapons that could without a doubt repulse any and all invasions? Do you know, Mr. Schnell, that this is not what she intended?"

"I know nothing for certain."

"Thank you. Mr. Schnell, you may step down."

His plea for acquittal rejected, Mr. Laughlin began Mildred's defense by asserting her right as an American citizen to criticize the late President Roosevelt and to be anti-Jewish.

"My God!" Mildred complained to him during the recess. "How dare you describe me as 'anti-Jewish!' Get this straight—I am not and never have been anti-Jewish. One of my dearest relatives is a Jew! With your help, my dear, bumbling attorney, I'm certain to get the death penalty!"

Perhaps convinced that government prosecutors had an ironclad case against her, Laughlin seemed to lose interest. He called only four witnesses on Mildred's behalf.

Oddly, the first of these, Gunnar Drangsholt, had been scheduled to testify for the prosecution. But while awaiting Prosecutor Kelly's call to the stand, Drangsholt, a veteran from Chicago, had displayed bizarre mannerisms. Sporadic outbursts, giggles and incessant knuckle-cracking earned stern looks from Judge Curran and a bailiff's reprimand. Prosecutor Kelly was no fool, he decided against putting this obviously disturbed young man on the stand.

Drangsholt had attended the trial every day. How confusing it must have been for him, as it was for Mildred, to see his name moved from the rooster of prosecution witnesses to the rooster of defense witnesses.

"Mr. Drangsholt," Laughlin began.

Startled by the sound of his own name, the witness shot up out of his seat, stood at attention and saluted. "Yes sir!"

"No, no, Mr. Drangsholt. You may be seated."

"Yes sir!"

Drangsholt plopped down, and, leaning forward, grasped the microphone as if it were a lifeline.

"We all understand your apprehension at testifying in court," Laughlin said softly. "Would you like a glass of water?"

As though offered castor oil, Drangsholt reared and shook his head. "No! I have to take a piss."

Judge Curran ordered a ten-minute recess.

With nature's call answered, Drangsholt returned to the stand. Laughlin tried again. "Mr. Drangsholt, I understand that during the war you were an inmate of Stalag 2-B in Germany."

"Yes sir! Yeah, I was. I was. I was there. I was there."

Again Laughlin came up behind Mildred's chair and placed a hand on her shoulder. "Mr. Drangsholt, did this woman, Mildred Gillars, pose as a Red Cross worker when she visited you there?"

Drangsholt squirmed, ran both hands through his hair and then began pulling on his fingers, cracking his knuckles. His eyes darted to Mildred. "No!"

It was not the answer Laughlin expected. "No? Are you saying that this woman, Mildred Gillars did NOT visit you in that prisoner of war camp—that she did NOT provide you with a means of getting a message back home to your mother?"

Drangsholt jumped up and began shaking his fist. Oblivious to the banging of the gavel, he cried out, "No! She came to see us. She threatened us." He tore at his hair. "That woman right there! That whore!" Drained by his outburst, he slumped down onto the chair.

Outrage at seeing the young vet's face streaming with tears

caused everyone to glare at Laughlin. Indignant protests spiked the still, hot air.

"Leave the kid alone!"

"'Fer chrissakes, he's suffered enough."

"How dare she put him through more agony!"

Drangsholt had to be helped from the room. The judge, glaring at Laughlin, ordered another recess.

Laughlin called Erwin Beckman. A former propaganda writer for Goebbels, Erwin had authored many of Mildred's scripts. He answered every question emphatically. "Yes, of course Miss Gillars was forced to read every script handed her—and to read them verbatim and with the indicated emotion. Not one word of her own dare she utter—no ad-libs. She—we were *all* threatened and coerced. They told us, 'one false utterance and you will be kaput—executed!'"

The truth at last! Mildred's heart leapt.

Judge Curran broke in. "Mr. Beckman, do I understand you correctly? You actually saw Miss Gillars threatened and coerced?"

Erwin looked confused. "Well... no... I... but of course she was... we *all* were."

"One more point of clarification, Mr. Beckman. You are testifying under oath that you were present when, as the defendant claims, she was forced to sign an oath of allegiance to Germany?"

Erwin chewed his thumbnail. "No, I was not present. But again, *all* of us—we were made to sign such an oath!"

Face beet red, arms outspread, and screaming "Objection! Objection! Objection!" Laughlin raced to the bench.

"Very well, Attorney Laughlin! Objection sustained; however, the court, hereby declares Mr. Beckman an uncooperative witness and rules his testimony inadmissible!"

Next, Laughlin questioned Emil Christiani, the radio engineer who had driven Max and Mildred from stalag to stalag and recorded Mildred's interviews with American prisoners of war. Although Emil thought Max a pompous ass, he'd always gotten on well with Mildred. A trained singer, he tried once to pick up her spirits by singing *The Marriage of Figaro* at the top of his lungs as they motored through the countryside.

"You'll get us shot!" Max had protested.

"For my bad voice or for my good Italian?"

Laughlin's first question struck Mildred as inane. "Was it your impression, Mr. Christiani, that Miss Gillars was a traitor to her country?"

"No! On the contrary! Miss Gillars ceaselessly professed her love for America. She wanted only to go home."

"Then why didn't she?"

"Why, there was no way! Absolutely no way! Her American passport had been confiscaded. She was afraid and, she had no choice... she was forced to broadcast the scripts they handed her... she felt ashamed for having read them over the air. Besides, no one quit Hitler."

Johannes Schmidt-Hansen had brought pressure on Mildred to sign a statement affirming that she had read and agreed to Nazi sanctions imposed on all broadcasters within the Third Reich. Assured Schmidt-Hansen would testify on Mildred's behalf, an unknown benefactor had paid for his passage from Germany to Washington, D.C.. Without explanation, Attorney Laughlin ignored the prospective witness's presence in the courtroom, letting him cool his heels day after day and did not call him to the stand.

Sensing the man's frustration, Prosecutor Kelly rocked the courtroom by calling the would-be witness for the defense to testify for the prosecution. "Mr. Schmidt-Hansen, did you ever pressure the defendant to sign an affirmation that she would broadcast verbatim what she was handed."

Schmidt-Hansen took a deep breath and, in the rapid-fire

monotone of an actor desperate to get off the stage, answered the question. "Although I believe it was a matter of routine to require such an affirmation, my broadcasters were never pressured into signing one. I never pressured Miss Gillars."

"Never?"

"Never."

Headlines on evening editions of February 23, 1949 newspapers cried "Hitler's Mouthpiece to Take Stand" "'Axis Sally' to Tell All!" and "Traitor to Sing!"

As he led the defendant to the stand the next morning, Laughlin squeezed her hand. "Brace yourself, my dear—this is it."

"Ah yes, 'my turn in the barrel.'" It was his metaphor, not hers—one he'd used to prepare her for this day. He'd had her imagine herself a rodeo clown compressed in a barrel, relentlessly attacked by a maddened bull. "I won't lie to you. You'll get knocked about something fierce—every question a thrusting horn—a poke—a probe—a wound. You'll feel impaled, bruised, bloodied—but in the end..."

"The clown goes to the electric chair?"

"No dear, he prevails—he always pops-up victorious to wave at a cheering crowd."

Laughlin spent four days laying the groundwork of her defense, establishing her character and asking her questions to rebut statements made by prosecution witnesses that she had willingly and without fear served as Hitler's propagandist.

On the fifth and sixth day, he systematically addressed each of the eight charges. Asking questions honed to establish her innocence, he repeatedly drew from his witness the same unwavering testimony: She was not guilty—not of a single count—she'd been forced—she had no alternative—everything she'd done, she'd done under threat of death.

The specter of a modern-day Mata Hari on the stand caused a media frenzy. Hoping for a glimpse of her, reporters and photographers mobbed jail and courthouse entrances. Newspaper articles called her smile "wicked," her manner "haughty" and her expression "defiant." Present during Mildred's fifth day of questioning, Journalist Walter Winchell noted in his evening broadcast: "Such pathos! Such drama! Watching Mildred Gillars defend her actions is like watching Ingrid Bergman play Joan of Arc!"

Prosecutor Kelly tore into Mildred like a piranha. His razor-sharp insults, hurtful innuendos and pointed, trap-hidden questions shredded her resolved to stay calm. "Tell us the truth, Miss Gillars. You were *not* forced or threatened—everything you broadcast—every word of it you broadcast of your own volition, isn't that so?"

"No, that isn't so! I..."

"Yes, we know what you did. Do we ever!" He pointed to the men seated in the front row. "We have but to look at these poor veterans whom you visited in Hitler's prisoner of war camps—these veterans whom you lied to—tricked—tried to seduce!"

"No!"

"And that's not the half of it! You were all for the Nazi movement—for incinerating Jews by the millions—for being a traitor to a country who's President, you gladly told the world, was a communist bent on selling out the American people! Our beloved F.D.R.!"

Kelly showed no sign of letting up. On day two, question after question begged the answer that she'd relished breaking down American morale. You made them up yourself, didn't you Miss Gillars? Those little earfuls you laid on our fighting men?" He strode to a table, picked up a sheet of paper and rolled it to simulate a microphone. Forcing a note of femininity into his voice, he pretended to broadcast. "This is your gal 'Sal,' coming to you courtesy of Radio Berlin. You poor fellas–out there spilling your blood in some God-forsaken foreign trench while, at the same time, big shots back home are making money hand over fist. Not only are they profiting from your agony and enjoying a comfy life–they're running around and doing who-knows-what-else with your wives and sweethearts."

He wadded up the paper microphone and hurled it into a wastebasket. "It stinks! What you did stinks to high heaven! And you did it, didn't you? You wrote and broadcast that filth! Of your own free will. In fact it was your idea to masquerade as a Red Cross worker, to interview our brave, imprisoned soldiers and to splice the taped interviews with lies certain to destroy their folks back home! Tell me I'm lying!"

"No!... Yes!"

He turned and, at the snap of his fingers, an assistant rushed up and placed a thin, red-covered pamphlet in his hand. "Do you recognize this?" he said, holding the pamphlet inches from her eyes. That she squinted and, unable to read the cover's printing at such close range, shook her head, egged him on. "Ah, vanity! Sooner or later, Miss Gillars, we all have to succumb to reading glasses." He backed away, slowly increasing the distance between her eyes and the print. "Now...? Now...? Now...?"

At last she nodded. "Yes, I wrote it.

"Ah, you wrote it! Please, in a loud, clear voice–your 'broadcaster's' voice–read for us the title you chose for this literary effort."

She cleared her throat and stared at the jury. "My Vision of the Invasion–How I Tried to Save Thousands of Young Men from Dying in America's Worst Blunder."

"Let me get this straight..." He grabbed the pamphlet from her and started thumbing through it. "You had an inspiration–God wanted a play written so that, upon hearing it performed, soldiers about to storm the beaches of Normandy would turn tail and run!"

"But that's not..."

"This play, 'Vision of the Invasion,' you were its star, were you not?"

She straightened. "Yes."

He tossed the pamphlet on a table then wheeled around. "So! Max Koischwitz, your Nazi lover, knowing of your lifelong obsession with becoming a great actress, writes you a play in which you can shine!"

"No! They liked my voice—the records I played—those boys—they were headed for certain slaughter. And for what? Germany was already on its knees... if only they'd turn back... I tried to convince them... we were... the bombings—hunger—everything in ruins—it was just a matter of time!"

"Bravo! I must admit, my dear, you are quite an actress! Let's go back to your last line for a moment. 'It was just a matter of time.' Of course it was! Hitler is beginning to worry: 'Oh my gosh, what if the unthinkable happens and the invasion succeeds? I need more time—a few more months and I'll have in my arsenal the super-weapons being developed at Pennemunde—then let them try their invasion'" Kelly spread his arms. "Ah yes, as you so aptly phrased it, Fraulein Gillars, 'It was just a matter of time.'"

Kelly lunged at her. "Admit it! Your Nazi lover Max Koischwitz wrote the play for one reason and one reason only—to give Hitler the time needed to produce his super-weapons! That's it, isn't it? Isn't it?"

"Yes, that's what he thought—but I'd tricked him into writing it. Max didn't know what I was trying to accomplish... he... Max didn't... he... Max..."

Laughlin saw it coming. At the first of her tormented screams he made a dash for the stand. Blinded by exploding flashbulbs, she pitched forward and collapsed sobbing into his arms. He held her close as the courtroom erupted. The judge, his face scarlet, pounded his gavel. "Order! Order! Order, or I shall clear this court!" Then, pointing a finger, "Attorney Laughlin, such theatrics disgust me! You will have the defendant back on the stand and ready to continue at three o'clock!"

Escorted by the bailiff, Laughlin and Edna Mae helped Mildred down the hall to an unmarked door. The bailiff produced a key and opened the door for the women to enter.

It was a small room. Dull light filtered in from a high window. A straight wooden chair stood at the foot of a narrow cot. On one wall hung a clock and beneath it a yellowed copy of the Bill of Rights. Another wall accommodated a sink and mirror. Edna Mae led Mildred to the cot and, after some coaxing, got her to lie down.

Mildred eased her head onto the pillow and covered her face with her hands. "I'm so sorry... so sorry..."

"Please, try to get some rest." She walked to the sink, wet several paper towels then returned to the cot. "Close your eyes," she said, laying the cold compress across Mildred's forehead, "Try to think of happier times. Think of... when we were kids... of Greystone... of when you and Momma..."

The words, as they washed over Mildred, slowly merged with the clock's ticking and the drone of traffic passing on the street below. Her eyelids grew heavy and, closing, fluttered for a moment against bursts of retinal stars. They came slowly, the images, slowly and as though backlit by the smoky afterglow of fireworks. A golden-haired child appears. Smiling, her curls bouncing, she plays a tune on a miniature piano. An angry voice mars the music. Cringing, her notes a discordant jumble, the child fades. Momma appears... young and dancing at first... then older... laughing as she strolls arm-in-arm with Ira Rosen. The couple steps aside to marvel at a passing car. It is Andre at the wheel of his Bugatti, his arm around a young and beautiful Mildred. The wind whipping her hair turns hot... smoky. It howls. A city burns... eyes the color of jade fill with tears. Bombs fall... shrapnel rips bodies apart. A woman, her head covered with a scarf, walks down the side aisle of a church and enters a confessional. "And what is it you seek, my child?"

"I... I..."

"Do good to others... do good..."

Startled awake by the sudden wailing of an ambulance, Mildred sat up wide-eyed. "I tried... I tried to do good... God help me, I tried..."

Edna Mae reached out and touched her sister's cheek. "I know you did, Sis... I know..."

At precisely three o'clock, Kelly resumed his attack. "Miss Gillars, when we left off you were, I believe, about to admit that you took part in the play 'Vision of the Invasion' to forestall the Allied invasion of Normandy until Hitler could produce his super-weapons. Is that not correct?"

"No!"

"Tell the truth! You wanted those super-weapons to assure an even greater slaughter, didn't you? The truth! The truth!"

Mildred sat straighter, took a deep breath and squared her chin. She looked at the clock. Then, as though seeing herself reflected in their eyes, she looked at her audience: spectators, reporters, witnesses, lawyers... the judge. Her eyes came to rest on the jury. "The TRUTH is, I was FORCED to broadcast Nazi propaganda. In hopes of saving tens of thousands of American boys from certain death, I tricked Max Koischwitz into writing the play 'Vision of the Invasion.' I then participated in the play of my own free will. I..."

"You're excused, Miss Gillars. No further questions."

AXIS SALLY DIES

COLUMBUS, OHIO (June 1, 1988)–Mildred Gillars, known during World War II as "Axis Sally" for her Nazi propaganda broadcasts, died at age 87.

Ms. Gillars died at a hospital in Columbus, where she lived in an apartment on the city's north side. Neighbors said the spinster had lived a quiet, private life.

After World War II, American military officials found her living in the cellar of a bombed-out building in Berlin. She was shipped home in August 1948 to stand trial for treason.

On March 10, 1949 the jury, after deliberating seventeen hours and twenty minutes, returned a verdict. Found innocent of treason on counts one through seven, she was found guilty of treason on count eight, that of portraying an American soldier's mother in the broadcast drama, "Vision of the Invasion."

On May 20, 1949 an appellate court upheld both her conviction and her sentence of 10 to 30 years in federal prison. A model prisoner during her incarceration at West Virginia's Alderson Federal Prison, Miss Gillars on occasion played Casino with fellow-inmate, Iva Ikuko Toguri, a.k.a. "Tokyo Rose."

Paroled in 1962, Mildred Gillars worked for more than 25 years in a Catholic Convent teaching music to kindergarten children. She left her teaching post only once–at the age of seventy to finish her college education. Deemed, upon her graduation in 1973, "the oldest person ever to graduate from Ohio's Wesleyan," she, once convicted of treason for her spoken words, received a Bachelor's degree in Speech.

Acknowledgements

To my editor, Maria Keith, whose dedication,
determination and superior editing skills
brought this work to print.

To Ron for his unflagging faith and encouragement.

To the charming and gracious Ruth Carlson,
who always knew this book would be.